WALTER MACKEN

Sunset on the Window-Panes

BRANDON

A Brandon Paperback

Published in 1999 by
Brandon
an imprint of Mount Eagle Publications Ltd.
Dingle, Co. Kerry, Ireland

First published by Macmillan and Co Ltd., 1954

10 9 8 7 6 5 4 3 2 1

ISBN 0 86322 254 4

This book is published with the assistance of
the Arts Council/An Chomhairle Ealaíon, Ireland

Cover painting: *Móin ón gCam* by Liam O'Neill, reproduced by permission of the artist and Greenlane Gallery, Dingle, Co Kerry
Cover design: Steven Hope
Typesetting: Red Barn Publishing, Skeagh, Skibbereen
Printed by The Guernsey Press Ltd., Channel Islands

One

H E WAS SITTING on the stone wall. The field behind him sloped. First it was green, then it became darker green where the ferns were beginning to embrace it.

He wore grey trousers and a white open-necked shirt that seemed to be blinding white in the sunshine. The wall was a boundary of the yellow road. When he looked left he could see the road twisting and winding back into the valley between the tall hills, until it ended at the lake. The lake was untroubled by wind. It was like clear glass. If he looked to his right he could see the calm sea stretching away to the horizon.

It was very hot. There were beads of perspiration on his upper lip. He wiped them off with the back of his hand and rubbed a finger along his eyebrows and flicked it. He watched the bead of sweat falling in the dust and vanishing.

He saw the girl coming out of the valley with the donkey ahead of her. She was a long way away. He paid no attention to her or the donkey. They were a common sight on the road between the big valley and the sea. He was looking blankly at the fields stretching away in front of him. They were neatly divided by stone walls. They were cared-for and cultivated. It was undulating land rising and falling. Some fields were barren and in others the cold stones peered through the thin grass. There were black cows grazing in them, and sometimes they raised a head curiously to look towards the white-shirted figure on the wall.

His eyes didn't see all those things. He was listless. He was bored. He barely tasted the cigarette he was smoking.

The figure of the donkey and the girl came nearer and nearer to him. The donkey's unshod hooves landed in the dust with a gentle clop. There were two baskets on his back, and as they swung emptily, the straps tying them to the pannier creaked.

The girl saw the figure on the wall long before she reached him. She knew him. She felt colour rising in her cheeks. The sight of him made her heart beat faster. All because everyone was unknowing. She had heard that he was home. This was June, this was the time when everybody came home.

She kept her eyes looking ahead, but now and again she would peep out of the sides of them to see if he was noticing her. He wasn't noticing her. His teeth were bared in a grin of thought. They were white and strong, and looked very white in the dark face. His hair was tightly curled and clipped close to his head. He had a good-shaped head and a thick neck rising out of a round strong chest. She knew what his eyes were like. They were steel-blue in colour and there was always a reckless sort of glint in them. There were some who said they were never without a sneer in them.

She passed by the unseeing eyes.

"Hello, Mister O'Breen," she said as she passed by. He paid no attention. She was sure he would pay no attention, but all the same she was a little disappointed. Then she heard his voice. It was a deep voice, sort of rusty.

"Here, Breeda," he said. "Come here."

She turned. She had to walk back to him. It was a good way. She thought it was a very long way. She was terribly conscious of the eyes on her. Looking her over, taking her apart. She hadn't her best dress on either. She had only the old blue cotton thing, that had been washed so often it was almost white. But she had outgrown it a bit if she only knew. Her body was shaping it better than she thought. She had good strong sunburned legs and they were bare like her feet. She needn't be in bare feet, but she liked to be. She liked the silky feel of the dust. Her hair was brown and it was straight, but it always shone. She wore it long around her face. Her face was narrow, her eyes were deep-sunken and seemed to glitter from cover. I won't blush, she thought. I won't blush. This is one time I won't blush – but

6

she couldn't stop it from rising in her cheeks. The blush seemed to start in her toes and rise all the way to her brain. She couldn't stop her fingers fiddling at the sides of her dress. She was furious at herself. After all she was over sixteen, practically, and he wasn't a nun who had called you from the body of the class to stand before her blushing and shamed and fiddling with your dress. She should be more poised like the sisters told her.

She found it hard to meet his gaze, but she raised her eyes. There seemed to be two bits of steel boring into her. His face was big and broad. All strong it seemed. All strong all over.

"What's the idea of calling me Mister?" he asked.

She was confounded.

"Well . . ." she said.

"Well what?" he asked.

"Well water," she was going to say, but bit it back. It was so schoolgirlish but it was the answer to end answers when people well-ed you. So she dropped her eyes and scuffled her feet.

"What age are you now?" he asked.

"I'm nearly seventeen," she said.

"You are like hell," he said. "You're probably nearly sixteen."

"I'm over sixteen," she said

"All right. I'm nineteen. That's a three-year difference. Why do I qualify for the Mister?"

"Well . . ." she said.

"What, again?" he asked.

She laughed and her blush went away.

"You seem to be a man," she said. "That's why. And when a person is a man he should be called Mister, I suppose."

"Where are you going?" he asked.

She flung her arm out in a gesture. "Down to the sea," she said. "Down for some seaweed."

He got off the wall.

"I'll go down a piece with you. I'm bored."

He walked beside her. He seemed to be towering over her. He wasn't, just that he was bulky. He was looking down at her bent head. She had full red lips under a thin nose. He knew from the look of her skin that it would be soft to the touch.

7

"You have changed a lot since I saw you last," he said.

"That was a year ago," she said. "I was only a child then." I mustn't gush, she thought. Walking like this beside Bart O'Breen was a sort of fulfilment of a daydream. She was thinking that when she went back to school this year, she would really have something to dream about. He was quite close to her. She could smell tobacco from him. His shirt-sleeves were rolled. The bare arm near her was very brown from the sun. The skin was smooth on it. Muscles were leaping in it. "Will you be long home?" she asked him.

"For ever," he said.

"What do you mean?" she asked.

"It means that I'm not going back there," he said. "They don't know that at home yet, but they will, they will." This grimly.

"Oh!" she said.

"It's all a cod," he said. "I wasn't cut out to be a teacher. Can you see me teaching?"

"I can see you doing anything," she said. Trapped, she looked up at him wildly. But he hadn't noticed. He wasn't even listening.

"It was the first thing that came into my head, when I was asked," he said. "Do you know why?"

"No," she said. He wasn't listening to that either.

"It was your father," he said. "He was a great teacher. He really knew how to teach and he made it look easy and a good thing to do. You remember him teaching?"

He had stopped now, looking directly at her.

She didn't want to talk about her father. It still hurt her. Did she remember him teaching!

"Yes," she said. "I remember."

"That's why I came this way now," he said. "Remembering back. It was a good life those days only for the home we had. I liked school. But it was your father really. Down here." He turned down a lane that led off the road. It was a little-used lane. There was grass growing in the tracks of the cartwheels. He stopped when she didn't come with him. "Come on! What's wrong with you?" he asked her roughly.

8

"I don't want to," she said.

"Don't be neurotic," he said, going back and taking her hand and practically pulling her down the small lane after him. She resisted a little and then followed him. She thought he was very cruel. She was sorry he had been on the side of the road when she passed by. They came out of the lane. The house was before them. It had been a two-storey house. The roof was half gone. There was no door. It was used as a stable. She felt she was suffocating as she looked at it. There had been a winding gravelled drive. You could barely see it. There was a grand stretch of green lawn. It was still there. The cattle had clipped it and manured it. The windows were blind. There was no glass in them. The rhododendron bushes grew wild, flinging their blossoms in all directions. All the other shrubs had been eaten or destroyed.

"You see, that's all that's left, nothing," he said. "He was a grand man, your father. It's a pity he had to die. All the good people die. Come on," he said abruptly and turned out of the lane again. She followed after him. She wanted to scream. Or kick him or something. That he should have been so unfeeling. But then he was a Mister no matter what he said.

Out on the road again, he looked left. It was as if he was expecting something.

"I thought so," he said.

"What?" she asked.

"Look at him." He pointed back down the road to the valley. "There's brother Joseph, like he has the hot foot coming after me. I was thinking she would send him for me."

She was bewildered.

"We will sit and await his coming," he said, "and see what message he brings from Garcia." His jaws were tight.

"I have to get the seaweed," she said.

"Sit down beside me, Breeda," he said, indicating a stone.

She obeyed him. Her thigh was nearly touching his. She could feel heat and vitality pulsating from him.

"The donkey will be happy cropping the grass," he said. "The donkey is far happier than you or I."

"I'm happy enough," she said.

9

"Well, the donkey is happier than you will be some time in the future," he said.

The thin figure of the boy was tolling on the hill. His hair was dark and fell over his eyes in streaks, and he would raise a lean hand to push it back over his high narrow forehead. Even though it was a very hot day he wore a black suit and a dark cardigan and a white collar with a black tie. His face was pale. He had a pleasant mouth and his eyes were dark and shy. The two waiting for him to approach knew all this about him.

Bart was impatient for him. He moved restlessly on the wall. Breeda thought he would get up and hasten Joseph's coming.

Joseph was pleased to see them. He had forgotten his message.

"Hello, Breeda," he said. "You are home. I am pleased to see you."

He was breathless.

"Well, well, well," said Bart. "Trot it out. Don't keep me waiting all day."

The smile went from Joseph's face. His eyes became troubled.

"Mother wants you, Bart," he said.

"I was expecting that," Bart said. "Did she get a letter?"

"She did," said Joseph. "He just brought it. She told me to go and find you."

"Well, you have found me," Bart said. "Can't you go home and tell her that you have found me?"

"She wants you," said Joseph. "She said to tell you to come home straight away."

"Well, I'm not going home straight away," said Bart, jumping off the wall. "I'm going picking seaweed, with Breeda. Amn't I, Breeda?" He caught her arm in his hand and pulled her towards the donkey. She had to run to keep up with him

"Yes," she cried, "you are."

"Can I come too?" Joseph called after them.

Bart turned round to look at him. Joseph's head was on one side. He was looking at Bart appealingly. If he had a tail it would be wagging, Bart thought. "Don't you want to go home and tell your mother about the disobedience of your half-brother?" Bart asked.

Joseph just looked hurt.

"All right, all right," Bart shouted. "Come on. We'll all go and collect bloody seaweed."

Joseph caught up with them and walked the other side of the donkey. Breeda was glad. She liked Joseph. She wondered how two boys who were bred from the same mother could look and be so totally different.

"You know the story about the Joseph in the Bible?" Bart was asking. He bent down and took up a heavy rock and heaved it into the field. It seemed to relieve him. He wiped his hands on his trousers. "He was his family favourite, just like you, Joseph. The very same as you. The old man left him an inheritance and favoured him above the others. Not his father, but his mother. She was the one. You hear that, Joseph? Well, you know what happened to Joseph. He ended up down in a well. Maybe I ought to put you into a well. What do you think of that, Joseph? Will I fire you into a well?"

"You can if you like, Bart," said Joseph.

"A meek Christian," said Bart. "A goddam turn-the-other-cheeker. I'm sorry I like you, Joseph. Do you know that? I'm sorry I like you. Sometimes I'd like to do violent things to you and I would, only I like you."

"You didn't finish the story," said Breeda. "Joseph in the Bible ended up all right, but the brothers that put him in the well had bad ends."

"You're for him too," said Bart. "Tell me, what has Joseph got that makes everyone for him? Tell me that, Breeda."

"Can't you leave him alone?" she said. "If you want to hurt someone for something that's disturbing you, why do you take it out on Joseph?"

He caught her and twisted her violently towards him. He looked down into her face. Her eyes were angry. A strange thing happened to him then. He felt her breast heaving against him, and he was suddenly conscious of the feel of her bare arm in his palm. Why, this girl is a little woman, he was thinking. The violence went out of him. His body seemed to go rigid. He saw the anger fading out of her eyes and a strange, disturbed, shy look

11

taking its place. The colour rose in her cheeks from her neck and she dropped her eyes. Her eyelashes were very long. He saw them resting on her cheek. She moved and he released her and walked ahead. He heard the two following him. He knew, if he turned, the picture he would see. Tall thin Joseph with his hand on the donkey's back, and then the donkey with his head bent and the baskets waving, and the girl on the other side with her eyes cast down, red in her cheeks and her breast heaving. He had suffered heaving breasts before. He knew about them.

He had to alter his picture of her.

She was a little girl who came to school with her father. He kept her up near the top of the classroom. She had a hard life in school. She was the master's daughter. But she was cheerful under it. A small scattery little girl with pigtails tied with purple ribbon. Then she was a girl sent away to school and coming home in gym frocks and black stockings. Then she was the tragic little girl in black at the double funeral of her father and mother who had died when fishing for pollack. Now she was this.

He turned and waited until they caught up with him. He looked at her closely and with interest. She met his eyes.

"You have changed a lot, Breeda," he said.

"Have I?" she asked.

"Yes," he said. "You have. I didn't know you until now." He felt excited. The other thing was nothing. That could come later. Have it out with his mother. All that. But this was something new. He recognised the look in her eyes too now that he came to think back on it.

The road came on to a tarred road that ran straight as men could make it in this rough land. There were no houses bordering the road, just the stony fields, with potatoes growing between the stones, and bare fields with grey ponies or cattle. They walked this road for a bit and then they turned off it on to another yellow road that went towards the sea.

Joseph was watching the sky. It was a pale misty blue with white clouds on the horizon. The sea was shimmering. There was no wind at all. There seemed to be no life in the day except for an occasional planing seagull. He fell back and walked behind because the laneway was narrow. He liked the look of his brother's back. He called Bart his brother. He always thought of him as his brother. Bart always said "half-brother". This hurt Joseph a little. He admired Bart. The straight back now, with the heavily muscled shoulders moving under the cloth of his shirt. The powerful graceful neck with the curls growing low on it. He was pleased to be with Bart. He liked always to be with him, but it happened rarely. The things Bart did were vigorous things in which Joseph could rarely join, because his chest was weak. That was what had his body thin, his face pale. But he was strong enough except for that. He wished he had always been strong. It would have been a great thing long ago, to climb trees with Bart or row currachs with Bart, or ride bareback on ponies across the dangerous ground.

He knows, Breeda was thinking. Now and again his hand brushed hers as he walked beside her. She could feel a shock going up through her arm. This is very strange. But not so strange. Her world seemed to have always been filled with his big figure, the restless eyes, the white teeth. Vacations from school were going home and maybe seeing Bart, more than just going home.

"We'll go out to the cliffs," said Bart, leaping the low wall.

"We'll get down that way to the beach. It's shorter." She followed him laughing. "You come after with the donkey, Joseph," Bart ordered. Then he took her hand and ran. She was a good runner. She was as fleet as himself. He was light on his feet. The field was riddled with rocks and the briars pushing up beside them and the waving bracken, until the place started to rise and they came near the sea. Then the grass was very green and cropped short by sheep. The sheep ran away from in front of them. Rabbits scuttled inelegantly out of their way. Breeda's hair was out on the breeze like the mane of a pony, but she was laughing and her eyes were glittering. They came to the edge of the cliff. There was about five yards of it cut off by sagging posts held together by barbed-wire strands. He stopped and put his hands under her arms and swung her over the wire. He felt the softness of her. Then he jumped too and threw himself down on the grass with his face out over the cliff. She joined him there, lying on her stomach looking over.

The cliff wasn't very high. About fifty feet. The tide was in. It was very calm except right at the bottom of the cliff where it broke over rocks. The rock weed was waving in it. They could see cliffs to the left jutting out too, going back for about half a mile. Gravel cliffs they were. You could see the strata of the different levels where thousands of years ago they had formed the bottom bed of the moving glaciers that covered the land. To the right of them the cliffs ended abruptly and there was a long yawning beach of silver sand, with the tide licking at it, and up-ended currachs lying above the high-water mark, like shapely black beetles.

"Nice?" he asked.

"Yes," she said. "I always remember this when I'm away."

"You remembered me too?" he asked, turning on his side so that his face was close to hers. She had the nerve to face him.

"Yes," she said, "I remembered you."

"Why didn't you tell me?" he asked, reaching a hand and putting it across her. That alarmed her. She moved restlessly under his hand and turned and sat up. His hand moved with her. "Let's go," she said breathlessly, and struggled to get to her feet. Suddenly he was angry.

"What's wrong with you?" he shouted. "What's wrong with you?"

"Let me go, Bart," she said.

Why should she be panic-stricken? She didn't know. Maybe it was because she was so young. Suddenly she was afraid of Bart O'Breen, because he was too direct or too vital. He stood up too. He had his arms around her. He felt as if he was holding a struggling bird. His hard jaw brushed her cheek. She screamed. It was like a nightmare. It wasn't necessary. "Shut up, for God's sake!" he shouted at her. "Let me go. Let me go!" This she screamed, punching at him with her fists. Joseph had come to the barrier. His eyes were wide at the sight of the two of them seeming to be struggling there inside the wire.

Joseph went over the wire. He reached between them.

14

"Bart! Bart! "he shouted. "Let her go. What's come over you?"

"Damn ye! Damn ye! Damn ye!" Bart shouted. "Leave me alone!" and he pushed himself free and the two of them were gone. They went in a sort of slithering as three feet of the green grass and the gravel under it carried them away. He heard her scream. He couldn't believe his eyes. He looked over. He saw the two bodies hitting the water far below, and then holding his nostrils with his fingers he stepped off and jumped so that when he landed he would land clear of the boiling place that covered them.

Two

OR ONE SECOND before he hit the water, he thought: Suppose I land on a rock. He imagined the impact of it against his legs. He imagined his legs breaking off at the knees. Then he felt the water. There was no rock. He wondered if Breeda had hit a rock; if Joseph was dead.

His feet and his body hit the sandy place below. It wasn't very deep. There was no undertow. He kicked himself to the top and turned. He saw Joseph. Joseph was swimming. He looked bewildered. There was a fresh stream of blood pouring from a wound in his head. Then he saw Breeda. She was out of the water, her face to the sky, and she was being dragged towards the foot of the cliff by a single crashing wave. It caught her and took her and he saw her head being stopped by a rock that came from the water and gleamed wetly in the sun. Then she was gone, but he reached her and went under and found the stuff of her dress in his hands. He hauled her to the top and holding her with one hand clung to the rock with the other. The waves were washing at his back and crashing over his head.

"Are you all right, Joseph?" he shouted.

Joseph nodded his head, then Bart turned and hauled himself and Breeda around the rock. He swam a bit under the cliff, and made towards the gaping stretch of silver sand around the turn. It wasn't far. It wasn't difficult. Soon he felt the sand under his feet, so he raised her in his two arms and walked clear of the tide. He laid her on the sand. She wasn't dead. She was breathing freely.

He remembered vividly her head being bounced off the black rock. He got on his knees beside her and raised her head in his palm. He felt the wet of the sea and a stickiness. He turned her over on her side. His palm was sticky with scarlet blood. He parted her hair. The cut right at the back of her head was deep and bleeding freely. He hauled his wet shirt out of the band of his trousers and tore a strip of it away. He went down to the sea and wet it again in case it wasn't wet enough, and came back and kept bathing the cut until his piece of shirt was no longer white. He took another strip and did the same. A good part of his shirt was gone before the wound stopped bleeding. He didn't dare press his hand around the cut. He was afraid he would hear the creaking of bone. Joseph was standing beside him, looking down at the girl stretched at his feet. The water was dripping from him. He was shivering.

"Go and get the donkey, Joseph," Bart said.

Joseph nodded and trudged up the strand. His shoes were squelching, so he sat and took them off and the dripping socks and walked stiff-legged holding them in his hands.

"Breeda! Breeda!" Bart was calling her, as soft as his rusty voice would allow. He was sitting on the back of his legs. Her head and shoulders were resting on his thighs. Her hand rose. Went up to her forehead.

"Breeda! Breeda! Are you all right? Tell us you are all right." His voice was urgent.

"My head is paining me," Breeda said. "I can't open my eyes with the pain in my head."

"It'll be all right, you'll see," he said. "It was only a crack. You have a hard head. All the Boola Valley people have hard heads."

She sat up. It hurt her. She gasped and brought her two hands up to her face. "Oh!" She sucked in her breath. "What happened, Bart? Why have I such a pain in my head?"

"It'll be all right," he said. "Listen, Breeda, I'm sorry. I don't know what happened to me up there. I'm in a fever, I tell you. About things that don't matter. Breeda, I wouldn't have frightened you for all the money in the world. I didn't mean it. You know I didn't mean it."

17

"All right, Bart," Breeda said. "It's all right. It's all mixed up. It was my fault maybe. I don't know what happened. But I wish I hadn't such a pain in my head, Bart."

"Here," he said, helping her. "Get up and it might go away. Walk about a bit at least. Even in the hot sun you shouldn't be lying still in wet clothes."

She got to her feet. She took her hands away from her face. He noticed that her fingers were long and slender. She opened her eyes. They were wide open.

"Bart," she said, and there was fright in her voice. "I don't seem to be able to open my eyes."

Bart felt his heart missing a beat. Her eyes were wide open.

"You will," he said, "you will, Breeda. There's a cut on the back of your head. We'll have to get to a doctor. It'll have to be stitched, that's all. Here, I'll tie a bandage around your head and we'll get away." He rolled a piece of his white shirt into a pad. He placed it over the cut. Then he bound a wrapped-up piece all around her head, covering her eyes and the pad, and tied it off at the side of her head.

"I'm covering your eyes," he said. "That way you won't feel the pain. It's better to keep them shut. Come on, Breeda, we'll go and meet Joseph." He caught her and swung her into his arms and headed up the strand. What remained of his shirt was flapping around his body. There was terrible urgency in him to get home. It was a long way home. But he didn't rush. He only rushed home with his mind. He didn't want to frighten her.

What kind of a person am I at all? he was thinking. What end can there be for a person like me who can do violent things like I have done?

"You're very strong, Bart," Breeda was saying. Even under the bandage he could see her face creased up into wrinkles of pain, even though he was very careful about her head. It was on his shoulder. He could feel her wet hair on his skin.

"I'm not strong enough, Breeda," he said. "It will take me a long time to forgive myself for to-day."

"What did they do to you, Bart?" she asked him.

"Nobody did anything to me," he said. "It's what I do to people. There was a teacher at the training college. I didn't like him. He was a sneerer. He was a superior sneering bastard. So I hit him. I wanted to wipe off the sneer, that's all. That's why there's no more college. But I took it out on you, Breeda. You know that. That's the terrible thing, that is."

"Oh, no," she said. He saw tears coming from under the bandage down on her cheeks, beside her nose. "It's hurting awful, Bart," she said. "Sure it's not bad, is it? Sure it's not bad?"

"No, no," he said, "on me oath. It's only a scratch, I tell you."

Joseph was coming down with the ass. "You better sit on the back of the donkey, Breeda. It will be quicker. We'll get home quicker." He put her down. He tore the baskets from the panniers and raised her on to the padded straw. "Hold his mane," he said, "and bend forward. Let your head hang, just as if you were an ass."

"I am an ass," she said. Her hair was in streaks. It fell around her face below the bandage. Bart hoisted one of the empty baskets on his shoulder. Joseph took the other. They weren't heavy. They turned on to the road. Bart was behind. He hit the donkey on the rump. "On with you," he said. The donkey went on obediently. Joseph stayed at his head leading him.

"How is Joseph?" Breeda asked. "Is Joseph all right?"

"I'm fine, Breeda," Joseph said, turning back to her as if she could see him. There was dried blood on the side of his face. He hadn't wiped it all away. It was only a scratch anyhow, he knew. He had scraped a barnacle on the side of a stone when he was coming up from below.

God, what a picture we are! Bart thought savagely.

They had to go through the main street of the village. There were only ten houses in it, five on each side of the street. Four of them were thatched and six of them were new grant houses with blue slates on them. The doctor lived in the far slate house. He was in. His car was in front of the door. He opened the door to them. Bart had lifted the girl from the ass. She was standing there.

"We had an accident," Bart said. "We were up on top of the

19

cliff below and it caved. She has a deep cut at the back of her head."

"I'll look after her," the doctor said. He was a thin man with grey hair. He had a grey suit on and his collar was crumpled and thick horn-rimmed glasses fell down on his nose. "I'll look after her. Go up and tell her aunt to get her dry clothes down here as soon as she can."

"It'll be all right," Bart said. "Everything will be all right."

Then the doctor had taken her in and he was looking at the closed door.

As soon as it closed it opened again and the doctor put his head out.

"Here, you," he said to Joseph, "I see blood on you. Are you all right?"

"I'm all right. Honest, I'm all right," Joseph said. His hands were behind his back and he was stepping away.

"It'll only take a second to look at it," the doctor said.

He caught his head in his hands and pressed back the hair. He probed it with his fingers.

"All right," he said. "Put iodine on it when you get home. Don't forget."

The door closed on him again.

I should have brought him in, he was thinking, and dressed it for him, but he was too worried over the girl. He was looking at a coloured chart of the skull. Principally he thought of the occipital lobe and thought confusedly about visuo-sensory and visuo-psychic agencies. "In here, Breeda," he said, leading her into the white-walled room. There was a couch and bottles, big and small, and glass-fronted cupboards with more bottles. He called "Mary" , and his wife came in rubbing her hands on her apron. She gasped when she saw the soaked and shivering figure of the girl. "Take her into the kitchen and dry her off and give her something to cover her," he said.

"Come on, dear," Mary said. She tried to cheer her. "You look like the daughter of an Indian chieftain," she said. "Do you know that, Breeda?"

"I don't feel as hot," Breeda said, her teeth chattering.

"Stand in front of the fire," Mary said. "It's as hot as hell. It's such a hot day out and I have to do the washing. That's why the range is going." She quickly had the dress over her head. Breeda felt her hands on her. The hands were warm, but they were hardworking hands. Then she felt the towel rubbing her all over. It was a soft towel. It seemed to bring heat back into her body. All the time I will think only of things like that, and maybe the terrible panic in my stomach will go away. She was afraid if she thought too much that she would vomit. It was queer to have her eyes covered so that she couldn't see, only feel, and the terrible pain in the back of her head was as bad as ever. Then Mary was carefully putting the opening of a soft silky dress over her head. "It's one of my own summer frocks," she was saying. "It's just right for you and imagine it's only three years ago that it was right for me. I'm getting a terrible figure and God knows I don't know why. I work hard enough to keep slim. John says I eat too much."

Breeda laughed.

"Sit down now," Mary said, "in front of the fire." It was odd that you should try and look around before you sat down, but that didn't matter now. The doctor was in the kitchen. She felt him raising her hand and putting a glass into it. "Drink this," she heard him saying. It was hot. It was faintly spirituous, she thought, and had to laugh a little and then almost gagged as it caught her throat. "I'll deal with the bandage now," she heard him saying. She felt his fingers at the knot Bart had tied. Where's Bart? I wish Bart was here. Then when she thought of Bart, she felt air under her feet and she was falling, falling, and afterwards something hit her on the head. The bandage was off. She felt him removing it. But he couldn't have removed it altogether, because there was still some of it blocking her eyes. "You still have some of it over my eyes," she said. The doctor avoided his wife's eyes. He knew the look of shock and horror that would be in them. His wife always suffered more for his patients than the patients themselves did. He lied then. "I'm just leaving it on for a little time more, Breeda, then I'll take it away." He wasn't sure yet anyhow. He couldn't be sure. "I might have to cut some of your hair," he said. "Will that offend you?"

"You can take it all," Breeda said. "It's only like rats' tails anyhow."

"It is not," said Mary indignantly. "It's beautiful long silky hair. I have always admired your hair, Breeda."

"You are very kind," said Breeda. What was that note in the voice of the doctor's wife? An odd note. Pity? It was kind of her, but it was only a little cut. It didn't feel half as bad now, so it didn't. The doctor was glaring at his wife. "We'll go back inside now, Breeda," he was saying. "Mary, you bring the water." His hand was on her arm guiding her. He didn't make it too noticeable. She felt the edge of the couch at the back of her legs and sat down. "Bend forward now," he said. He hurt her. He seemed to be a very long time swabbing and swabbing. Even though his hands were kind his probing seemed to be inexorable. "It only took two stitches, Breeda," he was saying then, "you are lucky. You can straighten up now." She sat up straight. He was shining the concentrated light of a pencil torch into her eyes, but she didn't know this and his heart was sinking very fast. It may not be, it may not be, he was hoping, but he knew. Anyhow, he thought, the final business can be put off. Who am I to say? There are the eye doctors in the town and X-ray photos. "I'm putting a fresh bandage over your eyes," he said.

She could feel the touch of the cotton on the sides of her face. "I'm going to College next year, doctor," she told him. "Guess what I'm going to be?"

"A teacher," he said, "like your father."

"No," she said, "I'm going to be a doctor like you."

"What put that thought into your head?" he asked.

He felt her then stiffening under his hands.

"You didn't take off the old bandage," she said.

What could he say? He was silent.

Breeda had a good brain. She had a very fast one. Her thoughts whirled around in her head. "Don't," she said. "Don't put on that one. There was no old bandage at all. It was just that I couldn't see. Tell me the truth now."

"There was no old bandage," he said. He saw the smooth face that was as soft to the touch as the petal of a flower pull itself into

22

crinkles. The deep-sunken eyes were very wide. But they could not see. But they could cry. The doctor felt very sad. He felt very helpless. Her head fell.

"Look, Breeda," he said. "You can never tell. We'll go into the town in my car as soon as your aunt comes and we'll get X-rays done. It may be just the shock. You never know."

She raised her head. Her face was fiercely eager.

"I don't believe it is serious," she said. "It couldn't be. It was only a small bash. I don't believe it. Things like that don't happen all the time to the one family. It can't happen. It was enough that thing that happened to Daddy and Mammy. It will be all right. It will come back. I know it will. I even see a bit of light now, so I do."

"We'll go when your aunt comes," he said. "First we can have a sup of tea. Will you make tea, Mary? Mary!" He spoke to her very sharply because she was standing there above the girl crying and wiping tears away with the edge of her apron. She was always like that. As soft as feathers. And she loved young people. Not that she was very old herself, but they had no children. Who knew why? Because both of their sides of the families had been as prolific as rabbits.

Breeda wanted to say, "Let's go off now before my aunt comes. I want to be gone before my aunt comes." But she couldn't say that out. You didn't say things like that out.

Bart was talking to her aunt.

He had to go down the street and cross over the stone bridge and instead of going straight ahead to their own place turn up to the left along the yellow road that wound. He paused at the cross.

"You go home, Joseph," he said. Joseph didn't seem to hear him, was walking along beside him still holding the donkey's bridle. "Joseph!" he called.

Joseph looked back at him. There was a vague look in his eyes.

"Yes, Bart?" he said.

"Are you all right?" Bart asked.

"Yes, I am, honest I am," said Joseph. He wasn't all right. He had a frightful pain in his head and his wet clothes drying on him in the hot sun were making him shiver almost uncontrollably. I should go home with him first maybe, Bart thought, and then thought of the girl in the doctor's. "You go home, Joseph," he said, "and change your clothes and if you feel bad get into bed."

"All right, Bart," Joseph said and turned off obediently. When his face was hidden from Bart he squeezed his eyes closed and said over and over with his lips barely moving: "Jesus, Mary and Joseph, help me." It was his infallible remedy for everything that beset him. People didn't know he prayed. They would meet him and salute him and he would be gone a bit before their greeting penetrated to his mind, then he would turn back slightly confused and say, "Oh, hello, yes, it is a grand day, isn't it?" Some said he was cracked. Others said he had a slate loose. Some were slightly awed by his introspection. "Ah," they said, "he's going to be a priest anyhow and that's what's wrong with him."

Bart watched him for a moment and then he threw his leg over the donkey's back and clucked with his tongue and hit him a blow across the ears with the thick rope of the reins. "Up our that!" he said. The donkey was startled and raised his ears, but when he got another blow from the rope he ran. It was uphill, the road, and the weight on his back was very solid, but he didn't like to be beaten about the ears, so he ran. The remnants of Bart's shirt were fluttering in the breeze. He thought what a figure he must cut. There were some people in the fields at the hay. Most of them were away in, but the nearest to him were the Brendans, young Willie with the black hair and his big brother, Suck. Suck was leaning on the handle of a hay-fork. That's why they called him Suck. Nearly every time you saw him with a spade or a sle·n or a fork in his hand, he was leaning on it, so they said he was a great man for giving suck to the spade, meaning every time you saw him he wasn't working. But he was a big man and he could do more work in an hour than another could do in a day and he could afford to give occasional suck to the spade.

They were near the road.

Willie shouted, "Hey, Bart. We can use you as a scarecrow."

The bastard has no reticence, Bart thought. He has to say out everything he notices.

"Ha! Ha! Ha!" Bart said savagely. "Very funny." Then he hit the ass again and they went over the hill in a cloud of dust.

"What's up, I wonder?" Willie asked his brother.

"Something odd," his brother said, and they remained for a long time looking after the tattered figure on the donkey. All the pleasure was gone out of work for them. They had to know.

Bart knew that the whole valley would be buzzing. There were faces at the windows in the houses in the village. He was thinking all these things to keep his mind off Breeda. He thought of her aunt. What he would say to her. A few hours ago, Breeda was a slight girl he saw but rarely noticed. Now his whole life was going to be coloured by her and what had happened. It was nothing. It was just all the shock. By God, it would be indecent if anything had happened to her eyes. That would really fix things up.

The house was surrounded by a neat stone wall. It was very white. It was very simple. A slate roof and another neat wall separating it from the out-offices and the hen houses. He tied the donkey to the gate and went in. He nearly sneered walking up the cinder path. There was cut grass on each side and flowerbeds. Imagine here in this bleak land where a wind from the sea in March would wither anything in its path. The door was open. He went in. There was nobody in the kitchen. It was wide and clean with the concrete floor level and well scrubbed. Her husband had been a good handyman. He had built the house himself, laid the floors, and was just in time to have it all finished for his funeral, they said. There's some finger on these people, there's no doubt. He called.

"Mrs. Heron! Mrs. Heron!"

His voice was deep, it reverberated through the house. The delph rattled in the cupboard.

"Yes, yes," he heard the soft sibilant voice. She was in the room. She came down. She stood. blinking. She couldn't quite believe the sight of her eyes. Young Bart O'Breen standing there in her kitchen, with the shirt tattered on him, his trousers

25

wrinkled and bedraggled, so that she had to turn her eyes away from the shape of his thighs and his body. But his big bronzed chest was very visible too. His eyes seemed to be looking at her hotly from over the big jaw. Dear, dear! They called her Dear. Her name was Bidelia. It maddened her if anyone shortened it to Biddy or Delia. She wanted all the syllables in, so she did. "What's wrong? What happened, dear?" she asked.

She was in her early thirties. She was well built. Her face was smooth, her hair was brown with no grey in it and it was settled around her face from a loose bun at the back. If she kept her mouth shut she was the picture of a good-looking, physically attractive woman. But that sort of sharp sibilant voice ruined the whole effect, he decided.

"Breeda had an accident," he said.

Her hand went up to her mouth. She gasped. He knew she would do that. "Oh no," she said, feeling around for a chair. She sat. "She's dead."

"No," he said impatiently, "she's not dead. We were on the cliff. Part of it caved. We fell. The three of us. Breeda and Joseph and me. She got a cut on the back of her head. She's at the doctor's. You better go down."

"Oh, my God," she said. "What it is to be mixed up with the Coopers! It's true what people say that the finger of God is on them. First her father and mother. Both together at once, and then my dear Pat. He was the brother of Breeda's mother, you know. I'm dry of tears. Honest, I'm dry of tears. If Breeda had been dead I wouldn't have a tear left. Is she bad? What's wrong with her?"

"A cut she has on her head," Bart said loudly in case he would shout at her for God's sake to get moving. "But she was wet. Bring her some clothes to change into. She will be all right. And hurry, ma'am, for God's sake. Will you take the ass?"

"No, dear," she said, "I'll run."

She went fussing. He started counting. He knew all the fussing she would do. She went five times into a room when once would have done. Then she fiddled around the kitchen. She was ready with a parcel of clothes and her own coat over her dress and the coloured apron. Then she had to take off the coat again to take off the apron and then she had to put on the coat again. He shut the door behind her and closed the gate. He told her to walk ahead and he untackled the ass in the yard and drove him into the mountain field behind the house. The donkey didn't like him. He shied away as soon as the bridle was off him. Bart threw the bridle on the wall and ran after the woman.

How in the name of God did I become involved in this? His own story about the collapse of the cliff was beginning to sound right to his ears. It was the only feasible way it could have happened.

Down ahead he could see the lake shimmering in the sun. That was Boola. It was a big lake. There were seventeen tree-covered islands on it. It wasn't as big as the Corrib lake further below, but it was big. On the left sloping away was the great Beann Boola mountain. It seemed to rise sheer up from the lake. You'd think only flies could stick to it. But you could see the white dots that were sheep and an occasional black bullock cropping. Opposite the mountain, on the other side of the lake, the land rose to a plateau and it was bisected by a gorge in which you could see a white stream that fell rather than flowed from the Upper Boola. All this on the left and then on the right the road and river running six miles to the sea. He didn't want to think of the sea. He felt shut in. He felt things were taking hold of him.

The woman was talking, talking.

"My darling, my darling," she was saying. "If anything happened my darling I would die. She is all I have left of the lot of us. So happy we were, the two of us, in the little house and the few acres. What would happen?"

She is a big soft pluddery woman, he was thinking. She has no control. He thought of Breeda. Breeda had control. It would be terrible if she was like her aunt. But then she wasn't her real aunt, but one by marriage.

He walked with her to the doctor's house.

The doctor was glad to see Bidelia. "Oh, you have come! Come in! Come in!" Bart didn't go in. He stood there until she was gone. Then he said harshly, "How is she?"

The doctor resented him. He felt that whatever had happened Bart was behind it. Whenever anything out of the way happened in Boola you could take it for sure that Bart O'Breen was behind it.

"She's not good. I think she has lost her sight," he said.

"Oh, no," said Bart. "That's not possible."

"Ah, so," the doctor said, his lips tightened.

"What are you going to do?" Bart asked.

"I'm taking her to the town," the doctor said resentfully, "to have them confirm by X-ray something that I am certain of already. And if I were you I would go somewhere and pray that I am wrong. I don't know who was to blame for what happened, but it is going to cause many people a lot of unnecessary suffering."

He closed the door then.

Bart turned and walked away slowly. He put his hands in his pockets and then pulled them out again. The pockets were wet and soggy.

He can't put troubles on to me, he was thinking. I have enough troubles of my own.

Then he went home to face them.

Three

DESPITE THE PAIN in his head and his discomfort, Joseph didn't like going in home. His steps dragged as he approached the house.

It wasn't one house. It was a conglomerate lying at the foot of the mountain. One time there had been two houses here; the farmhouse of Dempsey O'Breen. That was a two-storey slated house, stone built, and a good house against the weather. On the left of this there had been the shop of John Willie Baun. Now they were joined by a narrow two-storey edifice that had been erected between them to make them an awkward ugly one. The shop was two-storey but all the upstairs rooms were now used for storing goods. The fronts of both rooms were whitewashed and gleamed in the sun. On the front of the shop two tin advertisements had been nailed, one advertising a brand of stout and the other advertising cigarettes. One was scarlet and the other was green. Some of the enamel had been battered from the tin and they were rusted in spots, and careless whitewashing had left drops which had eaten into the enamel. The whole front of the place was a cobble-stone yard. Sometimes you would have to cover your ears with your hands to shut out the noise of ironshod wheels rattling on the cobble-stones. All the doors and windows were painted a dark iron-oxide red. Joseph could see a blue trail of smoke rising from the kitchen chimney. It was the background of the towering mountain behind that made it easy to see the smoke.

He hoped his mother was in the shop as he lifted the latch to go into the kitchen. He liked his mother very much, but there

29

were times, and this was one of them, when it would be better if she didn't see him, because it only meant more trouble for Bart.

She wasn't in the kitchen. Katie was there. She was fixing the turf fire on the hearth. She was humming and bending down and presenting an enormous backside to his eyes. Her legs were bare and fat and the shins of them were raddled with ABC's. She turned when she heard the latch. The tongs were still in her hand. Her eyes opened widely and then her mouth. She had some teeth missing, her mouth was big and a great laugh emanated from it.

"Beggars!" she screamed. "Who put you through a mangle?" She slapped her thigh. It made a dull clucking smack. She laughed again. "God, if you could see yourself! You're like a dog comin' out of a drain."

He was used to Katie. Katie had no inhibitions. She had no figure. Bart said to her face that she was like a gowleog of hay somebody had stuffed into a sack. Clothed any old way. Hair any old way. But she was a good worker and she had a good heart.

"Where's mother?" Joseph asked.

"In the shop, I suppose," Katie said. "Here what happened? There's dried blood on your head too."

"An accident," Joseph said. "We fell into the sea. Give me a basin of hot water, will you?"

"Fell into the sea!" she echoed. "What kind of going on is that? I'll bet it was Bart. Did he fire you in or what? That fella is up to anything. Wait'll your mother gets him. Over the letter." All the time she was pouring the water into a white enamel basin. "Here, I'll get you a clean towel. What kind of childer are ye at all? Yeer all grown up now or did ye know it?"

"All right, all right," he said, taking the basin. "Don't say anything to mother about me," he cautioned her as he went into his room.

"Divil a fear of me!" she called after him. "Not that it'll be any good anyhow. She'll know all about it anyhow." She laughed after that.

It was a small bare room. A single iron bedstead, a table with a white cloth to match the white quilt on the bed. There was shining lino on the floor and the walls were boarded and painted dark brown. There was a white washstand and a large jug with a red rose painted on it standing in another basin. He poured the hot water into this and started to strip off his clothes. It was a great relief to get out of them, but every time he bent down his head whirled. He didn't want to think of Breeda. He tried to keep her out of his mind. As he rubbed and rubbed himself with the towel his eyes fell on the little altar over the table. He prayed that Breeda would be all right; that nothing wrong would happen, that his mother wouldn't be too severe with Bart. He dropped the towel around his waist as the door opened and Katie came in. "You forgot the soap," she said. She took her fill of the thin body in front of her before she backed out. She wasn't embarrassed about seeing him. "You haven't a pick on you," she told him now with a measure of disdain. "You want to ate more stirabout and red meat. I think your mother is coming in."

She closed the door.

He quickly turned to the basin and using the corner of the towel he wiped away all the dried blood from the side of his face and his hair. He could see a small cut on top of a large bump. That was all. There was a curtained cupboard in the corner where his clothes were. He started to change into them. He was in his trousers and buttoning up his clean white shirt when the door opened and his mother filled it.

"What happened?" she asked.

"Nothing much," he said. "Just we were on the cliff and it caved and we fell into the sea."

"It was his fault, wasn't it?" she demanded.

"No," he said. "It was nobody's fault. It just happened."

"You're covering up for him again," she said. Then she noticed the towel with the bloodstains on it.

"You're hurt," she said. "What happened to you, Joseph? Is it bad?"

She came over to him. She caught his shoulders in her hands. She was taller than he. He had to look up into her eyes. There was a smell of the shop from her, spices and stout and bran and corn and red soap.

He tried to free himself. She wouldn't release him. "No, mother, honest, it's only a scratch, I tell you."

"Come down into the light until I look at it," she said. She forced him out of the room into the kitchen. She looked at his head from the light of the window. "It doesn't look bad," she said, "but there is a lump there. Are you sure it's not hurting you more than you say?"

"No," he said. "No. It isn't" – wishing he could go back to his room and lie down on the bed and rest his body and his head on a pillow so that the pain of it might go away. It was an effort for him to keep his eyes open.

"I'll bet he is without a scratch," she said. "I'll bet nothing at all happened to him. Nothing ever happens to him. Why didn't he come home when you gave him my message?"

"He was going to help Breeda with the donkey, that's all. We all went. That's all."

"That's all," she said grimly, going over to open the door and look out. "And the girl, what happened to the girl?"

"She got a bad cut on the back of her head. The doctor is stitching it."

He looked at her standing there in the light from the door. One time her hair was red, now it only remained a little red on the top of her head, the rest of it had turned a muddy grey. She wore it cut short and combed back over her ears. This was the way it had always been. It showed a very strong jaw and a straight chiselled nose and folded lips that could tighten. She was a tall strong woman wearing a dark blue overall with a leather belt from which keys jangled. Joseph loved his mother. He had always done so. He never remembered her being angry with him. He had never done anything that could anger her if it came to that. She had worked hard all her life. She had married Dempsey and his farm and borne him two sons, Luke and Bart. Joseph didn't remember him. The picture in the sitting room didn't disclose him. Just the head and shoulders of a large fair-haired man with a moustache and a large smile. He had been the father of Luke and Bart. Then he died. Hewn down like a great oak. She had worked very hard after that too, until small John Willie

Baun with his shop had made the tentative proposal that they should join the farm and the shop and themselves. Joseph was the only son of John Willie.

She turned and looked at him. Her eyes were soft.

"Go on in and lie down, Joseph," she said. "Katie will bring you in a bowl of hot soup."

"Katie will not bring him in a bowl of hot soup," Katie said. "Haven't I enough to do? The pigs aren't fed yet and I have all the dinner to get. Hasn't he a pair of legs?"

"Shut up," his mother said without looking at her.

"All right, ma'am," Katie said and shut her mouth tightly as if she would never open it again.

"It wasn't really Bart's fault," Joseph said as he turned to go into the room.

"All right," she said, her lips tightening.

I've done the best I can, he thought as he closed the door after him. It was real pleasure to rest himself on the bed and let the feathers of the pillow cushion the weight of his head.

His mother looked at the closed door, then she looked out of the kitchen door again. There was no sign of her son.

"When he comes," she told Katie, "tell him I am in the sitting-room." She went in there. It was a small cheerless room with a mahogany table and six upholstered chairs and a sideboard with an eight-day clock ticking. It smelled damp and cold because it was rarely used. She sat at the table and took out the letter and read it again. She looked up at the picture of her first husband. He grinned down at her. Bart was the spit of him, she thought. There isn't a bit of me in Bart. He had always been like his father. Careless and reckless, never pausing to count the cost of anything. He would earn a year and drink a year in a week. It was she who had built the farm until it was the best one in the valley. It was she who had used the spade and the plough and the horses, had limed the land and got it drained and built up the stock. Had snatched many acres from the breast of the mountain, so that now if you looked out of the back window you could see the long green fields creeping up the mountain inside the shelter of the grey stone walls.

33

It wasn't easy. He wasn't easy. He resented system and decorum and she had to fight the careless way out of him. Physically too, because he was a man who would raise his hand to a woman in anger and think nothing of it. He had raised it to her often until she disagreed and hit back. She could still see the startled look on his face with the blood flowing from a wound in his forehead. "You hit me, Mabbina," he said. "You hit me!" and he could hardly believe it until he explored the wound with his fingers and saw the bright blood on them. Yes, she had mastered Dempsey and she would master his son Bart. She squirmed when she thought of it. Why should it happen to her? She owed no man anything. She never bought that she didn't pay. In all her dealings she was just and honest. That was the way the world should run.

Bart was in the shop. He came in around by the back way.

There was nobody in the shop except John Willie, who was polishing glasses. There wasn't much light in there, only the diffused light from two small windows shining through green bottles.

"Crisscross, Bart," John Willie said. "Murder!" John Willie never finished sentences. He said "Crisscross" often because one time he used to say cross of Christ until he saw the hurt in the face of his son Joseph. Willie wouldn't hurt an animal, not to mention a human being. John Willie liked Bart. He liked him just the same as if he was his son. He was small, never wore a collar, just the brass stud holding his shirt tightly to a scrawny neck. He always wore a brown cap with the peak pulled down over his eyes. Most people wondered if John Willie wore the brown cap in bed.

"Where is she?" Bart asked.

"Athin," said John Willie.

"Rattle out a pint, John Willie," Bart said, climbing on a stool. The drinking part of the shop was in a corner. There was no separation between the drinking part and the grocery part. On the shelves in the middle of the shop there were three very big dark-green canisters with sloping lids, that said TEA, SUGAR, COFFEE.

John Willie went to the door of the shop leading into the house and peered into the passage before he poured the pint. If Mabbina caught him giving Bart a drink there would be blue murder.

"Bad, bad, Bart," said John Willie, shaking his head.

"I'm in trouble, John Willie," Bart said.

"Never out of it, man, never out of it," John Willie said. "Crisscross!"

He kept holding his hand out. Bart put the pint glass to his head and drained it, pausing in the middle for breath.

John Willie whipped it away and proceeded to wash it with a sigh of relief. Now let her come, his face said.

"You know the little Cooper girl, John Willie?" Bart asked.

"Yes," said John Willie. "Grand girl. Great father. Nice mother. Pity."

"More pity is needed now," said Bart. "We fell off the cliff below. You heard that?"

"Yes, yes, man. Heard you threw both of them over."

"That's a lie," said Bart.

"Sure, man, sure," said John Willie.

"I don't care," said Bart. "But she's hurt. I'm afraid she's hurt bad. If she is hurt as bad as I think she is, some of the colour is going to be taken out of the world for me. You hear that?"

"Yes," said John Willie. "Sad. Very sad. A grand little girl. She would have grown too. Into a beauty."

"She can still grow," Bart said. "She can still grow beautiful, but what good will that be, John Willie, if she can't see her reflection in a pool?"

"Crisscross!" John Willie said.

"And now I'll go and see your wife," Bart said, rising from the stool.

John Willie grinned. Always between themselves, John Willie called Mabbina "your mother" and Bart called her "your wife". John Willie felt warm with the sympathy that lay between the two of them.

"Don't answer back, Bart," he said. "Remember that. Don't answer back. All things equal, don't answer back. Hold your tongue between your teeth."

"Right you are, John Willie," Bart said, and went out of the shop and walked the few yards and turned into the open door of the kitchen. Katie was bending over the fire. Bart approached her and slapped her. Katie was unperturbed. She turned. Her face was red from bending.

"Jakers, we all know who that is," she said. "Hersel will kill you. She's up in the funeral parlour." Katie laughed at this. She had seen the words once in an American magazine. She thought it was funny because people around here rarely used their parlours unless they had a funeral.

"Is Joseph all right?" he asked her.

"Him!" said Katie. "Course he is all right. What'd be wrong with him? Mammy's darling. God, you look a sight! Like you were ripped be a thorn-bush."

"Fine," Bart said, then he went into the parlour.

She looked up from the letter. He felt the antagonism in her eyes. He always wondered at it. He wanted to be liked by her, while he was with her. In the many cases where he had been before her, like a schoolboy before a headmaster, he had always been tongue-tied. Not because he didn't want to say something, but because when you did say something in extenuation it always sounded to his own ears like impertinence. That was the feeling she gave you. She was a good woman.

He was nearly naked down to the waistband of his trousers. His chest was big. It was hairy. The hair was growing thickly almost down to his navel. He could have been his father, she thought, if he was a little older and had a fair moustache and a big smile. The permanent smile was the only thing that Bart didn't have. She didn't think that she was the cause of that. Mrs. Baun had no sense of humour, everyone knew. She was a good woman but she had no sense of humour. Bart didn't smile often either.

"I'll read out this letter," she said.

He waited there unmoving, one hand still on the knob of the door. She shouted at him suddenly. "Come in and close the door and sit down!" she shouted. Her eyes were narrowed with anger. He closed the door, quietly, he came to a chair and sat down. All done quietly, he thought, and yet it seems fearfully insolent.

Dear Mrs. Baun," she read, "We wish you to withdraw your son Bartholomew from the College. We regret to inform you that he is unmanageable, and given to outbursts of uncontrolled violence. He committed a brutal assault on the Maths Master, Mr. Fitzgerald. There was no possible reason for such an assault. The consequences for him could have been more serious if we had not persuaded Mr. Fitzgerald for the good of the College not to prefer charges. In the matter of compensation for the injuries your son inflicted on him, Mr. Fitzgerald's solicitors will be in touch with you. That is out of our hands.

"Your son would never have made a teacher. This action alone is sufficient proof of that statement, but his behaviour generally, apart from that, was never such that one could hope he would be successful. He is not amenable even to mild discipline. Rules, for him, are there to be either openly circumvented or broken. His example could be disastrous to better-balanced students. In several cases he has left ineradicable stains on the minds of some of the younger boys who professed to admire his 'freedom'. He has never shown the slightest sign of being contrite or even moved by the consequences of his actions. We regret the necessity of this letter. We are reluctant to inflict pain on you but there was no other course open to us. Yours sincerely."

She folded the letter slowly into its original creases.

Bart was thinking of Mr. Fitzgerald. Mr. Fitzgerald was a moral sadist, Bart thought. He had the most delicate way of inflicting pain on the mind. They didn't say anything about that, of course. Maybe they didn't know, but Bart knew the suffering that Mr. Fitzgerald had caused, almost as ineradicable as the stain he was supposed to have left on the minds of his few friends.

He saw Mr. Fitzgerald at the board with his sneer. He was called up. He was handed the chalk. His fingers brushed Mr. Fitzgerald's hand. It was like touching the skin of a snake. Behind him he heard the voice as he tried to wrestle with the problem on the board. "Mr. O'Breen will of course . . ." "Mr. O'Breen sees nothing . . ." Mr. O'Breen . . . all that and they were practically grown men. Why should they have to submit to this? This was no imparting of knowledge. So he spoke over his shoulder. "Shut up!"

There was a deathly silence. "What did you say?" "I said if you want me to concentrate on the thing to shut up and let me concentrate on it, and not be yapping away behind my back like an old woman with a viper's tongue." At that point Mr. Fitzgerald made a mistake. He lost his temper. He had never lost it before. His face was red. He reached for the round heavy ruler and he raised it and brought it down in a blind rage. Bart took it on the upper arm, and then with the chalk clenched in his fist he hit Mr. Fitzgerald with great satisfaction. He hit him in the right eye and before he reached the floor he hit him twice more, in the left eye and in the mouth. Then he walked out and went up to the long dormitory and packed his things and left. So I am a sinner. So I am willing to pay for my sins.

"You have shamed us," his mother said. "There's nothing I can do about it. There is no way I can punish you. I wish I could. If you were smaller I'd strip the clothes off you and beat you black and blue. I'd try and beat some of the sin out of you. Don't you feel yourself that you have done wrong? Is there not the slightest feeling of sorrow inside you for what you have done?"

"No," Bart said, and thought, I should have kept my mouth shut.

"I see," she said. "Well, you will stay at home. You will work in the shop and you will work in the fields when your brother Luke needs help."

"I don't want to do that," he said. "I don't like shops. I don't like fields. I want to go to the University. I want to finish my education."

She hit him, reaching up, half crouching, from her chair. There were sparks coming out of her eyes.

"I'll educate you, you lout," she said. "You with an education! What has all the money I have lavished on your education done for you to date? The only education you'll get is the education of sweat, something you never had, something your dirty idle body needs. Get out of my sight, will you, before I hit you with something harder. Get out of my sight and may God forgive you for making me lose my temper."

He went out of the door, his face tingling from the crack of her hard hand. He closed the door softly behind him. He wondered at his calm. Katie was looking at him, her eyes wide. He winked at her. Katie started to cry and turned away. Katie was always crying over lame dogs anyhow. She was a sucker for sentiment. He ran up to his room. It wasn't a tidy place. The small window was looking out at the mountain. He took off his clothes and rubbed himself with the towel. It felt good. He put on another pair of trousers and a shirt and tennis shoes and then climbed out of the window. He didn't want to go down the stairs. He didn't want to run into her again. There was a drainpipe outside. He went down the drainpipe fast. It was weak in spots, but he knew those spots and kept his weight off them. He jumped into the yard, startling the chickens who chortled indignantly at him. He went out of the gate into the haggard where the big hayshed was almost empty after the year, and then he ran towards the foot of the mountain where his brother was gathering hay in the field. He had to jump six stone walls to get there. He wondered if Breeda was in the town by now and what they were doing to her. It all comes from impulse, he thought. I am a creature of impulse. That sounded good. It explained everything, except how you should feel pain for inflicting pain. He didn't. It was all ordained. These things were meant to happen. Why should you wear yourself out worrying about them?

The hay was crisp in the sun. Luke was drinking tea out of a bottle. He was buried in the butt of a gathered cock. There was a girl with him, although it was stretching things to call Martha a girl. She was nearly thirty, he supposed. Luke and she had been going together since they were both attending the national school.

"Hello," he said, and sat.

"Hello, Bart," Martha said. She wore her black hair severely. It was bright but tied too tight in a bun. She had a good body too but she seemed to have that tied up as well as if she was ashamed of it. Nothing undulated when she walked.

"I have to work for you, Luke," Bart said.

Luke was wary. He was a big solid man, with great forearms and heavy thighs, and a face that never seemed to show emotion.

"What's up?" Luke asked.

"I've left off being educated," Bart said. "It's the plough and the slean for me any more and penny packages of bull's eyes."

"Are you home for good?" Luke asked. He didn't seem too pleased.

"Yes," said Bart. "Aren't you pleased? Or are you afraid she will have to divide things with me so that you'll only get half instead of whole?"

"Don't talk like that," Martha said. "Luke is not like that.

"I know," said Bart. "It makes talk anyhow. When are you getting married?"

There was silence. Luke dropped his head.

"Your mother doesn't like me," Martha said. "You know that."

"That's nothing," said Bart. "She doesn't like me either. Listen. Face her. Go on, Luke. For God's sake get a bit of backbone. Life will have passed you by. What can she do? She can do nothing but accept. Where is she going to get a man to do things as well and as cheaply as you do them?"

"Leave me alone," said Luke sullenly. "Mind your own business."

"One day Martha will leave you, you know," Bart said. He was lying on his back feeling the sun hot on his eyes. He was chuckling inside himself. It was so easy to manoeuvre with Luke. Luke hadn't much brains. He was honest and integral. He had startled him. "She might say she won't, but one day she will be tired, and she will be walking at night-time by the lake or a lonely place and another young man will meet her and put his hand on her and you will be whistling for Martha."

"You dirty devil," said Martha. But there was no bite in it. She was so tired of waiting for the approval of her future mother-in-law. What had you to do to gain her approval? Wait until you were forty or fifty and you were too old to be anything but barren and no fun behind you. Because Luke was very honest. The missionaries said: You must not embrace a girl if you do not intend to marry her, and even when you intend to marry her you must not commit sin with her. You must not see her too often

40

or you will drift into sins of impurity. Purity is the basis of good marriages. So Luke, perhaps on account of his lack of imagination, could always resist temptation. Sometimes Martha wished he wouldn't. But she loved Luke. He was so indefinite except where hard work was concerned. He was only happy when his body was moving to the farm rhythm of the seasons. She often thought of her devotion to him. It was like as if she was his mother. She wanted more though.

"You shouldn't say things like that," Luke said. He was hurt.

"Why shouldn't I?" Bart asked. "I bet it's a thought that often comes into your mind. And I'll leave you with it. I'm going up the mountain. I'm going to run up it until I have no breath in me." He was gone almost as soon as he had said it. They looked after him for a time as his figure became smaller and smaller against the slope of the hill. Then Luke looked at Martha. She was regarding him steadily. His eyes fell.

"I better get back to work," he said.

Bart's wind was good. He got a long way up the mountain before his breath came in short pants. That was a joke they kept repeating. He lay back in the heather. The hill was dry. He could embrace the valley with his arms, it seemed, if he wanted to. He could see the lake below spread at his feet and the rising plateau behind with the Upper Boola lake cradled in it. You couldn't see that lake from below. And he saw the road that went from the village to join the main road at the sea, and you could follow this main road for many miles before the shoulder of a distant hill cut it from your sight. He watched this road.

They will have to come back by that road, he thought, and I know the doctor's car and when they come back I will go down and see her.

Already the peculiar light of evening was overcoming the horizon, just as if light brush-strokes had been drawn across the sky. He knew he had some hours to wait so he closed his eyes and slept. He would wake in time.

Four

B UT SHE DIDN'T come home.
He timed his run down from the mountain as soon as he
saw the bonnet of the car appearing around the distant
bend of the sea road. He was glad to run. He was cold. Waves of
cold ran through him. The sun was gone and had left a chill June
nip in the air. The way down was deceptive. He ran instinctive-
ly. He didn't plan what he would say. Bart never made plans. He
could go without eating for a long time if he wanted to. He
always let things happen.

He was waiting outside the silent house when the car stopped.
He was well back in the shadows, so that he would have time to
decide what to do. He saw the bulk of Bidelia coming backwards
out of the car and then she was talking. "Thank you, doctor. The
blessings of God on you. You are very kind, dear. No, no, I will
be all right, dear. Who would trouble me?"

She turned to go in and Bart was in front of her. She started
back from him, her hand on her heart. The gesture annoyed
him. It wasn't dark. She knew well who he was, but these little
startled ways of hers were the instincts of a spinster, although she
wasn't one. She knew what it was all about.

"Where is she?" he demanded.

"Don't come near me, you monster!" she said, her hand held
out dramatically, warding him off. "What you did to my little
girl! May God forgive you, Bart O'Breen, because I never will.
Oh, Breeda! Breeda!" and she started to cry. They were real tears.
He could see them glinting in the fading light.

42

"She's not dead?" he asked, gripping her upper arm. She winced in his clasp. Yet she enjoyed it. She didn't pull away.

"No, thank God. But it's little but she is. They are taking her away, further into the big city. God forgive you. The thing you have done to an orphan girl!"

"Ach!" he said, and flung her arm away and passed her, his jaws tight. He saw that the doctor had turned the car and was coming back.

She staggered and called after him. "Keep away from here for ever, you hear. I don't ever want to see you again, you hear. Remember that, dear. Remember that" and then she went in the gate, rubbing her wet eyes with the back of her hand.

He made the doctor stop. He stood in the middle of the road. He leaned in the window.

"What happened?" he demanded. It was nearly a bark.

The doctor didn't resent it. He was too tired.

"What I thought," said the doctor. "The back of her head was crushed. She's lucky to be alive. But she will never see again. That's sure."

"How the hell do you know?" Bart asked. "Are you God?"

The doctor thought. He thought about God having billions of people on His mind. Here he was with only a few dozen and look at the trouble they were. "No, thank God," the doctor said. "I have enough on my plate as it is." He let in the clutch slowly. The car started to move. Bart ran along beside it. He banged the door with his fist. "But you can't be sure! You can't be sure! There are better doctors. Is she seeing better doctors?"

The doctor stopped the car.

"Look, Bart," he said. "You don't have to be a good doctor or a bad doctor to know for sure when something is certain, something so completely elementary that even a moron could see. You don't want anything serious to have happened to her, because it was probably your fault. You'll have to face up to it now for once and for all. Something serious has happened to her. Breeda Cooper will never see again. That's flat, Bart. She is gone to see better doctors. Better hospitals. Better equipment. But nothing under God can change the fundamental fact that her seeing

43

equipment has been as irreparably destroyed as if two red-hot needles had been poked into her pupils. Right in. Now, Bart, is that clear? If so, please let me go. I'm tired. I want something to eat. I have several sick calls to make yet."

Bart fell back from the car. His hands were hanging by his sides. There was a bleak look in his eyes.

The doctor said, "I'm sorry, Bart. Honest to God, I'm sorry. If I was rude to you way back at the house, I'm sorry. I'd give a lot that I possess if it wasn't true. But it's true. Good night!"

This time he really went.

Bart stood looking after him. He thought for a time. Then he became conscious of emptiness. He was hungry. It had been a long time since he had eaten. He thought of things he could eat.

He went home to eat.

Breeda had insisted on the departure of her aunt. She had become very determined. She didn't want her aunt fussing around her. She wanted to be alone. She insisted on being alone. They took her in the ambulance for a long long trip. She was five weeks in a place she never saw. She barely smelled it. They could do nothing with her. She wouldn't talk. There were many people who sat by her bed and talked to her. She let them talk. Rehabilitation? She wanted none of that, even from kindly experts who talked it over with her. All she wanted was for them to do something to take the bandage from in front of her eyes. She got that into her head, fixed. That all they had to do was to remove a bandage, and they wouldn't do it. They were very sorry for her. She lacked resignation. They said that. She lacked all the things that strong people should possess when they have to fight.

Finally they told her it would be better if she went home. They would send for her aunt. She didn't want her aunt. They could put her on a train, and her aunt could meet her at the other end. She fought for it. She talked more over it than she had done about anything. They dressed her and put her on a train. She was huddled in the corner. There was nobody there first. Then she felt people come in. She turned her head to look out of the glass window beside her. They would think she was just looking. Not one word of thanks had she addressed to any of the people at the hospital. Not one word of thanks. They talked over that for a long time. They said people from the west of Ireland were queer. You wouldn't know what to make of them.

The passengers who travelled with her were repelled by her silent rigidity. Their talk barely penetrated her mind. She remained sunken in her own created lethargy. She wouldn't think. She wouldn't hear. Because if she started to listen it meant that she was truly blind. If she didn't use hearing and feeling and touching, then she would see sometime. If she gave way to the knowledge that she was blind, she thought that she could never bear it. The passengers wondered who the good-looking sullen girl could be and why she never turned her head to even look at them. She was even lacking in curiosity. She had no pain in her head any longer; the wound was completely healed. Her hair had grown.

She stayed in the carriage until the train had come to a cold standstill, and everybody was gone. Then she heard the voice of her aunt, "Breeda! Breeda!" and she was in the carriage embracing her, touching her, asking her questions which required no answer. Then the hateful part. Leaving the carriage. Her aunt's hand tight on her arm. Overdoing it! Overdoing it! Careful the door, dear, and careful the step, dear, now down, now up. She spoke viciously, plucking her arm away: "Leave me alone, do you hear! Leave me alone!" She heard her aunt's gasp, her moan of remonstrance. "But Breeda . . ." and then she had to stand still and wait until her arm was caught again before she could go on. "I'm sorry! I'm sorry!" she said, but she didn't mean it. "This way," her aunt said. "It's the dear doctor. He is so kind. Imagine he came all the way in with me to meet you!" She heard his voice. "Hello, Breeda," he said. It was a kind voice. It accepted her as she was. "I'll sit in front with you," she said. "All right," he said. Bidelia got in the back. She was blowing her nose. Her eyes would be red.

The doctor thought that this wasn't the young girl who had gone away. She seemed to be a different person. He didn't like

45

the look of her compressed lips. He wished he could see expression in her eyes. He would know then how she felt. But there was no expression in the eyes. They just looked. He thought how easy it is for a blind person to conceal their thoughts. That is truth. It is always the eyes that give away the emotion behind the voice.

She felt every mile of the way from the town out home. She had done it so often before that it was instinctive in her. Here she would have been so overjoyed coming from school. Passing through the town to see what shops had changed their fronts, what kind of clothes were in the windows, and afterwards waiting to see the sea. Because the school was midland and all around it flat dull fields. Now she could smell the sea at the point where it should be. Each wind of the road brought her nearer to home and she didn't want to go home. She didn't want anything, any more. The doctor didn't speak at all. He had a feeling that he shouldn't ask questions. She wasn't even grateful to him for that. Her aunt chattered for a while and then she stopped under the burden of the charged silence. Bidelia wondered if this was Breeda at all. She was bottled up with love and pity and embraces that she wanted to pour over her, but she wasn't permitted. Bidelia had had a different picture altogether of what this meeting should have been. It wasn't working to plan. She was bewildered. She was a little afraid.

Breeda's body tightened as the noise of the car changed. It had been in open country with the sea noises on the left. Now it was reverberating as it passed slowly through houses that threw off its own sound. This was the village. Her body was tight. She could picture them at their doors, watching, waiting, perhaps coming forward to tell her they were sorry.

She felt for the doctor's arm.

"You mustn't stop!" she said. "You mustn't stop!"

"I won't stop," she heard him say.

She knew when they went over the bridge. She could feel the car mounting it. And she knew when they turned left and climbed the hill, and she knew when the car stopped outside her aunt's house. She sat there trembling. The doctor got out. Bidelia

46

got out. She felt for the handle of the car door herself and found it after fumbling and pressed it and she stepped out. Then she had to wait. She felt Bidelia's hand on her arm. She walked around the car and then she knew that there was somebody else standing in front of her. She could hear heavy breathing. She could even feel waves of heat coming from the body of him.

"Breeda," Bart said.

"Go away!" she said.

"But listen, Breeda," he said.

"Go away! Go away! Go away! Go away!" she said. She said it in a low penetrating monotone. He started to talk again. She went on, "Go away! Go away! Go away! Go away!"

"Come on in, Breeda," the doctor said. He had taken her arm. He guided her skilfully. Bidelia came running after them and turned the key in the lock and she was inside. "Now, Breeda," the doctor said. "There you are. If there is anything you want from me let me know," and she heard him going.

"Breeda, dear," her aunt began.

"Please, aunt," Breeda said. "Just let me go to my room. I want to lie down."

"But you'll have to have something to eat, dear," her aunt said.

"I'm not hungry," Breeda said. "I only want to lie down."

"All right, but don't take it so hard, dear. It's the will of God. You'll get over it in time, you'll see. You must pray for grace."

"I want to lie down," Breeda said almost in a shout.

"Yes, dear," her aunt said, and took her arm, and led her to the door of her room. Once the door opened she knew it was her room. She could feel the familiar things in it. She felt the bed behind her knees and she sat down. "Leave me alone, now," she said.

Bidelia kept silent and went slowly out. Breeda heard the door closing behind her and she laid herself down on the bed.

Bidelia expelled her breath when she got outside the door. She was almost wringing her hands. Then she saw Bart standing in the open door. The sun was dying behind him. It was late July. She went over to him. She put her hands on his shoulders. She

47

whispered, "Oh, what are we going to do, dear? What are we going to do? She is so changed, so changed." She forgot that she held Bart responsible.

Bart patted her hand.

"All right," he said. "Maybe it's natural for her to be that way. But I didn't expect her to be. She seemed to be sort of the wrong kind to take things that way. Look, Mrs. Heron, can't you go and do some shopping or something and let me talk to her?"

"Oh, no," Bidelia said. "That would be cruel. That would be so cruel. You saw the way you affected her."

"Let me try anyhow," he said. "Go on and tell her you are going out."

She looked at him and then walked back to the door of the room. She knocked on it. She wondered at herself that the day should dawn that she would be knocking at Breeda's door.

"I'm going down to the village, dear, for a message," she said loudly. She waited for a reply. There was no reply. "I won't be long."

She turned back to him, and made a gesture with her hands. "I'll have to fix the fire," she said. "I'll do that," he said to her, going over to it. He took the tongs and raked the ashes from the hot coals and backed them with pieces of turf, placed the hot coals against them and then blew the fire into flame. By that time she was gone. He looked at the door for some time, then he went over and opened it and walked in. He saw her body moving on the bed. It was hard to see her. The wallpaper on the room was cream coloured and it seemed to be golden now from the reflection of the sunset.

"Breeda," he said softly. She didn't say, "Go away!" She turned her face to the wall. She was wearing a blue costume her aunt had sent on to her and a pink silk blouse. The skirt was crumpled. It was the costume for a schoolgirl. It no longer seemed to belong to her. He wondered at the change that had taken place in her. She had lost weight. The cheekbone was very visible. Her hands were thin and very pale.

"You don't remember your father," Bart said. He was standing over her. "He was a great man. Ask anybody. He was the only man I ever admired. I will never meet another like him. He had a philosophy. There was nothing under the sun that could hurt him except another man's suffering. Everybody knows that. You ask anybody. Have you forgotten your father? Nobody else in the valley has. If there was one thing he was never sorry for, it was himself. You ought to know that. Where do you get it? My God, you're so goddam sorry for yourself that you could die."

"Go away!" she said.

"All right. I'm the cause of your affliction. I'm sorry. What else can I be? I can't give you my eyes because they would be no good to you. Why don't you get up from the bed and kick me on the shins and bury your nails in my pupils? Would that help you? Everybody wants to help you. Everybody in the place. They'd do anything for you. They'd do anything for you before you went away, but I doubt if anyone would be inclined to help a sullen bitch like you look now stretched out in a welter of self-pity on a bed."

"Go away!" she said.

"All right," he shouted. "I'll go away and to hell with you. Get up out of your bed and walk, girl. You can still walk and you can still feel and you can still hear and you can still taste, and if you still want to see there's nobody in the place that wouldn't be a pair of eyes for you. Your father would have walked ten miles to help a sick cow, but he wouldn't have walked half a yard to help himself. He had courage and simplicity and patience and humility. You're as proud as a bloody cock. You ever see a cat with a disease? He just stretches himself in front of the fire and he lies down and he dies. All right. You go ahead and be a cat."

"Go away!" she said. She heard the door banging.

He went away. He got as far as the gate. He was angry. He could have taken her by the shoulders and shaken her head off.

She didn't want to remember her father. Because she remembered him too well. If she wanted to remember she would have to go over all the business of the telegram to the school and the going home and seeing the bodies of her mother and father side by side. Both dead. Both drowned. Because her father had gone fishing for pollack and he was not afraid of the sea. He was afraid of nothing because he trusted in the gentleness of everything. She couldn't go back into all that. That would be too much. Because it meant that her own end was inevitable like her affliction. He was a big man with brown hair thinning and the blue gentle eyes. He was always doing something. Never at rest. She got off the bed. He wouldn't be lying down under this. That wasn't what got her off the bed, but that movement would stop her thinking about them. That was all. She groped her way to the door. She knew it was on her right. She felt it with her hands and the cold brass knob was in her fingers. She opened it. She felt that she might be on top of a cliff and that if she moved another step she would fall into the sea and meet the terrible blow on the back of her head. She moved out towards the heat that was coming from the fire. Was it dark now? That didn't matter. Her mouth was dry. She wanted water. The water was over near the dresser. She started to move towards it. It was on her right directly opposite the fire.

Bart was watching her from the door. He didn't come in. He just stood there and watched. She went to the dresser. The corner of the dresser hit her in the stomach. She bent forward to avoid the pain and her forehead cracked loudly on the edge of the dresser. She put her hands to her forehead, moaning, and stepped back. The stool was behind her feet. She fell, hard, on her back.

Bart made a move and then stopped himself. His teeth were clenched as he watched her. She got to her side and then she got to her knees. She was crying. She didn't stand up. She crawled her way to the door of the room and she went in and she pulled herself up on the bed and she lay there face down crying, and she cried out loud, "Oh, God, I want to die. I truly want to die."

Bart ran away from the house.

Five

"ARE YOU SURE, now?" Martha asked.

"Yes," Luke said, and she could discern no hesitation in him. "I am sure."

They were walking one on either side of the horse. It was a golden August evening. The horse was tired. He walked stolidly with his head bent and the harness was jingling. Sometimes his shoe struck a spark from a stone. You could see the light of the spark in the darkening. Martha was holding the reins near the muzzle of the horse. Sometimes the back of her fingers brushed against the soft part of his mouth. She wondered at the velvety feel of it. She was happy. It was a long road she and Luke had travelled but now at last there seemed to be an end of it. She suddenly stopped the horse, pulling on the reins. He remained docile, his head bent, while she crossed him and went close to Luke.

She knew Luke was tired too, like the horse. He was almost as docile. He looked at her. He was in his shirtsleeves, a rather ragged waistcoat over his shirt and a soft battered stained hat on his head that he used to protect him from the sun and the rain. The arms under the rolled sleeves were powerful ones, and so black from constant exposure that they were almost shadowed. She reached down and took one of his hands. He let it go with her. It was a hard heavy hand.

"You're sure, Luke?" she asked. "You're sure that you're right about me? This is the last time I'll ever ask you. Just to be sure."

He raised his free hand and rubbed it on her hair.

"I'm sure, Martha," he said. "Honest I'm sure. I'm not like Bart. I have no words to say it. But I am sure. I was always sure, since we were young, long ago. That was the way I wanted it. I'm slow, you know that. Maybe I've done wrong not facing it before. I should have faced it before. But now I will, and there can be no end to it but the right one."

"All right, Luke," she said. "That's good enough for me."

They went on.

They walked into the yard and around by the back of the shop and she waited while Luke stripped the horse and hung the harness on the pegs in the shed. He freed the horse into the field behind the haggard. The horse accepted his freedom and awkwardly lowered himself on the dusty patch inside the gate and rolled there three times on his right side and three times on his left side. There was no grace in the way he did it. He was like an old country woman who comes to the sea and flounders on the edge in a great white heavy linen nightgown.

Luke took her hand as he walked with her.

"She will be in the parlour," he said. "This is the night she does the books."

Martha had never been in the house before. She had been in the shop to buy things. She always hoped that it would be John Willie who would serve her. If it was Mrs. Baun, she would be angered by her tight-lipped silence, the studied disdain, the way she put her purchases on the counter. There was a little of glee in Martha's feelings now as she thought that at last she would be going into the house and facing the old woman. Here was something that she would find it hard to get out of.

Luke admitted to himself that he was afraid, and that the nearer he came to the house, the drier his mouth became and the harder his heart beat inside his big chest. But at the same time he was determined. He had always been afraid of his mother. His whole attitude of life had been to avoid displeasing her. When they were young she had a hard hand. He had never got over the feeling that any minute she would reach up for the stick on the top of the dresser and say the bit about This is for your own good. You will thank me later when you are grown up that

I took the stick to you when you deserved it. Remember that. I inflict as much pain on myself as I do on you, but it is necessary. She could hurt too. After all, thought Luke, I am over thirty now. Things are not the same. What could she do if I left her? She cannot afford to be without me. And I want Martha. I want something out of life besides hard work.

The kitchen was empty. There was a bright fire burning in it but some of the corners were in shadow. He saw the light under the door of the parlour. "Come on," he said and turned the knob.

The paraffin lamp hanging from the ceiling was lighted. His mother was at the far end of the table. She was wearing spectacles that hung down a little on her nose. On the far side of the table Joseph was bent over a thick book. His head was resting on his left hand and his eyes were moving backwards and forwards with the lines, slowly, and his forehead was furrowed with concentration.

Mrs. Baun looked at them over her glasses, then she looked down again. Luke said, "Mother, I'd like to talk to you." That made her look up. Joseph didn't look up. He didn't even know they were there. He was trying hard to concentrate. The words of *The City of God* needed concentration and he was beginning to think that his concentration was not what it used to be.

His mother said, "Joseph!" She had to repeat it. Then he looked up. His thoughts were confused in his eyes. "Yes" he said and saw his brother and Martha. "Hello, Martha!" he said. Martha was not favourably disposed towards him. She had always thought that Mrs. Baun had favoured him too much over Luke. After all he wasn't her first son. She nodded her head at him.

"Would you go outside?" his mother asked. "I have business to attend to." She underlined the business.

Joseph said, "Yes, mother." He wasn't even thinking of what the business might be. He just closed the book, got up from the chair and walked to the door. Martha thought he could have looked at them if only to sort of sympathise with them. Even an idiot would know that there was tension in the air.

53

Joseph was thinking. He was thinking: There is something wrong with my memory. What's wrong with my memory? Katie was back in the kitchen. She was hefting a bucket of milk on to the table. She was about to pour it into the cream separator. His hand was on the door, when he thought, No, I'll go out into the fresh air. Maybe I'm trying to concentrate too hard. Maybe that's what's wrong. Maybe I should let it go. He turned back and went out the front way. "Cracked," Katie said after him with a grunt.

"Well?" Mabbina said. There was no encouragement in her voice. None at all.

"Martha and I are going to get married, mother," Luke said.

"Oh," said Mabbina. "I see. You have thought it over?"

"I have had nearly ten years to think it over," Luke said a little bitterly. She looked at him sharply. His eyes didn't fall. She was face to face with it now, she knew. She had thought by ignoring it that it would wear away all the years. A look into his eyes told her no, that the crisis had come. Had she slaved and served so that the patrimony of her eldest son should be won by this slut?

"You have thought over what people will say, how they will jeer?" she asked. Martha paled but she told herself that this was part of it. She knew she would have to go through this.

"Why should they jeer?" Luke asked.

"You are going to marry a bastard," his mother told him, almost gently. "The girl has no father. Nobody knew her father, not even her mother. Does this not make you ashamed?"

Red rose on his cheek-bones.

"No, mother," he said. "The only thing that makes me ashamed is what you have said. That's all." That's why I love him, Martha thought. That's why it is worth going through what I have to go through in order to be near him, to work for him, to watch over him. She took his hand in hers. She raised it to her cheek. Mabbina's eyes dropped to her books. "We told you," he said, already sorry for his moment. He didn't want to hurt his mother. That's his weakness, Martha thought. He can't be strong all the time. He vacillates. She dropped his hand. "If

54

you don't want me to stay here, well, we'll go away somewhere else. We can live. I'm strong, we can make enough to keep us."

"There is no need for you to go away," his mother said.

If your mind is made up there is nothing I can do to stop you. I will just have to make the best of it. Will you wed soon?"

"After the banns," said Luke, almost suspiciously. Surely his victory had come too easily.

"All right," said his mother, and then she raised her voice. "Katie! Katie!" They waited, looking at one another in surprise. What could Katie have to do with this? Katie came in. She was grumbling. She had too much to do without answering calls as if she was a cuddy.

"Well, ma'am?" she asked aggressively. "What do you want now?"

"I just want to give you a month's notice," Mrs. Baun said.

"What?" Katie shouted.

"I'm giving you a month's notice," Mabbina said. "Take it or leave it. It will give you time to look around for another job."

"Are you mad?" Katie asked.

"No," said the woman. "I'm more than sane."

"You mean you're firing me out without a by your leave when I've been eight years slavin' for you? Is that what you mean?"

"You have been eight years, but it isn't slaving," she was told. "You are too insolent. You have always been too insolent. You never appreciated all I did for you. You have no gratitude. You have no control over your tongue. I will be glad to see the end of you."

"Well, you doughty oul bitch," said Katie.

"Shut up!" Mabbina shouted. She was on her feet. "Shut up and get out of here and don't let me hear that loose tongue of yours working again."

"All right, ma'am," said Katie. "Very good, ma'am. All I can say is that I'm sorry for you. On me solemn oath I am. And for you too," she said, turning to look at Martha. "I know what all this is. I know her. If you are here for the reason I think you are, don't stay. Get out. She'll crucify you. I know."

"Get out," said Mabbina.

Katie went. She banged the door after her.

So it was too easy, Martha was thinking. If she was different she would take Katie's advice now and go. Mabbina was looking at her. They spoke so easily with their eyes, the two of them. I have a new servant, I have sacked the old one. That was the burden of her look. Martha decided she would take up the challenge. Some day Mabbina Baun would have to die and then Luke would be the master. That might be worth suffering for.

"Since Luke wishes to marry you, you are welcome to this house," Mabbina said. "You can have his big room upstairs. Bart can move into Katie's room and we will fit it with a double bed."

"Thank you," Martha said.

Luke was bewildered. He had had his moment and the things that happened afterwards he didn't understand.

"Will you come as far as the house with me, Luke?" Martha asked.

"Yes, yes, sure," Luke said. Martha went to the door. He followed her. He turned back to look at his mother. "Thanks, mother," he said. "You took it well. You took it better than I thought. Thanks." Then he followed her out. He was sorry about Katie. He liked Katie. She seemed all right to him. She worked hard too, dammit, he thought.

When they were outside in the night, Martha said: "It was nice of you to thank your mother for insulting me, Luke."

"Oh no, Martha," he said. "She wasn't too bad. I thought she'd be much worse."

"My poor Luke!" Martha said.

They were silent as they crossed the bridge, walked through the village and turned off back left where there was a small house that was set back from a stream that ran towards the lake. It was a neat house, single-storey, slated. Martha's mother was knitting thick woollen socks. She knitted a lot of socks, pure white ones, and a mixture of white and grey. She got six shillings each for them. The wool cost two shillings. She washed too for one or two people in the valley and for the fishing hotels farther back. She was a hardworking woman. Her hair was grey, her clothes were neat, her body thin. Martha thought how much she loved her mother as they stood for a moment in the darkness outside looking in through the open door at the woman in the lamp-light.

"Hello, mother," Martha said. She looked up. She laid aside her knitting, wiped the seat of a chair with her apron.

"Yeer welcome, yeer welcome, yeer welcome," she said. "Sit down, Luke, amac. I'm glad to see ye."

"Thanks, Mrs. Cleery," Luke said, sitting in front of the fire. He liked Martha's mother. Sometimes he wished that his own mother was as poor as Martha's mother and with as much tolerance and patience in her.

Martha spoke. "Luke talked to his mother," she said. "She has agreed to it."

"Praise be to God," Mrs. Cleery said, raising her palms. "I never thought she would, God forgive me. She is such a just woman. Forgive me, Luke."

"You've said nothing, ma'am," Luke said.

"She threw your sin in my face, that was all," Martha said.

"Shush, girl," her mother said.

"Ora, Martha, don't," said Luke. He wanted peace.

"So well she might too, Martha," Mrs. Cleery said. "I was a sinner. I was a wild one when we were young, Luke. Your mother and I went to the same school. She went more often than I did. God forgive me. But she was always just and I was always gay. There was mebbe more to it than that too, but them times are past now, God be with them. We're in the present now and let us get on with it. Let us have no hard feelings. Let us all sit down and have a sup of tea. Eh, Martha? Have a sup of tea, child."

"All right, mother," said Martha. "We'll have a sup of tea."

57

Six

WHEN JOSEPH CAME out of the house he turned left and walked the road that climbed up towards the plateau. It wasn't a good road. It started to peter out the farther up it went. It had no boundary walls, only two shallow bog drains to run off the water. It only served two houses, which were two miles apart. The road ended at the street of the farther house, the Brendans'. It was a two-storey, stone house surrounded by a belt of spruce and larch trees with one silver fir that was bent wearily away from the west wind. The moon was coming over the shoulder of the mountain. It was very big and round, a fair imitation of the morning sun.

Joseph didn't see it. He was thinking hard, his feet stumbling in the ruts of the road. He was saying to himself: I must recall the words because if I don't recall the words how can I ever make out what it means? He stopped and fisted his head hard. He tried to see the big pages and the words written blackly. One by one they came to him as if he was squeezing them out of his brain. "Neither the notes of metaphysical birth (no, no, not birth, truth) metaphysical truth, nor the objective laws of criteriology, nor the necessary possibility of possibles, nor their unlimited . . . unlimited what? . . . unlimited, unlimited number, that's it, number, supply an immediate sufficient reason for the existence of a necessary and infinite Being."

He stopped then and took his fists from his head and breathed hard. His body felt tired. He was sweating coldly. That's it, he thought, and now what does that mean? What does what mean? What I have just worked out, what does it mean? Say it again! He tried it over again but he couldn't think of it, the beginning nor the end, only the last word, and in order to recapture it he would have to start all over and fight it out of his mind. I'm tired, he thought, my mind is tired. I'll leave it alone. It'll come again, maybe to-morrow.

He was turned, looking back. The moon was higher and not so large. It was assuming its normal shape and gleaming more brightly. The lake below was a sheen under it. His attention was caught by the sound of stones rolling on the road behind him. He peered closely before he could see the figure that was following him up the hill. First he thought it was a dog, because it seemed to be walking on all fours, and then he saw the body straightening itself up and he saw that it was a woman, a woman walking very hesitantly and slowly and with infinite care. He waited there as slow realisation of who it was came into his mind. That looks like the body of Breeda, he thought, and then he recognised her fully as the moonlight showed one side of her face. He went down. She heard him coming and stood in a tense attitude.

"Breeda!" he said, not loudly, hesitantly, as if she was a shape that would vanish from in front of him.

"Yes," she said.

"It's Joseph," he said. She relaxed.

"Hello, Joseph," she said.

He wanted to ask her what she was doing on the side of the plateau in the dark of night, but he didn't want to. He was very shy and her affliction had wounded him deeply, but he never had the words to express himself like that. He had prayed a lot for her. She had never been out of his thoughts. He wished talk would come easy to him.

"You are out late," was what he said. It was a stupid thing to say. It didn't mean anything until he said it and then a wonder dawned on him. What was Breeda doing on this lonely hill in the late night? He went closer and reached for her arm. It stiffened under the touch of his thin fingers, so he pulled his fingers away. "You came all the way by yourself?" he asked.

"Yes," Breeda said. She didn't say anything more. She wanted him to go away.

"I'm glad to see you are out," he said.

"Yes," she said.

"Will you be all right on your own?" he asked.

"I will," she said. "I will be all right on my own. Good-bye, Joseph."

It was a dismissal. She wanted him to go away. Why? So that he wouldn't see her stumbling limbs?

"Good-bye, Breeda," he said quietly and passed her, going down. She didn't move. She wouldn't move until she could no longer hear him. She would remain there glued to the ground, listening. He turned and came back. "Breeda," he said, "I didn't like to go down to the house to see you. I wanted to give you something, but I didn't like. I have it here. Will you take it?"

"What is it?" she asked.

"It's a book," he said. "A small book."

She laughed. It wasn't a nice laugh. "A book!" she said as her laughter died.

He persisted. He came close to her, reached for her hand and put the small black book into it, closing her fingers on it. "I know," he said. "You can't read it. But sometimes when things are very bad, stand by the side of the road and let it fall open and when you hear footsteps say to the passer-by: 'Would you mind reading the open page?' Do that, Breeda, will you?"

"You're mad, Joseph," Breeda said. "Take back your book" She was holding it out.

"No, no," he said, backing away from her. "Please, Breeda, just to please me. That's all, just to please me. I wanted so much to give you the book, but I didn't like to go to your house. Please keep the book, even if you don't want it to read it. Please, Breeda."

"Joseph!" she called angrily. "Come back!"

"Please, Breeda," he called. His voice seemed to come to her from a misty distance. "Please, Breeda." She stood there listening, enraged, trying to pierce the blackness of her seeing. She listened and listened until she could hear him no more. Then

60

she hefted the book in her hand. She raised it to throw it away, but didn't. Instead she pulled at the neck of her jersey and let it fall between her breasts. It can come too, she thought then, and sobered and continued pace by pace to climb the hill. She knew from the smell of the pines that she was near the end of the road by the Brendans' house. When she reached that she turned left off the remaining piece of road and felt for the drain with her feet and walked into it. Water and brown mud came up to her knees, but she pulled her feet, sucking, out of it and clawed her way up the bank and stumbled on straight across.

Joseph had stopped below. He watched her. She was out of sight in a dip in the road for some time, and then he saw her against the horizon. He saw her stepping into the drain and then she was gone and again she was walking tall against the horizon, her hands held in front of her. She was stumbling.

The hair rose on the back of Joseph's neck.

He had felt something terrible there as he talked to her in the middle of the road. Something frightening. Why should she cross the drain and head blindly across the bog towards the upper lake? Once she got into the middle of the great plain, she would never get out of it without aid. So why was she persisting in fumbling her way in? There was nothing in there but the black Upper Boola, deep and dark, with the river between, which in places had cut its way down fifty feet until it had found the hard granite under the soft muck of the boglands.

Joseph turned and ran down. He almost called out, "Bart," but it was too far away. Bart was the only one who could solve it or do anything about it. He fell once, slithering. The gravel and rocks of the road raked his body from chin to shin, but he got up and ran on. He was very pleased to see the yellow light from the window and the open door of the shop shining on the cobbled yard.

It was Confession night for the village men, so there was a good crowd in the pub. John Willie and Bart were busy, mainly serving pints. Tomorrow was the monthly Confraternity Sunday, so they were all sparked out in their best clothes. They always came in for a courage drink before going to Confession

61

and came in for a relief pint afterwards when they had got rid of their sins. Bart was adept at pouring pints, but he didn't like it. Sometimes he liked the noise and the conversation and the slow talk. Most times he felt like throwing bottles, or pulling the place apart with his hands. He saw Joseph in the doorway. He was very pale, trying to peer through the fug of smoke that encircled the lamplight. His clothes were muddied as if he had fallen. His searching eyes found Bart. There was relief in them then. He signalled with his hand.

"Excuse me," Bart said and hopped over the counter. "What is it, Joseph?" he asked, going close to him.

"It's Breeda," said Joseph. "I met her up the way. She turned in off the road and went into the plateau."

"Breeda!" Bart was surprised.

"There's something wrong, Bart," Joseph said, catching Bart's shirt in his hand. "I know there's something wrong."

Bart thought.

"Yes, all right, Joseph," he said.

"She was stumbling across," Joseph said. "How can she ever get out of it by herself?"

"All right," Bart said. No use running off at half cock. "You get behind the counter, Joseph," he said. He pushed his way back through the crowd. He went over the counter. "John Willie!" he called. Joseph's father came over to him. Bart lowered his voice. "We'll have to go up to the lake above," he said. "Something serious has happened. We'll have to go now and we'll have to go fast."

John Willie removed a canvas apron very quickly and reached behind the counting desk for his coat. He pulled it on. No words. That was John Willie. "I'll whistle up the dog," he said.

"Right," said Bart. "I'll get a torch." Joseph was inside the counter. "We won't be long, Joseph," Bart said. There was comment amongst the men. "What's going on? By God, there'll be a load there for a priest to hear between the two of them. I'd like to listen in to Bart's, so I would, heh, Bart." That was Suck Brendan. He had an enormous capacity. "That's right," Bart said. "That's right, Suck, I'm a bigger man than you any day, sins or deeds." He was pushing his way through them.

Then they were gone.

Joseph was behind the counter bewildered. The men winked. They ordered drinks. Joseph mixed them up. He had to say, I'm sorry, oh yes. Is that right? Did you hear this one, Joseph? they say, winking at one another. What is it? Joseph asks. About your man that came from the fair and there was this lassie in the pub and she says ... It was a very obscene story. They laughed, watching his face. It didn't register with Joseph. He said yes. They tried again. It became a competition. One worse than another. But it didn't penetrate to Joseph's sensibilities at all. They found great amusement watching his face. They nudged one another. Joseph was moving automatically. His mind was thinking about the silhouette on the hill and his lips were moving. They gave it up as a bad job.

John Willie's dog was a mixture of every dog that ever nosed birds on a hill. His head was setter and his body was cocker and his tail was pointer and there was a facility in him for turning sheep if he wished.

He ran silently ahead of them, delighted to be out on the hill. It was an unexpected treat.

"If she went in by Brendans'," John Willie was saying, "she must be heading for the lake. She can't take it fast. If we go in here and take a diagonal line we might get there ahead of her."

"We'll have to get ahead of her," Bart said. "That's all."

"Right," John Willie said. "Keep after me. Try and keep as close as you can and jump where I jump. We can't use the torch. If we flash it we'll have to slow up afterwards, and that'll be worse."

He leaped the drain and set out. John Willie knew all the land around like the palm of his hand. He was a good shot, and he was successful because he had studied the habits of all the game on the hill, so that he could find them where others would fail. It was very bad land they travelled. It was nearly all soft. Rarely were there outcroppings that would support the body. For the most part it was quaking sedge that moved under your weight, and if you were unlucky there were sedgy spots that would let you through as soon as you put a foot on them, so that the water

63

would seep up to your thighs if you didn't succeed in getting your leg out fast enough. And it was all uphill. In ten minutes Bart's chest felt as tight as if it was being squeezed in a vice. His tongue was almost hanging out. The physical effort was good because it took his mind from his black thoughts. He could just distinguish the body of John Willie, jumping, testing, side-stepping and jumping again, with the dog loping ahead, his nose to the ground.

Everyone knew that Breeda was in a desperate state. If they didn't, her aunt told them so. She told them in a welter of self-pity. All she was doing for the girl and no thanks for it. How she wouldn't eat or she would eat at peculiar times. She wouldn't wash. She wouldn't change her clothes. It was only for the last week that she had taken to going out in the night-time. Never as early as this. Always after midnight. I open my eyes, and I feel that there's something wrong. And I get up and I light the lamp and go into her room and the bed is turned back and there is no sign of her. My heart sinks to my boots, dear, and I pray and I go to the door and I look into the night and I call, Breeda, Breeda dear, where are you, where are you? Sometimes I walk the roads for a little. Only very little because it's not safe for a young widda woman to be by herself on a lonely road at night, dear. Think of all the things that could happen to her! The girl won't answer me. I wet the doorstep with my tears calling her, and one night her voice comes out of the dark. Go home and go to bed, Bidelia, for God's sake go in and go to bed, Bidelia. To her own aunt, that's minded her like she was her own since the death. Devoting her whole life to the girl and what thanks?

She comes creeping back sometimes. Where have you been? Just out, just out, just out, as if I had no feelings, dear. Just out. And leave me alone. What am I to do? What is to become of us? Why hasn't God given her the grace to put up with it? I have the grace, thank God. If you only knew, dear, the things I do for that girl.

A snipe ran from under Breeda's foot. She could hear its wings, its peculiar cry as it zigzagged away. How well she could see that, so clearly! She sank again. One leg into the muck and

64

she falls forward. She can feel the wet right up her thigh and soaking into her clothes where she is lying on it. She pulls herself to her feet. See what happens when you notice things like the cry and fly of a snipe. She has the river in her ear. That is what's guiding her. The river comes out from the lake in a deep broad sweep, silently, and then after about two hundred yards it falls. Straight down it falls and lashes the rough unyielding stones fifty feet below. Not even centuries have worn away the big granite boulders. They bear the shock of the white spume without effort, without wearing. This is the fall nearest the lake. The gorge is where a lot of trees grow out. Whitethorn principally that is there as long as man can remember, stunted, mossgrown and gleaming whitely in every part of the year. There is bracken too and tumbled briars and all around the forms of the hares. It is a lonely place and it thunders day and night; even when the big wind is coming from the sea it cannot top the thunder of the falls. She hears it now and it is her guide and is calling her straight to it. Once she reaches this there is no trouble to get as far as the lake.

The thought of the lake seems immensely calm and welcoming to her. She had often climbed up here before. To reach the lake and sit on the bank. The banks of this lake were high all around and steep, so that there was a fall to the water below and it was rarely ruffled by the wind, only the middle part that the wind could sweep over. On the far side there was a small sandy beach, but it was hard to reach it because the land all around it was very soft. You come to the lake and you are alone in all the world. You can throw yourself on the heather and you can cry yourself to death and nobody will disturb you. You might attract the attention of a soaring hawk spotting for a succulent young grouse, or you might be regarded by the cruel eyes of a greyback tearing at the putrefying wild dead. But the heather is sweet and it is soft for your body and the water is peaceful. You could lie dead for a long time before anybody could find you, or you seem so high that on a good day with low fleecy clouds you can reach up with your fingers and touch heaven and your anguish can be softened and you can see your father's face in the sky, laughing, and hold your mother's hand that is reaching down to you in the form of a trailer from the mists of the valley.

She fell. This was no bog fall. The thunder of the river was all around her and her grasping hands held and closed on the barbed branches of a thorn tree. She felt them lacerating her hands but she held tightly. Her heart was beating too fast. She didn't want to die on the cruel stones. She could feel the spray from the river fall rising and enveloping her from below. She raised a leg, flailing until it found solidity and heaved with her arms, and she reached further and scrambled and scrabbled until she fell out into the soft ground, and then she turned and walked with the river as her guide on her left. The thorns were in her arms, in her hands. They had broken off. She could feel them. She thought how little it mattered. What is pain? Pain is a physical thing. It can only hurt you on the outside. Outside pain doesn't matter. It's inside. That's what kills you. That's the pain you can't get away from. It keeps after you so much that if you don't kill this pain, then this pain will kill you. She swung wide so that she wouldn't fall into the river. It would be smooth here and silent-flowing. She would know when she came to the bank of the lake. She knew she would know. If you closed your eyes long ago you would know about the sheet of water under your feet.

She knew she was there. She got to her knees and reached her hand and there was nothing under her hand. No regrets. No regrets. Long ago when kings were maimed they could not be kings. They were put away. That was the best thing to do with maimed things. There was nothing under the sun for them. Of all the maiming that could be done, this was the worst one. What was the use of feeling what you couldn't see? Never again. If they had given you some hope that some day a blow that blinded could recur to bring brightness, but not this way.

She stepped out and into the water.

Below they had seen a slight sign of her. It was only a movement because the moon couldn't show up there. A slight movement and the barking of the dog. The dog barked and ran.

Bart, almost exhausted, his feet leaden weights, got new strength. He ran after John Willie, who was racing after the dog.

Her head came out of the water. She could feel the book bulking against her breast. What am I doing, she wondered, in the water? She was treading. She thought: in order to die I have to put my hands in the air and go under and swallow water and keep swallowing it. She was swimming. The water was cold to her hot body. It was refreshing. It was washing her. She thought of the past weeks in her room; of her aunt's voice enveloping her in whimpering and complaining and praying and admonishing, and in rubbing her the wrong way, all the time. She thought if she could have seen her face and body in a mirror, the tangled dirty hair without a shine, the creases of dirt in her face, the feeling of dirt on her fingers. Her body unclean, the smell of her jersey, the sight of a tangled and wrinkled skirt. And now she was washed and she was swimming in the lake and she wanted to go home. Home? How? She was in a lake. It wasn't a small lake. She was swimming around in circles. How could you get out of it? How could you swim to a bank when you were blind? If you reached a bank how did you get out when the top of the bank was seven or eight feet from the surface of the water? There was the sandy end, but where, what side, north, south, cast or west? Panic hit her then. I don't want to! I don't want to! She swam and water went into her mouth. It was brown boggy water.

She trod water and she screamed.

"Bart! Bart!" Her voice was terrible.

"Well, what the hell is wrong with you?"

That was Bart's voice. It couldn't be.

"Bart! Bart!" she called almost doubtfully.

"All right," said the voice. "What are you getting so excited about?"

"Are you real?" she asked, wondering if she was dead.

"I am," the voice answered her, "and I'm bloody awful hungry. I came up here without my supper."

"Oh, Bart," she said.

"Are you going to stay swimming there all night?" he asked her.

"No," she said.

"Well, come on in so, for the love of God," she heard, "and let's all go home."

"Where are you?" she asked.

"Where you are looking now," he said. "Come on. Straight ahead."

She started to swim towards his voice.

"Am I right?" she called.

"You can swim well," he told her. "Where did you learn?"

"In school," she said. "There was a funny old sailor fellow used to come once a week to the school pool."

"That's a lie," said his voice. "Everyone knows that sailors can't swim."

"Oh, honest, this one could," she said. The effort of swimming made the words come in short explosions from her. "He had a woman tattooed on his tummy in blue and green and he could make her dance by moving his muscles."

She heard him laughing, big loud bellows of laughter.

"Am I near?" she asked.

"Two yards," he said. "I'm leaning down. When I tell you, stretch up and you will feel my fingers. Now!"

She reached and felt a hard hand grasping her own. She felt safe. The hand would never let her go even though it was squeezing the thorns in her palm.

She was lifted out of the water bit by bit. She was lying on her back on the bank.

"All right?" His voice was over her, very near her.

"Yes, yes," she said. "Who's with you?"

"That's John Willie," he said.

"Hello, Breeda," John Willie said.

She felt a tongue licking her face. It startled her.

"Sure that's not you, John Willie?" she asked. They laughed. She laughed herself. She raised her hand and stroked the coat of the dog.

"What's that sort of noise I hear now?"

"That's a grouse," John Willie said. "He's mad that we disturbed him. Listen to him. Gurgle gurgle, and then he says Go-back, go-back, go-back."

"That's it," she said. "I heard that too just before I . . . just before I went for a swim."

"Better get up," she heard Bart's voice. "We'll go down home. If you wanted to go swimming you shouldn't have gone in in your clothes."

She sat up. Then she stood.

"Lean forward now," she heard him say. She did. She felt his body under her. "Put your arms around my neck," he says. She does that. Then he rises up and she is riding on his back. She feels his hands feeling for her legs and securing them, hefting them around his waist. "We'll get down quicker this way," she hears him saying. "Are you right?" "Yes, I am right."

"Then we'll go home," he says, and John Willie whistles up the dog and they move off.

Seven

JOSEPH SAW BART standing in the door. He beckoned to him. His heart was beating fast as he got out from behind the counter and went over to him.

"She's out beyond," Bart said. "Go out and go home with her."

He pushed past him then, taking off his coat. Joseph noticed that the back of his coat was wet.

He went out. It was hard to make his eyes see after the lamplight. Then he saw two figures pulled back on the far side of the road. He went over.

"Ah, Joseph," said John Willie. "Good man! Nobody will know if we slip back. You go home with her."

"All right," said Joseph.

"Bye, Breeda," John Willie said. "I'll look for you again. You know what I said. You'll be better to me than a dog, hah, on the hill. No eyes means better ears. Laugh at that. Eyes no bloody good on a dark night. Ears better. All right?"

"All right, John Willie," she said. "I am grateful to you."

"Crisscross!" said John Willie, heading in for the shop, the dog still at his heels.

"You have a nice father, Joseph," she said.

Joseph was surprised. A nice father? Yes, he was a nice father. Only it was hard to see him somehow behind the shelter of his mother.

"I wanted you to come home with me," she said. "Will you take my hand?"

He took her hand. It was cold to the touch. She was shivering now. Bart hadn't talked to her all the way out. She just clung to his back, feeling the muscles of his chest moving under her clutching fingers. He carried her all the way out. Sometimes she had to press her head to the side of his face when his legs stumbled in the soft ground. Sometimes he cursed. But she felt safe with him, although she was tongue-tied. She hoped he would forget the night. She thought that Bart was so strong that he would despise weak people. She hoped he would think differently about her later on.

When they reached the road he let her to the ground. Her legs were unsteady at first. There were pins and needles in them where his strong hands had a firm clutch on them. Then he left her alone. "Come on now," he said, and strode ahead as if she was able to see. She tried and might have stumbled on the hill if the unobtrusive hand of John Willie wasn't on her elbow now and again. Bart's behaviour filled her with indignation. Maybe that was what he wanted.

"Don't mind! Don't mind!" John Willie would say.

"What was that?" she said. "What?" John Willie asked. "I heard a swish of wings over to the right," she said. "That must be a golden plover," he said. "Crisscross, girl, you would be good on a hill at night. Must bring you with me. You be the ear and I'll be the trigger." He laughed. It made her feel good.

Bart was waiting below. She could sense him before his voice stopped them.

"Are you all right now?" he asked gruffly.

"Yes," she said, stiffly. "I want to see Joseph. Would you ask Joseph to come out to me? Maybe he'll come as far as the house with me."

He didn't answer. He just went away. She heard his boots on the cobbles. Some of the original hatred she had felt for him in the hospital came back to her. It was all his fault, all his fault, and she didn't care. She had seen herself meeting him for the first time and digging her nails into his eyes, saying, How do you like that, how do you like that, you cruel casual bastard? She had thought of other names for him that came from rare fair-day

71

overhearings. If she could see him she would like to dig her hands now into the curly hair and tear some of it away from his head, or beat with her fists at the cold scrutiny of his eyes. He was incapable of thinking of anybody else. His whole world was himself. He could reach out as if he was God and crush a creature and then expect the creature to love him for it. "Don't mind! Don't mind!" she heard the soft voice of John Willie say. "It is only his way! Only his way."

Then Joseph was there and John Willie was gone away with the dog. Funny, now that she listened she could hear the scrape of the dog's claws on the stones. Joseph walked slowly and carefully. She thought his hand was very thin and soft after the feel of the toughness and resistance of Bart's body.

"Joseph," she said. "You sent them after me, didn't you?"

"Yes," she heard him say.

"Why, Joseph?" she asked.

"I felt wrong," he said. "Just wrong. There was something wrong. You shouldn't have been away over the bog by yourself. That was all. Inside I was afraid, that was all. There were waves coming from you."

She wondered at the softness of his voice. It was his father's voice but different. It had the quality of awayness, as if it was completely divorced from himself.

"You must be a visionary, Joseph," she said.

"Oh, no," he said, horrified.

"You could tell fortunes," she said, teasing him, and squeezing his hand. Joseph was peculiar, she thought; what is so peculiar about him as if he doesn't belong?

"The book you gave me," she said. "I didn't throw it away. It's inside my jersey. It's all wet and soggy. I can feel it. Was it a good book, Joseph?"

"It was a good book," he said.

"What did you say I was to do with it?" she asked. "Back there, that time. I only half heard you."

"I just said," he said, "If you were in trouble that if you let it fall open and stop a passer-by and ask him to read, that it would be the thing to do."

"You believe that?" she asked.

"I believe," he said.

She reached inside her jersey and took out the book. It was very wet, the binding was very soggy.

"Can you read in the light of the moon?" she asked. "Let's give your book a trial." She flipped at it with her fingers, but it wouldn't open. The pages were stuck, then she hung it down and let it fall open and turned her wrist quickly. She felt the weight of the book divided, so it must be open.

"Is it at a page?" she asked.

"It is," said Joseph.

"Then read, passer-by," said she.

Joseph made out the number of the page and a few words from the soggy page and then he read it for her. He didn't consult the book at all but she couldn't see that. He knew the page.

> ". . . how small soever, if only it be suffered for God's sake, should pass without its reward.
>
> Be thou therefore prepared for the fight if thou wilt have victory.
>
> Without a combat thou canst not attain unto the crown of patience.
>
> If thou art unwilling to suffer, thou refusest to be crowned. But if thou desire to be crowned, fight manfully, endure patiently.
>
> Without labour there is no arriving at rest; nor without fighting can the victory be won."

His voice died away.

"You believe that, Joseph?" she asked.

"Yes," he said.

"Give me back the book," she said. He put it on to her out-stretched hand.

They walked together silently, over the bridge and up the hill.

"Will I leave you?" he asked, at the gate.

"Come in to the window," she said.

They walked there.

"Look in the window," she commanded, "and see what my aunt is doing."

He looked.

"She is on her knees," he said. "She has a rosary in her hand. She is crying and praying at the same time."

"I must have made her unhappy," she said.

"I don't know," Joseph said.

She felt for the door and put her hand on the latch.

"I'm all right now," she said. "Good night, Joseph."

She heard his feet on the path; the closing of the gate. He was well away before she opened the door. He was feeling good, only for the one thing. He hadn't told her all of the page, not because he didn't want to, but because in the middle of it he couldn't remember any more. Why was that? He used to remember so well, and now he couldn't remember. He tried to think back to the end of the sentence he had spoken and what followed it. All the way home he tried to remember, but it defeated him.

Before she raised the latch, Breeda thought: I must clean out my room, and tomorrow I must get the big tub and the washing-board and I must scrub everything I possess. That will be easy. You don't have to look anyhow, you can feel, and I must have more patience with Bidelia. I must not let her annoy me. I must be patient with my aunt.

And then she opened the door and allowed herself to be enveloped in tears and lamentations.

Eight

LUKE WAS MARRIED in the spring.

It should have been a joyous day for Martha and it was in a way, but her mind started to stack up all the things which were wrong.

It was all right going down in the cars to the church near the sea, and getting married, that was fine. Luke looked very well. Dressed in a blue suit and a white shirt and highly polished boots he was as good and as fine-looking a man as you would wish to see. And it made her almost cry the way his huge hand was trembling as he put the ring on her finger. That was the place she was really happy, when she was inside the altar rails with only Luke and herself, and the priest who was saying the nuptial mass. But she didn't fool herself that from here on everything would be fine. She was too conscious of her mother-in-law behind her on the front bench.

Holy Joseph wasn't there. That was what she called him in her own mind. She didn't know why she felt an aversion for him, but she did. She thought his thin pale look and the faraway eyes were hypocritical and when he couldn't come to the church for the wedding, because he was lying in sick with a terrible splitting headache, his mother said, she thought she could see what he was after. He always wanted to be the centre of attraction in the world of his mother, and he thought that Luke and Martha were taking the limelight, so he goes sick to get more attention.

Joseph at home in the darkened room with his hands, holding his head and twisting his body from side to side would not have agreed with her.

She was wearing a grey costume. It went well with her brown hair. It was bought in the town and it should have looked better on her than it did. Bart could have told her that. She was too tightened in, he could have told her. If she loosened her body up a bit and let something go free she would have looked better. But there would never be anything loose about Martha. She would look after that.

Mabbina kissed her afterwards. It was a cold kiss on the cheek. Most of the guests from the village kissed her too, not so chastely, and decided amongst themselves afterwards that there was no give in her and that she would be a cold proposition in bed. There was nothing bawdy about the dialogue. It was just a cold-blooded summing up of a human animal as opposed to the ones they bought and sold at the fair.

Mrs. Cleery would never have a better day. Mabbina of course wanted to put up the do, but Mrs. Cleery wouldn't agree. She practically beggared herself to do it, but then since she was always a beggar, as she said, she was entering no new state.

Martha watched the two of them in the spotless clean kitchen of her mother's house.

Mabbina was very cold. Her mother was warm, and ignored the coldness with patient charity. Mabbina sat at the white-clothed table and pecked at the roast goose and the ham and the jellies, and touched a wine-glass with her lips, before she rose to go, saying about Joseph, how ill he was and how she didn't like to leave him.

As soon as she was gone everybody started having a good time, and when Martha and Luke had taken themselves away to the south of the country, where they were going for a week, everybody really loosened up.

Bart proceeded to ply Mrs. Cleery with strong drink.

Down below, the young people were gathered in the kitchen making tentative efforts to start a dance in the broad light of the spring sun. They would succeed. In the room around the table were Mrs. Cleery with Bart and John Willie and Breeda's aunt Bidelia. John Willie looked odd without his cap. His hair was cut closely to his head. He had a narrow well-shaped head.

Anyone who saw it on the rare occasions it was uncovered would recognise that Joseph got his narrow neat head from his father. John Willie only drank one glass of whiskey. He rarely drank. He said if you sold sweets in a shop all day could you eat sweets, Crisscross?

"I was very beautiful when I was a girl," Mrs. Cleery was saying.

"I'll bet you were," said Bart. "You'd have knocked spots off your daughter, Mother Cleery. Have another."

"You were a pretty brown girl," said Bidelia. "I remember when we were only school-girls, dear, seeing you walking the road and . . ." She stopped, slightly confused, and put a glass to her lips. She thought of a ringing box on the ear because she had been seen talking at the crossroads to that thing, Una Cleery. Why is she a bad thing? Tight lips. You mind your own business. "She lifted the skirt once too often," cackled the old man in the corner of the fireplace. "Hee-hee." "You shut up, Gran, you dirty old thing! Fitter to be saying your prayers than talking like that in front of the children." Bad luck to it, she was a better bit than any of ye!" he cried, banging his stick on the concrete. "Better be far. Then ye crucify the girl because she done what none a ye had the courage to do but ye had the feelin' for it. More power to her, I say." Bidelia was shushed out like the chickens. "You were very pretty, dear," she said.

Mrs. Cleery laughed.

"I was that," she said. "I was that. I had gay times, I had. The world was just a big pink laugh, the world was, believe that."

"That's the way the world should be," said Bart.

She poked him in the ribs with a finger. "You're another one," she said. "You be careful, boy. I know the look of you. You're another one."

"I'm another what?" he asked.

"Another one," she said. "You know. I met you before, long ago." She started to hum an air.

"Go on," said Bart, "raise it."

"Oh, you devil," she said. There was a flush on her cheeks, a slight glaze in her eyes. She suddenly started to sing. Her voice

77

was thin and wavering, but it was the startling way she felt what she was singing that brought a tenseness into the room. Outside in the kitchen the young ones hushed their rising talk and gathered at the door of the room as she sang. Suck was there with a pint glass drooping from his fingers, and many of the other young people, reaching over the men's shoulders to peer.

She sang:

"Oh, far the road to Ball na ndé,
I sang and laughed on a dew-spring day.
My breast was young and my face was fair,
And the sun was bright on my silken hair:
Where the tip of the hills do touch the skies
I met the man with the golden eyes.

'Oh, lovely maid, come down with me
Where the finches couple be the whitethorn tree,
I'll wind my wrist in your silken hair,
And seal your lips with the lover's prayer:
Oh, come down, maid, come down with me,
And we will wed by the whitethorn tree.'

The road is bleak where I go my way,
My breast is old and the sky is grey,
The curlews cry on the lonely hill
And the fickle finches' song is still.
Rent and weary the thorn tree dies
Where I wed the man with the golden eyes.

A lovely maid I went with thee
Where the finches couple be the whitethorn tree.
You wound your wrist in my silken hair,
And you sealed my lips with the lover's prayer.
'Oh, come down, maid, come down with me,
And we will wed by the whitethorn tree.' "

Bart looked around at them. They were all affected by her singing. There were tears coming out of her own eyes. Bidelia was sniffling. John Willie had his head in his hand. It must be the drink, Bart thought. Then he clapped her on the back and broke

78

it up. "Great woman, great woman," he said. "Did ye hear that, fellas? That was something." They agreed. She wiped her own eyes. "A bit pagan, dear, that song," said Bidelia. "That was fine. Great stuff," said John Willie. It's because their lives are empty of romance, Bart thought. Most of them had only business arrangements like John Willie and his own mother. That was why people like Mrs. Cleery had to be reminded all her life that one time she had sinned and she must never forget it. She must never be allowed to forget it. She had forced colour into her life.

"Who was the fellow with the eyes?" he asked her. "A nice fellow, eh?" thinking that Martha was very dour and straitlaced to be a love child. This made him laugh.

"I'll tell you," said Mrs. Cleery. "They all have the cut of you, Bart. They have tangled locks and gleaming eyes and – and they are restless. Yes, they are very restless. They have to move on."

"Well," said Bart, "if I had been about your time I wouldn't have minded being the one with the restless eyes."

"It's not the eyes at all that are restless," said Suck from the door. "Not the eyes at all." The people behind him laughed and they all pulled back into the kitchen.

"Have another," said Bart, pouring a drink for Mrs. Cleery.

"I must be going," said John Willie, rising. "I will be back again later maybe. Maybe. Thanks, ma'am. Great do. Great do indeed. Powerful send-off. On me oath."

She winked at him boldly. They had a secret. John Willie smiled. Most of the drink was smuggled out from the shop. Under the counter. Otherwise it mightn't have been such a successful wedding. Everybody agreed it was one of the most powerful weddings ever. The old ladies said that Una Cleery must be up to her tricks again to be able to provide such doings. She couldn't have paid for it all honestly. But she was a good woman. She just knew a man with a kind heart. That was John Willie. If there was a left hand in Ireland that didn't know what its right hand was doing, that belonged to John Willie when it came to doing kindnesses under the counter.

He was pleased to get into the fresh air. He thought of where he was going and it pleased him even more. He bet she would be very surprised when he gave her the thing he had made. She would be very surprised. It was worth while having Luke married to get a free day. The shop was never shut, it seemed to him. Maybe Christmas Day, but even then there was always some lazy one who hadn't bought in enough and who had to come down. John Willie will oblige, they said, but keep out of the way of herself.

He had a workshop at the back which was his property and his only. It was a small shed with a window. It was full of shavings and feathers. He shot the birds in the winter and preserved the feathers for making trout flies and salmon flies for the summer. Things like that. Mending rods or engines or broken dogs' legs. He also obliged by ringing pigs, castrating calves or using a bicycle pump on a cow with milk fever. He didn't mind doing these things because he had worked out ways that it didn't hurt so much. He looked again at the board he had made with the slots in it. He wrapped it carefully in a sheet of brown paper and then closed up the shed. He was in the yard walking away when he thought a little and went in the back way into the kitchen. Katie was there. She was very sullen. Sometimes she forgot to be sullen and lackadaisical and worked like a slave for a day or two to make up for the studied neglect of the other days.

"Hello," she said.

"How is the boy?" he asked.

"Oh, him," said Katie disdainfully.

He knocked at the door of the room. Mabbina was sitting on a chair facing the door.

"How is he?" he asked.

"Not too bad," she said.

"Hello, Joseph," he said.

"Hello, father," said Joseph. John Willie thought that he looked very pale and drawn. There were purple shadows under his eyes. He had always been a bit delicate anyhow. John Willie never felt at home with his son. He wanted a son that could walk twenty miles on a mountain after strong grouse, or sit in soaking wet on a snowy evening waiting for the geese to come in. He

80

hadn't got him. John Willie felt sometimes as if he had never had anything to do with the birth of his son Joseph.

"Is it bad now?" he asked.

"No, no," said Joseph. "Fine now, father. Fine now."

"You left the wedding early," said Mabbina.

"The young ones are there," he said. "They have better times without the old people."

"Humph!" she said. "Better times won't get them far."

"We are only young once, Mabbina," he said.

"That's all," she said. "But we worked hard when we were young. I did and you did. And Una Cleery didn't. And now she has more honour than if she was honest and pure and industrious."

He didn't argue with her. He never did. That was why they got on well.

"Anything you want, Joseph?" he asked.

"No, father," said Joseph.

"Fine," said John Willie, and backed out of the room. Joseph never needed him when he had his mother. He never needed him anyhow. John Willie thought he didn't need anyone at all, the way he thought and lived inside himself, so that sometimes you could shout at him and he wouldn't hear you. He knew that people said that Joseph had a slate loose, they said, a cracked tile, but Willie knew they were wrong. It wasn't too little Joseph had inside his head, but too much.

He closed the door softly after him.

"Any sign of a job, Katie?" he asked.

"What do you think?" she asked scornfully. "When do I get time out to go looking for a job?"

"I have one for you," he said. "I'm sorry you have to go. I know a man, over the way about. In a hotel. Nice place. All right?"

"You're very kind, John Willie," she said. "I didn't bother to look. I knew you'd do something."

"All right," he said. "Sorry, Katie. Sorry."

"Not that I'd have stayed anyhow," Katie said in a loud voice, hoping it would penetrate through the door. "No thanks, working like a slave. Me finger skin as raw as a carrot, and me back

81

broke. For nothing. For nobody to say thanks or how are yeh. All right. Some people that think themselves Christians. And what are they? Turks, that's what they are. Just Turks."

"Bye, Katie," said John Willie as he sidled out of the door.

Outside he wiped his forehead and headed over the bridge towards Breeda.

He heard her singing when his hand was on the gate. It stopped him. Breeda singing? It must be. Bidelia was down getting a little squiffy, and there was nobody else around with a light sweet voice. It was a happy song. John Willie opened the gate and went up the path and looked in the window.

She was at a table. She was washing dishes. Then they were washed. She walked back to the fireplace and took a glass-cloth off the line there. She walked back to the table, reached for a cup, dried it off and still singing walked over to the dresser and hung it from a hook. Then she went back again and dried a saucer and placed it on the shelf. It was all done so that you could forget there was anything at all wrong with her. The light from the window shone on her long straight hair, and it was gleaming. The bones of her face were still showing too much, but there was a kind of glow on her skin. She was wearing a white blouse that was very clean and a blue skirt swinging from her hips. She was a different girl.

He opened the door and went in.

She didn't look around. She stopped her song.

"Hello, John Willie," she said.

He laughed.

"How the hell did you know?" he asked.

"Ah," she said. "That's because I have eyes in the back of my head."

"Well it's powerful" he said.

She came towards him.

"Ah, I was fooling you, John Willie," she said. "I am as good as your dog now for hearing. I heard your footsteps coming up the road and by the time you had your hand on the gate, I was singing, and washing the delph. I knew I'd surprise you. I was only showing off."

"Listen," he said, "no matter the reason, do you realise how good? Crisscross, a bloody miracle, man!"

"It wasn't a miracle," she said. "It was a lot of hard work. One step, two step, three step, fire; one, two, three, four, dresser; one, two and a half, table. I know this house like all the squares of a draughts board. I did it the hard way. I have more bumps on my anatomy than the road up to the bogs, and I can get as far as your house and over to the cliff by the sea. At night, that is. I haven't tried it much in the day. You are afraid people will see you and come over and hold your elbow."

"It's powerful, powerful," John Willie said.

"Was the wedding good?" she asked. A little wistfully, he thought.

"Ach, the usual," he said. "Don't like weddings. Makes you want to get drunk." He sat on a chair near the fire.

"Bart was there?" she asked casually.

"Yeh, yeh," he said, "everybody there, everybody. Una Cleery sings a song. Nice old lady. She and Bart get on well."

"They would," said Breeda. "Two free souls. I haven't seen Bart for a long time. I mean I haven't heard him for a long time. Did that night, you know that night, did that disgust him or what?"

Cautious now, thought John Willie.

"We see just as little of him," he said. "Every weekend he is gone to the city within. Every free day. Sometimes he goes away and doesn't come back for a week. Red eyes on him then. Trouble with his mother. He's restless, he is. Restless. Can't stay put."

"He's insensitive," she said. "He wants a good pain, Bart does. He wants a good pain, more than anybody else I know. But he will never have a pain. People like Bart never have pains."

"Don't know," said John Willie. "Never know, girl. People like them, it doesn't show on their faces what's going on inside them. Not like us. Open books, hah? Listen, I made a gadget for you."

"You did?" she asked. "What is it?"

"Wait'll you see, man," he said, unwrapping his parcel and holding it up. "Look at that!"

"It looks lovely," Breeda said. She laughed. John Willie remembered then. He laughed too. He thought her face looked very well when she laughed. Her teeth were white and her gums very red, like her lips. Pity, oh, it is a great pity!

"It's a board, see," he said. "Here, take it" She did. "Now in here you put a sheet of paper from a writing p , see. Then there's a little crossbar that fits into slots on each side. Now you sit down with your pen and you have the paper on the board and you put the edge of your hand on the bar and you write a line and then you pull down the bar a click, click and start another line, and when the bar can't click-click down any farther you know you are at the end of the sheet and you take it out and put in another one."

Her face was shining. Her eyes would have been if they had sight.

"I should be able to write so, with that," she said.

"Chance it now," he said. "If it doesn't work, cut my throat." She was over at the table.

"Here's the paper," said John Willie. "Only drawback is that the paper must be certain size, like this, hah, and the only place you get the right paper is in our shop. So I do myself good by this thing. You have to buy all the paper from me." He laughed.

He put a sheet of paper in the board. She was sitting at the table. She had got a fountain pen from the window behind the table.

"I feel the board," she said. "I feel the paper in the board. The bar is up as far as it will go. Now I write a line near the left of the edge of the board. How is that? How am I doing, John Willie?"

"God above," he said. "It's straighter than the flight of a bullet."

"Now I am at the end of the line," she went on, "and I click-click the bar and I continue with another line. How is that, John Willie?"

John Willie could have jumped.

"Man, it's the thing!" he cried. "It works. My, but it's a great thing. All it wants is practice. Now what did I tell you!"

She click-clicked again and she was on a third line.

"It's great," she said. "It's really great." She wrote on. He stepped back looking at her. He felt good that it worked. He felt that all the hours he had put in on it were not wasted.

She pulled the sheet from the board. "How is that?" she asked.

John Willie took it. He read it.

"John Willie Baun is a good man," he read.

"John Willie Baun has a heart of gold."

"God bless John Willie Baun."

John Willie reddened. He was glad she couldn't have seen. But she knew anyhow how he would be, shifting his small feet.

"Ach," he said, "I must go home. The boy behind is not too well."

"What's wrong with him?" she asked.

"Head, head," he said. "All the time he gets bad headaches."

"I'll go over with you," she said.

"You will?" he asked.

"Yes," she said. "Everybody is at the wedding. So nobody will see me stumbling except you, and I don't mind you. Thank you, John Willie. You have given me a great gift. All the people I can write to now. All the girls who were at school. Everything. I won't forget."

"Ah, Crisscross!" he said with a throwing-away gesture of his hand.

He let her go out of the door.

He closed it after him. He could see her lips moving in a sort of counting. She looked back triumphantly when her hand touched the gate. "I knew," she said. "I knew exactly where the damn thing would be. The last time it nearly banged in my stomach."

"Great, great," said John Willie.

It took them a little longer than usual to reach the house, but she got there without guidance.

Nine

I T WAS LATER in the day that Bart found himself in the kitchen with a girl in his arms, twirling and shouting as he swung her off her feet to the sound of the fiddle in the corner. They were all shouting anyhow. They were all a little drunk. Bart was in good form. He felt like shouting. It wasn't a warm day but he could feel sweat on his body. It was the fixed look of the girl that finally brought his eyes into focus. She kept looking into his eyes. She had big eyes with short lashes, very dark, and her eyes were blue. The top of her head came to his chin. He hadn't noticed her particularly. He had just grabbed a girl and gone dancing in the kitchen. It was hard to dance. There was no room. There was just a squash. She was well built. Her body was firm under his hands. Her hair was near black and wavy. He saw that. Her breasts were full. She would be young.

The music came to an end. It had to sometimes, while they refreshed the fiddler. They still stood close to one another. They couldn't help it. He closed one eye to get a good look at her.

He tried to draw up her name from his memory. Of course you knew everybody. If you paid attention. Sometimes he didn't pay attention, and he had been away a lot at school and things. And little people grew up and changed. One day they were children and the next day they were seductive women. Mass on Sundays was a great place to see and know them. But he was generally late for Mass and always stood with the crowd at the back of the church. You could only see the backs of heads that way, and women's heads were always covered in scarves or hats or yokes. The face was strong enough, with red curled lips and a nose that looked as if it had been slightly broken, but it wasn't. That was a family characteristic and on her it looked well, while on Suck it looked tough. That was it.

"Sheila Brendan," he said.

"I thought you'd never tell," she said smiling. "You're a great one. It took you long enough."

"How are you?" he asked.

"I'm well," she said. "Why was it so hard to remember me?"

"What does it matter?" he asked. "Have a drink. Lashin's of drink."

"No," she said. "I don't drink. I have a pin. Look." She fondled the small pin at her breast. It was made in the form of a shield with a red heart in the middle.

He snorted.

"That'll keep you pure," he said.

"There's no point sneering," she said. "People have their own opinions."

"Not sneering," he said. "Don't give a damn if you never drank water."

He moved to go towards the fireplace where one of the old men had a half barrel of porter on tap. She caught his arm.

"Don't be cross," she said.

He turned back to her. He put a hand up to her cheek. Her skin was soft.

"Not cross," he said. "I have no emotions, girl. You hear that? None at all. You have two hearts, one out and one in. I have none at all. Do you believe that?"

"No," she said.

He laughed.

"You hover and you'll find out," he said. "That was my trouble. I was born without a heart. That's a strange thing. I can crush beetles, kick dogs, goad cattle, crush people under my thumb, and no pain. Imagine that!"

"I don't believe it," she said. "Why don't we go out an' get some fresh air? We'll all melt in here." She raised a hand to the front of her dress and pulled it away to let air in. She blew into her chest with her lips. "I'm passin' out," she said.

87

"All right," he said, and caught her arm and raised his arm to make a way through the throng. He had to lever a way, pushing down his arm, inserting his shoulder and forming a gap through which he thrust, pulling her after him. He noticed that her hand was hard but it was small. Who had soft hands? Nobody in the world except ladies in picture magazines sitting in front of mirrors with transparent garments, putting pots of cream on themselves. He tried to see old Una Cleery, the courtesan of the village, doing that. It made him laugh. He laughed outside the door, the cold air smiting him.

"Is it funny?" she asked.

"Yes," he said, "it's very funny. Your hands are hard." He took one in his own hand to look at it. It was well shaped, but it was undoubtedly hard. He rubbed his fingers along her palm. She shivered.

"It's cold out here," she said, "after the heat." All the time her eyes were looking into his.

"What's wrong with me?" he asked. "Why do you keep looking at me?"

"Nothing," she said. "This is the first time I have been this close to you." She could have told him that most of the girls she knew wanted to be a bit close to him. His eyes were blurred with the drink. There were locks of curly hair falling over his forehead. His skin was very clear. He had a boldly chiselled face. I suppose, she thought, most girls would be soft with him. She told herself this would be foolish. His chin was too hard and his nostrils flared a bit too much. There's a lot of suffering with a handsome one like that, the old people would have said, even if he was steady, which he wasn't. There was no tranquillity about him.

"Why wouldn't my hands be hard?" she asked. "I have to work. If my hands weren't hard what good would I be?"

"Plenty good," he told her. "Plenty good."

He saw the men then, a little out from them in a field on the right. The grass looked green under the sun. One of them was in his shirt-sleeves, poised, swinging on one leg, hurling a large rock from his shoulder.

"That's Pat," she said.

"Let's go," he said.

He walked with quick strides to the low wall and leaped it. He came over to the men. They were measuring the mark.

"Beat that," Suck said, rising up and striking his chest with his hands. His chest was nearly bursting the buttons off the waistcoat of his blue suit. His sleeves were rolled.

"I'll beat that," said Bart, approaching them.

"Look who's here," said Suck. Then he saw his sister coming behind. "You keep away from Bart, Sheila," he said. "Or you'll end up over a cliff."

"Do you want a fight?" Bart asked him.

Suck bent his head and looked at him from one eye. Bart was taking off his coat. His collar was loose. He had a thick neck going into powerful rounded shoulders. A fine bit of a man, Suck thought, but stocky. He could call any man stocky because he was so awful tall himself.

"Not yet, Bart," he said. "Too soon for a funeral after a wedding."

He thought this was very funny. He laughed, slapped his thighs.

Bart liked him. He had a great open face, wide eyes well spaced. He was always friendly as big men are. They rarely have any need to be anything else.

"How is it that the nose on Sheila looks good," Bart asked him, "and on you it looks terrible? Like a big gorilla."

"You beat that mark," Suck said, "and leave me alone. Because I'm handsome is no need to insult me."

There was a bunch of men there. They were all in their Sunday clothes. They were all a bit tight. Some of them grinning foolishly. Bart went to the mark and got the stone. It was a very big stone. It was granite and heavy but it fitted well into the hand. He walked back with it to where a line was gouged out of the grass by a stick. He thought, This is going to madden Suck. He knew well he could put the stone farther only because there was a trick to it, which he had learned in school from all the athletics. Suck had only main strength and ignorance.

89

"I'm sorry for you, man," he said to Suck as he tentatively swung a leg.

"We'll see," Suck said.

The stone flew from Bart's shoulder. They watched its heavy flight. It came down six feet beyond the last mark.

"Bow, wow," one of the men said. "Man, but you're dead, Suck."

Suck's forehead was creased. "It couldn't be," he said.

"Ah, but it is," said Bart. "You have to acknowledge your betters."

Suck took up the stone again. He walked back to the mark. He took in a deep breath. The tendons were leaping on his arms. He flung the stone. It landed short of Bart's mark by four feet.

They laughed at him.

"It's a bloody trick," he said. "I'm a better man any day in the week."

"Only in a bed," Bart said. This convulsed them. Suck was married for five years to a nice young woman from back the way. They had four young children and another one on the way. Suck laughed too, showing his big white teeth.

"I beg your pardon, Sheila," said Bart, bowing solemnly to her. "I forgot there were ladies present."

She didn't like being the centre of attention then.

"You're a wonderful man," she said. Her face was flushed. Her eyes were angry. She liked her brother too. She didn't like him being made a fool of.

"I could break him in two with one hand," Suck said.

"Go on," his brother Willie said. "Let's have some blood out of him."

"Can you break my grip?" Suck asked Bart.

"Of course I can," Bart said. Suck was holding his hand, palm open, out from his body. It was a very big palm. Bart flexed his fingers and put his own hand into it. Suck was grinning. His palm closed on Bart's. They were facing one another, right hands clasped. Bart's head just came to Suck's chin. There was terrible power in Suck's grip. His hand was as hard as an oak board from his work in the fields. Bart held his grip for a count of ten and

90

then knew that if he didn't submit the bones of his hand would be crunched. He couldn't admit it, so he put a leg behind Suck's leg and heaved with his shoulder and as Suck fell he fell on top of him. They rolled on the wet grass and soon their white shirts were wet and dirty. The onlookers were excited because they knew something else had entered into the original challenge. Bart was furious that he was on the point of being defeated. Then they were on their feet. Suck's arms were around his body, pressing, pressing, squeezing on his ribs, raising his body off the ground. He put his palms under Suck's chin trying to push back his head to make him fall and break the grip. He found that there was not enough power in his strong body to push back Suck's head. He thought, This Suck is a terrible strong man. He only broke the hold by digging in a knee into his crotch and breaking himself free. He was breathing hard. His next instinct was to go after Suck and beat at his face with his fists.

Sheila was between them.

"Are you both mad?" she asked. "What's got into you? Look at the state of your clothes."

She saw a sort of mist fading from Bart's eyes. She had been right. He was really angry. Suck wasn't. He was placid and cheerful.

"Now who's the best man?" he asked.

"It's not decided," Bart said.

"What the hell are we doing out here," Willie asked, when all them other fellas will have the porter drank?"

Most of the men scurried towards the house when they had half digested this thought. Suck and Bart put on their coats and straightened themselves up before they followed them. Some day I'll tumble him, Bart was thinking with one part of his mind, and the other part was wondering what it was all about. Suck was a stronger man. He would always be a stronger man. What was the point in not acknowledging it? I don't care, Bart thought. Some day I'll tumble him.

He danced again with Sheila. He thought once, I must go home with that girl, she's a nice girl, but in the end he was too drunk. Most of them were. It was nearly the next day before they went home. Bart thought once of Luke and Martha. He wondered how they had passed the night. With a twisted grin he thought that. Bet they had shaken the holy water on the bed before they got into it. This amused him mightily.

Martha was all right. She was thinking fiercely: Now he is really mine and I will fight for him and for his rights. He is not going to remain a slave, a dumb ox for his mother. She enjoyed his love fiercely because she wanted a son. She was sure of a son, so that nobody could take their inheritance away from them. She was a far-seeing woman.

Bart didn't see Sheila again until a few months later when the young priest was driven into the valley.

It was evening. A nice evening. It had been thirty-five years since they had had a young man, newly ordained, out of the district. He lived in the other valley at the back of Boola mountain, but in order to get there he would have to come from the coast road into Boola and then get on to the road that wound over the bridge and go back beyond Breeda's house and away.

Joseph had climbed the side of Boola with Breeda in order to get a good look at the lighted valley. In the street of the village there were gay little flags fluttering in the soft wind, and big banners with FÁILTE written on them in green and red. Breeda had the laugh on Joseph, because she could climb up the side of the mountain with less stumbling. It was dark. The due moon hadn't arrived yet. It was remarkable how she could feel forward with a foot and get secure purchase before she brought the other one forward. Some of the ground was soft and her sensitive foot rejected these spots and sought a harder place.

Joseph had to follow in her footsteps.

She stopped once, hearing that he was a good way behind her.

"What's delaying you, Joseph?" she called.

"It's hard," he called to her. "I can't see."

She laughed.

"Neither can I," she said, "but I am doing much better than you."

There was a sheep-track further up. She knew from the feel of it. It was a narrow track. If she shifted a foot, she could feel the coarse sedge higher on each side of the path. A sort of instinct guided her feet. You could know it was late spring from the smell of the mountain. The heavy sedge was dead and had been blown away by the wind, and the new green was erect. All the dead seed of the heather had been blown away. She thought you could nearly hear the heather growing. The patches of gorse were in bloom. She knew that, when it brushed her hand and she withdrew it quickly from the needles that hurt. But in the needles there was the soft feel of the vivid yellow petals. She wished she could see the yellow gorse under bright sun. She remembered how it looked if you stood down near their house and looked up at the hill. The yellow blazing blindingly. She felt sad for a second and then she threw it away. She was practised now in throwing away the sadness of the heart. Sometimes when you thought of a beautiful thing, and you remembered the beauty of it: the blue sheen on the lake, or the green colour of the sea under a hot sun, or the view of the valley from this high hill, or the sight of a bog lark fluttering, or the blazing purple colour of this hill heather in the autumn, ah, there were thousands of things that when you thought about how they looked your heart would miss a beat and you would have to bend forward in case you would suffocate. All that. But if you went into it every time it happened you would be worn out with sadness. So she could hear, and to hear could be beautiful too, because there are so many nice sounds that you never hear because you are looking at them. They have become part of your eyes. She knew the footstep of every person in the place. Every one. It amused her to call them by name as they were passing by. They thought it was miraculous. But it wasn't. She could distinguish between the jingle of the harness on an ass or a horse or a jennet. And then there were smells. Oh yes, she told herself, there are so many compensations, and if these things weren't meant to be appreciated, the thing would never have happened to her. The footstep she knew least was the footstep of Bart. But she let that go too.

She knew from the feel of the air that she had reached the cleft in the hill.

This was a deep cut in the hill where the sheep sheltered from

93

the worst of the storms. It was a great high block across the mountain. It reached up, fifty feet of solid granite, blocking the way. You would have to walk around nearly half a mile to avoid it. It jutted out above and there was always a drip of water coming down from it. But it was sheltered and you could sit here on soft grass and look down below. The grass was soft because the sheep constantly fertilised it and kept it cropped.

She stopped here. Joseph joined her. She heard his panting breath.

"Oh," he said, "that's a terrible climb."

"You must take more exercise, Joseph," she said, "if a climb like that loses the breath on you."

She heard him sitting down. She knew that his head was resting on his knee from the sound of his voice.

"Maybe I'm too skinny," he said, "to have much lungs."

She sat too.

"What's it like now?" she asked.

Joseph raised his head.

"The moon is coming up over the lake," he said.

"Are there any bonfires?" she asked.

"Ooh, yes," said Joseph. "Now, almost just now when you spoke. There's one has sprung up, oh, miles and miles away. It must be over near the sea road. Like the spark of a cigarette in the dark. Now another. And another and another and another and another, and they all nearer and nearer to home. Now there is an enormous one down below under us at the cross beyond your house. It looks marvellous. You can see the whole shape of the road from the fires blazing. Up hill and down hill. There must be nearly fifty of them. He must be coming in."

She could imagine the pattern of the fires on the floor of the valley. She wanted to put up her hands and tear away the veil from in front of her eyes.

"It must look grand," she said.

"Oh, it's really lovely," said Joseph.

"It's a grand thought, that way, to welcome a new young priest. One year soon, Joseph, they will be welcoming you home like that too."

Joseph was silent.

"Well, won't they?" she asked.

"I pray to God they will," Joseph answered, "but sometimes I am afraid."

"What are you afraid of?" she asked.

"Only of a silly thing," he said. "My own stupidity."

"You're not stupid," she said. "Don't be silly."

"I thought I wasn't," he said. "But each year that passes something is happening to me. I just seem to be growing stupid instead of becoming learned. I can tell you, Breeda. It's – it's a sort of lack of concentration. Sometimes I am good. Sometimes I am helped. But there are times then when we are in the classroom and the professor in his way drives home his lesson and only a moron could not assimilate it. And five minutes afterwards when he asks me I can't recall it. Not a bit of it. I have to sit there, and inside my whole soul is in a panic. And in my mind I know that I know and yet nothing can come from my mind. Nothing. It's like as if a door had closed and I am red and stupid. I can't help it, Sometimes that happens. It is hard to bear."

"Do you still get the headaches?" she asked.

"Sometimes," he said. "Not as often now, but sometimes."

"Joseph," she said then. "You remember the time of the accident to us, down on the cliff? You fell too. You were hurt. Look, Joseph, you weren't hurt more than you thought then, were you?"

"No, no," Joseph said. "That had nothing to do with it. In the College the President was worried about my headaches. He sent me to Dublin. They X-rayed me. There was nothing. They could see nothing. No, Breeda, nothing like that." He suddenly became cheerful. "It's just that I have a thick head, that's all, and it's hard to get knowledge into a thick head." He laughed.

"I don't believe that," Breeda said.

"Look," said he then, rising, "the car has come in from the coast road. You hear? Listen! I can see it in the bonfire outside the village. Like a little toy car it is, and the people. They have a band."

She could hear it faintly, and the cheering voices of people.

"Don't you mind Joseph," she said. "One day you'll come home like that too."

"With the help of God," Joseph said gravely.

They were very busy in the pub. They could always count on being busy on occasions like this when men had to gather together. Funerals were good for business of course, when the corpse was being taken to the church and when the corpse was buried. Saturday nights before the men's confraternity were also sure as the men went to or came from confession. Missions or fair days also counted. It was very hot in the pub. Bart and John Willie were sweating in the pub part. Mabbina was selling the groceries. She was nearly always in the shop now since Martha had come to live in the house. Martha had nobody to help her except her own hands and feet. She had to cook and keep house for five persons and herself. It was not easy.

The pub cleared when a little boy ran in and shouted.

"The first is up," he said. His face was excited. The men hastily emptied their glasses and left. Bart grabbed his coat and vaulted the counter and went into the night.

The sky near the sea was red. The hill covering the first bonfires seemed to direct their red light into the sky. As he watched, the fire on the far side of the village suddenly blazed. He could see the figures around it falling back with the cans in their hands. It was taller than a tall man, the fire, and it reached greedily for the sky. Bart wondered why the sight of a bonfire could give you a shiver up your back.

He went towards the bridge.

That fire was not up yet. Just beyond the bridge at the cross it was. It was very tall. He could see the men throwing cans of paraffin on to it as he came closer. Then somebody lit a paper from a match and threw it and the whole thing exploded and burst into bright flame. There were tall trunks of willow piled high in a triangle, and chunks of bog deal and spitting conifers all placed one on top of the other. It was a terrific sight. The people said O-oh and A-ah and scurried away from the flame.

The sound of music could be heard in the distance.

96

John Willie heard a car pulling up outside the shop. He was alone now. He thought, This couldn't be the priesteen. It wasn't. It was a strange man with a light coat on him and a brown gabardine suit and a very light-coloured grey hat.

He came in. He was pulling a camera out of a case.

"Jeepers," he was saying. "It'd make you cry. I'll have a drink."

John Willie poured whiskey. The man gulped it. He wiped his lips. His face was fresh-looking. He wore glasses without rims.

"You don't know me?" he asked.

John Willie shook his head.

"I don't blame you," he said. "I left from the place below there. Thirty-five years ago. Imagine that. And when I come back I walk into this. It's home, so it is. It's more like a welcome home to me than that young priest. I followed all the way. Man, it's something. You hear the fife and drums. You can't realise what it does. It reduces me to a jelly. Can you believe that?"

"I can," said John Willie politely.

"I'll have to get a picture," he said, going out to the door. John Willie went to the door after him.

"We never spoke anything but Irish at home," the man said. "I hardly knew how to talk English when I went away. I learned it. I thought I would never remember the Irish. Help me, I did. And the first day I am home and go in for a drink with the men, Irish comes spouting out of me as if I had only left home yesterday. It's a miracle."

The band had entered the village at the side above and was coming down the hill. The houses were lit up with penny candles in every window. The doors were open throwing squares of yellow light on to the street. The moon was adding faint light too, and the people of the cortège were like red dancing devils as they passed by the top bonfire.

The man just stood there staring as the sounds of the drums reverberated off the house walls, and the thin fifes wavered a sturdy sustaining and wailing background to the march. The man just said Oh, Lord! Oh Lord! and it wasn't a curse with him but a sort of prayer. John Willie couldn't believe in the man. He

97

was genuinely moved. John Willie admitted that a band always gave him a shiver up the back, but the man was petrified with emotion. There were actual tears in his eyes.

The band came on. The kettle-drummers held themselves tall and rattled and rattled, and the man with the big drum had his coat off and was trying to bang the skin of the drum to death. It thundered and roared and behind the man there was the first car. It was a small car that had a sliding roof and the priest was out through the roof and sitting up there waving. He was young. His hair was fair and his face was thin and the lights were gleaming in his eyes. There were other cars behind too, and the children were running along beside the cortège, shouting and cheering, and the women were at their doors waving and clapping their hands. John Willie gave the young priest a special wave and got one specially back. No wonder, he thought. John Willie had taught the young priest all he knew about trailing wild geese in December in the new moon.

Then the cortège had passed by and the street was empty.

The emotional man had never taken a picture.

"I couldn't," he said, "I couldn't. It brings back so much. It stuffs you up. Why didn't I come home before? Listen, could I go after them? Could I talk to that young priest? Would they take exception to me if I followed them to the house and talked to him?"

"Indeed no," said John Willie. "Everyone is welcome. It'll be open house for the rest of the night. Nobody is a stranger."

"Thanks," the man said. "I'll do that. I'll never forget this time. Never. Wait'll I go home and tell them all about this."

He left. He got into his car. It was a new gleaming one. It roared after the procession on over the bridge.

If he had to stay at home now, John Willie thought, as he went back in, the stars would soon go out of his eyes.

Maybe I'd be the same if I came back home after thirty-five years, he thought then, in fairness. He had never wanted to go away. If you drew a circle of fifty miles with Boola as its centre, that was as far as John Willie had ever been from home. He didn't want it any other way.

As the procession came down towards the bonfire Bart felt a hand on his arm and turned. Sheila was laughing at him.

"Hello!" she had to shout over the approaching din.

"Hello!" Bart said. He put an arm around her as they pulled back from the throng. He felt very friendly towards her. Like as if he had been talking to her yesterday. "I'm sorry I didn't see you sooner," he said.

"I am too," she said, still looking him full in the eyes.

"Still got the pin," he said, flicking it with his fingers.

"Yes," she said, laughing.

They watched the procession pass by them, the children and the band and the line of cars, and when they were gone around the bend heading towards the blazing bonfires springing up around the shoulder of the hill somewhere away behind the mountain towards the house of the young priest, a violin beside the fire started to wail. A longdrawn-out note and then it changed and went into the fast notes of a dance and everyone looked over where the fiddler was, and he was bowing away for dear life, and the next thing all the young people were out in the middle of the road dancing and dancing and cheering, and away from up the village too the young ones came leaping and shouting as they heard the notes of the fiddle and soon the whole cross was a mass of dancing young people with the hot flames of the fire gleaming on white teeth and shining eyes and flashing limbs and roaring laughter.

It had happened very suddenly although somebody had obviously arranged it. It didn't matter now. It was a pity to waste a good bonfire. It was as good as St. John's Eve.

It would go on until the early morning when the fire burned low. But they would dance and sing and laugh.

Sheila was the first to tire. The dance was interminable, back and forward and swing and stamp and change around in a ring and back to your girl and swing her off her feet. It was very exciting in the light of the fire and a starred sky above with a moon hanging brightly in it now. She pulled out of the dance and she pulled him with her.

She ran back a bit. Over the wall there was a sheen on the tumbled river below. She fanned her face with her hand.

"It's so hot, so hot in there," she said.

"We'll go down to the river," Bart said. "We will be cooler."

"All right," she said.

He helped her over the wall and held on to her hand.

There was a grove by the river, a mass of willows and laurel hanging and kissing the water. It was a shallow river. It sang songs in the night as it went over the stones.

Down there Bart suddenly pulled her around to face him.

"Why didn't I know you before?" he said.

"I don't know," she said.

Her mouth was slightly open. He could see her teeth. His face was close to hers. He could feel her breath on his chin. He found himself short of breath himself. This amazed him. Why so suddenly should this happen to him? He had no heart. He bent over her.

As soon as they heard the faint notes of the band Breeda and Joseph had come down the mountain. It was easier to go down than to come up. Joseph had gone on to the bonfire. Breeda had remained behind. She just got far enough to feel the heat of it on her face and then she stayed in the field inside the wall. She didn't want to be trampled on. She would have been defenceless and deprived of her sense of direction in a crowd. So she didn't pass the stream. She had sat there and tried to hear and distinguish the noises. She had heard the band passing and the cheering and the cars and then she had heard the music and the dancing and it set her own feet moving so that she danced in the grass of the field twisting and humming diddle-deedi-dee di deedle dum, diddle dee di dee di deedle dum, diddle dee di dee de dee di dee di, diddle iddle iddle iddle ee di dum.

She was on the other side of the grove. She had sat down laughing. Then she heard the sound of feet on the ground coming nearer and she heard voices, and she stiffened.

She recognised his voice and what he was saying.

Bart said very softly: "You remember the wedding in Una Cleery's?"

"I do," Sheila said. "I will never forget it."

"Do you remember the song she sang?" he asked.

"I do," Sheila said. "That pagan song, Bidelia called it."

"That's right," said Bart. He said it softly. "'Come down, maiden, come down with me, where the finches couple be the whitethorn tree, and I'll wind my wrist in your silken hair and seal your lips with the lover's prayer.' Do you remember all that stuff?"

"I remember," Sheila said.

He caught her hair in his hand and wound it around and around, and as he wound, her face was pulled back and he drew her close and kissed her.

Breeda felt like an animal caught in a trap. But she got to her feet and started to move away, slowly, cautiously, slowly, cautiously, holding her breath, feeling panic-stricken, and when she thought she might be far enough she reached down and took off her shoes and ran in her bare feet and ran and ran until the low wall met her knees and toppled her and made her lose her panic, so that she had to stop and think, Where am I now? and then she found her way. She could no longer hear the voices but she could hear the sound of the violin and the scuffling of leather in the dust and the cries of the excited young people.

Ten

AT THE BACK of her house Bidelia's husband, for the short while he was in the world after the wedding, had carved out a garden. It was rugged soil and it had cost him a lot of endeavour, but he had levered the big stones and hustled them to the sides and made two walls going down to the end of the place where blackberry bushes intertwined with wild woodbine tendrils curled and twisted around four stunted sycamore trees. This blackberry patch was very useful for hanging clothes on to dry. Sheets placed on the bushes seemed to dry out very white, and the only thing you had to remember was to shake the earwigs out of the folds before you brought them dry into the house. The garden was bisected by a stone path. He had carted the flat lime-stone rocks from the lakeside to make the path fairly level.

Breeda had a picture of all this in her mind as she walked down the path with a bucket of wet clothes.

She knew she was near the end of the garden when the air around her legs became a little colder, because the thicket kept the heat of the sun from that end of the garden. So she placed the bucket on the ground and took out the sheets and the blous-es and the other things and she stretched them out there. It must be hot. It was a sweaty July day. It didn't feel burning hot, so that meant that the sun must be shining from behind a layer of cloud. She tried to remember back to when she could see, and how she had felt on a day like this, and she saw in her mind the sky hazed over as if a thin layer of gauze had been pulled right across it. The birds weren't singing very much.

She heard the voices at the top of the garden. Bidelia's voice, twittery, so she must be talking to a man. "There she is," she heard, and then the call, "Breeda, there's somebody here looking for you." Then she heard his voice, "All right, I'll go down to her." "What a lovely day, dear," she heard her aunt say. Even though her hands trembled a bit when she had heard him, she controlled them now, and hardened her emotions. After all, she knew. And what could have brought him now? So she didn't turn around.

He was behind her. She could feel his presence.

"The maid was in the garden hanging out the clothes," he said, "when up came a blackbird and pecked off her nose. Aren't you afraid of blackbirds?" he asked her.

"No," she said. "It is humans who are dangerous."

"All right," he said. "Would you like to come fishing?"

He has a deep musical voice, she thought. A pleasant voice with the undertones of harshness in it. Sort of husky harshness, a sort of take it or leave it. So he could say commonplace things and they sounded like adventures.

"I have a lot of work to do," she said.

"To hell with the work," he said. "Your aunt says it's all right. You can come."

"You got around her easy," she said.

"All right," he said. "You don't want to come fishing." She knew he had turned away on the last few words. She knew he would walk away up the garden and go fishing. She would like to know what had impelled him to call on her.

"I'll go fishing so," she said, "if you wait until I am ready."

He had stopped. "What ready?" he asked. "It's only fishing. You're fine as you are."

She turned and walked towards him with the empty bucket in her hands. How does he see me, she wondered. She was wearing a light flowered frock and over that she had a wet apron from bending over the tub rubbing the clothes on the corrugated washboard. Her hands would be white and the flesh on them sort of crinkled up from the water and soap. She had to stop when she felt him unmoving before her. "I'll carry the bucket," he said. She felt his hand beside hers, as he took the bucket away. "My, what gallantry! What poise! What breeding!" she said. He didn't answer her. He had walked on. She put her hands behind her and freed the apron-strings. She was about to get angry and then thought that if she did she would lose her way and she would have to be helped and that would be worse, so she didn't lose her temper.

"Isn't it nice of Bart?" she heard her aunt say. "He's taken the day off specially, dear. It will be nice for you to have an outing."

To hell with him, she was thinking. He has some other purpose. He just doesn't do things without a purpose, or maybe he only does things from instinct like an animal today I hunt, today I sleep, today I eat, today I'll pick up that blind girl and bring her fishing.

"I'll have to do my hair," she said defiantly.

"What's wrong with your hair?" she heard him say. "Your hair is fine. There's a shine on it and it's not falling into your eyes and who'll be looking at it anyhow except the birds and the trout?"

"I'm going to do my hair!" she said.

"All right," he said. "But hurry it up for God's sake or half the day will be gone."

"It's only ten o'clock in the morning yet," she said.

She felt her way by him. He was standing in the doorway. She had to push by his body. It felt hard and sort of throbbing. That could only be Bart, like he was a dynamo discharging vitality. She went into her room. She went over to the dressing-table. It amused her sometimes to think she was standing in front of a mirror. She felt for the comb, ran it through her hair. Her hair was crackling, so it must look well. She tightened it up behind and tied a ribbon on it to keep it from blowing across her face. She heard them talking. Bart was flattering her aunt in the careless offhand way that was a sort of sneer. But Bidelia was preening herself. Then Breeda went down.

"Good-bye, dear. Look after her well, Bart." Bart didn't answer that. Look after her well. With Bart looking after her she would probably end up having a leg amputated. "How about something to eat?" "I'll look after that," Bart says. Which means that I'm going to be hungry tonight.

"We will be back early," he says. She goes to the door, lifts the latch. She feels the hotness about her body again as she steps from the shelter of the kitchen. There was no wind at all to alleviate the heat. "Where are we going fishing?" she asked. "On the sea or the lake?"

"On the lake," he said. "We'll have to go off by the river and get some bait first. Take the right turn out here."

She turned right. She walked about a hundred yards. He was walking beside her. He wasn't silent. He was humming. He had no music in a humming voice. Like the drone of a bee off key. She laughed at that.

"What?" he asked.

"You can't sing at all," she said. "You have a voice like a crow."

"I like crows," he said. "I'd prefer crows to nightingales. You know where you are with them. In here," he said then. She felt his palm on her elbow. His hand wasn't hot. It was cool. The skin was firm and hard on it.

Over a wall. Then into the green sandy way where the river wound. Gently rounded hillocks, terribly green from the limestone deposits, up and down. She knew where the river wound and had piled up great heaps of sand and gravel that most of the people used for building houses and walls and things. Later the ground became a bit soggy. Here there was a weedy drain running off towards Boola. "You hold the can," she heard him say. She felt the thin handle in her hand. There was water in it. "Come along behind me," he was saying. "When I get a bait I'll pop him into the can."

She heard swishing and gurgling.

"What's that?" she asked.

"I have a small mesh net on a long handle," he said, "and I am digging it deep into the drain among the weeds, and when I lift it up like this I am hoping there will be a couple of fat minnows among the mud. Ah, yes! one two three. Not bad." She heard them being flung into the can in her hand. The can seemed to be alive for a moment as if there were mice running around in it. She nearly dropped it. "What do they look like?" she asked.

"The minnows?" he asked. Then he paused. I know, she thought. He was going to give a rude answer and then he looked up at my face and changed his mind. His voice then hadn't changed, but it was as kindly as Bart could make it sound. "They're small little fellows," he said, "as long as your little finger, but not as fat. On top they are brown and underneath they are sort of golden, like the sheen on the belly of a goldfish, and the trout love to eat them."

"How horrible!" said Breeda.

"That's life," Bart said. "We are all cannibals."

He used the net again as she heard, and this time he failed with a disappointed grunt. The next dip was successful. She felt the can vibrating as the little fish ran round in it and knocked against the tin with their snouts and their tails. "They are funny in the can," she heard Bart say. "When they settle down, they can see themselves reflected in the tin and they go around nosing away at the other fellow just like themselves they can see, but however much they try they can't get in to them. Like a pussy cat looking into a mirror."

She laughed.

"We have enough of them now," he said. "We'll go down to the boat."

They went back the way they had come, passed the house again and went the road to the lake. She could do this walk blindfolded, she told herself with a smile. There was barely a breeze but she could hear the lazy lap of the waves. The boat was pulled up on its side on the short sandy beach. She heard him loosening the chain from the rock and the keel grinding on gravel as he pushed it out.

"Get in now," he said, "and sit at the oars. You can pull away while I am fixing the lines."

His hand was in hers. "Step," he said. She did and found the bottom of the boat with her feet. She walked forward until she felt a seat against her shins. She walked over that one and felt for the next with her hands. The wood was hot to the touch. She sat on this seat with her back to the way she had come. "I'll push off," she heard him say, and felt the boat moving violently under her. She held tightly and then it was rocking on deep water. "I'll turn her out," she heard. The horizon twisted. "The oars are near your hand now," he said, as he put them in the pins. He crossed her, his hand resting heavily on her shoulder, and the boat went down a bit by the stern as he sat there. "Pull away now," he said. Her hands were on the oars. They were fixed ones. She bent forward with them. She was indignant. How am I expected to row a boat? I rowed little enough when I could. But she let the blades of the oars into where she judged the water should be, and pulled and the boat moved. She tried it again. It was fine. Now that she came to think of it you never looked at oars when you were pulling them anyhow. You just raised them and bent forward and they went back and you let them down and pulled towards you and that was that.

"Is that why you took me fishing?" she asked. "So that you could have somebody to do all the work for you? I don't think it's fair."

"If you don't pull your left a bit now instead of talking," she heard him say, "we'll end up back where we came from."

She had to laugh. It could be only Bart who would take a blind girl fishing and then set her to rowing. Her laugh rang out over the water.

"That's better," he said. "You were like cold water for a while."

"What are you doing?" she asked.

"I'm about to kill one of the little minnows," he said. She heard the can making music as the fish dodged and twisted from his fingers. "Ah, I have one. Now I raise him in my hand and bang him down on the bottom of the boat [she heard the gentle thump]. He lifts his head and his tall and they quiver and now he is dead. I take him up and I open his little mouth and I shove the end of the spike of the spinner into his mouth and right down through his little body. Then I take one of the spikes of the triple hooks and stick it into his side and I get the other one resting by his tall and I tie him on to the spinner with red thread. Now he is a nice-looking bait. If I was a trout, I'd eat him myself.

Now I kill another of the little dears in the same way as the first and put him on a spinner too."

"You are cruel," she said when she heard the thump.

"You are too sensitive," he said. "The whole world is that way. I like minnows. I like the colour of them and the size of them, but we have to go fishing."

"Why?" she asked.

"That's silly," he said. "If we don't get a trout, we don't eat."

She heard more noises. "What are you at now?" she asked.

"Letting out the line," he said. "It goes out for thirty yards with the minnow spinning at the end of it. Then I fix it to this ash pole and stick it out at the side of the boat. There's a little bell on the line near the end of the pole and when the big fish bites he will ring the bell and then we haul him in. I do the same at the other side, and when I have that done, I can relax."

"I'm glad," she said.

Shortly, he said "Now," and she knew he was leaning back in his seat. "Not too fast now, Breeda," he advised her then. "Too too slow. Nice even strokes, so that you can allure the fish. This is nice. I'm glad I took the day off."

"I'm getting tired," she said.

"Already?" he asked. "Your trouble is you don't get enough exercise."

"What made you call for me?" Bart she asked.

There was a pause.

"I don't know," he said. "There was a nice day in it. I was fed up. I thought, I'll go fishing. I said to John Willie, I'm going fishing. Then I thought I will call for Breeda, I'm sure she'd like to pull me around the lake, so I went and collected you. I'm glad I did. You look nice there out from me leaning on your oars. It's a fine day. The colour of the lake is sort of steely blue. That I don't like. It should be clear. Apart from that everything is fine."

"Just an impulse?" she said. "And you were sure I would answer your impulse. Does everybody come running to your impulses, Bart?"

"Look, Breeda," he said. "Don't let's go into things. Just enjoy ourselves. Just the day. Maybe we'll never get another one. Take the crease from between the eyes and the furrow from the forehead and the jut from the chin. Let's just pretend to be happy for a day."

She relaxed her face.

"All right," she said. "Let's be happy."

She felt him moving.

"Go back to the stern," he told her, his hands on her shoulders, "and I'll pull for a bit." She obeyed. He held her hand until she had manoeuvred and felt the seat under her. Then the boat moved easily. "Stretch out your left hand," he said then. She did so. "Higher," he commanded. She raised her hand and felt the line. "Pull it," he said. She did so. The little bell tinkled. "Now you hear what the fish will do," he said. "Now reach for the line on the other side." She did so, found it and tinkled the bell. "When you hear that again," he said, "you can stretch and pull in a fish."

"I'd be afraid," she said.

"The fish will be more afraid," Bart said.

The water was slapping gently against the bow of the boat. It was very peaceful. But it was hot.

"I'll remember this day," she heard him say.

"I will remember the feel of it," she said.

"Poor Breeda," he said. "It's tough, is it?"

She was silent.

"I don't know. You might be better off at that," he said. They passed an hour in silence then. She was conscious of him. If she stretched her legs her feet would hit against his shoe. It was a very silent day anyhow. She could hear his breathing. She could hear a dog far far away barking. She could hear the far-away call of a lake gull. The world seemed to be stretched senseless under the heat.

And then the little bell tinkled.

"Breeda! Breeda! the one on the left!" she heard him calling. She was confused. She was excited. First she stretched her right and then her left and floundered with her fingers until she felt the line. "What will I do? Oh, what will I do?" she asked.

"Pull in the bastard," Bart shouted at her. "I'll haul in the other line." She turned, facing back, and pulled on the line. It was jerking in her hands. There was terrible force trying to draw back from her. She started to pull hand over hand. "Oh, Bart," she said, "he'll get away." "Pull, pull, you devil!" Bart shouted. She kept hauling in the wet line, She felt it wet on her knee where her dress had dragged up. It was cold and wet but she was excited. She felt the line not only jerking but moving backwards and forwards. Then it was free. There was a big splash behind. "Oh, he's gone, he's gone!" she cried. "No," Bart shouted, "he only jumped." The strain was back again on her hand. "Closer! Closer!" she heard Bart saying. "Easy! Easy!"

He was beside her, kneeling. His body was crushing hers. "A little bit more," he said. "Just a little bit more and I'll have the net under him." She pulled in more and then she heard him shout and she heard the clumping of the fish on the boards. "Oh, a beauty!" Bart was saying. "A bloody beauty!" "Let me feel him," she said, holding out her hands. Bart put the fish into them. Her slender fingers closed over his thick length. The fish jumped. "Ugh!" Breeda said and dropped her hand. The fish was jumping all over the boards. Bart was laughing. She was rubbing her hands on her dress. Then she heard a dull clump and the fish was silent.

"That was great work," said Bart. "Man, if we had more time we'd make a fisherman out of you."

"I did all right," said Breeda complacently.

"And now we can go and eat," said Bart.

"Are we going to eat him?" she asked.

"Why the hell did you think we came out here?" she heard him ask.

"Well, if we hadn't caught him, what would we have eaten?" she asked.

"Och, I have a few oul biscuits and things," Bart said.

Their laugh ran over the lake.

It was very exciting. The keel shortly grounded on a beach. Bart got out, and she held tightly as the boat was pulled up. "You sit on the ground over here," he said to her, "and leave the rest to me." She did. The grass was coarse where it met her exposed skin, but it was soft. She smelled the wood fire burning before she heard the sound of it crackling. Nice smell. Of alder wood and beech and hazel. He was more efficient than she had given him credit for. He made tea and fried the trout in butter and he had two plates and cups and he hadn't forgotten anything. He had filleted the fish. She ate it with her fingers. It was very nice. It is always nicer when it is just fresh. He fried biscuits too in the butter, and though the tea was a bit strong it was very nice. Then the two of them lay side by side in the sun.

She wanted Bart to bend over her and make love to her. She wanted to be made love to with all her heart and body. Once she thought he would make a move towards her, but he never did. What's wrong with me? I'm good-looking. I have a nice figure. My skin is soft. I am not as buxom as the girl he had down by the river. She had heard about Sheila. Her aunt had told her. Did she know the latest, that that Brendan girl and Bart were great? Great what? And I love him, because his was the last face I ever saw, and I loved him before anyhow, no matter what he does to me or anybody else, or what he is like or where he comes from or where he goes or what he does. That's all. Am I a destroyed king? Like long ago if a king was afflicted he couldn't be a king. He had to go. Was that it? Like you would hesitate to kiss a girl with leprosy, or consumption, or who was armless or legless or voiceless or eyeless.

All he said was, "This is nice. I am very happy." But it wasn't enough for her at all. He said it mildly and sleepily as if he was half asleep. He wasn't of course. She couldn't know that. He wasn't asleep at all. His head was turned and he was looking at her. All over.

On the other side of the mountain a breeze was born at sea. It started small and sent off a puff that travelled not too fast and met the mountain and was awed by it and climbed it, and scooped down the other side and ruffled the lake. But this small breeze had only been the precursor, because many more like it and then greater than it in every way started to come in from the Atlantic. Away out there, there was a bank of heavy cloud that was being driven very fast. The breeze followed the breeze and behind that was the heavy rain, and suddenly Breeda felt cold.

111

And she shivered and sat up and felt the wind on her face. The waves were playfully slapping the hard stones that edged the island.

"Bart," she said. "The wind is getting up. Maybe we ought to go home."

There was a pause. He was looking over beyond the shoulder of the hill.

"Yes," he said, "we better go home. Wait a minute." She felt his hand brushing her legs. Both legs. And then her arms. "The ticks," she heard him say. "You wouldn't know you had them when you can't see them."

"Thanks," she said. He still held her hand. He pulled her to her feet.

"Thanks, Breeda," he said. "For this day. I'll always remember this day."

She had nothing to say. They got into the boat.

This wasn't the same at all as coming out. She had to hold very tightly to the sides of the boat with her hands once they were launched. She could hear Bart grunting. It wasn't too bad at first, but then the wind rose strongly, and she felt very cold in her light dress. Sometimes a lash of wind-driven water would hit her full in the face like a blow. The boat was rising and falling, rising and falling. When it rose the water came in and drenched her, when it fell it fell hard and bounced her on the seat and rattled her teeth. It must be very bad. Why had it come so quickly? But it always came quickly. She remembered the fishermen saying that. It was a treacherous lake, everybody said.

She was suddenly filled with terror. She thought of her father and mother. That had been on the sea. He was an odd man, they said, because he was never seen without his wife. That was an oddity in a place where men rarely showed signs of public affection, in case people should think they were queer. Her father was queer. He always took his wife wherever he went. Fishing on the seas in the evening. But once the sea rose like now, and he was not a professional and he didn't know what to do with the sea. It swept down on this hopeless amateur and swept himself and his wife out of the world with a flick.

She was sure now she was going to drown. The waves must be monstrously high. She was panic-stricken.

She screamed. She couldn't stop herself and she went on her knees and held out her hands until they clutched Bart. One of the oars hit her on the forehead before he let them free. His arms were around her shoulders. He was shouting.

"Breeda, get back! Get back!" he shouted at her. "It's not bad, on me oath it's not bad."

But the boat had swung around when it was not controlled by the oars and it yawned and the wind whipped the water into its mouth. She felt the water all around her. She thought they were gone. She screamed again. She felt Bart's hand on her hair. His mouth was close to her ear. "Breeda," he said, "go back to your seat. Go back to your seat. If you don't go back to your seat, we will be gone. Breeda, go back to your seat. I can't do anything if you won't go back to your seat."

"Bart! Bart!" she said. Her face was pressing into his chest. His shirt was wet. She could hear his heart thumping steadily.

"Breeda!" he said again. "Go back to your seat! I swear it's all right if you go back to your seat."

He pulled her hands away from his body. "Go back now," he said to her face. She sat in the bottom of the boat. The water was around her thighs.

"Can I stay here, Bart?" she asked.

"Fine," he said. "Duck your head a bit." She was between his legs. She leaned down. He got the oars in his hands. He had a struggle to get the bow into the wind. She could feel him struggling. "It's because of not being able to see, Bart," she called. "It's just because I can't see. If I could see I wouldn't mind. Honest, Bart, I wouldn't mind if I could see."

"All right, Breeda," he said. "Take it easy. It's not too bad. It's just a hard row. It will be slow. But we'll get there. It's not bad. It's just bad enough to make your blood hot. Honest. Man, I'll show you. Who's the best man in a boat in Boola? Bart O'Breen. You wait."

The boat was creaking. She could hear the pressure of his straining feet cracking the footboard. The boat was groaning. It rose and fell with terrible thumps, and the water spattered in now and again and drenched her. But her heart settled down. Her limbs ceased to tremble. The battering became no worse. It remained at about the same. Why did I make a show of myself? She wished she had Joseph's book, so that she could let it fall open and read. Who would read? She thought of having the book in her hand and allowing it to fall open and saying: Would you mind reading this, Bart? Just when he was straining to hold the boat against the wind. What would Bart say? She was sure that he would curse horribly. This sobered her. She pulled her body back until her shoulders were against the seat, and then she raised herself on to the seat and sat there.

"Good girl," she heard Bart say. "Good girl." It was said through his teeth.

An hour of time can be long or it can be short. This was a long hour.

They were in the lee of the land. The water stopped hitting her in the face. She heard Bart resting on the oars, from the muffled sound of his heavy breathing. "It's over now," he said to her then, raising his head. "We are very near home." He had turned his head to look towards the beach. Then he turned back to her. There was tenseness in his voice.

"Breeda," he said to her, "as soon as the boat lands you run home, you hear. You run home and change your clothes and dry yourself, you hear."

"I will, Bart," she said. Why did he say that? She would have done that anyhow. "I won't be able to go with you," he said. "It's straight home. You can't miss. I have things to do."

"All right, Bart," she said.

She felt like a drowned rat. The day had been so good and so promising. What was left of it now? Just a drowned rat. Wasn't that the way things always happened with Bart? Everything started out fine and seemed as if it would be perfect and then at the end of it there was always something to destroy it. Bart hadn't created the wind, and he hadn't created the rain that was fiercely pouring now with the wind behind it, but it was part of him.

The keel of the boat ground on the beach. She stayed until she felt him pulling it up, and then she stood and his hand was there to steady her. She stepped out. His hand pressed hers strongly for a moment and then he said, "I'm sorry, Breeda. I always mess things up. Go on now, straight home."

"Goodbye, Bart," she said. Her feet were on the track up to the right road. It was an easy walk. She was some yards away when she heard Bart's voice. It was low, and there were no pleasant notes in it. She heard him say: "Well, Suck, what's worrying you now?"

Eleven

HE HADN'T LOOKED directly at him while he spoke. He was tying the chain of the boat. The rain was heavy. He looked after Breeda. She was walking slowly up the slope to the road. Her dress was clinging to her body. Her hair was sticking to her head, and falling in rats'-tails. The last time he had seen her like that hadn't been so good either. The sight of her forlorn figure made his heart warm. He wished that the business with Suck could be postponed, but he supposed it couldn't be. He felt very tired. It was a hard struggle to bring the boat home against the wind and the weather. He didn't feel very energetic.

Suck was watching him, saw him looking after the girl.

"Are you going to put her up the spout too?" he asked. His voice was grating. He spoke coarsely.

Anger flooded into Bart. He looked up. Suck's face seemed as if it was on fire. His body was crouched, his great hands were clenched into fists. I mustn't get mad, Bart told himself. If I get mad things won't work out at all. They'll only end up all wrong.

He controlled himself with a visible effort. He stood up.

"All right, Suck," he said.

"All right! All right!" Suck jeered at him. He was very angry. His eyes were slitted and looked red. Suck was trying to restrain himself too. He wanted to go over to the curly boy and beat him into the ground. Beat him into the ground and stamp on his puddings. But it mustn't be that way either. It would have to be the nice way, the polite way. Give it back fifty years ago and there would have been no nice way about it. There would have been only one way.

His going into the house. His old father was there, white about the nostrils. Not so old. A nice sixty-five and he was as straight as a whip. And the soft old woman the mother, bending over the fire, sitting on the small stool: and her check apron thrown over her head and she crying, crying, crying. God almighty! Why did it happen to them? They were decent, weren't they? They paid their Christmas dues and their Easter dues and their harvest collections. They went to Mass on Sundays and Holy Communion once a month and people respected them. People had always respected them. And Sheila of all. She was good. She was bright. She was well educated. She knew about everything. He loved her. They always had fun. She was over near the dresser. She was pale. She wasn't defiant. It wasn't all that. But it took away. It took away the way you held your head or walked among the people or talked from a good heart. Like potatoes in a pit. All good but one with a mark on it. And bit by bit the mark grew and it was a bad potato and beside it the other became bad, and another and another, till all around it when the pit was opened there was this black mess. Dirty soft black mess of nothing but putrid potatoes. It hurt him. It hurt him right in. How could a good potato that came from a bad pit ever be the same? Even if it was healthy and right they would always say, There's a good potato that came from a bad pit. And now he looked at the present and the future and the things that would be said, the silences that would fall on groups when you appeared. No laughing it off, it was too dirty. And you with the pin, he said as he raised his hand and hit her with the back of it across the face, and as she staggered he hit her with his fist in the stomach. She had seen that blow coming and had pulled in her body, so that its full force didn't land deep in her belly. But she couldn't breathe. Her hair was falling over her face. She was on her knees waving and she was moaning. And his mother got up and cried, "Oh no! Oh no!" And a wave of sorrow came over him and he got on his knees beside her and put his long arms around her and he said, "Sheila, girl, don't cry. I'm sorry, Sheila.

117

It will be all right. It will be all right." But of course he knew that it would never be all right. Never again.

Joke, they said. Laugh, about up the way. The Brendans. Hear about the girl? A mark, man. Watch it there. Who'd have thought? Who'd ever have thought? But they are all the same in the dark. My wild Irish rose, they sang, and then the obscene bit ending in "clothes". He could hear the pubs resounding with it. Healthy clean people were brought in there even. But once unclean, think of the way. Every pint that was drunk and relieved of, the talk would be good. Hear this. Hear this. Oh, man, but it's the boy Bart, the curly ram. Ha! Ha! Ha!

He went out of there, and he expended himself on the hills. Up after the sheep. Right up to the top of Boola, and looked down at the dirty world. Even if you were a mountain, rain and wind could wear you away given the time. Given the tongue. Wouldn't the tongues of men if they came up and licked take away a mountain just as easy? Just licking it with their dirty tongues, they would wear away a whole mountain. What would they do to a man's name? A man's name's a precious thing, to be down in the dirt and they scrabbling at it like the snouts of pigs shoved into shit. Goddamn him! Goddamn him from a height, from the greatest height he could damn him. He was up on the mountain and his arms were reaching to the sky shaking his fists. I better stop or I'll go mad. Can the loss of respectability drive a man mad?

He was down, coming down, thinking of Sheila bent over on her knees. He was crying. A great big man. But he was crying. He loved Sheila. He was big when she was small and it was nice having a small wee sister. Small little fingers she had and tiny feet, as soft as the feel of flour in his big red hand. That way. What a thing! What a thing!

He went in to John Willie.

There were people there, but he didn't mind. His hands were trembling as he put the money on the counter. John Willie was worried looking at him. Where's your man? Who? Who? Bart. Where's Bart? He's out fishing, I think, on the lake. He should be in soon. You know! You know! I know? What do I know?

118

What do you know? You know everything, John Willie. You know what that curly bastard done to my sister. Let's have it in the open. Right out in the open now, so that never again can it be sniggled and scrabbled about in pubs. Let's be clear now. Shish, man. Please, Suck, let's take it easy. No taking it easy. No taking it easy. Let's face it now. Get it washed in the open in the clear air. He knew Mabbina was down at the grocery counter. He knew that there were other people there. But he didn't care. Let them listen now. Let them listen. Let ye listen now. Because this is the beginning and the end of it. I'll crucify people after this. You hear that. Crucify the tongues. The tongues should be crucified.

Then he was out. The rain had come. It fell on his hot face and he welcomed it. He went towards the lake.

He stood on the shore. He could see the boat far out, rising and falling. He saw the battering it was taking from the wind. About thirty gusts would run along the backs of the high waves and scoop up water and whiten it so that it seemed from the spray as if hot springs were boiling from below. It took a long time for the boat to come in. He was breathing easier. He wanted to look at his face.

He saw the girl in the boat. The girl. Another one. The world knew what he had done to her. Wasn't it all his fault that she was like that too? He saw your man turning his head once to look in. He knew he saw Suck waiting for him. It gave him a feeling of savage satisfaction. Satisfaction.

If he hadn't walked the mountain he wouldn't be as calm as he was now and he facing him.

All wet, the fellow was, but the curly hair and the good-looking face were still there, tanned by the sun, a shine on the straight bone of the nose. I'll crooken that for him. The eyes looking at him. Clear. As if he wasn't what he was.

"What's a little education?" he asked out loud. "Does it give you the right to go around taking like you were an old lord? A half-educated bastard like you. Who do you think you are?"

"Look," Bart said. "If we want to talk let's go somewhere else. And stop the name-calling, Suck. I won't stand for it."

"You won't stand for it! You won't stand for it" He spat on the wet ground. "Why did you do it? Why didn't you go into the town and pick up something there? Why did you do this? Did we ever do anything to you? Why do you have to soil us? We are decent. We were always decent. Your father before you was no good. You are no good. Why do you do that to us?"

"Maybe I didn't do anything to you. Maybe I didn't." The veins were swelling on Bart's neck. "Why am I supposed to be blamed? How do I know she wasn't ditching with every bloody man in the place?"

"Oh, God!" said Suck.

"You go, Suck," Bart said. "Leave me alone. I'm sick of the sight of you."

He was lost now. There were waves of rage running up and down his body. He would say things now that he would have to believe afterwards if he ever said them at all. He didn't want to say them. He didn't want things to be this way. He wanted them to be different to this. He walked past him, close to him, determined. The hand caught his shoulder and pulled him back. The shirt ripped clean away, one sleeve hanging.

"Three weeks," said Suck. "Three weeks is what you have. That's all."

"Listen, you can go to hell. What do you think I am? Nothing doing. Not going to be saddled with other men's sins. Let her go to hell. Let her end up a happy hoor, like Una Cleery."

Suck aimed a wild blow at him. Bart dodged it and hit him in the mouth. The teeth cut into his knuckles, and blood appeared on the other's lips. He hit him again in the stomach. If I have to fight him I'll make him sorry. By God, I'll make him sorry. He danced back on the sand. Suck came after him. Bart hit him again, in the belly, and hit him on the side of his head. It had no effect on the other fellow. There was a look of joy on his face. The hand reached for his other shoulder, caught it, held, and then Bart couldn't dodge the great fist that was raised like a club and came down on his neck. He fell on the sand. He thought he was choking. He saw the nailed boot coming and turned on his side and took the kick on his upper arm. His arm

120

seemed to go numb. He turned and turned and then got to his feet again. He was convulsed with rage. He ran into Suck. He couldn't raise his right arm at all, but he hit and hit and hit with his left and the force and energy made Suck go back. It was no good. A great fist went up and fell, up and fell, while the other hand was gripping his numbed arm. He felt the blow on his nose and waves of pain went through his upper face. He felt the blow on his mouth as his teeth cut into his lips. He felt the blow on the temple that laid him on the sand, so that his cheek was hugging, the wet sand. Then he was lifted up and hit again and again and again, and while he was lying after that the boot came into his ribs. His sides pained him.

He wasn't unconscious. There was a glimmer left to him.

He felt Suck's breath on his face.

"I'll give you a week," he heard him. "One week, and then I will come after you again. I will beat you next week and I will beat you the week after. Every week at the same hour."

Then Bart was alone.

Suck walked up the slope. Up there a bit away near the road there were people standing looking. Suck bent down and picked up a stone. He flung it towards them. He was shouting. "Go home! Go home! Go home, ye pigs! Go home and wash yeer tongues and yeer eyes in soap." He bent again to get a stone but when he straightened they were gone. He turned at the top of the slope to look back. Bart was still lying on the sand. His clothes were wet and blood-stained.

Then Suck turned his back on him and walked his own road.

Twelve

HE PULLED HIMSELF up from the ground. His hip had made a hollow where the rain had gathered. It had soaked into his skin. Not that the rest of him was dry. He had gone in the morning wearing only the shirt and the grey flannel trousers.

He was on his knees resting on his hands, shaking his head. He was hurt. Then he got to his feet. The wildest imaginable feelings flooded him. Shame and rage and a deep feeling of humiliation. It warmed him. He didn't feel the cold. He saw in his mind the gun hanging over the fireplace. It was a thirty-inch barrel with a hammer. It was always well oiled. It was an old gun. There were a few pits in its gleaming inside steel. But it was very accurate. John Willie could shoot anything with it. He saw himself taking the gun down from over the fireplace and taking a number one cartridge from the drawer of the dresser, and opening the gun and putting in the cartridge and then going after Suck and finding him and blowing his face off.

It was pleasant and he was determined. It was the only way he could get his health back.

He walked. Nobody had ever done it to him before. Not this way. He had been hurt before. He had had black eyes and sore cut lips and sore limbs from fights and from football and from games. But this was terrible. He rubbed the blood from his upper lip. His nose was sore. The blood was running into his mouth. The whole side of his face was sore. His right eye was closing. Every inch of him seemed to be injured. He saw the way home. It seemed endless. His imagination was running ahead of his body. He tried to run but his ribs were too sore. If he breathed fast or put effort on them the pain seemed unbearable.

He went into the house by the back door. He would go straight to the gun.

He went in by the back door, but he didn't go to the gun.

His mother was standing in front of the fire. Martha was near the table. Joseph was sitting on the stool beside the fire. Luke was standing near the dresser, his long arms hanging awkwardly by his sides.

His mother's face was bitter, her lips tightly closed, her eyes were cold. He hadn't thought of the kitchen being full when he came for the gun. He had seen it empty.

His mother said: "You have ten minutes to go to your room and gather your clothes and get out of this house."

He couldn't believe his ears. He stood staring at her.

She shouted, "You heard me! You heard me! Go on and go, go, go, go!" She went on like a gramophone record that was stuck.

She felt desolate with bitterness. She saw her life back over. The lean years with his father. She saw herself in the fields in big boots following a plough. Herself with her own hands. She had used the scythe and the slean and the spade. Herself over the years. All that in the fields, and cook too and wash and rear the children up, fighting and husbanding and buying and selling, a struggle that would have gone on and on and on if John Willie out of pity professed as love and regard hadn't taken the toil out of life for the lot of them. She was bitter about that. Because she had found a husband and a haven, but there was deep in her the sense of loss that remained as wild despair deep down in her for the laugh and the twink and the genuine love that had come to her from Bart's father. A feeling that shamed her, that should have been rooted out, rooted out, and John Willie and she had nothing to say to each other except the pleasantries of companionship that didn't make up for the wild love of the other. She saw in the son the incarnation of the father. His whole lower face splotched with blood, altering the whole shape of his face. The narrowed eyes, one of them closed. His shirt in tatters, with the pink spatters of rain-washed blood. A picture like this. She had seen it before, after rows in pubs or long absences, when he came back, his eyes apologetic, wanting a shave, and the charm that emanated from him calling to her heart. She would have to quell that and harden herself for the sake of her children and her own sanity. He was no good and the boy was father of the man.

"A good name," she said. "I had a good name always, and you have taken it and walked on it. No sense of decency. No sense of right or wrong. Only what is good for you. No thought for others. Just take, take, take and take, and in the taking kill, people and good names and morals and all that is decent. You! You! Long ago I should have put you out. Long ago. If I had the courage. If I had the hardness of heart. Now there would be less people unhappy. Now get into the room and get out. Ten minutes. I swear it. Ten minutes or I'll throw them out."

"Mother, mother!" said Joseph, plucking at her sleeve. She flung his hand off violently.

"Shut up!" she said to him. "Shut up."

Bart looked at her for a long minute. The fire in him had cooled. His eyes no longer sought the gun over the fire. All he could see was the blazing eyes of his mother, accentuated by the pale face, the veins in her neck, and the red hair that was dusted over so that the colour was gone from it. She was a fine figure of a woman. He could admire her. His sore lip twirked at the corner in a sort of smile. It maddened her. She came over towards him, her hands clenched. That smile at the side of the mouth. How well she knew it! Knew that all that she had said made no impression. That she might have been talking to the air. He would have his own thoughts and believe them, while he listened to the truth calmly and didn't hear it.

"Doesn't it mean anything to you what you have done to that girl?" she asked. "Does what her life is going to be mean nothing at all to you? The agony she will go through for you and the shame and the misery of her existence on account of you. Doesn't it mean anything at all to you? Anything at all?" She was beseeching.

124

He could have said: I would be almost married to her now if Suck and you had minded your own business. He could have said that. That was his intention. It was just that it was put away until he had to take it out and do it, and he would have done that, the right thing as they called it, just as impulsively and enjoyably as he had done the other. But not now. They themselves had destroyed the girl.

"She is on her own now," he said, and walked past her into his room.

It didn't take long. He had the old school case, brown fibre with his name written inside in indelible ink in big unformed handwriting: Bartholomew O'Breen, Boola. It smelled of mothballs and pencils and books. One suit, one shirt and a pair of shoes. He threw off the wet clothes and grimaced with pain. He washed his face as well as he could in the basin, and rubbed it gently with the towel. He hardly knew himself. Put on a shirt and trousers and a sports coat and over that an old raincoat and then he was free. He stood at the room door, looking at his room. An iron bedstead with a white quilt. And shelves with things from away back. Bits of wood that had been the frame of a first fishing-line, and a box with tangled gut skeins in it, with queer awkward feathered flies that he had unskilfully put together, pulling the feathers from a bantam cock he had chased. Lumps of lead and hooks and bits of funny stones and a four-leaved clover stuck on a Christmas card. That made him smile. It had brought him a lot of luck, he thought, that four-leaved clover.

Then he closed the door behind him.

The light in the kitchen was going. It was later than he thought.

He spoke to Luke. "Goodbye, Luke," he said. "So long, Martha. Good luck, Joseph," and then he went out the back way. He couldn't face walking out the front. It was still raining very heavily. He pulled up the collar of his coat. There wasn't a lot of light in the sky. The clouds were enveloping the hills. Right down. You would think you were living in a flat land.

Inside, his mother was saying, "Come back, Joseph, you are

not to go after him. Come back when I tell you." But Joseph followed him. He was crying inside of him. Why should things like this happen? Where was the love and affection that Christ had died to implant in the hearts of men? Nothing but sorrow and sin and desolation.

"Bart!" he called. "Bart!"

Bart was climbing over the wall when he heard the thin call. He climbed the wall and stood on the other side. He waited.

"What is it, Joseph?" he asked.

"Bart," said Joseph, "don't go away. Things will work out. If you go away things will never be the same. Things will never be worked out. There will be too much bitterness and hate. Mother doesn't really mean it. Give her time, Bart, and everything will be all right."

"Poor Joe!" said Bart. "No, it won't be all right, Joseph. That's because everybody is not the same as you. You haven't the feet on the earth, Joe. You have the head in the clouds. We are all only sinners, boy. That's nature. We have to do things as we see them."

He felt sorry for Joseph. The rain made him look so thin and small, flattening his dark hair, running down his thin face. He was all eyes that way, like a fish, big dark eyes in which tears were welling. Not for himself either. He doubted if Joseph knew now that he himself existed.

He put his hand on Joseph's face.

"Don't take it too hard, Joe," he said. "You read too many books where man is laid out like a dissected frog, where he should answer to a fixed set of rules. He never will. He is never like the books, Joe. You are too thin. Go and drink some porter and fatten yourself up. Goodbye."

He turned then and left him.

Joseph called after him again but he didn't turn around. He only waved a hand in the air.

Joseph turned back to the house. He was bent down. The rain was sloshing in his shoes. If Bart had waited things would have been all right. He shouldn't have gone away. Things were out of hand, out of hand. His mother was standing at the doorway.

126

Inside the kitchen Martha was lighting the lamp. Its light was already closing out the night. She pulled down the blind to close out the eyes of the people. Martha was thinking, her heart hard: Well, that's one of them gone. She surveyed the figure of the other as he came in from the rain with an expressionless face. The misery of his face and appearance left her unmoved.

Joseph went into his room. Mabbina was hurt by the reproach she felt from him but she knew she was right, and that he would get over it.

Bart wasn't going through the street. He would make his way behind the houses and join the road farther out near the sea.

He was on his way there when he hesitated. He thought of Breeda. He didn't mind never seeing any of the others again, but he liked Breeda. He thought he couldn't go without at least seeing her. He turned off. The rain was easing. The night had almost fallen. The dark clouds were racing across the sky. They were broken. It would ease for a while and then the heavy mass would close in again. It would be a nice wet journey to the town unless he could chance on a lift.

He went in her gate. He stood back in the shadow after he had knocked. Bidelia came to the door. She was peering. He pulled back from the light of the lamp. "Who is it? Who is it?" "It's me, ma'am. Tell Breeda I want to see her out here for a minute." "Oh, Bart, you bold boy, dear. She was drenched to the skin. Why didn't ye come home when ye saw the rain?" "Why didn't we? If everybody came home when they saw the rain coming nobody would ever do anything." "Come in," she invited. "No, I just want to see Breeda for a minute." "Is there anything wrong with you?" "No, just in a hurry." "Breeda! Breeda! Bart to see you. He won't come in." She backed away. Breeda came down from the room. Her hair was fuzzled and tangled from the drying of the towel. There was colour in her cheeks, in her lips. She looked well. She had looked well in the sunshine pulling on the fish, with the big mountain as a background behind her.

"What is it, Bart?" She was worried. There were creases on her smooth forehead.

"I'm going away, Breeda," he said.

127

"What's up?" she asked.

"You'll hear," he said. No bitterness. Just a statement of fact. "Just thought I'd see you. Now I have seen you. Goodbye. Don't forget me."

He was going.

"Bart!" He was turning back.

Like that. Don't go like that. I want to talk to you.

"No, no, no time. Too much talk. It was a posh day, Breeda. I did like today. It was grand. Nicest day I have had. Until the end of it."

"But are you going far?"

"Where is the end of the earth? Know where that is, Breeda? That's where I'm going."

"Oh, Bart, for ever, like that for ever."

"Yes, for ever. I suppose for ever. What's for ever? It's like the end of the earth. If you keep going round you come back. I don't know."

He came back to her. He put up his palm, rested it against her cheek. I'll remember that. So soft and smooth. She always had that soft smooth skin, like a child or like velvet. He remembered Sheila. She had smooth skin too but just behind her elbows the skin was coarse when you held it in your palm.

"That's it, Breeda." He took his hand away.

"Bart, write to me, send me a message. Do something."

"I don't write. Never wrote in my life. I might. I don't know. Goodbye." He was at the gate. He listened to the running feet coming up. Watched, his hand tense on the timber, until the figure of John Willie emerged. Slowed down.

"Thought you might be here," John Willie said. "Just thought. Going off, Bart?"

"Yes," Bart said.

"Not say goodbye to me. Crisscross, what did I do to you, man?"

"Nothing, John Willie," hitting him a blow on the shoulder. "I like you, John Willie. Maybe I don't want to say goodbye to you, hah?"

"Blast it to hell," John Willie said. "Here's a few quid for you.

Until you get started." Holding out the bundle. Saw Bart hesitating, his jaw muscles hardening. "A loan if you like!"

"Thanks," Bart said, taking it, and then he opened the gate and walked away, walked away and went down the rise and crossed the river where it was shallow at the stepping-stones. He mounted the slope on the other side and headed away behind the village. Then he was hidden. Then he was seen again, and then he was gone.

John Willie went in the gate.

He stood by the door, beside Breeda. He saw the tears coming out of her eyes where the lamplight caught their glisten.

"Don't cry for Bart, Breeda," he said. "I'm afraid he is not worth it."

"Have you no doubts at all, John Willie?" she asked.

"That's the trouble," he said. "I have."

"What happened?" she asked. "It was Suck Brendan."

"It was," said John Willie. "In the pub raving today. Then he went down to the boat. Met him coming in."

"I heard the beginning," she said.

"Suck gave him a terrible beating, from all accounts," John Willie said.

"Beat Bart?" she asked.

"That's right, the great Bart," John Willie said. "Beat him into the dirt. You wouldn't know Bart's face, they say."

"Why are you so cold about him?" she asked.

"I don't know," he said. "Maybe because I like him so much. But what he did was wrong."

"Did his mother hear?"

"She did," John Willie said. "She put the run on him."

"I don't know," said Breeda. "Did nobody at all try to stop and listen to his side of it?"

John Willie considered that.

"Bedam," he said then, more cheerfully. "Nobody did. First they bet him and then they run him."

"Bart is not meek," she said. "Bart is not humble. Maybe they should have given him a chance to open his mouth. And so Bart was really beaten?"

"He was."

"I wonder if he was hurt."

"Oh, he was hurt. They say he must have been hurt bad. Suck is a big man. He doesn't know his own strength."

"I'm sorry Bart is gone. I'm not sorry he was hurt. I hope it will be to the good and not the bad. Good night, John Willie."

"Good night, Breeda," he said, and waited until the door closed behind her. Then he walked away. He was torn with conflicting feelings. He was indignant when he thought of that nice little Brendan girl and the big tortured Suck. And he was sad when he thought of the mixed-up Bart he had known so long. To hell with it, he thought, desperately. But I didn't see his face. I kept my eyes off his face.

Breeda was in bed listening to the new rain banging on the window-panes. She tried to sleep, but all she could see was a figure with a suitcase walking the wet road by the sea, as lonely as hell and as proud as the devil, and she couldn't feel glad.

Thirteen

IT WAS AUTUMN and the black-cassocked figures were walking on the gravelled drive by the river. The drive was lined with enormous copper beeches. The copper colour of the leaves was turning faintly green and they were falling listlessly on the grass.

Joseph walked by himself, his hands held in front of him, his eyes on the ground. Off to the left there was the sound of laughing young men and the sharp click of a leather ball meeting the base of a hurling stick. Joseph stopped and looked over at the field.

None of them were wearing togs because it was only the time of the short recreation. They had their cassocks tucked up and were swiping the ball between four of them in line from goal to goal. He saw the fair head of Larry, could hear his deep voice and his laugh. The walkers on the drive were two-by-two, some of them talking, some of them reading, some of them conducting animated conversations with waving of hands.

Nearly always Joseph walked by himself. He was not free with conversation. He always made a great effort to conquer his shyness, but the greater the effort he made, the more awful became his embarrassment, and the embarrassment of his listener. It was an ease to both of them when one or the other drifted away. Joseph felt best on his own. He liked to think and to conduct brilliant theological conversations in his own mind. He knew that they would never come out of his mouth but they were good in his head. On assigned days all conversations had to be conducted in Latin. Joseph could write Latin well, but when it came to talking it, making up phrases that never existed, faking up the Latin words for things like "radio" and "film-star" and "bicycle" and "tandem" and "electric razor" and "Okay" and current slang phrases, he was a dead loss. The others got great pleasure out of thinking up a new one and springing it on the unexpected occasion, in order to make the Professors laugh. He tried so hard to be as he ought to be, but he could never succeed. But he had to persist, because all human failings are barricades to be overcome on the road to God.

So even though he was more frequently alone, he never felt lonely. Not here. He was always more than pleased to come back after holidays. He thought this was a fault in his nature too, that he often did penance for. But the atmosphere of his home was not easy. There was all the business about Bart hanging over the home like a black cloud, and he was eternally conscious of his mother's dislike for Luke's wife. He had tried to talk to her about it, but she wouldn't listen. She never spoke to Luke's wife. She spoke at her, through somebody else. There was that. But there was his father whom he liked to sit without on the wall in front of the house on a summer's evening, sitting in silence. He would have liked to see more of his father, but he didn't like to go into the shop. The smell of porter nauseated him, and the sight of men becoming drunk and drooling was something he could never become accustomed to. Occasions he often felt like taking a whip like our Lord did to the money-changers in the temple. And then the thought of him striking around him, and what would happen, like one of the big men taking him up in one hand like you could take a dog by the loose skin of the neck and putting him out of the door, that thought made him laugh weakly.

So he liked here, with the great green lawns and the stone-built, nicely weathered buildings, the polished block floors and the stained-glass windows, shouts on the playing fields that always seemed distant, the peace and quiet of the night-time, when you could focus your eyes on the stars and the moon moving in state through the heavens, and you'd think of where you were standing, on a piece of ground that was part of a world that was not only spinning but revolving, and that if you could overcome gravity and fall off you would never end anywhere at all, that there was nothing under or over or around the earth to hold it in place except the will of God, and that all and every one of the stars were little worlds like this one, all revolving or spinning and nothing around them or above them or below them, and he looked at all this sky and he thought what fun and pleasure God had out of creating it all, and he would feel very peaceful and very content, and he wished this scholasticism could go on for ever and never end, that he could just be a struggling scholar for ever, and never have to go outside the walls, into the world. But he would have to if he was good enough. If he was good enough! Joseph had doubts about his goodness. He tried very hard, and he had the will, but his advance was very slow, oh, very slow. He was two years behind what he should be now, because he just couldn't seem to assimilate. There was nothing in the world he desired but the day to come when he would be able to say, and he freshly consecrated and finally fit, *hic est enim corpus meum*. He saw it all, himself vestmented at the altar bending over the Host, but lately he seemed to be looking at the vision through a telescope, the narrow end, and the figure of himself at the altar seemed to be so far away, miles and miles and miles and not coming any nearer, any nearer at all. And he closed his eyes tightly where he stood and said in himself: Please, if it is Your will. If it is Your will, please.

A hand hit him gently on the shoulder.

"Dreaming, Joseph?" the voice asked him.

He opened his eyes.

"Hello, Larry," he said. Of them all Larry was the only one who could knock anything out of him. He was tall and lithe and had fair hair and a sort of crooked twist to his lips that was most appealing, and very bright blue eyes, that were always watching, always dancing. Larry did everything well, threw himself into everything. He had a bright brain and his body was built for doing. It would never fatten, his body. It would never build a corporation because it would never have a chance. He was all that Joseph was not, and yet he liked Joseph. He felt a great friendliness for him. He saw his lonely life with sadness, because Larry couldn't imagine anyone like Joseph, so tied up with nervous embarrassments. If there was only anything he could do he would do it, but he knew there wasn't much anyone could do. Here each man had his own battle, guided by the generals who knew what they were doing. But he could alleviate it maybe with talk or gesture or by the liking in his heart.

He had a hurley on his shoulders.

"Have you the sermon ready, Joseph?" he asked.

Joseph stopped walking. His hands gave him away, and the nervous blinking of his eyes.

"Not today?" Joseph asked.

"I'm afraid so," said Larry. "You and me."

"Oh," said Joseph. He didn't complain. It was an ordeal in which he nearly always failed. He went through it while cold sweat covered his body. But he always approached it as an ordeal, as a penance. It was cruel to see him.

"Don't take it so hard, Joseph," said Larry. "Why do you take it so hard? Why can't you relax over it? The world is not going to come to an end because of it. You are not murdering anybody over it."

"Only the prose," said Joseph.

Larry was so surprised that he stared at him and then he let a hoot of laughter out of him.

"That's it, Joseph," he said. "That's the way to approach it."

Joseph was smiling. He had actually made Larry laugh. But inside he wasn't smiling at all.

"Anyhow," said Larry, "I have to go first and that'll make it easier for you."

"It will," said Joseph. "That will make it easier."

But it didn't.

The Professor was standing at the back looking out of the tall windows. When they were all seated, after a little clattering and talk and confusion, he caught Larry's eye and nodded, and Larry made his way to the rostrum. The Professor was a tall thin ascetic-looking man with a severe mouth, rimless glasses, and a

134

dark saturnine countenance. He was very brilliant, and so just a little inclined to be impatient of dull understanding. It was all so clear to him, he had to call on all his powers of humility to bear with students who were hard of understanding.

Larry cleared his throat and looked at faces watching him, covertly, gleefully, encouragingly, winkingly.

"Dearly beloved brethren," said Larry and then paused.

"Thou shalt not steal. Thou shalt not covet thy neighbour's goods."

At this point the door opened and one of the priests beckoned to the Professor. He nodded, looked at Larry, said "Pray continue," and went into the corridor. Larry thought that if they were all younger they would start a terrible hullabaloo as soon as the master showed them his back.

"Which is the greatest of the seven deadly sins?" Larry asked them in his deep pleasant voice. "Some theologians and Fathers of the Church will say pride. Others will say lust, others gluttony, others sloth. But out of the deep suffering of my own personal life, I tell you that the greatest sin of all is covetousness, allied to plain stealing. I will illustrate this by condemning to the depths of hell the ignoble person, the *persona ignota,* who removed a humble Gillette safety razor from its place in my cubicle and returned the same with the edge of the blade as blunt as if it had, in its brief absence, been used to mow the moss on the front lawn. This is not a laughing matter, my dearly unloved brethren. Can you appreciate the agony of your brother's face as he endeavoured to utilise this blunt thing on his gentle skin? Agony! You think it is nothing to steal an edge? That is what this sinner did to me, and his sin is all the greater because of all the things in the world he could steal this is one thing that he can never return. You can steal the edge off a blade but how can you ever return it to its owner? Impossible! I can only be ameliorated, and give this individual absolution, if before tomorrow morning he begs, borrows or steals a new blade to replace the one which he has so rudely ravaged.

"Whilst I am engaged on this commandment I would also refer to the nether regions the unmitigated and obviously

135

hopeless scoundrel who, without my permission, mark you, without a by your leave from any being, entered my press in the pavilion and took from there my freshly laundered togs, spotlessly white from the loving hands of the laundry, and with malice aforethought and a singular lack of humility, donned these togs, used them in the mud and the rain, and returned them, utterly deprived of their pristine beauty, a horrible mess of mud and dirt and terribly torn in two places. Can this person be forgiven by God or man? No. I can see only one end for this person, whose name I know. He can replace these togs, or be at the expense of their being freshly laundered and invisibly mended and returned. But his sin is great. He has taken away one day in the life of these togs. Can he return that day? No, that day is lost for ever. I will try to forgive him, if I receive suitable compensation, but I will also punish him. I will meet him in the gymnasium at the big break tomorrow evening, where we will don the gloves, and although he considers that he is the boxing pride and joy of the college and about twice my height and three times my weight (which is the reason for the rents in the togs) I will nevertheless forgive him by the letting of his blood."

They were laughing heartily when the door opened and the Professor came back. The laughter died away except for an odd chuckle. The Professor looked up at Larry. Larry's face was without guile. The corner of the Professor's mouth twirked into a smile.

"Humorous sermon?" he enquired.

"No, Father," Larry said. "I was illustrating my point with a little moral to get the congregation into good humour before I pulverise them."

"H'm," said the Professor. "Proceed with the pulverisation."

"Yes, Father," said Larry.

He preached his sermon seriously.

Joseph thought that Larry preached a very good sermon. It was like himself, simple and without guile. It wouldn't stir great congregations to cheering and admiration, but more important, it might make them uneasy and examine their consciences. The sermon fulfilled all that Larry had been taught, and all that he felt himself. It was successful.

136

The Professor, looking out on the great lawns, the grass scared a little from the yellow autumnal touch, the black-and-white well-fed cattle nuzzling the grass, the great beeches being stripped almost obscenely of their clothes, all these things before him but not seeing them, hoped that Larry would go on and on talking and postpone as far as possible the ordeal that Joseph was about to undergo. The Professor didn't exactly dislike Joseph. He felt uncomfortable about him and his lapses of memory. By rights long ago he should have gone to the President and reported that Joseph Baun would never pass the examinations. But he hadn't, on account of the uneasy feeling he had about the boy. He had devoted extra time to his tuition, after hours, and after classes, and some days he would think that at last he was getting some place, and then the blank would descend on him. Sometimes the Professor wondered if the boy was half-witted. He chided himself with impatience when he thought that way. He would look into his eyes that seemed to be set so far back in his head and to be just wells of dreaming, mystical eyes. He was aware that the other students referred to Joseph as The Mystic, but there was a touch of malice in their nickname. The Professor in his student days, in his reading, in his philosophy and theology, was always more at home with the men of mind than with the mystics. The practical and cogent arguments of real reason leading to the Godhead, by the, to him, simple paths of step-by-step philosophy, the reason of St. Augustine and St. Thomas and the modern theological thinkers. Those men. He felt as if they were in his study sitting beside him in a leather upholstered armchair, sharing a pipe of tobacco.

He sighed.

Larry was finished.

The Professor paused, caught Joseph's eye, nodded, and Joseph raised himself from the seat and made his way to the rostrum. Larry sat into his seat and dropped his eyes. A tension seemed to pass into everybody in the room, hold their breaths. Will it be the same? Hoping it wouldn't, Larry praying it wouldn't, that Joseph would be helped from some source.

The path to the rostrum seemed to Joseph to be five miles long. He had been sitting in his seat, going over his points. In the night-time they were clear and simple and lucid, they flowed from his mind as clear and inevitable as the water flowing over the rocks of the river at home, the river coming from Boola Lake. But it was always that way, and then as soon as he rose from his seat, his legs started to tremble as if they would never support him, his mouth became as dry as the sand on the shore above high-water mark, and in his head, in place of lucidity and order, words and sentences chased one another panic-stricken. He could stop and turn and say: I can't go on, and the Professor would say: All right, another day. He would say it kindly. There would be no reproach. Everybody, Joseph knew, would be immensely relieved. But then there would be no suffering for him. And Joseph knew that he would have to suffer if he was ever to attain the wish of his heart. No man who had been granted his desires had ever received them without suffering. Only the good was granted through suffering. You could have the bad with no effort at all.

He faced them on the rostrum. He was very pale. They saw that. The students at the front could see the tiny beads of sweat on his upper lip. His face was very thin, his eyes were very big, and the panic in them now seemed to have made them an enormous size.

"Dlylodren" was what his salutation came out like. Then all shrunk into their clothes. Some of the more sensitive held tightly to the wood of their seats. Larry gripped his hair, felt the sweat pouring down his chest. One or two of them nudged and grinned. They weren't very sensitive. They enjoyed his discomfiture.

"Thou shalt love the Lord thy God with thy whole heart and thy whole soul."

That quotation came from him clear and solid. They thought that he had hold of himself and that it would be fine now. But it wasn't. Joseph saw all the words neatly written in his angular handwriting, clear as headlines on a children's copybook, saw it all, but it wouldn't come from his mouth. The Professor saw it written. The sentences were simple, the feelings utterly sincere, the expressions gauche, but it was good. It was better expressed than a lot of sermons he had listened to. But what good was that?

He was incoherent. His words refused to come. Some of them stuck in his throat, others pushed past the ones that were stuck and came forth like small explosions. He stuttered and stammered, but he didn't go back. He kept ploughing ahead, turning the pages of the clear script in his mind. It went on for ten minutes. It seemed to his listeners like half an hour. To Joseph it seemed like five years out of his life and ten from the strength of his body.

Then he was finished. An audible sigh was in the room as their minds and bodies relaxed. Thank God, it was over. Joseph was in his seat. He was rubbing his palms in his handkerchief. The Professor, who had turned, saw the pale white hands twisting, turning. With his eyes and his heart he felt a terrible pity for the sight of him, but his mind rejected and disliked the picture that he made.

He walked up to the top of the room.

"We will have criticism," he said. The students rustled.

Fourteen

JOHN WILLIE GOT the note late on the Friday evening.
It came with Bidelia of course.

She always did her shopping on the Friday evening. She was a dooderer. She started off in the morning deciding that she would go to the shop early today as sure as heaven, dear, and it always ended up by her getting into the shop before closing time. Then she had all sorts of little notes in all sorts of pockets, and she would search around when he had it all totted up and say Oh, dear, didn't I forget all about the chicken mash, or about the strawberry jam or the tin of treacle, and John Willie had to exercise extreme patience with her. Then she always had a tot of sherry, and all the hiding and shuffling she went on with to pretend she wasn't having a glass of sherry, or so that she wouldn't be seen having it, would drive a saint to distraction, and John Willie admitted he was no saint. He had a way of getting rid of his fevers by going out to the store at the back for the mash or the bran or the rice or the oatmeal, and standing there and cursing fluently for a few minutes, and then he felt better and was quiet, cheerful, and patient when he returned.

She was out of the door and half-way home when she remembered the note. She came back. "I forgot, dear. I don't know what's wrong with me. Breeda asked me to give you this."

John Willie read it.

"My dear John Willie," it said.

"Could you make your way down to the sea after you close? I heard from him! I'll wait for you.

Breeda."

Him could only mean one person. Crisscross, John Willie thought. After all this time. How long was it? It was over a year. A year. He could have been dead for all they knew. Did anybody care?

It didn't take him long to close. Bidelia was the last customer. He blew out the lamps and locked the doors and scooped the money into a paper bag and went through into the kitchen and locked it in the sideboard in the parlour. Then he whistled the dog up and walked towards the sea. The longest day wasn't very far gone, so it was quite bright. It was a very clear evening, as calm as the heart of an old nun. The dust was deep on the road. The dog raised little puffs of it with his pads. The sun was just gone. The world was encircled in pink and above the pink the sky was the colour of a pippin apple, and that was giving way to a dark blue that was almost purple.

John Willie breathed the air into his lungs. It was fresh from the sea, the air.

Once he crossed the main road he saw her standing on the cliff this side of the beach, a tall thin girl with the horizon behind her. Her face was turned to the road. He was a long way away when he saw her waving her hand. He called to her. It always surprised him how acute her hearing had become and how she could distinguish between the steps of different people. That was the law of compensation, he supposed.

He crossed the wall and went over to her.

"You came, John Willie," she said. She was very pleased.

"Well, I'm not at home," he said.

"I thought you'd never come," she said. "Maybe I'm wrong. I got the letter this morning. Bidelia was going to open it and read it, but I knew somehow. I wouldn't let her. I'm sure it's from him. Here. Look."

He took the letter.

It was bulky. The address was scrawled impatiently all over the envelope. There was hardly room for the stamp. It was an Irish stamp. So. "It's him, all right," he said. "Nobody could stretch a name like he could." The envelope wasn't very clean. It looked as if it had been carried in somebody's pocket for a long time, and then taken out and shoved into a letter-box.

141

"Sit down," she said. "I come here often. It took me a long time before I could walk near the edge. But now I do. I know exactly." She was sitting swinging her legs over the drop.

"The Lord save 's, be careful," John Willie said. He approached carefully himself and sat down.

"It's a nice evening, John Willie, isn't it? It's a real summer's evening, isn't it?"

"Fine, fine," John Willie said.

"I knew he'd write to me," she said. "I knew he'd have to write to me. I'm in his blood, John Willie, even if I'm only on his conscience. I don't care. I knew well he couldn't forget me."

"We'll see," John Willie said. "Will I open the letter?"

"Do," she said. "Where is it from?"

"I can't make out," he said, peering at the blurred marking. "But it's somewhere in the country."

"Go on," she said.

He shoved his thumb under the flap and tore it across. He levered out the pages. They were long thin ones as if they were torn from the duplicate page of an invoice book. Both sides written on. There were quite a few pages. "No fixed abode," said John Willie. "That's the address he has on it. No fixed abode."

"Oh," she said. "Well, go on." She was sitting on her hands. He glanced at her. There was a very eager look on her face. He shook his head slightly before he went back to the letter. It was darker now. He had to hold it up and read it off sideways against the light in the western sky where the departed sun was leaving an area of brightness.

" 'My dear Breeda,

" 'Before I move on, I write to you. You know why? Because you are not able to read. That's good. You hold this in your hand and you look at it and you know it's from me. How do you know? I don't know. But you know. What are you going to do with it? You can't ask your aunt to read it. She might be shocked. So what do you do? Stop a passer-by and ask him to read? No. You put it under your pillow and try and dream the lines out of it. Only one solution. You never read it at all or you go looking for John Willie. Am I right? I bet I'm right. Hello, John Willie!'

"Ho! the bastard," said John Willie. "I'm sorry, Breeda."

Breeda laughed. Put her hands up to her mouth as if she was lacking teeth and laughed through her hands. "It's all right," she said.

John Willie coughed. He went on reading.

"I nearly achieved respectability. Said, I'm a bad sinner and until I become respectable I am useless and hurt all around me. Become respectable and stop hurting. Came to this town how long ago? It seems like years. Not that long, six months say. I have letters and introductions. To this fellow. An honest man. This is funny. He sells things, another shop, but not like John Willie's. Kiddies' clothes and ladies' doodahs. Oh, a laugh. There is a long mirror. Sometimes I see me in the mirror. Oh, very respectable. I have a grey suit and the pants is lovely creased and a red pullover and white shirt with a hard collar, and a grey and silver tie.

" 'I am living with the man. He is tall and straight and he has thin lips and his head is growing out through his hair. A tall brick place. Shop below. Living quarters above. He has a wife and three children. The place. You should see it. The parlour is all full of stuffed sofas and stuffed cushions and stuffed birds. An owl, moulting under a glass cover. A piano, with the keys yellowed. I live in the very top. Used to be an attic, or a place where the tweeny had to hide herself at night. Sometimes I look up at the skylight and I think I can hear the tweeny's ghost sniffling. I bet she had a tough time here long ago. See, I'm apprenticed! That's a laugh. Get two pounds a week and keep. This in the big city. But I have firmly determined that I will crawl to the lowest depths of respectability to acquire it. This torture I think I owe to you and John Willie and maybe to Suck Brendan. Not that I've forgiven that son of a bitch. Just wait. If I fail to become respectable, I'm going to find out a way I can crease that fellow. I'll find a way. He hurt me. It took three months for him to stop hurting me. But time will go around.

" 'Doing fine, until I suddenly take a dislike to the boss. Not a boss like John Willie. Should see the eating. Subdued family.

143

Wife is thin and grey hair before it should be. She used to be an apprentice too, until he fiddled her in a corner. I'd swear it. Three children. Eldest nine. All wear thick glasses. One boy, the youngest. Afraid of their lives of Mr. M. No word spoken at meals. Stand. Say grace. Then eat and stand and say grace. A saintly man. Except that his wife is frightened to death of him and his shadow is enough to silence the children. He carries a banner in the church when they have processions.

" 'This Friday morning. Before I get up I hear commotion down below. I get up, look over the banisters. It is payday. That's all I know. The wife is saying now, no, please no, he did-n't mean it. He can't help it, he is so young. She is following Mr. M. down the stairs. He is going into the parlour. He is very determined. She is sort of holding her hands out beseechingly. He is shaking his head. He goes in, he comes out, he has a stick in his hand. His lips are tight. He is going into the room where the boy sleeps. I can see the boy in his bed through the open door. He is crouching back in the bed. He is pale with fear. The man reaches for him and pulls him across the bed. The wife holds his arm. He fires her away. She falls to her knees. She stays there. She covers her face with her hands. She is moaning. He pulls up the little boy's nightshirt. His little bottom is bare. It is not a plump bottom like the babies we know. Mr. M. wallops it until it is blue with the stick. Until there is a drool from the side of his mouth. You know a sinister thing. The little boy does not cry. There is no word or cry from him. Mr. M. is exhaust-ed. I am exhausted. I am holding the banisters with my hands. I wonder if I have crushed the wood to pulp. But I have won my battle. If that was me the sinner, I would be down there, beating Mr. M. into a bloody pulp. But I don't, see, so I am winning the fight for respectability and I go back and dress and I whistle while I shave.

" 'I am good all that day. I look at Mr. M. dealing with his customers. He is a nice man. A pretty girl comes collecting for charity. She is rattling money in a box. Mr. M. puts twenty shillings into the box and pinches the girls cheek. He is a good man. I am paid. My two pounds. With this two pounds I have nearly forty, all in my pocket. This I do so that I show myself how I can carry temptation around with me.

" 'I always eat out on pay night. I go out now when the shop is shut. A city on Saturday night. Not so busy. Buses and neon lights and couples. Long queues outside picture houses. Here I go. I join. It is not a good picture.

What is a good picture? I get out of there. Over opposite there is a place with a light outside it. I go in here and I call for a drink and I get the drink and I go over to a table and I sit down. The table has a marble top. It is cold on the wrist. I notice that I am being watched. A man at another table. He looks sort of familiar. But there are thousands like him, a black bowler hat and a soiled-looking raincoat, and a high starched collar and a gold tiepin. He has a moustache that is grey and sort of scorched looking in the middle. He rises, and comes over carrying his glass. I will sit with you, he says. It is a free country, I say. You are mistaken, he says. It is not a free country. It's god-ridden. All right, I say. I recognise him. In the street of Mr. M.'s shop, over on the opposite side there is a small lock-up place, that sells fruit and vegetables, soiled looking. This is the man. He talks and we drink.

" 'It goes on. Has this man discovered the secret of living? That God is a myth? Maybe he has. We are put out of that place. The streets are crowded. I feel fine. It is not all we have drunk. This man has the germ of a great idea. I join the long scrabbling place for the bus. We are passing down by the river. The tide is out. There is a terrible smell from the river. There is a fug on the windows of the bus. I rub it with my elbow. The bus is stopped at a cross place. I see a woman on the pavement. She is under the light of the street lamp. She has no hat. She is sort of fat. Her coat is held together with a safety pin. She is carrying a basket in her hand. Her face is held up, and tears are pouring out of her eyes. She is crying, crying away. She is not drunk. I can see that. She is just standing under the street lamp in a big city waiting for a bus to pass so that she can cross the road, and she is crying her eyes out. Why? The bus jerks away. I want to get out and ask her why she is crying. Is somebody dead or dying or has she received a message saying that some-body belonging to her is killed?

Or is she crying because she has suddenly discovered that there is no god?

" 'I have to knock to get in. That is the rule. He opens the door. He has no collar or tie. He has a long stringy neck. You're late, he says, and as I pass, he says, You're drunk. I tell him to mind his own bloody business. That shakes him. I am going up the stairs. He closes the door. He says: You'll go out of this house now and stay out. I come down to him. I shove my face into his. He pulls back. He is frightened. Gleefully I see that he is fright-ened. How easy it is to frighten him! I take his shirt in my hand and shake him a little. Leave me alone, he says. So feeble. You are a hypocrite, I say. Of all the things in the world I hate it is a hypocrite. You are a sadist. I saw you beating that child. I am going to beat you now. With my fists. I'm going to dig my knuckles into your face, and I'm going to kick you in the belly so that you will be rolling around the floor in agony. Leave me alone, he says. Leave me alone. You'll rot in your own hell, I say, rot in your own hell. I hear the woman's voice behind me. Please, please, she is saying. I really mean to beat him. I just fire him and he goes back down a step or two and collapses in the hall. He is looking up at me. I can see the whites of his eyes. I go upstairs. I pass her. For you, I say, but you should have let me hit him a little. I go to my room. I put in the things I have. Not many things but enough. They are not there when I go down. They are upstairs, waiting fearfully for the door to close. So I open it and I close it. But I don't go out. I go back the back way and I get into the shop. Where he keeps his things. Where he has the takings. I force the place silently. There is a lot of money there. I hear my friend's voice telling me. I say to myself, I am god, this is dross. I am god, so I will punish this fellow in the only way he can be punished. I will deprive him of money. But the lesson is not well learned. I close the place. I am not yet qual-ified. I'm only an initiate. I go away.

" 'The streets are deserted, and I go down and down to the place where they are unloading the ships under the are lights.

146

That's the place. Well, I tried. I tried to be respectable. Didn't I? I'm not respectable. It's too boring. Where does it get you? What will you do afterwards? I will go down to the sea in ships. Open up the world with a new philosophy. Or will I? I don't know. I'm sorry for you in your little hole in the hills.'

"That's all," said John Willie. "He didn't even sign his name."
"Poor Bart!" said Breeda. "Poor Bart!"

Fifteen

"ALL RIGHT, JOHN Willie," Luke said, "you can go in to your supper."

John Willie was glad to see him. He was hungry. He had had a hard day. It was always the same on Christmas Eve. Nobody seemed to get what they wanted until the last minute. And it was a lovely frosty evening and the moon was on the wane. He thought, I will try and trick him into it later, when I get a look at the weather. It was mainly drink now, all the grocery business was finished with. Luke was slow in the shop. It took him a long time to count up change. Some of the customers would jeer at him for it. But Luke was very stolid and painstaking and jeers went away from him like water.

"Good man, Luke," he said. "I'm glad to see you. It will make a good frosty evening, will it?"

"It will," said Luke, "powerful."

"Could you wait a biteen after," John Willie asked, "if I was to run up for a shot?"

Luke smiled.

"I will wait," he said.

"Ah, good man," John Willie said and went, rubbing his hands. His place was set at the table. Martha was over at the other table. She was stuffing a goose. Outside the light was not gone. In fact the descending sun was shining into the kitchen through the window. It was getting big now though. He had the time gauged nicely as he looked out at it.

"The fry is on the hob," Martha said.

"Thanks," he said, and went to it. The plate was resting in the pan covered by a tin lid. It steamed when he took off the lid. Chopped onions fried in butter with two eggs. Pity it's a fast day, he thought, a rasher would go nice with that. He put the plate on the table and brought the teapot with him. The cake was cut. He buttered it thickly. "You make bloody nice cakes, Martha," he said.

She stopped her stuffing to look over at him. "I'm glad you like it," she said. He looked at her. Very thin tall figure, chest flattened. There were lines, deeply embedded, by the side of her mouth. The poor bitch, John Willie thought kindly. No life. No life worth much. She was a very silent girl. She would speak when she was spoken to, but that was all. Her eyes never lit up with emotion, her lips never poured out talk that might come from her heart. She hadn't much of a life. Unless up in the big top room with Luke. That was the life. What did they talk about? Did they talk about the fact that there was no sign of a child? If they didn't, then he hoped they hadn't heard the heartless talk of people, a smile caught here, a word there, or a slow wink.

"I like Christmas," he said through his food. "No work and roast goose. I like roast goose. I'm going up after the wild ones tonight. If I can get one or two we'll have them roast for New Year's Day."

"You don't have to pluck them or clean them or stuff them," Martha said. She had a threaded needle in her mouth. She was holding the gaping skin of the goose, ready to stitch it.

"Oh," said John Willie. "Don't you like that? I thought women didn't mind that."

"I don't like that," Martha said. "I hate puttin' my hand into their puddens."

"I didn't know that," he said. "Next time I'll do it for you."

"No, no," she said. "It's all right. I'm just complaining."

"You don't complain enough," John Willie said. She looked over and then stuck the needle in the goose, left it there and came over to the table. She sat on a chair opposite him, resting her bared arms on the wood and looking out at the dying sun.

"Why do you say that?" she asked.

What's come over me tonight? John Willie wondered. Maybe it's Christmas.

"I don't know, Martha," he said. "You work hard. You have a hard time. Was it worth it?"

"Yes," she said after thinking. "Not now maybe, but it will be worth it. It can't always be like this."

He thought: She has quite good bones in her face when she relaxes that mouth. And there were nice glints in her hair. She probably thinks too much. "Maybe you think too much," he said out loud. "Maybe you think more than you ought to. Maybe you shouldn't take things too seriously. Maybe you ought to take more time off and go out for a walk."

"That's easy," she said. "Who does things then? Does Luke throw the plough on one side too and come walking with me? What will people think if they see a man in the middle of the day going for a walk with his wife?"

John Willie thought about that. Then he laughed.

"Man, murder!" he ejaculated.

"I'm willing to wait now," she said, "as long as there will be a better future for Luke. John Willie," she said loudly so that he had to look up and meet her eyes. "There will be a future for Luke, won't there?"

John Willie felt faintly sick. She could have turned her thought from the future and material things. If she had the courage to accept her lot instead of fighting it, if she had the courage to be happy in herself despite all the things that were wrong, like Breeda, she could be happy and in the end she could have weaned Mabbina. Mabbina wasn't that hard, as John Willie knew. Mabbina could be won over. But Martha was engaged on a struggle for existence, an unnecessary one. Would Luke be all right? Would he come out number one or number two or number three in the splurge for material things?

"I have no intention of dying yet, Martha," John Willie said. There was no bite at all in his words, just a statement made in a kindly way. "But when I do, Luke will come out all right."

He commenced eating.

He heard her sigh, and she rose from the table and went back to the goose. It was always the same way, if he tried to get her out of herself, to start talk about anything at all. The future, the future, the future. To hell with the future, John Willie thought. Damn and blast the future. What she wants is a bit of religion, not the religion you pick up by carrying out the bare necessities of the laws, but something more fundamental, that when you got hold of the tail of it, left you feeling that the future could look after itself if you looked after today.

He finished his meal. He hadn't removed his cap. He reached for the gun over the fireplace, broke it, looked through the barrel. Then he went to the dresser and opened the bottom press and took a handful of BB cartridges out of it, and shoved them into the pocket of the heavy jacket hanging behind the kitchen door. He stripped off his other jacket and put this on. It was full of pockets. If he distributed meal in all of them he had room for a few stone of it. He smiled at this thought as he exchanged his light boots for the rubber ones. Then he slung the gun under his arm and went out the door. Once outside the door he curled his bottom lip under his top one and let a piercing whistle through his teeth. The dog came running. He paused and then when he saw the gun he nearly went mad. He ran around in circles whining and then came and put his paws on John Willie's chest and jumped up to lick his face, then he ran around in a few more circles and came back again. John Willie patted him, saying, "All right, all right, we're going all right," and then set off past the shop up the road towards the big flat above Boola lake.

He stopped when he heard somebody calling him. He looked back. It was Joseph. He had come from the bridge direction. He was waving his hand. John Willie wondered what was wrong. He waited. The skies seemed to be slowly burning all around, as if somebody had set a match to them. Joseph paused and slowed as he came nearer. He had his hand to his chest where his breath was caught. It always worried John Willie to see him doing that. But then they had doctors at those colleges and things and if there was anything wrong they would look after him.

151

"What's up?" John Willie asked.

"Oh, nothing, father," Joseph said. "I just thought I'd like to walk up a bit with you."

John Willie warmed. "That's nice, Joseph," he said, and slowed his pace. "That's nice."

Joseph was a little embarrassed. It was just a feeling he had, when he saw the figure of his father bending forward walking up the hill. A sinking feeling he got in his stomach and the automatic call. Very strange. John Willie thought that Joseph looked well now. The blood had flushed his face. He didn't look as pale as he usually did.

"Do you like shooting things?" Joseph asked.

John Willie cocked an eye at him.

"Are you going to give me a lecture?" he asked.

Joseph laughed. He put his hand on his father's arm.

"No, honest," he said. "It was just a question. I can't bear to see things killed myself. I just wanted to know."

"I don't like killing things," said John Willie. "It's a nice thing to see a bird in flight. Then you get a fever, see. Even when you are walking with no gun on a road. You see a bird. You estimate his speed and his direction and in your mind you are always leading him with the gun. Like that. It's a sort of instinct. You don't care about killing sort of. Just to see can you bring him down. That's the excitement. After that, not so good. Don't like to see a fleet bird turning over and over like an ugly bundle, and bouncing on the ground. A grouse coming down wind that is hit. That's bad. A bird like that hits the ground hard. Once that happened. He bounced six feet. All the puddings were knocked out of him. He was empty inside. That wasn't good."

"I'm glad I didn't see that," said Joseph.

"A wild duck, now, a fine sight flying. No matter how often you wait for the wild duck flighting, or how many you kill or how many you miss, you always get a terrible exciting thumping of the heart when you hear them coming. The low sibilant whistling of the wings. That's what excites you, and then they are over and you aim and they fall. After that you see a drake with

152

his colouring lying on ice, or a green field or brown soil. Vivid sort of, and you feel sad. Until you are eating him. You have forgotten your excitement. You have forgotten your sadness."

"I see," Joseph said.

"Ah, but the wild geese," said John Willie. "Ah, man, them are the thing. You have forty great geese flying low over your head calling and cackling and you are experiencing the most beautiful thing in the world. You follow me?"

"I think I do, father," said Joseph. "It isn't the killing. It's the seeing and the getting. I would like to see, but I'd never want to get them. Just to see them. Is it geese you are after tonight?"

"That's right," said John Willie.

"I'd like to go," said Joseph wistfully.

"I wish you would come," said John Willie.

Joseph looked at the great stretch of soft ground leading into the flat on the left where the lake was. "Ah, no," he said. "I'd never make it. I'd frighten the geese on you I would be so slow, and then you would be cursing me."

"I'd never do that, Joseph," John Willie said.

"I know, father," said Joseph, "only, ah, I wouldn't be able to manage it. Some other evening maybe you'd bring me, and we'd start early."

"That's a promise," said John Willie delightedly, "and we'll forget to bring cartridges for the gun. How's that, hah?"

They both laughed.

"Ah, that'd be just right," said Joseph.

"I'll turn off here," John Willie said.

"Don't go a minute," said Joseph impulsively. "Sit for a minute on the stones."

"All right," said John Willie very gratified. He could afford five minutes anyhow, his hunter's eyes told him, looking at the sky. His father's eye told him he didn't give a damn even if he missed the flight of the geese. They sat on the big rocks bordering the rough road. John Willie lit a cigarette. "I will have it now," he said, "because I won't be able to inside. Them geese are the cutest divils. They'd see a wink of a fag ten miles away." Joseph was looking down below at the village. "You're happy,

153

Joseph, there's nothing worrying you, is there?" He was trying to account for the behaviour of his son.

"Thanks, father," said Joseph, "I'm happy. At least I'm as happy as I will ever be trying to be happy."

"Crisscross," said John Willie, "that's involved. No trouble at College? Nothing?"

Joseph frowned a little.

"No," he said then. "Nothing that I can't overcome with the help of God."

"That's fine," said John Willie. He thought, After all it's a good thing to sit down by the side of the road and have a real son sitting beside you. Not that John Willie was in awe of his son, but there was something not quite ordinary about him, that was all. John Willie might have understood a son, if he had had one like Bart, better than he would ever understand Joseph, but all the same, he thought, he wouldn't give Joseph for all the ordinary sons in the world. Even if they didn't talk much or exchange confidences, there was a sort of tenuous line between them, a call of blood that made Joseph a bit of him. Joseph thought how lucky he was in his father. Because he was an honest man, and because he had a heart and was kind to everybody who demanded kindness. He was a good man.

The dog had run into the flat land and had poked about sniffing for birds. Now he was back again. He was nuzzling John Willie. He was whining. He was practically beseeching him to come on for goodness' sake or the evening would be gone.

"Look at him!" said John Willie, laughing. "He's mad to be gone."

"You better go, father," said Joseph, standing up, "or he'll never forgive you."

"Better be off all right," said John Willie. "Have to be there before they get in." He stood there. "We'll have a good day tomorrow, Joseph," he said. "I like Christmas."

"Me too," said Joseph.

"You'll be eating a killed bird all the same," said John Willie laughing.

"I'll forget that when I'm eating him," said Joseph.

"Well. . ." said John Willie.

"You better go," said Joseph.

Strange, this reluctance to part from him, John Willie thought. That's Christmas. He waved his hand then and turned his face towards the flat.

Joseph stood there a long time looking after him. Why be depressed? There was no need to be depressed. But he stayed there until the figure of John Willie was lost in a fold of the bog, and then he went slowly down the hill homewards, his hands in the pockets of his black suit, kicking the loose stones ahead of him.

There was a layer of frost over the bog. John Willie liked the feel of crunchy frozen bog under his boots. You had to walk to keep warm. He was cold from the short sitting on the stones. He thought about Joseph. He wondered what it would be like to have a son a priest. He turned then to look back. He was on the last hillock before the bog fell towards the chasmed river. He could see the figure of Joseph going back down the road. He turned to walk and stumbled. The bog was soft there. His right boot went into the mud. He saved himself from going further in by stretching his left hand and using the barrel of the gun as a support. When he straightened himself he knew that there was something he must do, and then he forgot as he saw Joseph coming into the valley in the gleaming glare of hundreds of bonfires. That would be a proud night. It would be a great night. He thought back to the stranger moved with emotion who had watched the coming of the last young priest into the valley. He thought how nice it would be to have Joseph coming with him an odd night after the wild fowl. They could talk of many things then. There were such a lot of things he could teach and show him. All the bog plants that were used long ago for healing and purging and dyeing, and all that, when people were very poor and had to make do with what God had provided for them without getting it all out of bottles that were churned out in gigantic medicine factories, working night and day spitting dirty fumes into the sky. And he could maybe get inside the mind of his son and get to really know him. Not that that mattered so

155

much. He knew enough of him to know that he would be all right, whatever happened. John Willie sensed that Joseph might be closer to a better parent than himself.

He preferred to be out alone. He liked to be alone after the almost permanent company of the shop. There where you were in the middle of other people's loneliness and sorrow and complaint, where it was all too easy to see men's failings as their hidden nature peered out, often leering, over their loosened thoughts. It wasn't nice in a way. Maybe when Joseph was a priest, he would give up the business altogether, buy more land and just let Luke and himself farm it. Maybe keep on the part of the shop that had only the food of the people and let off the drinking part to somebody else.

He was at the lake before he knew it, but his thoughts were still busy. That was unusual for him. He was always conscious of where he was and the things he had to do to be successful. Now he only went through the motions mechanically.

Where the bank fell steeply to the lake, there was a sort of hide made. He crouched in here. The lapping water was at his feet, and his sides and head were covered in by the heavy heather and the faded coarse grass. It was a favourite bay for the geese, this place which his gun commanded. He could see ice forming on the water in front of him, and also the long lines of geese-pickings that had been washed ashore by a former wind. The pickings were fresh, so there was a good chance they would come tonight. He slipped a cartridge into the gun, so that he would be ready for them, and then let his thoughts trail off into other channels.

He wondered where Bart was and what he was doing now.

He felt sad about Bart, very sad, because there was good in him, if it could only be brought out to supersede the bad. But sure only himself could do that, there was nobody else at all who could help him. Breeda would have helped him if he had sense and seen, but that was complicated too.

It was very cold. He had the collar of his coat pulled up around his neck. The cold seemed to be seeping into his bones. It was always like that anyhow. You had to get used to that. He smiled as he thought about the advice an old hunter from the other side had given him. It was a recipe. You take a small bottle of good poitin when you are going, and when you reach the lake you pour a little of it down one boot and a little of it down the other boot, and what's over you pour down your neck. So your extremities are heated and your belly is heated and since your belly is the fount of your body, you will be warm and glowing and toasted. Man!

Then he stiffened as the honking of the geese was heard in the sky. He knew how deceptive the honking could be. You would think they were right beside you and if you looked they might be two miles in the sky in a great V flying away. That was very true of calm nights like this when sound travelled far. But now what? He listened. They could be by-passing the lake and going farther back the way. If you looked from a height on to all this land you could count hundreds and hundreds of small, lonely, almost inaccessible lakes they had to choose from. There was no guarantee that they would choose this. But they did. He knew it when he heard them circling.

A cackle and then silence for a few seconds. And then a cackle again, and more silence. They were circling. Shrewd and wild eyes were looking below at every fold of ground, at every hump and shape. They would see any moving thing at all. If it was wild they would ignore it, but just in case. But the dog was an old campaigner. If and when the geese died he would swim away for them and return with them.

Now! The great swishing. A terrible thing to hear. Great wings beating the air to death over your head, right over your head. That's where you might lose your head, getting so excited that you moved your body or a hand or the gun. They were right over him going into whatever breath of wind there was to case their landing.

They came low and he was looking at their tails and their great wings backbeating as they landed out from him with very little splashing. Then they were settled in a confused mass, and he rose to his right knee and levelled the gun on his shoulder, released the safety catch and pulled the trigger, and just as he pulled the trigger he remembered what he should have done.

When he had stumbled in the bog he had helped himself with the barrel of the gun. That meant the barrel of the gun was stuffed and it was too late. All he could think was, I have been shooting for nearly forty years and I never did anything wrong. This was wrong.

The gun exploded.

The geese cackled madly and honked and threshed the water and spread their wings and beat and beat with them until their terrified bodies were airborne and they swung backwards and forwards and across and into the wind. It took them nearly five minutes to circle and rise higher and higher and go back into the bleaker lands, or over towards the other great lake where they would be as lost as a pebble on a sea beach. And then they were gone and there was nothing to disturb the night.

John Willie's dog was barking, barking.

John Willie's head was resting almost in the water. His cap was off. His skin was white where the cap had covered it. His hair was grey. Only the side of his face was in the water, but it was staining it. I have so much to do, John Willie thought. I have so many people to look after. He felt no pain. He just said, bubbling the coloured water with his lips, "Oh, my God," and then there was no sound on the night except the frantic barking of John Willie's dog.

Sixteen

THIS WILL MAKE you laugh, John Willie. Don't know about Breeda. Long time now is it since last? Don't know. Time doesn't matter most times. It's just a sort of divided thing, of night and day and weeks and months and years, and that's nothing when you add it up. No beginning and no end. In the beginning no sense and in the end none either.

"What happens? I end up a soldier. That's a laugh. Despise soldiers. All the Irish did ever. The tailor and the soldier. They said that tailors and soldiers are picked up on the wrack of the sea-shore. Not these soldiers. Red coat. Imagine! And black pants and white yokes and high polish and great smothering hat. That was the kind of a soldier. Discipline. That's it. That's what you want, O'Breen. Put in three months of it. Fine, a new man. Until one day in the autumn.

"Here I am outside a big gate. Beautiful precision metal work. But familiar now. Sick looking at. Standing there to full regulation height. Just made it for height. But there are thick soles and heels on the black boots as well to make height look bigger, that's how they do it. It is evening. Up and down the great walks black cars are gliding. Girls in grey dresses and veils on them like nuns wheeling great luxurious prams.

"But this is different. Two fellows. Peering. Coming up to look as if I had a smut on my face. I look then. Two Irish kissers if ever I saw. Where, where, where, as I do the regulation clump and clamp, and I pull one of the faces out of the past. In college. A wild boyo. I don't think he ever made it either. I think his father got a note from my mother. That's it. Red curly hair, and pale freckled face. Frail-looking body but as tough as a tinker.

"He is talking now. Then he slaps his hand on his knee. And he throws back his head and he laughs. Oh, ho-ho, well, will you look who it is for the love of God almighty? Bart O'Breen. Oh, man, who ever lived to see the day? He comes close beside me. He walks. I am looking over his head. Bart, you bastard, he says, don't you recognise your own friends? I say out of the side of my mouth what I want him to do. Now I know it is you, he says, but at first I wasn't certain. Here he says, Meet my friend, Paddy, the bould Paddy. Here, shake hands with the man, will you? What kind of a mutual friend are you at all? They are both half drunk. I see this. I tell them to go away, for the love of God. I know the fellows with the red bull-binders on their caps are behind, watching. Go away, go away. See you at six. Hang around at six. They catch on. So I walk and I turn and I walk and I turn. They stand away a bit looking on. They have hands on one another's shoulders, supporting their laughter. My neck is red. How would you feel, John Willie?

"When I am off they are waiting for me. Oh, Rory, I remember you well, why wouldn't I, and what are you doing? Farming he is, this down south. He is prosperous. He can't believe his eyes. Is this where I have ended up? I resign at that minute. I think of how terrible it is to be a soldier.

"Let them fight their own bloody wars. What was I doing there anyhow? Right, man. No sense to it. I'm late anyhow. Because I am in Rory's hotel and it would be too late, too late now to go back. Over the wall. Notice up. Don't care. Lend me an oul suit, man. Not so old the suit. Tight under the arms, and mustn't bend, and over that a light raincoat. Fine. Down we go into the midnight. Roaming the streets. Laughing. Do you remember. All that shine. We come to a big bridge spanning the river. A nice bridge. Well built and broad and over that goes the lovely uniform, a brick tied up in the middle of it. It makes not much of a splash and then it sinks and we see the policeman making our way, so we are off again and quiet.

"I am with him three days and then he is gone and I am alone.

He is generous. As much as he has left he gives me. It's only fools have a sense of shame about taking money from friends. I decide that. Now I am a pebble on a beach. I am waiting for the tide to roll me where it will. Loneliness is a thing that is inherently part of a man. You are one place and you want to be some other place. That's why you drink in warm company. New things to take. So that you can destroy the sense of loneliness that is nothing really. You are lonely in a city like this when you think. But then all other millions are lonely too. Don't know what for. Is it a home? You go home, you are fed up. You want something badly and you get it and it doesn't please you.

"This fellow in the park is talking. He is a big fellow with horn-rimmed glasses. He is standing on a box. There are about twenty of us around him. It is nice in the park. The sun is shining. People have come out into the sun like rabbits out of burrows. Behind outside there is a ceaseless roar of traffic, traffic. Maybe like the sea at home beating on that famous cliff in a south-west wind. But different. Just roaring. No fumes there. No people. But much more bloody lonely. Much more bloody lonely.

" 'Scientists tell us,' this chap says, 'that there is no such thing as a soul. They say that the thoughts of our mind come from cells in the brain. When you sin and have shame, your thoughts are not the lash of an afflicted soul, but little murmurings from individual cells in a brain. What is a brain? A brain is matter. You have seen the brain of a sheep on a butchers block. Some of you have eaten the brains of an animal. Most of this generation or the last have seen the brains of human beings open to the air on many a bloody battlefield. There is the brain of a sheep. You have eaten this. There is the brain of a man. You can eat this too if you wish when it is properly cooked. That's matter. Well, tell me, friends, if you can eat a man's brain are you telling me that you are also eating his thoughts, that man's thoughts are nothing but the bits of soft tissue you are eating. And if a man's thoughts are separate from the matter that is his brain, doesn't it follow that it belongs to some other unseen part of him, his spirit that gives rise to his thoughts? Can spirit die? Can something that is not matter die?'

161

"The trouble about this fellow is that he keeps torturing himself over nothing. I know this. There is one simple solution if he will see it and everything falls into shape. See what he is heading for. Is he ever going to know peace of mind? Stop fighting. Stop figuring it all out. Because it all ends in nothing in the end, all the talk and all the torture. Is there any point in going on with it? I am about to argue with him but I keep my mouth shut when I notice out of the side of my eye that I am being watched. Closely. Not so good. Two big fellows with the red caps. I know one well. He can't but know me. The only thing is that I am not wearing a hat and so he mightn't be sure. It's funny how seldom he could see me without a hat. So I sidle away to the other side of the crowd. They are coming after me. From the crowd there is a long place with heavy shrubbery and I go in here and when I am covered I look back. They are behind me. This is good. This is excitement. I run as fast as I am able through the shrubbery and out the other side into the elm trees. I pass from tree to tree, running so that men behind if they are following won't see too much of me. When I come out into the open I saunter. By a stretch of water with one or two boats out on it, and over a humped bridge. But they are coming after me. I have gained on them. If I can work to one of the gates I can get lost in the crowds in a side street. But I don't want to do this. It is far better to be pursued. I think that if I am caught I will go to jail. What would jail here be like? It might even be interesting to find out.

"The chase lasts many miles. It is all at a saunter, with an odd fast run when sheltered by trees or shrubbery. Then I come into the last open. A big round pond, with children sailing boats. No, not children, but big grown men, with rubber boots on them. Out there with little chugging boats, little tugs or battleships or yachts or liners, all beautifully made. It seems odd to see big men in there in the water. There is a little curly child with a small wooden boat which he is poking with a stick. There is no breeze so the sail is dead. I hear a voice from behind calling the child to be careful now, boy, be careful, I tell you. This is a Irish voice. Soft and drawling. I turn and go back to

162

the voice. She is sitting on a chair. There is another chair empty beside her. I sit into this. I say, Hello, how is every bit of you? Her face is stern and forbidding when I sit, but it softens now. She has a white starched yoke around her neck. But her face is nice and a lot of brown curls, real ones. You're Irish, she says, are you long over, what part do you come from, tell me. Oh, I'm years and years over here, years and years. I tell her where I am from. She is disappointed but she bucks up. She knows a girl that knows a girl that came from a place twenty miles from me. Do I know this place? I say I do and it's a pity I didn't know her place and what was it like, and she talks throwing her arms up and laughing and remembering and I see the two fellows on the other side of the pond, but I have my arm on the back of the girl's chair and she is bending forward with her talk and I have my coat off, so they look and look all around and they shake their heads and move away. You're not listening to me at all, she says, sitting back. You're watching something else. I'm overpowered by the magic of your voice, I say. She says I have a fellow already and he's very nice and he comes from my own part, not ten miles away. I say I am glad, thank you for your company, and she says You're not going like that, and I say I am, and she seems disappointed with her face up to me, so I bend down and kiss her and it's like kissing a bit of bog, very soft and tasty, but I am seeing down the place where there are hundreds of ships, line on line, waiting and panting to go to sea. Any place in the whole world you can go from here, any place at all. Even hell. So I am going. Goodbye. Keep your finger on the trigger, John Willie, and don't let Breeda's footsteps stray."

"Why are you crying, Breeda?" Joseph asked her.

"It's poor John Willie," she said. "Him not knowing that poor John Willie is dead. And John Willie was very fond of him."

Joseph had to swallow a lump in his own throat when he thought of John Willie. If only he had asked him to wait longer. If only he had gone with him. If only! But it was all arranged that way. There was nothing anybody could do to arrange it any differently. It was taking all of them a long time to become accustomed to the fact that John Willie wasn't around any more. To this John Willie might have replied, Well, it will do them no harm at all to make do for themselves for a change.

They got up from the stones and started towards home.

Breeda was thinking: If only I could tear out of myself this feeling for Bart I would be very happy. It was a sort of surge that came over her like a tide. Of longing. If you could tear out a personal feeling. What did she want?

She wanted Bart to come home and live with her. Bart could never live with anybody. Bart was going farther and farther away from living with people. And then if she had Bart, what then? And after that, what then? What was it Joseph had, that made suffering intense for a short time and after that he seemed to emerge placid with his eyes calm? She knew that every day he set out very early in the morning and he walked six miles to the first Mass in the church beside the coast, and afterwards that he walked the six miles back again. If all the wishes of your life were fulfilled, what then? Would you be happy? She didn't think you would and why was that? Wasn't there a reason for it?

She said: "I'm sorry, Joseph, that I asked you to read Bart's letter."

"I'm not," said Joseph. "He wants somebody to be thinking about him. When he is like that. That's why he goes to the trouble of writing a letter. Even once in two years. That's why. Because he wants to know that there is somebody thinking about him."

They went into the graveyard on the way home.

John Willie had a new monument over him. The mound hadn't even settled yet. Joseph thought of John Willie at home when they took him down from the place above. He wasn't injured much. The piece of metal had entered his right eye and another few pieces had cut the right side of his face, but that was all. He looked quite peaceful, and Joseph had a terrible feeling that somebody should have put his cap on. Even when he was lying there. His cap was such a part of him that he didn't seem the same at all with out it. There were some early primroses in a pickle jar. That was Breeda. Joseph thought that it would be nice if there were some wild duck feathers or the white tail feathers of a cock. John Willie would like that. He could think of him below rotting away, but he was pinning his faith on his goodness, and his goodness would make him eternal.

Not the way some of them said, that he had already been seen on the hill with a shotgun under his arm and the dog walking ahead of him ranging with his nose to the ground. Because the dog didn't survive him for very long. Joseph thought the dog just died of old age and lack of exercise. People said he died of a broken heart. Joseph wondered about animals. The regard you could have for an animal. Was there only dust for them and nothing after? Many people, saints even, had written books about the love man bore for animals. Joseph hoped that John Willie in heaven could be provided, if at all possible, with his dog. And then he blessed himself and rose from his knees.

"We will go home now," he said to Breeda, touching her shoulder.

"Poor John Willie," Breeda said, sighing. "He was such a help to me. He was such a help to everybody."

Later Joseph was in the parlour reading when his mother came in and there was a girl with her. His mother had taken the death of John Willie harder than people thought she would. She had never been a talkative woman, but she talked less after his death. Joseph thought she had become much thinner. That her face was more drawn. She wasn't as active as she used to be.

"Sit down," she said to the girl.

The girl sat. She sat straight on the chair. Her face was set as if she was getting ready to take an insult.

"Why did you send for me, ma'am?" she asked.

"I will tell you," Mabbina said, dropping heavily into a chair, rubbing her eyes with her hand. "Before he died my husband spoke about you. I didn't listen to him at the time. Perhaps it was too close to what happened. I don't know. Anyhow he thought we should do something about you."

"I don't want anybody to do anything about me," the girl said. She didn't say it defiantly. She just said it in a soft voice. She could look after herself. Mabbina looked at her closely. Maternity had given her more flesh, had made her looked older. She was not very well dressed bur she as neatly dressed. "I consider myself married to Bart. When he comes home he will look after me."

Mabbina felt sorry for her, and then she was impatient.

"Nonsense," she said. "Bart is no good. Bart was never any good and he will be no better in the future. You can sit your life away waiting for him to come home and look after you, and that is as far as it will ever get you. I have something more practical. I want you to come and work in the shop. I will give you enough to support yourself and leave your home if you wish and look after your son. There it is. That's it."

She didn't really know why she was doing it, except that sentence of John Willie's some time before he died. She felt a bit impatient with John Willie. If he had kept his mouth shut, she wouldn't have this on her mind. But he had said it and it had kept nagging, nagging at her mind until she had to do something about it. Well, make her a barmaid. Men weren't used to barmaids in this part, but it might do something to make them hold their filthy tongues if a woman was serving them. If they wanted to travel six miles away to the next place for their drinks, then to hell with them. "Well?" she asked.

"It's very kind of you," Sheila said. "And I will take it." It raised a load off her mind. It wouldn't be so hard now. It wouldn't be so hard. "But I'll stay at home. My father and mother are old. I would like to stay at home with them."

"All right," said Mabbina. "Good girl! Thanks for coming, and you can start next week."

The girl went away, silently. Mabbina leant her head on her hands.

"The things I have to do," she said. "The things I have to mix myself up in. All because of other people. I wouldn't have anything to do with any thing or part of them if it wasn't for other people. You'd think John Willie was stretching himself out of the grave to get a bad girl like that fixed up. It was nothing to do with me. It was Bart. If she was a good girl it would never have happened to her. Why do I have to do things because other people sinned?"

Joseph had sense.

He didn't say anything.

Seventeen

JOSEPH WAS QUITE happy when he got the call.

He was down at the sidelines of the playing fields, watching a game. The field was muddy after heavy rain. Every time the ball was hit several pounds of mud were sent flying into the air, landing on the playing togs of the opposing players and often on their faces. It was a great test of near-priestly patience on their parts to refrain from using bad words. The hurlers on the fence were no help either, because they were either very partisan or loudly jeering.

He felt the young man's hand on his arm.

"The President, the President," the young man said. "Duty calls. Abandon games." He was the young man they called the Flying Monk, because he could never move at a slow gait. Every time you saw him his coat-tails were flying or his arms were flying. There was always some part of him flying. He was the dog of the place. He'd do anything for anybody as long as it meant he would be on the move.

"Thank you," Joseph said, and moved slowly towards the block. Always when you got a call to the President you started to examine your conscience. Joseph examined his, and found that it was as clear as he could make it at the moment. Therefore what was he wanted for? He didn't think too much about it. It was a fine day. Maybe somebody calling or something like that, although all the years he had been there only once had he been sent for, and that was when his mother had travelled all the way to see him. That was pleasant.

He hated to walk in out of the sun. He stood on the steps and looked back at the running men on the playing fields. You could just see the colours of their jerseys through the heavy leaves of the trees. The grass looked very green in the sun. Then he sighed and walked in the door and up the stairs. He paused then and knocked and the voice said, "You may come in." He went in.

The President had his back to the window so that Joseph couldn't see his face at first. Then he moved away from the window and sat at his desk. It was a nice room. Nearly all books, a big desk, leather-covered chairs and a red carpet on the floor. He was a tall man and well built and his hair was nearly all grey but very thick and he wore heavy horn-rimmed spectacles. Nearly everybody liked him. He wasn't forbidding; it was only the amount of his knowledge that made you cautious.

"Please sit down, Joseph," he said.

Joseph sat tentatively into the chair. He had to pull himself out to the edge of it or he might have disappeared into its deep hold. The President leaned back in his swivel chair. He had a green pencil in his hand, sliding his long fingers up and down it.

"You have been a long time with us," he said at last.

Joseph felt an empty space appearing in his chest. He closed his eyes for a second, until his breath came back, then he opened them and said: "Have I been too long, Father?" and the Father threw down the pencil and leaned his elbows on the desk and bent forward and he said: "Yes, Joseph, you have been too long."

So that was that.

The President was used to mortality. But there was always a different reason for it than the one he was faced with now. After two, three, four, five years you could see the weeds and pluck them from the grain, sometimes abruptly, sometimes infinitely slowly, so that they were out, roots and all, almost before they were aware of it, and in the process they would not be hurt. Often it was very difficult, when young men held desperately to vocations that you knew they did not possess.

He said: "Of the class that started with you, not one remains. There were twenty-two of your year; eleven of them have been ordained for more than three years and the others are scattered

169

abroad, and most of them doing well. We have tried hard, Joseph. We have been very patient. We have stretched rules and regulations until they were screaming. Now we think you ought to go home and think over it all for a year, or maybe two, to see if God will give you back the gift of retention."

There was a silence. Joseph's head was sunk on his chest.

He had a vocation. The President knew it. In his character there was absolutely nothing to deny it. He had true piety without display. He was utterly obedient. He had all and every single one of the qualities that would go to the making of a good priest. But of what use was that when there was no apparent hope of his ever passing the simplest examination? The President had seen his pitiful attempts at answering the set questions. One or two of them might be ideal as his brain seemed to flame into a fire of remembrance, but the others would be as halting and lame as a deaf and blind and lame donkey. And yet, had they done all they could? He thought they had. He had called all the professors together this morning and questioned them again closely until he had been sure and certain that this was the only course open to him. He rose from his desk and came and stood looking down at the slight hunched figure in the huge chair. If there was anything he could do. . .

"Joseph," he said, "there is nobody here who wouldn't give you his brain or his eyes or his memory if such a thing were possible to assist you. Maybe we did wrong to keep you so long when there was no hope. Maybe too long. There must be something else, Joseph. There must be some other reason. God doesn't create good things without a reason. They must have some purpose. There must be. When you go home and think and pray, maybe you will find the purpose."

"Thank you, Father," said Joseph, but he didn't look up, he couldn't look up.

The President pulled himself together. He went back to his desk. He tried to take the softness out of his voice.

"It's also possible, Joseph," he said, "that you were using the College as a refuge. Here you were happy in a way. You were cut off from the problem of living. You were putting it away from

170

you from day to day and year to year. Saying something will turn up. One day my memory will come flowing free and everything will be all right. Nobody can flee from challenge. Not from the challenge of life. Nobody can face it except yourself. You will have to face it, Joseph. I don't think you will ever face it while you are there."

"I understand, Father," Joseph said.

"You can go and pack your things now," he heard him say. "They are all on the fields. This is the best way. They will just come back and you will be gone. There is somebody here who will take you home. I sent for him."

He rang the bell on his desk and a knock came to the door. He called "Come in, please," and the door opened and Larry came in. Joseph didn't know who it was. He still wasn't looking up. The President nodded and Larry stood over him and spoke.

"Hello, Joseph," he said.

Joseph looked up at him. Larry was distressed at the sight of his wounded eyes, but he hid his distress and smiled.

"I'm glad to see you, Larry," Joseph said.

Then he stood up and walked to the door. He turned there and spoke to the President.

He said, "Forgive me, Father."

The President said, "If there is anything I have to forgive you for, Joseph, I willingly forgive you."

"I mean," said Joseph haltingly, "not accepting, with proper humility. I know, I know, that I was not fit. If I was wise, long ago I would have saved you the . . ."

He stopped. The three of them stood as if they were carved figures. Then Joseph went out. The President allowed his breath to leave his mouth. Then he rubbed his forehead with a handkerchief.

"You will see him safely home, Father," he said to Larry.

"Yes, sir," Larry said.

"And keep an eye on him," he said.

"I will, sir," Larry said.

"God bless you," he said, "and I pray that you will never be a President."

171

Larry went out and closed the door softly after him. He went to Joseph's cubicle.

Joseph wasn't a good hand at packing his bag. Larry took the clothes from him and folded them carefully and put them neatly away. Joseph sat on the bed. His long lashes were almost resting on his pale cheeks. Better say nothing, Larry thought. That was the best way. He just went ahead folding the clothes and putting them away and after that the little things. He thought: How would I have felt if before I was ordained I had been told to leave? The thought horrified him. Even though many a time since his ordination and since he had been appointed to a parish with all the multifarious and oftentimes vexing duties of a junior curate, he had often wondered what on earth made him become a priest, knowing quite well, of course, and it being brought home to him now, in the case of Joseph, how terrible it would have been and how grateful he should be to God that things had turned out all right for him. What a selfish thought!

"It's all packed away now, Joseph," he said.

"All right, Larry," Joseph said. He stood up, took his hat and coat and looked around him once and then went out.

"I'll go to the chapel," he said. "Will you wait for me?"

"I'll wait," Larry said. He carried the two bags down the stairs and out to the drive at the back. There was a small car there. It didn't look very good. Larry thought that the car looked decidedly sick, as if it was going to die any minute of old age. He opened the back door, which creaked protestingly, dumped the bags on the seat, and then sat in the front and waited. He could hear the voices around the front. If it had been a different visit, he would have seen a lot of the others. He would have stayed a while. He looked at the block of buildings and thought what they had meant to him, all the years, how pleasant, and yet how far away now, like long-ago schooldays. Joseph came down the steps. Larry thought how slight he looked, how pale his face was, emphasised by the dark hair. He looked like a boy masquerading in the long trousers of a big brother. Even though he was over twenty now like Larry himself. Had he ever grown up at all?

Joseph opened the other door and sat in beside him.

"Drive off now, my man," he said then. Larry looked at him. Joseph looked back. His eyes were much calmer. Larry felt pleased. He had thought it was going to be much worse than this.

"All right, your honour," he said, and touched the peak of his hat with his fingers. Then he laughed. The car exploded a few times as if there was a bomb under the hood and then it chuffed away, loudly, stopping and then starting ahead furiously as Larry pulled knobs and pressed yokes, and then it settled down into a sort of outraged groan that brought it around the buildings and out on to the broad drive leading to the main gate. The playing fields were on the left.

Said Joseph: "It had to come, you see. Deep down I knew. Everybody else knew years ago. I'm not alone. I'm as thick as a turnip, let's face it. I mean let me face it. I should have known. Why should I be sad now? It was just you remember all the cases of stupid ones like me who kept on and on, and managed to scrape through. I should have been born four or five hundred years ago, when you could have been ordained even though you had only the blessing of yourself in Latin, and logic and rhetoric and philosophy were things you only heard other people talking about. I was like a willow tree trying to hide itself in a mowed meadow. All that. But I thought, Well, others won through, very ignorant men who ended up saints for all their stupidity, and I thought, Well, if you pray and you pray and you pray, maybe the same thing will happen to you. And it could have happened. It could quite easily have happened."

He didn't speak very loudly. The engine was noisy. He spoke mainly so that he could not hear the cries of the men on the playing fields. He kept talking tensely until they had passed through the wrought-iron gates and turned on to the main road, and then it was all behind him.

"Prayer is never wasted," said Larry.

"That's right," said Joseph. "That's right," hunching himself up in his seat.

"For example," said Larry, "some of your prayers, Joseph, might get this contrary car to bring us home. We have a long

173

way to go, and I have never had such lack of faith in anything of this world as I have in this car. Unless a miracle happens soon and I can get rid of it, my immortal soul is in great danger from loss of temper. Every time when it misbehaves, which is terribly frequently, I have to grip tightly to myself and say: Patience and humility are two of the great virtues, and of these the greatest can be patience, so please grant me patience with this cursed, misbegotten implement of the diseased mind of man."

"Larry," said Joseph, "I don't mind so much, honestly. I will recover very quickly, wait until you see. But my mother. My mother is going to take this very hard."

"I suppose so," Larry said. "I suppose so. Well, I will talk to her."

"That's fine so," Joseph said. He thought of going in to his mother and saying, "Well, it's all over, mother, I can never be a priest." He tried to see her face. He shrank back into his clothes thinking about that. It would be so hard to explain, so hard, and that it wasn't such a terrible affliction, if you looked into yourself and thought about what it meant to you, and not to keep thinking of what it meant to you in the eyes of other people, which he was afraid was the way that his mother would look at it. And that way it could be very sore. Because he wasn't finished. That was one way just, he had gone on the road ahead of his heart and it had passed him by. The road was a dead end. There was no corner or a new road hidden around it. He would have to go back and retrace his steps and find another way. There wasn't just one road leading to one mansion. There were many roads leading to different mansions all made and erected in the same building. It was hard of course. It was very hard. It could be so unbearably hard that it took great effort and aspiration to stop tears from welling out of his eyes, and his hands in his pockets were clenched and the nails biting into his palms hurt him until he became conscious of them, and then he turned his eyes to the road and watched it unfolding.

It was a fine summer day. The land had been washed with the heavy rains. It was glistening. All this they were passing was flat land with an occasional mound to simulate a mountain.

The cattle were big and fat and the sheep were big and fat and the land was made up of great fields that you wouldn't see at home. Great long fat fields, with the corn growing in them well up above the earth. The clouds in the sky were white and woolly. The sides of the road held heavy tree-covered ditches, brambles and briars and ash trees with the wild woodbine, newly washed, creeping in a pattern of death all over the good and the bad. Larry weaved his way through droves of cattle and flocks of sheep being driven carelessly on the roads by people who wouldn't raise a hand to get them out of the way for you. Sometimes the road stretched away straight for miles and other times it wound tortuously, and they travelled with the sun which was going the same direction as themselves. Once they stopped at a place and they drank tea and ate sandwiches.

After that the sun started to win out on them as it went lower and lower towards the western sea, but they caught up with it before it died. They saw the sea just as it sank into it and it started to smoke and spit flame from the hot contact. Nearer and nearer they came to home and the light went out of the sky and the stars took over and Larry switched on the lights of the car. They weren't very good, they were only a feeble yellow glare, and Joseph thought that Larry's eyes would bug out as he peered through the glass. He thought what a fortunate chance it was that Larry had been assigned as curate in his own parish. What an odd welcome thing it was! He thought what it would have been like to have come this long journey on his own with the terrible end to it. Larry was fine. He would talk or he wouldn't talk. He would joke or laugh or remark. But it was all as peaceful.

They got on to the windy road by the sea and soon they would turn off to their own place.

His pulse beat faster. If only this was over! If only this was over!

He thought of Breeda and himself on the side of Boola and he watching the springing bonfires on the hillsides as the young priest came home. It would never happen to him now. That was too bad. He wouldn't have minded it. He would have enjoyed it for John Willie's sake maybe, if John Willie had lived to see it.

He wished John Willie wasn't dead. John Willie had a great way of putting everything into perspective. He would have made it easier for Mabbina. Joseph knew that. I am equal to my lot now, he thought. He thought of Breeda, and the way he had watched her for months and months as she fought her affliction. That had been a terrible battle, he knew. She had won out of it with a sort of calm and accepting lustre about her. He could do the same. His was an affliction but it wasn't a physical one. His was spiritual, and if he was blind to the way he would have to go, he could at least see the face of God in the sky and on the sea and the side of a hill. But not Breeda. That had been taken from her. She grew eyes inside of her that might be better than the ones she had outside her.

"I'm afraid we are here, Joseph," said Larry.

Joseph stared. The car was stopped in front of the house. He hadn't even noticed that they had got on to the road. He hadn't known they were passing through the village.

"Yes," he said, "this is it."

"May God put the right words into our mouths now," said Larry as he took the bags out of the back of the car.

"Amen," said Joseph, and they headed for the lighted doorway.

Eighteen

MARTHA WAS IN the kitchen. She was sitting beside the fire darning the heavy woollen socks. She looked up as Larry came in.

"Hello, Mrs. O'Breen," he said.

"You're welcome, Father," she said, looking at him curiously and at Joseph who followed him.

"Where's mother, Martha?" Joseph asked.

She nodded her head at the closed door of the parlour, biting off a piece of thread with her white teeth. It seemed to make her grin. She was wondering what was up. Why was he home without them having heard a word about his coming and why was the young curate with him? She had met Larry before when he had called to make himself known, and she knew the look of him well from watching him saying Mass on Sundays down below at the coast church. She didn't know if she liked him. She liked her religion without humour. Larry thought that she was an odd person. He found it difficult to like her.

Joseph went through the door resolutely. Larry put the bags down near the dresser and followed him, removing his hat.

Then they were both inside looking at Mabbina. She was sitting at the table, with account-books spread out before her, and she was looking up at them over the top of spectacles. She took those off and put them down and then rose very pleased and came over to Joseph.

"This is a surprise, Joseph," she said, taking his hands. "I didn't expect to see you for another week. Did they close the college sooner? Sit down. Sit down, Father. I'm pleased to see you. Joseph, tell Martha to put on the kettle. Good boy!"

Joseph opened his mouth to talk, and then closed it and obeyed. He went to the door and said, "Martha, mother says to put on the kettle."

He saw her eyes looking at him coldly. Then she nodded and hung the kettle on the crook. His heart always sank a little when he saw that cold look in Martha's eyes. He thought that it was weakness in any person to want to be liked, but it was a natural weakness. Then he went back into the room.

Larry was sitting in the chair near the fireplace. There was no fire. The empty hearth was covered with moss. There were one or two flower petals thrown on the moss. He thought it was a nice way to cover in a hearth.

"You picked Joseph up at the bus?" she asked. "That was very kind of you."

"No, Mrs. Baun," he said. "I was down at the College and I drove him home."

"That was very decent of you," she said. "I was going to write my weekly letter tonight, so now you have saved me the price of a stamp."

He was looking at her closely. She had clear skin, that was sagging at the edges of her jaws. The hair at her temples was almost pure white, and the hair on the top of her head was still red. It would soon be all white. She was thin and there were blue shadows starting near her eyes and ploughing a deep way down by the sides of her nose. He didn't think Joseph's mother looked well. He wished what they had to say now could be postponed for a long time. He dropped his head, thinking, How will I begin? What are the right words to choose in a situation like this? He hadn't been in this house often, but each time he came into it he sensed the tension. He knew the history of the house. It was a sad history. It seemed as if the family had been specially picked out to be afflicted in spirit or in the physical sense. He liked going into the other houses. They would be a little embarrassed first at your call, but they would pull out the chair, and the woman of the house would clean the seat of it with her check apron, and the man of the house would take off his cap before he shook your hand, and inevitably in this greeting he was always conscious of the burned part of the lower face and the white part of the uncovered head. He could joke a little with them, and take a sup of tea back in the room with a boiled egg and plain cake on the spotless table-cloth, but when they saw he was light of spirit they all cheered up and he could make them laugh and they could make him laugh heartily and the oldest lady could say: Well, you're the divil! And he could know that things were fine. He wondered now at the way he was holding in his breath, as if he was oppressed. He knew why Joseph felt so good away from here in the arms of the College, even though his mother obviously loved him devotedly. Her eyes now as she watched him. They were gleaming. Well, he thought, if she loves him well enough, this disappointment can be taken in her stride. Her love will be bigger than the disappointment.

Joseph broke out.

"I was sent home, mother," he said. "I can never be a priest."

Now he's done it, Larry thought. He hadn't the courage to raise his eyes.

It took her a long time to understand him, and then she didn't quite understand him.

"What did you say?" she asked.

Joseph sat in a chair opposite her. He had to. It had taken a terrible effort to say the sentence. His legs were trembling.

I'm telling you very simply, mother, that they sent me home. I cannot be a priest. I'm not fitted to be a priest."

Larry raised his head now and looked at her. Her mouth was open and she was staring at her son.

"He's putting it very badly, Mrs. Baun," he said. "What he means is that, by the will of God, Joseph is unable to retain, to assimilate. He cannot pass examinations, that's what it means. There is some physical or spiritual reason why he cannot pass examinations. It doesn't mean he hasn't a vocation. It just means that they want him to come home for a year or two to think things over and see what happens after that."

179

He shut up. He had put it badly too. He knew that. But the whole thing was so subtle that it would take a master of logic to place it on the table in simple language.

"I don't understand," she said. "You want to be a priest still, don't you, don't you?"

"Yes, mother," said Joseph. "I want to, more than anything in life."

"Then what's wrong? What's wrong?" she asked, rising from her seat. "Have you sinned? Have they found you out in something wrong? Tell me!"

"Mrs. Baun, have sense," Larry said. If it was anybody else he would have made a light remark. The idea of Joseph being a sinner was funny.

"Well, why did they put you out? What made them put you out? Tell me, Joseph. I'll forgive you. I swear I'll forgive you."

Joseph's voice was patient.

"It boils down to the fact, mother," he said, "that I am a bit stupid. I hear things and understand them but I can't remember them. It's just that."

"But you're not stupid, Joseph, you're not," she said. She hit the table with her clenched fist to emphasise it.

"Haven't I seen you night after night over the big books? You can read them. You can understand them. He's a liar to say you are stupid. We'll go down and see him. I'll go down and see him tomorrow morning. What does he mean!"

"Mother," said Joseph, "it's no use. Please, for my sake, understand. I cannot be a priest. I haven't the right things that make a priest. That's it, simply, mother. Please try and understand it now. I will never be a priest because I am not worthy to be one."

She sat down on the chair then. She was looking at him as if she could devour him with her eyes. Her hands were clenching the edge of the table until her knuckles were absolutely white.

"You too," she said. "You don't want to be a priest."

Joseph said quietly, "I want to be a priest, mother."

"You don't," she said. "You don't! If you did, what's to stop you? Nothing! Nothing! This talk of stupidity. Do you think I'm stupid? If God calls a person, He calls him, doesn't he?

There's no half-measures. You have deceived me."

"Mrs. Baun," said Larry.

"All these years," she said. "What had I in life? What did I get out of life? Nothing but slavery and torture and sadness and disappointment after disappointment. You were the last hope I had, Joseph. You know that."

Joseph looked at the tears coming out of her eyes and felt very miserable, but there was nothing he could say. He could only keep his eyes fixed on hers.

"Did I force a vocation on you?" she asked. "Did I insist on a vocation for you? Did I ever say anything to you that would make you think I wanted you to be a priest?"

"No, mother," said Joseph.

"Very well then," she said. "You were all that I had left. When the others, one after another, wounded me, I could always say, there is Joseph. Joseph will never disappoint me. I clung to you, Joseph. You were the only one I had left in life. I would have died many a long day ago if I hadn't you to hold on to. All the rest, all life would have been fine, but to see the day that you would be down in the church below saying your Mass and I could go to the rails and you could lay your hands on my head. That was all I had left to look forward to, and now you have taken that away when I am least able to bear it. You shouldn't have done it, Joseph."

"I'm deeply sorry, mother," Joseph said.

"Sorrow?" she asked. "I have enough of that. Enough of that. All the books and the clothes and the colleges, all for what. All for nothing. But they were nothing. It was you, Joseph. You. You were the anchor of my life, Joseph, and now you have proved yourself to be like all the rest of them. Just common clay, Joseph, like all the rest of them."

"Mrs. Baun," said Larry.

"All right, Father," she said, rising heavily to her feet, "I know you have good arguments. I know you would have good reasons. I know all that. But the fundamental fact remains. And that cannot be answered. I have been disappointed in my youngest son. He was a good one. He was the son of a good father. Not like the others. They had their father's nature in them to fight. He hadn't. His father was good by nature and by example. If I had known before! But to let it go this long. So near. This is too much. I'll get over it. I have got over worse things. But it's hard now. It's hard. If you forgive me. Martha will make a meal for you. I'll go upstairs. I don't feel well."

She went out. There was nothing Larry could say, although he knew there were hundreds of protestations he should have made. He looked at Joseph. Joseph had let his eyes drop at last. His head was bowed. Larry thought: Oh, my God, this won't do. It's not right, not right at all.

He rose to his feet and went into the kitchen. She was going slowly up the stairs, holding to the banisters. He spoke again, "Mrs. Baun, you'll have to let me explain." She didn't turn around. She just waved her free hand and walked up and then turned on the landing and was gone from his sight. He felt miserable with his helplessness. Martha was standing by the fire looking at him. Her face was expressionless.

"Will you have a cup of tea now, Father?" she asked.

He looked at her sharply. It seemed like a jeer, it came so apt.

"No, thank you, Mrs. O'Breen," he said. "I don't want any tea." He went back into the room. He went over behind Joseph. He put his arm across his shoulders. He bent over him.

"It's the hard road, Joseph," he said. "I'm afraid it's the hard road."

"I'm sorry, Larry," Joseph said.

"I'll go away," Larry said. "In the morning she might be sorry. She may spend the night thinking and the Lord will put her thinking straight."

"It's hard on her," Joseph said. "She was looking forward to it so much. She really hadn't many things to look forward to."

"It's hard on you too," said Larry. He took his hat from the table and stood a while. It seemed to have been a very long day. It must have seemed very much longer to Joseph. "I'll see you again, Joseph," he said then. "Things will be better tomorrow. Things are always better the day after."

"That's right," said Joseph. He rose. "I'll see you out."

Larry looked at him closely. His face looked old and only a few hours ago he thought he looked too young for his breeches. But his eyes were calm. The mind can only absorb so much, he thought, but his admiration for Joseph was increasing. He went ahead of him and stopped in the kitchen to say to Martha, "Good night, Mrs. O'Breen." He had his hand on the door to open it when they heard the thump that came from upstairs. The three pairs of eyes looked at the ceiling. It was a boarded ceiling. The boards were blackened from the generations of fires. There were many hooks driven into the wood, and from three of them flitches of bacon were hanging. He seemed to see all this clearly, the whitewashed walls with the pegs for the horse's collar and harness, the dresser with the gleaming delph, the comfortable white-scrubbed wooden furniture, the staircase painted red, and then he had thrown his hat on the table and had run up the stairs. They were steep. He headed for the noise and went into the opened bedroom door and saw her crumpled on the floor. Her breathing was heavy and forced. Her eyes were closed and one side of her mouth was pulled down. He left her there after blessing himself and ran to the head of the stairs.

"Joseph," he ordered, "go and get the doctor. Come up here, Mrs. O'Breen."

They obeyed him automatically. Joseph went out of the door and she mounted the stairs. He was back inside by this time. It was a big room, with a great double bed with brass knobs on it and a snowy white quilt. There were enlarged pictures on the walls, and starched lace curtains on the two windows. A dark cupboard and a table with a white cloth and a cross on it and a prayer-book and beads and a little glass bottle affair with a picture of Lourdes inside that seemed to have snow falling over it when you shook the bottle. Martha came in.

"We'll have to get her on to the bed," he said. She nodded. She was competent. They raised her on to the bed. She wasn't very heavy, he thought. She was a big-boned woman, but she had lost a lot of flesh. He said then, "I'll get the things from the car. I will have to anoint her." She nodded, started to pull the quilt over the woman, and he went out towards the car wondering what great thought had made him retain the holy oils in the car when he had set off for the College.

He was at the car when Joseph came back with the doctor. The doctor was in his shirt-sleeves with no collar and hadn't paused to change from his slippers. He had a bag.

Larry went with him.

"Sorry for my appearance, Father," the doctor said. "Always when I put my feet up, I am caught out. Upstairs, is it?"

"Yes," said Larry. The doctor mounted the stairs and Larry followed him. I knew it, the doctor was thinking. High blood pressure and hardened arteries or I'm a horse doctor. If only people would come and get themselves looked after in time. You couldn't go up on the street to them and say, Look, I'm not sure without an examination, but I think you have such a thing wrong with you. It'd be like drumming up business. You would probably be thrown off the medical register . . . but the doctor knew many of the people and what they would die of, seeing the incipient stages of old-age diseases or young-age diseases in their faces or limbs. What could you do? When you were going from morning until night. He tried to see himself facing Mabbina any minute before now, and saying, You ought to take it easy, Mrs. Baun, or you're for it. Nice times!

He bent over her.

Joseph was below in the kitchen, sitting on a chair, his hands dropping between his knees, his eyes staring in front of him, his overcoat collar crumpled about his neck. He was praying, Not now, don't let it happen now, because I would be the immediate and utter cause of it and that would be unbearable. Even until she can understand. Just that until she can understand, if it is Your will.

It seemed a long time before the doctor came down.

"She won't die yet, Joseph," the doctor said kindly. "It was a very near thing. I'll wait here for the night. I'd like a cup of tea. I came out without it. Would you go over to the house and collect my coat and shoes? Good man! "That'll give him something to do, he thought, keep him from thinking. He was very attached to his mother. He wondered what way she would come out of the stroke, as they called it. He could bring her out of this one, but he didn't know what would be impaired. There was always something impaired.

He sighed and went over to the fire and hung the kettle on the crook.

Nineteen

"OH, DEAR," SAID Bidelia, rushing into the house, "it's a massacre! You should see her, poor Mabbina Baun, up on the flat of her back and no life in her except the eyes, and that young man, Joseph, who would have thought common clay, dear, just like the rest of us and he thrown out of the College."

"That's a lie," said Breeda, sharply.

"Well, dear, it's what they say," said Bidelia plaintively.

"I'm only telling you. I myself believed he was a saint, but what is a person to think when they won't have him and he comes out, what is a person to think, and the poor woman went down with the shock of it, I tell you. She had her heart set on it, they say, that he should have been a parish priest before she died. And the shock of it struck her. She's really stricken, dear, and isn't it a terrible thing? The whole place is aroused. Not that I say it, but pride comes before a fall, they say, and there's little left of pride now in that whole family."

"And that pleases you," said Breeda.

"Now, Breeda, dear, what's come over you? My heart is melting for them. The thought of that boy Joseph is searing me. Having to come home and face his mother and all of us, after getting so near."

"Oh, stop it," said Breeda. "It's all different, all different, but what can a person say? It will be all taken and twisted and tortured so that the truth will be like a thorn in a bale of wool. Why do people just only see the worst of a situation? Nothing is ever like what the people think. I think people are stinking, stinking."

She made her way to the door, feeling with her hands. She was very angry. A blind anger because if she had her eyes there were a lot of things she might have done.

"Breeda! Breeda!" she heard her aunt wailing after her, but she didn't turn back. She walked down the road and over the bridge and through the village. She was called at on every side. "Hello, Breeda! Hello, Breeda! Great day, Breeda, thank God!" She could pass through another day and she wouldn't be greeted even once, so she had a vision of them all running around like ants, hugging their eggs to their breasts, or shuffling them with their legs, calling and whispering and sighing dolefully with great glee. It was only time would level it all off. They would forget the things but not the causes of the things. Familiarity would breed distorted forgetfulness.

She knew well what was wrong with Joseph. They had been together many times during his holidays. He had read for her from his tomes, and the next day while she held the things in her memory he would come back without the tomes and try and discuss what he had read yesterday. Sometimes he could, but most times it would be as if you had poured water on a hot stone and the water had evaporated in steam. There was no trick of memory that he hadn't tried, while she stood or sat, her whole body tense with the effort of his trying to remember. What did they know about that? How could you explain it to them? If you said it, they would say: Ah, so he's an idiot, a bloody half-wit! If only brash Bart was home to take it on himself. What a hope!

She fingered the newest letter in the pocket of her cardigan. It rustled deeply there. She wished he hadn't written to her again. She didn't want to know about him. He was as dead now as he ever would be. He had gone away farther than if he had died. All of him would have changed. Would he have a heart now for what Joseph must be going through or would he laugh at it? Would the sight of his mother paralysed in a big bed hurt him? Would it? Or would he be completely indifferent? Or would he say: Everybody who hurt the great Bart O'Breen is laid

187

low? She knew she had come to the place where she had often waited for Joseph before, when he was coming from Mass. She would come this far and walk back with him. She liked being with him. They talked about many things. He had a clear outlook on life, a very simple one that she couldn't reach yet, but being with him was like walking with a peaceful day. Even though he had suffered things, they didn't seem to make him sour or turn him into an introvert.

Now she wondered if she was wise in being seen often with him. Their filthy minds could turn that too as another handy stone to throw at him. That thought made her turn off towards the road that led to the sea.

Sometimes she was glad she couldn't see. She didn't want to see the looks on the faces of people. Just to listen to them sometimes was even too much. Because you could judge well the look that would be on their faces. The ears of the blind were terrible truth-gatherers, because every nuance of speech was recorded and every sentence that was tempered with malice or envy or hatred, however well it was hidden by the face, could not be taken from the voice.

She lay on the grass of the cliff. The sun was warm on her body. If only it hadn't happened to her. If only she could have gone away and seen. There was the sea unseen. Even if you went away on it, it would only bring you to places where the smell was different. People would be exactly the same. You could only smell new things and hear the sounds of different things. And what good was that? If only she could see Joseph, see his face and know about him. If she could see and follow Bart and talk to him about his selfishness, and his casual dishonouring of people and his mixed-up mind. She felt like tearing the eyes out of her head so that they might let in a chink of light. She sat up and took the letter out of her pocket and she opened the envelope and she tore each sheet into bits and she threw them from her so that they floated down to the sea below, the calm sea where they rested for a while.

That is the end of him, she thought. The end of him. I don't want him to write to me. I want my own life, crippled as it is.

Nothing to do with him. Nothing to do with him at all. She pressed her face into the grass and she clawed at it with her fingers biting into the ground so that she felt the hot earth all around her, and she couldn't stop sobs bursting from her, just as she knew they were sheer sobs of angry frustration.

Then the hand was on her shoulder shaking her, and Joseph's voice said, "What is it, Breeda? Breeda, what's wrong with you?"

That stopped her. She quietened down. She was ashamed that she should have been seen. Although it wasn't so bad when it was Joseph.

She turned her face away so that he shouldn't see it. She sat up with her back to his voice. "Just plain bad temper, Joseph," she said.

"Were you upset about my mother?" he asked.

"That's part," she said. "And I had a letter from Bart and I threw it into the sea."

"You shouldn't have done that," he said. "I would have liked to know how he is, where he is."

"He's gone to hell," Breeda said. "That's where he's gone. Didn't he say that the last time?"

Joseph bent over the cliff. He looked down at the water. He could see the torn bits of the letter waving on the gentle tide. In and out. Some of them had soaked and gone down. Others of them were on top. He could see the big bold writing, almost make out a word or two.

"I still believe you hurt your head that day," Breeda said.

I still believe that that is what's wrong with you. I don't believe you are stupid. How could you become stupid out of the blue? You weren't stupid before that. Stupidity is something that you are born with. You are not bright one day and stupid for ever afterwards. I believe that Bart blinded my eyes and blinded your intellect all at once. I believe that as true as I am here, that he was responsible for both of us. And when you are in trouble and could do with some help where is he? He's gone to hell."

"Breeda," Joseph said. "Let it rest. What has become of your resolutions? It all has a purpose. I keep telling you. It all has a purpose. Come on. Get up and we'll go home."

She got to her feet.

"Joseph, what is to become of us?" she asked.

"God knows," Joseph said.

They walked slowly away.

Below on the sea the torn letters wavered. Pieces of them came together to form jumbled words and sentences, unintelligible now, except to the writer. ". . . a foreign place you wake up, with your head muzzed, all muzzed and the strange accents of people outside in sweltering sun. Lying naked, sheer naked, because it is February and outside in the baked streets it is a hundred degrees in the shade. Where am I? you say. Every day near, you wake up and say where am I, and you are nowhere. All the places are alike. Baking seas and hundreds of ships out there. One yours where you work. Now in port and last night. About last night. This sort of building where they uplift men who go to sea. All the local society ladies. Sort of good work, to keep the sailors and their money away from the evil coloured women of the port. So this lady is with me this morning. Later I look at her. Remember the place last night. Coffee and cakes in this place and a well-corseted lady at a piano singing hymns. Oh, that was something. This other lady handing around the plates. Don't ask me how, I don't know, but she comes with me afterwards into places all over and we don't drink coffee. This lady of uplift. She's all right. She's a nice girl. She is fair and when she is dressed in expensive light blue gabardine she looks like a boy. Long shapely limbs like they all have, that is their line.

"She says: Oh, my God, what happened? She is sick. I don't care. She dresses and she looks after herself. She calls me names. Polite names venomously. What will I say at home? I don't care. I don't care at all. She has a home. She's lucky.

"Breakfast. Coffee. I hate coffee. I want tea like Martha's mother makes out of the boiling black kettle. They don't make it. Dip bits of bloody bags in hot water. I say, you can keep this country, anybody can keep this country. Give it away. It is so hot. There is no relief. I think of Boola on a February day. Probably frost, heavy frost. Delicious cold. Grand cold. Invigorating cold. We are down below. She has a car. It is a long blue car. Hardly

190

hear an engine. I will show you beauty, she says, because we are arguing. Why? To cover up despair. What is there in the world? There are good times. You have them and then what? You have more once you have got over being sick. Sometimes I feel I don't belong to me at all, at all. We go this long road out of the town heading away as straight as the long hair of a woman, into the blue. There is a sort of breeze made by the car. Pass sort of wooden houses back in great stretches of winter land. That's the climate. Last week a heavy frost and snow. Now it is as hot as hell. In front of the houses they have patches of plants covered with heavy canvas, to keep out the frost. Corn plants I think. Maybe tobacco too, I don't know. Coloured men on the porches resting in the sun, hats, big straw hats over their eyes. Other men with their bodies in the shade and their heads in the sun. Man, that's why they are coloured, I say. She calls them names. She doesn't like them. I think they are nice. They are just the same as we at home, lazing in the fields on a hot day. The car goes very fast on this straight concrete road. Big signs up. Speed limit 55. This girl is driving at eighty. I look at her. Her face is drawn, like my own, I suppose. Lines around her eyes. Looks tired. What is she looking for? We turn right after a long time. Go down a smaller road. Then far down we see little children by the side of the road. She slows down. Small little black girl with a pink frock and hair all done up in bits of ribbon. She is dancing around on the side of the road, clapping small black hands, singing, Jesus is my Saviour. We throw out money. The child picks it up, bows profoundly, and we go on and then I look back and see other badly dressed kids converging, looking at the amount. All down the road for miles there are the beautiful little black girls. The air resounds to Jesus is my Saviour, for miles and miles. Their Jesus is very gay dancing Jesus, clap hands Jesus. Not a bad idea to have at home. Make money. All little children out on the side of the road doing the same, what? Would that be approved? Ho-ho!

"This place then. Walk around. Near a man-made lake, place that has been flooded for dams or some such. Lovely walks by the lake. Flowers without number. Azaleas and flowers growing out of the forks of trees. The air permeated. Don't believe it. Or the cypress groves, all sort of swamps, out in shallow boats. Man pushing and humming behind. White trousers and blue uniform. All the trees growing out of the water and Spanish moss trailing from the branches right down. What am I doing here? I don't know. What does it make me think of? I don't know. I can see a girl in a boat out on a windy lake, catching a fish or bending to the terror of the wind, body lashed by wind and rain, her white teeth gleaming. Terror in her maybe. The pull of muscles in the arms. What's that? That's nostalgia? No good. Never be the same. Say you go back. All you get is a pain in the craw. Never be like your mind wants it to be.

"Back to the port. She says, You come up and meet the people. I object. She says, Come on. He likes to meet Irish. He was a tatterdemalion himself one time. Wants to see them low before they go high.

"Great big building. Up a lift. Whizz. Opens into a great room. On top. Somewhere over the rainbow. Carpet deep as the bosom of a nursing mother. Up to the knees. Soft lights. Bathroom as big as John Willie's shop. Laugh. Sweet scents. Am I presentable? Crumpled trousers and sweat-shirt. That's all. In there. A sideboard of drink. Anything from anywhere. Then he comes in. Low-size squat man. Blue suit. Red flower in his buttonhole. Sits looking at me with small eyes. Her brother too. Older than she. I notice her trembling. She is afraid of her life of this little squat fellow. Why? Everywhere I go. Small pig eyes boring into me. What am I doing? Where do I come from? Where am I going? You have good teeth. Why do they all when they come over have bad teeth? I say, To hell with teeth. Then a phone rings, always phones ringing. He listens. Then the pig eyes are on the girl. So! She is terrified. She has to sink into the soft sofa. I know her legs won't support her. Where were you? I can see. You were supposed to be somewhere else. You this. Terrible. Awful. Don't mind hearing them in the forecastle. Hear them here with your shins in carpets, that's not so good. I tell him things. Why am I always caught up like this? Dirty little man. He rings bells all over the place. People appear. If I am not out of the port in twenty-four hours things are going, to happen to me. I am thrown out. Out into the hot sun. I think of the girl up there, in the clouds of the building, ice cold from the man-made air, and what she is going through from this old devil. Where do you go? Why are we going? This place gives me a taste in my mouth. Going on. Don't know where. To the end maybe, who can tell? Your hole in the hills is not so bad.

Maybe it was as well they didn't read it.

Twenty

Luke stood in the bedroom doorway, huge and sunburned and awkward. The sun was shining in the window so he could see his mother clearly. Her face was emaciated. She didn't seem to be at all the woman he had known. There were severe hollows in her temples. Her hands lay outside the quilt. They were palely yellow, the fingers of the right hand feebly plucking at the knotty decorations of the quilt. But her eyes were clear and they were looking closely at him. He tried to keep his eyes from the way the right side of her face dragged, the distortion of her mouth.

"Come over, Luke," she said. She didn't exactly say it. The words were slurred. She couldn't emphasise her meaning with a nod of the head or a bend of the wrist. Luke walked carefully to the chair beside the bed. He felt big. He felt so big and full of rude health in comparison with the body of his mother that he could have cried. He was conscious of his heavy boots on the linoleum. The chair creaked when he sat on it. He didn't like being there. Luke always wanted to run away if people were sick or if something untoward was happening. He didn't want to be there. He didn't mind people telling him all about it afterwards.

"Where's Joseph?" she asked. Always Joseph, Martha would say. Always Joseph. Every time you go in to her, always Joseph. What did Joseph eat? Had he an egg for his breakfast?

"He's out at Mass, mother," he said. "He'll soon be home."

"Home," she said. "Luke!"

"Yes, mother," he said.

194

"Look after Joseph," she said. Her right hand turned over. He saw the movement. He knew what it meant. He slowly raised his own brown hard hand and he rested it in her upturned palm. The fingers of her hand pressed his. He remembered his mother's hand. From way back he could remember the feel of it on his naked body, time she would be bathing them in the galvanised tub in front of the fire. He remembered the hardness of it sometimes on the side of his face when he was being smacked, probably for the sins of his brother. He saw her hand in the pots, laying the table, skinning the spuds, holding the hoe, black with the brown mud of the bog that turned sticky black when it dried. She fetching the heavy sods to his cutting, arranging them on the barrow. He saw the muscles on her arm leaping to the swing of a spade. He even remembered her using the scythe. That was the hand he remembered. It bore no relationship at all to the piece of loosely wrapped ivory that held his own now. This made Luke sad. It made him want to weep.

"I will, mother," he said. "I'll look after him."

"Not like us," she said. Her words were very slow. Each one of them brought out as if her mouth was an oyster being irritated into forming a pearl. "Doesn't live in our world at all, Luke. People say odd. Yes. Not odd. Something else. Something I don't know. Shelter him a little, Luke. You promise that?"

"Yes, mother, I promise," he said, meaning it too, not even thinking, Well, Martha is the one, Martha will look after him.

"Everything will be yours, Luke," she said. "Farm and shop. John Willie leaves shop to me. I leave to you. You are my eldest son. Good boy, Luke. You were always a good boy. Remember. Never knew day's idleness. Like me, Luke. We were not the same as them. So now you will have it and you watch over my boy. You promise, Luke?"

"Yes, mother," said Luke.

"Good boy, Luke. Martha. I was hard with her, Luke. Sorry now. You know. Good wife to you. Hard work. Birth, that means nothing. What you make of it. That's it. She made the most of it. All right."

195

Martha came in. She was carrying a tray. She watched the hand of Luke holding the hand of his mother. She had a glass of warm milk on the tray. There was a little brandy in it. She saw the big eyes of her mother-in-law turning on her. She met their look, but slightly veiled her own. "I brought you the drink now," she said. I worked hard, she thought. I worked very hard. Many many years. Since Mabbina'd got ill she had worked hard with her too. All the unpleasant tasks that paralysed people demand, she had carried them out unflinchingly, patiently, of set purpose, with no grumblings to Luke, no hint of malice or triumph lying in bed beside him at night. Her mother-in-law had been brought low and she had served her well. She had served her very well. She was conscious that nobody in the world could have done so much with such good grace as she had done.

She went to the other side of the bed. She placed the tray on the small table. Then she put her strong right arm behind Mabbina's head and she spooned the warm drink into her mouth. It took patience, because the drink was inclined to dribble off again. It hurt Luke to see this, so he rose and went over to the window and looked out at the road and the village. Over at the end of it he saw the black-suited figure of Joseph approaching with a heavy gilt-edged missal glinting occasionally as it caught the rays of the sun. He walked with his head down. He always did that, as if he was tracing a map on the ground at his feet.

"Joseph is coming now, mother," he said, turning to her.

Martha restrained herself as she saw the pleased look that came into the eyes of Mabbina. Had Luke ever earned a look like that, she wondered, when he would come home late in the evening almost too tired to eat, nodding with physical tiredness over his meal? Would he ever earn a look like that when he had expended all of himself in toil? Joseph had never hurt his hands, they were as unblistered as the hands of a baby, and the sick woman from the depths of her near death could pulsate with pleasure at the thought of his return. It took restraint on Martha's part not to pull her hand away, not to do something to show her feelings.

196

"Thank you, Martha," Mabbina said. "You are very good, very good." Then she lay back in the bed and directed her eyes at the door. Martha nodded her head at Luke.

"I'll go, mother," he said. "I have to give the girl a hand in the shop. It's Saturday."

"Thank you, Luke. Good boy," she said. He stood for a while big and clumsy. What could he say? "Wish you were better and in the shop too," he said. "Everyone says it's not the same place without you."

She smiled. Luke was pleased at himself. He went out the door, followed Martha down the stairs. She turned below. She kept her voice low.

"Well," she said, "what did she say? Tell me what she said?"

"It's all right," he said. "I told you it would be all right. I'm her eldest son like I told you. She will leave all to us, but she told me to look after Joseph. That's a promise, I told her. I will look after Joseph."

"So she leaves you all," she said. "Thank God for that. I was afraid."

He moved uncomfortably.

"It's not right, Martha," he said. "These things don't matter. Not when she is like this. She'll never get up from there."

She went close to him. She held his arm.

"I don't mean anything, Luke," she said. "I don't mean to be unkind. It's just we have to think of tomorrow, that's all. And what's to become of us. And that we are rewarded. It's part of living, that's all."

"Just not now, Martha," he said. "Not now. Not at this time."

Joseph came in then.

Luke said to him, "She seems much better today, Joseph. She's talking quite a bit today. She might get better. I think she might even get better."

"With the help of God, she will," said Joseph, leaving his missal on the table and making for the stairs.

"I have your breakfast ready," Martha said. "I'm keeping it hot on the hob."

197

"I won't be a minute," Joseph said. "I'll come down in a minute for it." He went up, their eyes following him. Then Luke went through the door into the shop. Martha paused for a second, and then went over to the stairs and listened intently. She could hear nothing. The voices were too soft. She shrugged and went back to the fire.

Joseph was holding his mother's hand.

"You're stronger today," he told her. "I can feel your fingers squeezing."

She shook her head.

"Bit," she said, "little bit. Joseph, this the first time I ever lay on my back so long. Good thing!"

"Why, mother?" he asked.

"Thought," she said. "Before never time to think. Not very clear but just think. Way back. To Bart's father. And John Willie. Things I should have done. Too late like."

"Mother," said Joseph, "don't talk so much. He told you that. He said save up all your strength."

"Only little talk," she said. "Got little out of life. My own fault. Everything is there to take. Depends on the way you take it. Like John Willie. John Willie liked life. John Willie was good."

"Yes," said Joseph.

"Bart's father liked life too in his way," she said. "I should have laughed with him. I should have done that."

"Mother," he said, "nobody gets their life back over. Except a sight of it. Wait until you get on your feet again and you can worry it."

"Will I ever get on my feet again?" she asked.

Joseph was nearly horrified.

"Of course you will," he said. He was sure of it too. The doctor was optimistic. She could live for another ten years, he had said, once she came out of it, and she seemed to be getting stronger every day and she had the heart of a lion and a good constitution. And besides Joseph had found himself able to pray so fervently. He had no feeling about it. That time about John Willie. He didn't like to think about it too much. Of the wave of desolation that came over him as he saw his father trudging across the bog with the gun over his arm. No, his mother would live on and become stronger. He would devote his life to her. Maybe that was the answer to all the conflict. He wouldn't permit himself to think of her dying. It opened up a great void in the sight of his life, a big dark place where he would have to walk on his own.

"Read for me, Joseph," she said. "Read a bit for me."

He took up the small black book from the table and turned over a page and commenced to read.

She knew well the contents of what he was reading for her. Since she had become so ill he had read for her every day. He had a soft voice that didn't caress the words. His voice seemed just to slip on them, and the words themselves and their meaning rose very strongly. Back over her mind went roving in a colourful dream of golden days of youth and laughter in the midst of hard things. Children around a table and a great three-legged pot of potatoes turned out on the table. The potatoes mashed up then and the green stalks of the scallions mixed in with them and butter. Cally, and once a month the cuts from the beef kidney stewed in flour and onions. Black polish on Sunday and the carefully patched dresses and the big hats that covered every inch of the head and the hair. The terrified sight of a long thin man shaving the beard of her dead father to make his corpse presentable for the interminable wake with snuff and tobacco and the muted drunken voices. The great days in the hay and the sight of Bart's father, the fair man, a giant with golden hair on his chest, and his white teeth ever showing in sounds of laughter. Oh, the love of him and the heartache of him. What killed me was John Willie. John Willie should never have died, never at all, because I had not enough of life to show him what he meant to me, what he meant to all of us. She didn't want to hold on to life at all. She was tired, and she would let go if she didn't have to remain for the sake of Joseph. He had nobody but herself. She knew what he was aiming for. If he didn't know himself. When he would say, I don't feel like eating today, she would chide his paltry appetite until one day she had seen the look of hunger in his eyes as she had taken away his half-empty plate. That had shocked her. That and other things. The time recently, when she had dreamed. A nightmare, after John Willie had died. About Joseph on a great plain with mists swirling about him and he was calling, calling, his hands held out, a boy alone and calling, and she woke up sweating and she was sure he was dead too, and she had gone down to the kitchen with the lighted candle in her hand, and it splaying hot grease on the back of her fingers, to open his door tentatively, expecting to see him dead with his eyes open, and he was lying on the floor of his room with his arms stretched out. Her cry had awakened him. She had seen the long lashes opening and his head turning to look at her. It wasn't warm weather, it was very cold. His exposed limbs looked blue, and "Oh, Joseph!" she had said, and he had smiled sleepily and said, "Mother, I must have fallen out of the bed." Imagine falling out of the bed and sleeping on the floor. That time and other things that made her afraid. That made her think, that removed her mind from the scenes around her to other things. That made her afraid. That made him seem so weak and he was so strong in one way. She knew him and she didn't know him and she prayed, Oh, God, look after him, and on top of his face and the sound of his voice in her ears she saw the grinning dark face of Bart with the curls hanging down on his forehead. Oh, what will become of him? What will become of him? He was a lovely baby. They all said he was a lovely baby! He was fat and lusty and his eyes were bold. He was a lovely baby. Only why? And where? Oh, God, she said, bring him back to me. Bring Bart back and bring him out of where he is! Up to his neck in trouble. Always trouble as long as it is not fatal. Don't let it be fatal. Try and bring him back.

She was opening her mouth to say something to Joseph when she felt the load pressing on her head. The word froze in her mouth. She wanted to squeeze the hand which must be holding hers, but her fingers couldn't move. She wanted to stir her head, her body, her arm, to call him, but this pressure on her brain wouldn't let her. Her eyes opened to their widest. One exclusive thought filled it, just before she stopped breathing.

Joseph was absorbed in his reading. His soft voice spoke on and on.

He wasn't conscious of the noise below of the doctor and Larry coming into the kitchen and addressing Martha cheerfully. This time each day they both came. The doctor would minister to the body and Larry would minister to the soul. Each day, so that his mother was surrounded by all that was good for her.

He didn't hear them come up the stairs or see them stand in the doorway. The doctor was about to shout a cheerful remark, to break up the reading, when he saw her face and horror came into his own because she was so recently dead, and because her son was reading, reading, reading, good words, excellent words, and so engrossing that he didn't know he was holding the hand of a corpse. Until the terrible silence impressed him and he looked up to the door. And he saw the look on the doctor's face and he saw the look on Larry's face and then he turned his head and looked at his mother's face. And he dropped her hand and he rose and pulled away and the doctor thought he looked like a young animal that is looking at the corpse of its mother, lost, bewildered, looking for another hole in the ground.

Larry saw a different look and moved first towards Joseph.

A single person is like a smut on the face of the world that is simply rubbed out by the wipe of a finger. For a time the smut leaves its little mark until the rain wipes it away.

For many saw the signs of their own deaths in the death of Mabbina. The people of her own age felt a chill in their spines. And others thought of the money they owed her and wondered if the heirs would be quick about gathering in. And some said, She is as well away because she was ever a hard woman. And others said, She was a just enough woman if she was tight with the credit. And very few of them could think of her as a laughing girl who had been won by the O'Breen fellow. But all of them for many miles around took the day off in anticipation, and they took the polish and brushes from the corner and got to work on their boots, and they took their good clothes from the cupboards and brushed them with the miniature twigs. And the man far below pulled an unpainted coffin from his high pile and dusted

201

it off and prepared to add the fittings and the linings according to the best. And the diggers got the word and went up and measured the site and spat on their hands and dug the sharp spade into the well-manured grass. And there would be black crêpe and lighted candles and the big passenger car which when the back of it was let down would hold the coffin when it was tied a bit with ropes.

All that was the stain. But it would soon be gone.

The sun would still shine and the rain rain, and her daughter-in-law would look pale and gaunt in black, and the whole history of them would be dragged up for a few days into the light of men's mouths, and they would be told and retold about their failings and how the living forgave those failings now they were dead.

Dust would be raised on the road and a few tears shed and the car would go away and the bills would be paid.

The waters of Boola would rage and storm and die away and Joseph would have to try and discover what he had done that he was being swiped left and right. Get up, and swipe, and he is down again. What is the reason? What have I done? How have I offended God?

Twenty-One

MARTHA TURNED THE key and flung the door open
away from her. She left it open. The sun poured in.
The front window and the back window were red-
blinded. She took off her black coat and she flung it on a chair.
She threw her hat on top of it. Then she went to the back window and tugged at the blind. It rattled up, letting in the north
light. Then she let up the blind on the window near the door.
The fire had burned low. There were only white ashes in it with
a feeble trail of smoke up from them. Somebody had forgotten
to blow out the six candles that were in the brass candlesticks,
three on each branch. They had burned very low and a draught
had burned them crooked so that the melted wax ran thickly
around each holder. She blew on their guttering. There were
flowers fading in jars. She caught them and went to the back
door and threw them out. She left the back door open. Wind
swept in and out through the house. She welcomed it. It blew
upstairs too and wafted away the faint smell of death.

Her eyes were gleaming. There was nobody to see her. She
hummed a song. No music in her humming. No great sound.
Like a bee buzzing on a hot day. She cleaned out the fire, backed
it with sods of turf, then she caught the twig and brushed the
hearth. After that she went around collecting cups and plates and
glasses. She piled them all into a large basin and left them on the
table near the dresser. Then she attacked the floor. She brushed
out to the front and out through the back, flower petals and
pieces of mud from men's shoes and the smell of death and

flowers and stale stout. She stood at the back door and looked out at the fields and the lake and the land backing up to the mountain. It was the first time she had stood at the back door and thought: This is ours. All this is ours. Mine and Luke's.

Upstairs then she went, running. She let up the blind in her own room. It wasn't a big room. They were crowded into it. The double bed in it left little room for the big cupboard and the old chest of drawers where they had everything they possessed. They had lived their lives in a double bed and a chest of drawers. Only there could they be alone. To talk, to whisper. Even that, because the room next door belonged to her. The walls, the inside walls were not thick. You could hear, so even at that when the door was shut and the blankets pulled up to your chin you still had to talk easy. You were not alone. Now!

She went into Mabbina's room. She stood on the threshold looking at it. It was bathed in the red-blind light, muted, dead. The white quilt still bore the traces on it of the shape of the dead woman. She snatched it away and let it lie on the floor in a crumpled heap. Then she let the blind up. She tugged at the small window. Opened it top and bottom, and breathed in the air that was coming down from the mountain. The chairs were placed facing one another. The two of them on which the coffin had rested. It took little imagination to see the coffin between them and it unlidded and she inside in her habit, mainly folded white hands with the stark white face and the hair in the nostrils startlingly black, it seemed. She kicked over one of the chairs and the sight was gone. There were more brass candlesticks. But they were cold. There were flowers. She pitched them out of the open window. There was the white cloth on the small table with the jug of holy water and the feather in a saucer. She took off the white cloth, and the jug and the feather looked innocuous. She threw the cloth on the floor with the quilt. Then she ran at the bed. Almost feverishly she stripped it of the two white blankets and threw them away and the sheets and the pillow-cases. She piled all of them on the floor until the tick mattress lay naked and unsightly with the two stripped pillows lying squaw-ways on it.

She bent down then and encompassed the whole pile with her arms, gathered it in and went out of the door, and when she got to the head of the stairs she threw the bundle over. It landed on the floor, noiselessly, and then she went back into the room. The cupboard there was big. She opened both doors. Inside, each had a long mirror. She looked at herself. A tall girl, no longer a girl, with white excited eyes. She could see her teeth, though she wasn't laughing. It was just that she was clenching them and her lips were drawn back so that she could let her fast breaths in and out. Black silk dress and black woollen stockings and black shoes. She hated the sight of it and soon she would be done with it. She looked into the wardrobe. On top was a shelf. It smelled of moth-balls. There were hats there, three or four, old shapeless things. She threw them out, handling them distastefully. There were cardigans and a few boxes. They were cardboard shoe-boxes. She lifted the lids. Little bits of papers and a few letters and small faded things. She threw them down. Under the shelf there was a space where clothes were hanging. Dresses and skirts and one or two coats with severe black, well worn, shoes. She scooped all out. Underneath there were drawers. She pulled them open. More clothes, underwear, darned and well worn, nightdresses. It was surprising how few clothes there were there. She emptied the drawers, down on her knees, pulling and pulling until they were all piled beside her. She could smell the woman from them. Even though she was no longer there, she could smell her. She filled her arms with them and she went out to the head of the stairs and she let them fall. Three trips it took her, and when she went out with the third pile Luke was just inside the door looking up at her, his mouth open.

He looks well, she thought. He had a new black suit and a white shirt and a new cap and shoes, and there was a big black crêpe diamond sewn on his left sleeve.

He was looking up at her and his eyes were troubled.

"In the name of God, Martha," he asked, "what are you doing?"

"Getting rid of her," Martha said, throwing down the pile.

"Martha!" he said, turning quickly to close the front door and standing with his back to it. "Oh, Martha! She's only buried. You could wait. Suppose people saw."

"What about them?" Martha asked, coming down the stairs. "She's dead, Luke, and buried and we are free. Why should we leave any part of her to be reminding us? Let us do it now quick and start to live our life."

"God, Martha! "he said. "It's so sudden. You could have waited until tomorrow."

"No," she said. "This is tomorrow. Now. Here now. This is tomorrow. How long have we been waiting and saying and talking about tomorrow? This is tomorrow, Luke."

"Oh, my God, Martha," he said. "So soon! She isn't cold in the grave. Why do you do it? You don't hate somebody like that. You could have waited."

She came over to him. She put her arms about his waist. She pressed herself close to him. His eyes were still troubled.

"Luke," she said. "Even you don't know what I suffered, all these years."

"It wasn't that bad, Martha," he said. "It wasn't that bad. She was good in her way."

"She wasn't good to me," Martha said. "You don't understand, Luke. Your mind is too simple. You are happy when you can work and eat and sleep and don't let people trouble you. I was with her every day, every day. You can't understand what I suffered from her eyes. Just from her eyes, the way she looked at me. What did she do to me? She turned me into a skivvy. She battened me down with work. All the time. She tried to kill me with silence. With the looks of her eyes. So that I would weaken and go away. just that I would go away and be defeated. I knew what she wanted. She didn't want me here. She told you that. She hated the sight of me. What am I to do now? Do you want me to weep? Do you want me to tear at my breast? Do you want me to let down my hair and rake ashes from the fire and cover it? She's dead, Luke, and I'm glad. I cannot cry. She's dead and I'm glad she's dead and there is an end to her."

"Oh, Martha!" he said, pulling away from her.

She walked down to the fire, quickly, and she turned there.

206

"What's the use of being a hypocrite?" she asked. "I can't be a hypocrite. I hated the sight of her just the same way as she hated me. And I won't be happy until there is none of her left with us. Don't you understand, Luke? Have you no feeling at all of the things I went through for you?"

"I know, Martha, I know," he said. "But it wasn't that bad. She didn't mean most of it. She was a good woman in her way."

"No, no, she was not a good woman," said Martha. "That's a tale. That's a fable that ye'll build up now. Don't spit on the dead. I'm only saying these things to you. You are the only one I can say them to. For the people outside I can be demure. I can keep my mouth shut. I can draw a veil over my eyes. But not with you, Luke. You are the only one I can talk to. The only one. She rubbed that raw too. You don't know how she rubbed it raw. I prayed for a child. Every woman prays for a child. Is it my fault if we have no children? You can't know what it has meant to me, the agony I've been put through with only a glance at my belly and a glance at my eyes and a raising of the eyebrows. All that."

"Martha," he said, sitting into the chair by the table. "What's the use of hurting yourself? It doesn't matter any more."

"Oh, but it does," she said. "It matters to me. I have it inside of me and I'm getting rid of it in case I go sour. That's all. Maybe now we'll have children when she's not around watching and gloating."

He dropped his head in his hands.

She went up close to him.

"Listen, Luke," she said. "It's like being drunk to know that we are free. Just to know that we are free. What do you want most in your life? What is the single thing you have wanted most in your life?"

He didn't look up at her.

"She was only buried today, Martha," he said.

"It doesn't matter," she cried, stamping her foot. "That doesn't matter, Luke, what does that matter? This is our minute now. We'll never have another one like it. This first knowing that we are in a house and it is our house and that when we look out on the land it is our land and that we have a shop that is our

207

shop, and that from here on men will have to respect you. You, Luke, you hear! It's meaning a lot to you. All of them will have to look at you with new eyes. You're not just the great ox that worked the fields from morning until night, a great stupid ox, to whom you said, Good morning, Luke, and Good night, Luke, and Good day, Luke. You're Mister now, can't you see? You hold part of their year and their toil in your hands. If they want fertiliser, you have the credit. You can withhold it or you can grant it. You have part of their bellies and their thirst in you. Doesn't that make a difference? Why can't we look at it now? Why do we have to put it off until tomorrow to rejoice over it?"

She got on her knees in front of him and raised his head.

"It's not hate with me, Luke. You see it's not hate," she said. "It's just joy. That we are free. What does one day or two days matter to her? But they matter to us. This is the minute that will never come back to us. So what do you want, Luke? Tell me, what do you want?"

He was looking over at the wall near the dresser.

"What do I want?" he asked.

'More than anything else in the world?" she said.

"I want a tractor," he said. "I want one of them yellow tractors with the red wheels. Those long fields. Oh, those long fields, Martha, with the horse labouring in the drill. And this," he said, rising to his feet and going over and snatching the horse's collar off the peg. "You see this. All my life with this harness, I have been patching and scratching, patching and scratching, awls and waxed thread and needles and pieces cut from old boots. And the toil. I want to sit up on the seat of the tractor and the fumes of the paraffin all around me like. That's what I want, Martha. I want a tractor."

"Well, you go and buy one, Luke," she said.

"Buy one?" he asked.

"Yes," she said. "Can't you see? Tomorrow morning you can go into the town and you can walk into the place and you can say, Give me one of those tractors. And you don't even ask the price, you just take it and give him what he wants for it."

"Like that?" he asked.

"Like that," she said laughing and going over to him. "That's what I mean about it being our minute, Luke. You can have what you want. I can have what I want. Never again sink my elbows in bloody flour. Never again lug turf from the stack. Wash and mend and drain and dry and stoke. Never again."

"God, Martha," he said. "It'd be great to have a tractor. Buzz, buzz, and the thing is ploughed and the seed is sown and the hay is cut and you sitting all the time. Just sitting. Imagine that. Just sitting!"

"You'll get fat, Luke," she said. "You'll get fat and contented like a stall-fed bull so you will. And your eyebrows won't hang down from your forehead like they do." She smoothed his heavy eyebrows back with her fingers. "You'll tell people to do this and to do that and we will have a family of sons, seven sons we will have and the last one will have the gift."

"No, but a tractor costs a lot of money, Martha," he said. "A terrible lot of money. Man, with the thing itself and the plough and the belts and a trailer maybe and attaching things, why, man, it would cost near a thousand pounds."

"Well, you have a thousand pounds," she said. "You have much more than that. Can't you wake up, Luke? Think of John Willie. He was a careful man but at times he was a bit too generous. There was him and there was your mother. She always looked at a penny. You know that."

"Aye, for she had a hard time long ago," he said.

"You keep standing up for her," she said, walking away from him. "All the time. She was careful. She could have spent more. But she didn't and it's all yours and mine. I saw the books. You are well away, Luke, I tell you. Take a thousand pounds from what you have and what's in the future and it is nothing. These, all these clothes, I'm going to take them into the back and make a pile of them and pour paraffin over them and burn them, and that will be the end of her."

He stood worried, the horse-collar in his hands. He watched her bending over the pile gathering it up.

"It's so soon, Martha," he said. "She'll not rest."

"Pishreogs!" said Martha, taking a pile, walking to the back door and putting the pile into the yard. She gathered more. He stood watching her. He couldn't raise a hand to help her. She took three journeys and the clothes made a solid pile in the yard.

"You could give them away, even," he suggested, "to somebody that might have use for them?"

"No," she said. "No! And have me meeting them some time that I would be abroad and the sight of them making my heart burn. No! I will not. There'll just be an end. It's like a feast."

She got the tin of oil and she went out and she poured it over the pile. Then she came back and got the matchbox and she went out and she lit one and she threw it. The pile exploded and then flamed and black smoke rose from it. Luke was worried. She seemed to be feverish, her eyes were so bright.

"Now," she said, back inside. "Look at it! Now we will have a different life, Luke. I tell you the sun is going to shine in our house any more. You'll see."

She ran up the stairs again. She looked at the emptied room, gutted-looking with drawers and cupboard doors gaping. Nothing left, except the holy water and the feather and the two small prayer-books on the table. She gathered those up and she stood at the door and she went down the stairs with them in her hand. The front door was open and Joseph was standing there. He was looking at Luke, Luke moving uncomfortably with the huge horse-collar in his hand, his eyes not meeting the eyes of the boy, his neck red. Joseph looked from him to the burning pile he could see through the open back door.

Her face hardened. She came down the stairs. She drew his eyes to her. He has soft eyes, soft eyes like a dog, she thought. He better not forgive me. I don't want him to forgive me.

"We're clearing out a little," she said. Her voice was loud. "Just clearing out a little."

He looked at the pyre outside before he answered her. There was hurt in his eyes and then the look of them was veiled. If he would get angry and shout or something, she would feel for him. But he didn't. He looked at the books she was grasping in her hand.

"Would you let me have the books, Martha he asked. He didn't even reach his hand for them. If she went out and threw them on top of the burning clothes, he wouldn't have protested. She knew that too. That's what maddened her.

She walked down and over.

"Yes," she said. "You can have them." She held them out.

"Thank you very much," he said. "Thank you." He opened them. They opened at places, definite places. They were well worn. The years that fingers had turned their pages were evident from them. There were small holy pictures marking some of the pages. Joseph turned some of them very gently with his fingers and then he walked with them into his own room, and closed the door softly after him.

She was boiling. Her hands were clenched. Her eyes were slits with the anger that was burning in her. He had spoiled the day.

"Didn't he spoil the day? Didn't he?" she furiously asked Luke.

He was really alarmed.

"Martha, what's come over you?" he asked. "What in the name of God has come over you?" He threw down the collar. He walked over to her. He caught her shoulders in his hard hands. He hurt her.

She winced under his grip. Then she relaxed.

"I don't know, Luke," she said. "I don't know. I thought I would have it all done before he came home. Before even you came home. I had to do it. You understand that, Luke."

"Yes, Martha," he said. "Maybe I can see. But it's hard for him. They were very close. Don't forget that, they were very close. And I promised I would look after him. Don't forget that, Martha. I promised that, and I won't forget. Remember that, Martha."

"All right, Luke," she said. "I'm sorry. I'm sorry. Close the back door on the smoke and I'll ready something to eat."

She walked to the fire. He closed the door on it. It was burning well. It didn't take long to burn a person out of a house.

Then he went back to her. She was happy again. She was humming.

Twenty-Two

"IT'S VERY PECULIAR," Joseph said.

"How?" she asked.

"The sheets that it is written on. There is only one full-sized sheet, lined, from a cheap sort of copy. And there are stains on that. All the rest are bits and pieces. Thin paper, like the paper that cigarettes are made of, and they have funny smells too. Here!" He held one of the sheets under her nose.

"Funny," she said. "Sort of like the spices that you put in a Christmas cake."

"That's it! That's it," said Joseph. "The envelope is very dirtied and there are thousands of markings on it. It has come a long way. A very long way."

"Read it," she said.

" 'If you are still there,' " he read, " 'if you still remember me. Everybody in the world seems to be dead. A terrible thing happened to me. I think it is the worst thing that happened to me. Many things here happened to me. I think I have had everything that could happen, happen. You can go down and you can go up. It's easier to go down than it is to go up. So, even if you go up, what then? You are bound to be bored. That is what I tell myself. I was writing to you, wasn't I, and I was guessing that John Willie was reading me for you and interpreting. Yes, I remember that.

" 'I was very sick. You say you are strong, like I am a very big strong man. I am not afraid of anything. Once I think back to the brawl long ago, when that big fellow Suck beat me into the

212

ground. That time. Things I have seen and done since that make it look so honest. So easy. I think of many things that I have learned and I think of Suck again and of the things I could do to him. So easily. Maybe it is as well I didn't know all that before. Maybe it is. You know the rain. That rain that you call rain. That isn't rain. That's only a mist. The other rain. That goes on for many months. I know that rain. And then the sun. You think you know the sun. You don't know the sun. You haven't an idea about the sun. So you don't know the sun and you don't know the rain. Or the little fellows that breed in the sun and the rain. Once I saw them, little wrigglers. Some ship, that the surgeon says, Come in, and I go and we talk, time I was a sailor. He is young. He says, Look in there. I look into the piece and there the wrigglers. Too small to see on your own. Put the glass on them and they are terrible things. They can get into you. I got one, maybe a million. I don't know. You know the cold you get, the pleasant gentle fever of a cold. Just air whirling and blowing about your bones and you go to bed and drink hot poitín. Well, that's like the sun and the rain, you don't know anything about. This cold is really something. All the flesh is turned back from your bones so that they can blow cold winds on it. They even scoop out the marrow and blow on that and put it back. And then your flesh is drained away with the heat. When you get that you have to drink. That's what they say. It's the only poison, they say, so you drink to kill this. Not like you drinking and feeling it warm in your chest and down into your stomach.

" 'Other things too. To dream in the day. That's the thing. To dream the day away. Not lying back on the heather with the wind and the sun on your face. No, this is dirty. This is very sweaty and afterwards you are built around a hollow that groans and aches. Oh, things. One time I look at my hand. I can't believe it belongs to me. Terrible hands I used to have. Very strong. Could wrap them around an oar. What happens? So I wake this night. Where am I? I am lying on stones and there is rain and when I open my eyes I can see the feet of people passing by. Bare feet. Nobody bends down. Like the man in the Testament story. Nobody bends passing. Some of the feet are

213

wrapped. I hear strange calls. I smell queer smells. The sound of voices. Ununderstandable. Gibberish, but they understand one another. I try to raise myself to my feet. I only get as far as the knees. Then I go back again. I smell things that you do not know about. Strange fruits and strange foods and strange after-effects. All people are the same. Honest. There's no difference at all between people. That is profound. Makes you laugh. Hah? You travel all around the world to find that people are all the same wherever you go. This is not right. If people are different colours from you, damn it they should be different. If they have eyes turned up and high cheeks and thick lips or thin lips, if they are the colour of night or early morning or ivory or roasted pork or what, they shouldn't be the same as people you can remember. Why should a fuzzy with curly hair be exactly the same as a fellow you know at home with red hair and big teeth and the same laugh? This is funny, I am thinking, on my knees supporting myself with my hands. There is water flowing over my fingers in the channel. Odd things flowing with the water. Odd strange things. Then I see feet beside me and I am hefted up. One man on each side. Must be men. Very strong. Very strong. And I am loaded away. I feel the rain on my neck. I feel the clothes that I wear are sticking into me. Very light clothes. As if you had none. What am I doing? I don't care where I am going.

" 'You know when the sun comes out after three days' rain. Your sun, not this one. It is sometimes good to wake up. Sometimes you don't want to wake up. This is a bed. Haven't seen one for ages. I say hello to the bed. Coarse linen, like the lady that used to wear the flour-bag petticoat. That laugh. Feel a mattress too. Not soft. Kind of hard. All the light is coming into the place through slits. All slits letting in the light. Maybe I am at home. Like last time I remember in the rain and the water and the smells, I thought of what. Thought of many things but thought of home last time out on the lake with that girl. That was wind and rain, but washing rain and cleaning wind. Saw you then. Never forget you like that. Like a carbolic dream. See. All clean. All decent. All fresh. There is a rustle, rustle, rustle. So used to sounds. Can't open my eyes with the slits and the pain.

Rustle. I remember rustles. Many rustles through life. Life is always rustling. Paper and cloth and this cloth. I think back to rustles I have heard. Easy with the eyes closed. All wrong for here but I wager long dress, silky sort of stuff, rustling, and I open the eyes. I am very pleased. I was right. See the long black gown with sort of blue draped down it. Then look up. Starched affair. Hah. Right in the hands of heaven. There is a face. I look at this and I say a thing. I say, God, there's a real Irish kisser, and the mouth seems to open with a smile and I hear her calling, Sister, Sister, he's awake, what did I tell you? Didn't I tell you he was? Was what? Irish of course. I told them. How did you know? Oh, the curly hair, and besides, the curses. She put her hands over where her ears were beneath the cloth. Only the Irish can curse like that after all poor Saint Patrick did for them and all. What the hell are you doing in here, in hell I mean? You should be at home at home. Oh, home! she says. There, didn't I tell you? And there are two more of them. Where are you from, who are you, what part? I say I have no name. I have no country. I don't belong to time and place. I belong to the middle air. I have no name. He's raving, the poor man. Now wasn't I right about him? He won't talk, but I'll get it out of him. He shouldn't be talking. He should be sleeping. He's very weak. Tell us your name and the place so that we can write to your mother. I have no mother. Your father then. I have no father. I have no one. I don't want anyone. I just want to be alone.

" 'They went away. But they came back. Day after day. So nice. So polite. In this dreadful place, so clean as if they were scrubbed every five minutes. It's all wrong. Why do they end up here? The race has no business to be sending them out to places like this. They are everywhere like the locusts. That's right, the one says, the locusts of God we are and we'll eat you up too until we find out all about you.

" 'Then the terrible thing. One day she comes. An old paper she said. Bet there's a bit of news about your county in it even. Trying to guess from my accent, but it is too layered over with the scum talk of the continents. It is an old paper. It is years old. So strange to read it. All about things you had forgotten existed.

215

You see people doing just the things they always did centuries ago when you were human. I read this all of it. So strange. And then in the little bits of news, you know, the places where they put snippets that never are big enough to be good stories. There the little paragraph said about a man called John William Baun found dead near the lake with the gun lying beside him. How many years ago? How many years ago? Why didn't I know? It has to be him. There is nobody else but him living around that place. I don't know. All this way. Here and you read a little bit about John Willie dying like that. It can't be. Because he was indestructible. I think about him. And I writing and being smart, saying John Willie is reading the letter. Oh, John Willie. Why, she says, what's wrong with you? You're crying. It's a lie, a lie, a lie, I say. I don't cry. I have never cried. I am sick. I am weak. I am drained. I don't know what it is about. She takes the paper. She examines it from cover to cover. But she can't find it of course. Is it this, she asks, and is it that, and is it the other? I say, please leave me alone.

"'This is the end, see. You may not ever get this. I don't know. I have been writing it away while I sit in a cane chair under the veranda of this small hospital. I am getting better. I am very sorry about John Willie. I don't know where I go now. I have learned a lot of things. I have seen a lot of things, but all that it means to me is that I am about five stone lighter than I used to be. There doesn't seem to be any future in sin no more than there is in anything else. If it is sin. All life is a sin. We should be all squelched before we have a chance to wreak things on the world. The world would be better off completely unoccupied. A few maybe like John Willie maybe and maybe yourself, and perhaps Joseph and these daft holy dillies here who should be at home having babies instead of killing themselves over the heathens. I don't know. This is maybe the last now, because I don't want you to remember me. What happens a leaf when it is whipped off a tree? It's blown about a bit, I suppose, and its colour changes and it loses weight and it ends up somewhere, like closed up in a book until it is a delicate tracery skeleton, or mulched into the earth so that the same tree will suck the little good that's in it out of it. That's all.'

"That's all," Joseph said.

The seagulls were screaming below. You couldn't hear the sea, it was so far out.

"Soon, Joseph," said Breeda, "there will be none at all of you left. Bart is gone."

"No, I wouldn't think so," said Joseph.

"He'd be better gone so," said Breeda.

"Why are you so hard on him?" Joseph asked.

"That's only my mouth," she said.

"Oh," said Joseph.

She wondered if she could ever acquire Joseph's tranquillity. Was it tranquillity? She didn't know. She wished she could see his face. People said his face was very thin. No wonder, Bidelia said, and the way he is treated by that upstart. She had gone in to say a last word of sympathy coming home from the funeral and what did she see, dear? She saw that one actually burning up all Mabbinia's clothes. It was a scandal, dear, a positive scandal, and all the poor people that could have done with an ould skirt or a blouse or a dress even. All that gone up in smoke. A wonder she let them bury her at all, dear, that she didn't cremate her out in the yard. You mark my words. Having her victorious face leering at you over a half-pound of margarine. Oh, the good days are gone. It's only the best people that are taken away.

"Why are you tranquil, Joseph?" she asked.

"It's not tranquillity," Joseph said. "Is a fire tranquil or the sea even on a calm day? That's all. I have no words."

"Do you enjoy being made to suffer?" she asked.

"Not that," Joseph said. "It's something deeper than that. It's once you get the mind for the right thing, that nothing material matters, yourself less than anything perhaps, sort of."

"I'm sorry," she said.

"No, no," Joseph said. "It's just I haven't the right way of saying. For all I know I haven't the right way of thinking."

She sighed.

"We'll go back," she said.

Then she heard Joseph saying, "Why, hello, what brought you out this far?"

217

And she heard a small voice saying, "I saw you coming. I followed you. Mammie doesn't know."

"Well, she should know," Joseph said. "You should have told her."

"Who's that?" Breeda asked.

"Come here," she heard Joseph say. She couldn't distinguish a sound but she could feel the air being disturbed by a body.

"Shake hands with your Aunt Breeda," she heard Joseph say.

"Hello, Aunt Breeda," the voice said. She put out her hand and a small fat sticky hand was put into hers. A hot little hand.

"Hello," she said, "and who are you?"

"I'm Bart," the voice said. "I followed Uncle Joe."

I'm Bart!

"The gentleman shaking hands with you," Joseph said, "is about three foot high. He is not wearing shoes or stockings although he should be. His legs are fat and muscular and both knees are scarred with a few fresh cuts overlying the scars. Above that he has short trousers, blue in colour, that have recently been rent by briars. There's braces holding up the trousers, and the remains of what was once a white shirt, now, alas, sadly stained by the juice of the blackberry. Out of the shirt is growing a nice fat neck, well browned with curls growing well down on the neck. What can be seen of the chin and the lower face juts a bit with stern resolution. The nose is short and pug and the eyes are big and blue. And now tell us where you got the blackberries."

"Up the way," said your man.

She was still holding his hand.

"So Bart is not dead," she said.

"No fear," said Joseph. "I wish you could see him. He's so like that you could laugh. His bottom jaw juts out just the same. He has the soft eyes of his mother though."

"It doesn't matter what happens to us," she said. "There is always someone else."

"That's right," said Joseph.

"If you come back with me, Uncle Joe," the fellow said, "I'll tell her then."

"Ah, but," said Joseph, "that's sort of cheating. It means that you are afraid to tell her on your own, whereas you came away on your own."

"That's mixed up," he replied to that.

Joseph laughed. She was very pleased to hear him laughing.

"Help me up, Bart," Breeda said.

"Can't you get up on your own?" he asked.

"I can, I suppose," Breeda said. "But gentlemen are supposed to help ladies."

"That's soupy," he said.

"Lord, he is like his father," Breeda said, laughing.

"But I'll help you," Bart said then, "because Uncle Joe is making faces at me, and I suppose I'm bold again."

Joseph groaned.

Breeda laughed. She said, "No, he's making faces at you because I'm blind and that's why he wants you to help me."

"Oh," he said, after thinking it over. "That's it. You can't see at all?"

"No," she said.

"But you have eyes," he said,

"Yes," she said.

"You must be very old," he said, "like the sheep-dog we had at home with my grandfather. He was old. He couldn't see. It was sad. My uncle came with a gun. He's out under a tree. I put flowers with him."

"I hope you'll do the same with me when they come to shoot me," she said.

"Oh, no, they wouldn't," he said. "You're a person."

"Does the day seem far brighter, Joseph she asked as they walked towards the road.

"Well, it's not as dark as it was," Joseph said.

"Down a bit away here," said Bart. "I'll show ye the blackberries. Way in a bit. In an old place where a house was. Do you know?"

"I do," said Breeda. "We used to live there one time."

"Did you really?" he asked. "Then the blackberries must belong to you?"

"Oh, no," she said. "A man bought the house. They belong to him."

"Well, if he can't see us," said Bart, "it isn't stealing."

Breeda laughed and Joseph laughed as they followed him into the blackberry bushes.

Twenty-Three

HE PAUSED BEFORE he pushed the door. He looked at the two cargo boats lined up beside the docks. There was great activity: cranes clanking, donkey engines steaming, men shouting, the horses restive under the shafts of the coal carts, and road dust and coal dust rising over it all and nearly blotting out the spring sun. Then he pushed his way in.

He went past the grocery counter to the back where the high stools were.

"Hello, Joe," he said to the big bald man behind the counter.

"Ah, Carrymore," he said. "You're back, are you?"

"Have you the goods?" he asked.

"Where's the van?" Joe asked.

"Outside," Carrymore said.

"Fine," said Joe. Then he opened a door into the yard and roared out, "Hey, Palsy, load up the stuff in Carrymore's van. Have a drink while you're waiting. You were away on a long trip this time."

"That's right," said Carrymore. "Half over Connacht, Joe."

"Good deal?" Joe asked.

"Too easy," said Carrymore.

"Man, the way some people make money," said Joe. "And people like myself have to work for it."

Seven men came in. They greeted Joe with nods of the head. They greeted Carrymore boisterously. Mick, Pat, Jim, Jack, Jerry, John, Joe. Oh-ho and he's back. Where's the roller? Saw the hearse outside. Still going? Do you have holes in the boards and walk it or has the thing got an engine? There should be a law against it. Where away now, Carrymore? Where away is it? Back west this time. Oh-ho, that's new, isn't it? That's right, new ground. Completely new ground. Poor country though. Have to take it on tick. All on tick. No bloody fear. Eggs for jam, wool for lamb, fowls for towels, you know me – I carry more than any man in my van. Have to be going. In a hurry today. Very special. Man, stay and have another one. Are you running away? Soon be in the Pioneers. That's a laugh. Drink it out of a shoe. But he got away from them. Be seeing you. Keep it clean. Watch the peasant types. They'll diddle you. Gluggers and tar, that's the men to break the travelling shopkeeper. Laugh.

Palsy was putting the last of the stuff in the van. A thin pale man with a cap worn with the peak over the side of his head. Clothes too big for him. Big slack behind on his breeches. Always smiling and his teeth pointed and black. Carrymore assisted him with the last of the load, banged the doors shut, threw him a half-crown, and then got in behind the wheel.

He was excited.

The engine was in good form today too. It started on a pull of the wire and he let in the clutch and started away. He settled himself and went down by the docks. He waved at many men who greeted him with shouts from blackened faces, startlingly white teeth. Sometimes he liked the town. He liked to come back to it after having been away for long times in the country. He liked the warmth of shops and electric light in the windows. When he was away he most times slept in the back of the van with the groceries and oddments. It was funny to sleep in a place like that, but he had slept in worse places. Sometimes he slept in the house of a friendly man in the country. But he liked his own room that he had in the town. He liked to come back to it. It was all right.

Each month that passed he had meant to tackle the road to Boola, but he always found a reason for putting it off. Maybe because no place can be the same as your memory. Maybe because memory can be a painful thing. Maybe because he wanted to be orientated. It didn't matter now. He was on the road to it. He broke into song. He could hardly hear himself above the sound of the noisy engine, but there was a lot of sound in his chest, so he knew he must be singing.

He got the van cheap. He had fixed it up himself. He had a mechanical bent and he had learned a lot about all sorts of things. His provisions rattled behind him. There were spices and currants and raisins and soap and shoelaces and meal and sweets and hairpins, chocolate and paraffin, everything that a woman needed in a house that was far away from shops. He grinned when he thought what effect he would have in the valley of Boola which had always been served by the establishment of John Willie Baun. Well, John Willie Baun was no longer there and his heirs would have to take their chances in this hard commercial world. He laughed at that. Out by the long road the van went, leaving the suburbs of the town behind. Into green places and woodlands and long silver beaches glinting occasionally far away to his left. Up hills and down hills and winding ways. He could have stopped at many places, little villages and small towneens that served them, but he was anxious now to get to Boola and be done with it for once and for all. If you have something in your stomach you have to vomit to get rid of it and then your stomach is the better for it. But he wasn't the same man. That's why he was afraid to face it. But that didn't matter either. He had been to many places. He had seen many things.

Why should a small buried village mean anything to him, beyond what he had seen?

And yet when he turned off the sea road a long way back and chugged his way up the high hills towards it; when he saw the top of Boola emerging from a cloud; when he could nearly count the sheep that were grazing precariously up at the top of it, he couldn't restrain the quickened beating of his heart or the dryness that came to his mouth. This made him marvel. Wouldn't you think a fellow like himself had no emotions left, that the sight of an oul hill would leave him unmoved? Godammit to hell, he had seen mountains that Boola would have only seemed like a pimple on them. It wasn't a mountain in the proper sense. It was only a barren hillock if it came to that. All right. So there was nothing to marvel at.

223

Nor when he came to the top of the hill was there anything to marvel at, but because the engine was steaming from the climb, he decided that she would need cooling, so he stopped her and let her rest and got on to the road and looked below him, standing there, his hands on his hips, his teeth clenched, saying, Well, all right, there it is, a scruffy little village in the middle of nowhere. The sun was shining on the white houses. He could see the road in and the houses on each side and the river below the bridge and it with the sun glinting off it. All right. And he could see the long shape of the shop and the house looking up at him with blank unfriendly eyes. And behind was the lake and he could see the few boats drawn up on the shore and upturned so that the rain would run off them. And behind them the lake, lying peacefully embracing its islands, with the bare birches backgrounded by the green forest trees and the holly that remained green all the time. Over to his left he could see the road that went lazily to the sea, and the small square of ground where they buried their dead. Well, that's that, he thought, now I have seen it.

He got back into the van and held the wheel tightly. He wondered with panic, Will I go away? Will I turn on the road and go back the way I have come and forget this place? I have seen it. It would he easy to bypass it. Why? What fear was on him? He was a man that feared no soul or sinner on the face of the earth. He had met the best of them and the worst of them, and to hell and damnation with them.

The engine nearly stalled he started off so fiercely. Then he cooled off and let her coast down the hill, out of gear. The wind swished by his ears. He knew the road so well that he could let the car make its own way nearly. Who would be the first person he would see? The superstitions of the sailors were with him. He hoped it wouldn't be a red-headed woman. But then as far as he knew there was only one red-headed woman in the valley and from what he had heard she too was dead, so there could be no redheaded woman.

The hill came down almost into the village.

Where it turned into the street of the village he put her into gear and was going quite fast when the boy ran almost in front of his wheels. He was chasing a small pup. The pup had a ball in his mouth. The car slewed sideways as he shoved on everything he could and then it stopped, shuddering. The boy had swerved to the screaming of the rubber and the clashing of gears. He now stood at the side of the road. Carrymore leaned out of the window and shouted at the boy. "You bloody little bastard!" he shouted. "Do you want to be killed?" He expected the child to take to his heels but the boy didn't. He stood there with his hands behind his back and he looked boldly at the man that cursed him. His jacket and trousers were well worn and he wore heavy clog boots that looked a bit too big for him.

Carrymore got out of the van. He walked over to him.

"I've a good mind," he said, "to give you a wallop."

The boy just kept looking at him.

"Why didn't you look where you were going?" Carrymore asked him. He was more frightened than the boy was. That's what made him angry. It would have taken very little for him to be squelched under the wheels.

"How could I look where I was going," the boy asked, "when I was looking at the dog?"

"Well," said Carrymore. Then he thought there wasn't much answer to his logic unless he hit him and he wasn't mad enough now.

"Hop in there," he ordered him. "I'll take you to your oul fella and let him wallop you."

"In the yoke, is it?" the boy asked, very pleased.

"Yes," said Carrymore, and in a twinkling he was around and in the door with the door opened and banged and he was pulling at the gear lever.

Carrymore got in.

"Where?" he asked.

"Below," the boy said, pointing ahead. "What's that for?"

"That's the gear lever," said Carrymore. "There below?"

"And what's that for?" he asked.

"Godammit," said Carrymore, "where do you live"

The boy's eyes widened. "Down there," he said, pointing at the shop.

225

"Is it the shop?" Carrymore asked.

"Yes," said the boy. "What happens when you pull this thing?"

"That does," said Carrymore, pulling it, and the engine started.

"Oh, man," said the boy leaning back and pretending he had a wheel in his hands too and buzzing with his lips.

Carrymore coasted down to the shop, swung widely and drew up outside the door.

It was the same as ever. The same tin advertisements. The same whitewash, seemingly the same bottles and groceries in the window. "Come on," he said, alighting and taking the reluctant boy by the arm. "Is it right in the shop? What's he doing in the shop this hour of the day? Why isn't he out ploughing?"

He didn't give the boy time to answer. He went in the door and released him. There were no customers. Just a girl behind the counter with her back turned. He walked over and then she turned and she looked at him. Her eyes widened. Her hand came up to her throat, her face paled and her other hand held on to the counter.

"Hello, Sheila," he said. He sat on one of the high stools. He looked at her. She was still young, youth fading a little but still young. Her hair was short. It was shining. It was held back over each ear by two slides. One slide was pink and the other one was white. They were shaped like dogs.

"Bart," she said, "Bart," and then she rested her head on her hand. He could see her breast rising and failing, rising and falling. She was wearing a green blouse.

"You still got the pin," he said.

She looked up then.

"Yes," she said. "I still have the pin." She laughed. Not a laugh really. A sort of gasp of a thing. She put both elbows on the counter and she let her head fall into her hands. "It's so sudden," she said. "So sudden." Even with her eyes closed she was seeing his face. The curls gone far back on the forehead. The face very lean so that most of the bones showed. Hair gone grey at the sides, where it wanted to be cut about his ears. And over the

226

whole face a sort of yellow tan, lines deep drawn from the nose to the mouth; from the mouth farther out, down deep into the chin on each side; but the eyes were the same, looking and looking.

"Oh, Bart," she said.

"It's not Bart any more," he said. "Men call me Carrymore. That's me, see, Carrymore."

She looked up. She was calmer.

"I always knew you would come home some time. That you would come home always no matter what they said," she said.

"Did you?" he asked.

There was a hand plucking at his trousers.

"Hey," the boy was saying, "are you going to tell her?"

Carrymore looked down at him.

"Tell her, is it?" pointing with his thumb.

The boy nodded.

He looked at Sheila.

"This is yours?" he asked.

She nodded her head. She didn't have to add to it.

Carrymore turned on his stool. He pointed. "Go back there," he said to the boy. The boy was puzzled. He dutifully walked back. "That'll do," Carrymore said. "Now turn around." He turned around.

He hadn't properly looked at him before. He did now. The curly hair, the set of the mouth, the pug nose and the thick neck going into the shirt. Carrymore slapped his thigh, and then he started to laugh, slapping his thigh. She waited behind him. The boy was puzzled. He put his head on one side. He laughed, too.

"God," said Carrymore, "it's as funny as hell. Like looking into a mirror that can take you back over the years." Then he stopped laughing. "Come here," he said. The boy came over. "Now listen," said Carrymore. "If I ever see you running before cars again I'll kick the backside off you. Do you hear that?"

"All right," said the boy.

"What's your name?" he asked.

"Bart," said the boy.

"On my oath you are!" said Carrymore. "On my oath you are, and I hope you grow up to be as good a man as your oul fella." He winked at Sheila. "Will you have lemonade?" he asked him then.

"Yes," said Bart. "One of the big bottles."

"Girl," said Carrymore, "pour the gentleman out a large bottle of lemonade." Then he sat back a bit and looked at him again. "So you're Bart," he said. "Well, I'm Carrymore."

"Carrymore," the boy said.

"Why are you Carrymore?" Sheila asked. She was pouring out the lemonade. Her hand was shaking. The top of the bottle was hitting the glass. Carrymore reached one of his hands and covered her hand until the glass stopped tinkling. Then he took it away.

"Because I carry more than any other travelling man in Ireland, that's why," he said. "I have a van. I am a travelling shop. I am as free as the air." He paused then and said, "My mother is dead?"

"Yes," said Sheila.

"And John Willie?"

"John Willie too," she said.

"Everyone is dead," he said, "including Bart O'Breen."

"Oh no I'm not," said the boy. "I'm not dead," and then lemonade went up his nose and he was sputtering. Carrymore laughed. "No," he said, "fair enough you're not dead. Have you a gun, Sheila?" he asked then.

"A gun?" she questioned him.

"Yes," he said. "Wouldn't you like to shoot me?"

She shook her head. She turned away.

"All right," he said. "That's fine. That's a start. You don't want to shoot me. Who is in the shop besides yourself?"

"Luke's Martha," she said.

He got up, he walked about, looking at the shelves and the counters. He shook his head.

"What's wrong?" he asked. "It's not as good. Something wrong."

"Well, she's not John Willie," Sheila said, "and she's not your mother. She doesn't kind of know. She hasn't sort of the way. She's a bit abrupt."

"Ho-ho," said Carrymore, and then stood still as the door from the other house opened and Martha came in from behind. He stood where the light of the door fell on him. He saw her before she saw him. Her hair was pulled back tightly on her head. She wore a severe blouse, brown in colour, up around her neck. Her shoulders sloped. Her face was severe too. The skin seemed to be tightened on the bridge of her nose. He stood there grinning until her eyes found him. He saw the light of recognition leaping in them and then the light was veiled. She was very casual.

"Oh, it's you," she said. He could see thoughts working in her. He thought he knew her. What danger is there here? The second son. Will he claim anything? Will he live with us? Will he this, will he that, and how will I say this, and how will I say that, and I will watch, and watch.

"Aren't you very pleased to see me, Martha?" he asked, walking over to her.

"Naturally, Bart," she said. "We are all pleased to see you."

"That lightens the load," said Carrymore. "And how is Luke and the family?"

"Luke is well," she said, "and if by the family you mean Joseph, we rarely see him, but when we see him he is well."

"I see," said Carrymore. "No fatted calf, eh, Martha?" He laughed.

"We are pleased to see you," she said. "If you are staying long we will give you a meal."

"I'll take that," said Carrymore. "I'll take that. I'll go and rest my old eyes on the people. I'll be back, Sheila. I want to see you. Come on, son," he said then to the boy. "Come on and show an old man about this interesting village of yours."

Bart finished off his lemonade hurriedly.

"I'll take care of him," he said to Sheila. She was still looking at him as if he was going to vanish any minute. He laughed at her look, caught the boy about the arm and went into the sunlight with him.

Twenty-Four

SUPPOSE YOU ARE going on a great journey, and away at the end of it there is a tall hill with the vague figure of a person on top of it. You know that when you reach this figure you will have found rest and peace. So in order to reach the hill you have to go away from it, away, away until it is out of your sight. And you are cut and beaten on the way, but from each beating you rise afterwards. Sometimes you have to fight so that you will break free. And you will cross many thorny ways and deep-flowing rivers with terrible currents. You must go through those rivers and sometimes they are fast and clean and they don't dirty you, but sometimes they have only the appearance of rivers; they are really mud flats with a few inches of water flowing on top of them. All right. You wade through this mud that comes up to your neck. You are up to your neck in it and your whole body is soiled, and leeches below are sucking at you and draining you, and into your nostrils there comes a terrible stink of rottenness and disease, and yet you can pause in all this mud and embrace it with your body and feel its flaccidity on your lips and you turn your head away from the mountain in case you should be seen. But at the back of your mind, there is the sure knowledge of this clean person on top of the hill, waiting for you patiently, so after a time, reluctantly, you turn and claw your way out of the mud and go to the opposite side and set out once more.

It will take a lot of rain to clean your clothes and your body. Your body will only be cleaned by fevers burning it from the inside and a hot punishing sun burning it from the outside. And on you go falling to your knees and rising again until you have turned your face to the star that is shining over the hill that you cannot see. But you follow in its direction.

There is a terrible journey before you, of impenetrable briars that you must pull apart with your naked hands, and sucking swamps and places littered with big boulders, some of which you have to push aside with all the strength of your shoulders, but bit by bit and piece by piece you come in sight of the hill. It is there. You are looking at it from a different direction and you hurry and hurry, until it is nearer and you can see the person standing up on it, just the size of a pin sticking in a mound of matter. And you come out of the valley and you try to climb the hill. It is very hard climbing. More often you fall back three paces for the one you go forward, but gradually you claw your way up it, and your knowledge of the person on top of it becomes stronger and stronger. If it wasn't for the person you would let go and fall back into the valley and drown in a bog, because now there is no point in your existing unless you can reach the figure on the hill.

And you go up and up and up until you pull yourself over the lip. You have to lie there for some time just feasting your eye on the person. You are not seen yet because the blind eyes are look- ing over your head. You raise yourself to your knees and then to your feet and you gain strength and you walk forward and you say to her:

"Hello, Breeda!" And what happens?

"What happens?" Bart asked, almost savagely. "Nothing hap- pens. You just know I am here and it means nothing at all to you. Nothing at all to you."

"Please, Bart," she said. "I cannot help how I feel. I just don't feel anything. Anything at all. I just don't feel anything."

"Fine," he said. "Fine. If it wasn't for the thought of you, I wouldn't have come back. I was down in the dregs of the world and you were a clean person, so clean. And even that you were blind and I blinded you, that was good because if I hadn't blind- ed you, you wouldn't be clean, you would have been like all the others, just the body of a woman, and I'm sick of bodies, sick and tired of bodies. I've seen enough bodies to last four lifetimes."

"Bart," she said, twisting her hands, "you can't be blaming me for yourself. It's not my fault."

"All right, it's not your fault!" he said.

"You cannot put a person up on a hill and drag yourself to a person. That's not faith. That's all false faith. That's idolatry. If you turned your eye to God on a hill, that would be different. That would be much better. That might be your real answer."

"Gods!" he said. "Listen, I've seen them in all sorts and sizes. Bits of poles and trunks of trees; gods without hands and gods with twenty-four hands, all of them predatory and cruel and unconscious of the poor vomiting septic people that worship them. I cannot feel for a dream. I cannot have faith in anything except reality. What's wrong? Is it because of him, little Bart below? Is it because of him? Did that hurt you so much or what? What is it? I have never spoken like this to a living creature, least of all a woman. What is it?"

"Oh, no, it's not Bart," she said. "How could it be? Can't you leave me alone? Leave me up on the hill and go down away. Because maybe I'm up on a hill myself and that's where I want to stay, but I don't want anybody climbing up to me. Please leave me alone, Bart. Just don't be making me feel I am the fault of you."

He looked at her. She was crying. He bent on the road and took up a stone and flung it into the river below.

Little Bart looked up, startled, at him.

"What are you doing?" he shouted down to the child. "Jay," he shouted back, "I have a trout trapped here in a pool. I'm building a wall around him. I'll have him soon."

"Trapping a trout," said Bart. "All right, Breeda, forgive me. I'm sorry. Maybe I shouldn't have spoken. But to see you after all this time. You couldn't see me. You couldn't see the shine in my eyes or the panting in my chest or the way my legs trembled. And then your hand is cool and you just say, almost like Martha, "Oh, it's you."

She said: "I said 'Hello, Bart. You have come back.'"

"What's the difference?" he asked.

There was silence between them.

"Ah, well," he said. "That's what life is like. The thing you look forward to most, when you reach it and try to eat it you find out that it's only ashes after all, the ashes of the past, although it should be the present, like the Dies Irae, singing the song of the dead, hah?"

"Bart," she said.

"Right," he said, "we'll call it off. Where's Joseph? Where is he? What has been happening to him?"

"I don't know," she said. "I haven't seen him for a long time. They say he's not happy below. That's what they say."

He snorted. "Who's happy? Nobody. Maybe he enjoys that?"

"He's not like that," she said.

"Don't tell me," he jeered, "that holy Joseph was walking up my back with you while I was gone."

"That's not worthy of even the worst part of you," she said.

"All right. I'm sorry again. Hear that. How many times in all have I had to say to you 'I'm sorry?' Fine. We'll part. Next time we meet I might be more rational." He shouted. "Hey, young fellow, come on, we're going back to your mother."

"Aw, here," young Bart replied. "I almost got him, Carrymore. Another two minutes and I'd have got him."

"Why does he call you Carrymore?" she asked.

"Because that's my name," he said. "Big Bart is dead. They called me that in the town, the citizens. It's better that way. You call me Carrymore too, will you?"

"Yes," she said.

"Better be going. Come on, Bart!"

"Aw, listen!" the boy replied.

"Come on," Carrymore shouted, "or you'll get it. I warned you."

He started reluctantly to come out of the river, looking back.

"He's all right. You should see him," Carrymore said. "He's the only good deed of my whole lifetime."

Bart joined them by the wall.

"That's the lesson you have to learn, Bart," Carrymore said. "Even if you got the trout he would probably have been diseased anyhow or there would have been something wrong with him. Goodbye, Breeda."

"Goodbye, Bart."

They walked away from her. She could hear them. The boy was talking and Bart was answering him. There was a similar timbre in their voices. Walking away. Walking away. She couldn't make it feel that it meant anything at all to her. The hoarse voice that should have meant so much; that she had heard so often in her dreams. It was walking away on two legs and it didn't mean a thing to her. Am I dead of feeling? she wondered. Is my mind just nothing at all? What's wrong with me?

Bart turned once below to look back at her. The blind girl with the straight hair and the narrow face, lined now to his wonder (she should have remained always very young), and a blue blouse with a brown skirt, and bare legs already tanned a bit from the spring sun. It would happen to me, he thought, and then he turned away. He felt bitter about it. He thought of Martha below waiting for him. He would make her suffer a bit, he thought.

Then he thought: All the same, even if, it's good to be home, and he remembered the face of Sheila welcoming him with the pin in her breast. That made him smile and he rubbed the curly head of his son with his hand.

234

Twenty-Five

AFTERWARDS BREEDA WONDERED if events would have come to a head even if Bidelia hadn't lost her temper. They would have happened anyhow, she supposed, but Bidelia was the one who set the torch.

A Saturday in April it was that she went down to the shop to face Martha.

It was a busy day. There were about four women and three men, with their baskets and string bags and paper bags and canvas bags all waiting to get supplies. Martha was working and Sheila was working and Luke was out at the back trundling in the grain and the flour and the bran and trying to bottle stout and to weigh and put the sugar into the pound bags. He wasn't handy. It came hard on him.

Martha's hair had loosened from its bun and fallen straggling around her face. Sheila was sweating at the task. The unserved customers were being terribly patient about how they didn't mind at all and they were in no hurry, but there were a few sardonic looks. Martha saw some of those looks and they infuriated her, but there was nothing she could do about them, just clench her teeth and put up with them. Because things were not working out. It had seemed that there was nothing to do but take over where Mabbina had left off. There was nothing to keeping a few books. Until she started to try and keep them. To know what stocks there were and not be confused about them. Sometimes she ordered too much and sometimes she didn't order enough, so that people couldn't get what they wanted at

235

the times they wanted. Everything had been all right before. It wasn't now. It was all a terrible mix-up, because Martha had painfully and slowly to learn how to run a business. She was cheated by travellers, who loaded her with goods with the wrong percentages. She was upset by carriers. She knew nothing about anticipating trends, or about ordering things six months in advance to have them on hand at the right time. It couldn't be all learned in a day or a week or even a year. There was too much to be done and there was nobody with the knowledge of how to do it. There were no graceful days of living like a lady on the sweat and industry of her mother-in-law and the late John Willie. How John Willie would have hated the mess the shop was in!

Luke had to work the stores. He didn't like the stores. He was slow. He wanted to be out working his new tractor. He didn't have the time. They had to pay a man to work the tractor. It wasn't his own tractor so he was indifferent about it. It seemed to be always in trouble. Men didn't like porter that was fresh bottled. It had to be at least a few days in the bottles. With Luke so slow, they got it practically hot out of the barrels. They complained about it. Fewer of them came in to drink it. They hopped on their bicycles and went over six miles to the shop near the sea. The takings in the pub had fallen to a disastrously low level. Sometimes they hired men to help Luke, but they didn't last long. If they were good men they didn't get on with Martha, and if they weren't good men they flogged bottles of whiskey and things until they were found out and then fled to some other part of the country before she could put the law on them.

Customers didn't care for her attitude in the shop. She couldn't realise that a country shopkeeper simply has to give credit, sometimes from harvest to harvest and oftentimes skipping two harvests before payment comes. So Carrymore fulfilled a want at the right time. He gave groceries and things right on your own door once a week and if you hadn't money he took eggs or butter or he gave credit. Carrymore was injuring his own brother, his own brother! Martha would say indignantly. But the people often tackled up the ass and cart and took their good women the six miles to shop by the sea. They said they were sick of the woman. And it wasn't the same place anyhow. You couldn't get nothing in it when you wanted it. The shop was beginning to look like a place without order. There was no neatness on the shelves. Things weren't where you could lay your hands on them. Martha was sometimes up half the night trying to figure it all out, poring over books and credits and accounts and invoices. Luke couldn't help. Luke was not at home with these things. He didn't like them. Luke could add up the fingers on his two hands but after that he really didn't care.

So where were the peace and the leisure and the money and the case that she had been looking forward to? It didn't exist. She spent her days in a miasma of non-understanding. It should have been so easy. It should have worked out just as simply as it did before. But somebody had put sand in the works, and sand in the food too. She hadn't time herself to be in the kitchen. There were many servants in the kitchen one after another. None of them could cook very well. They were all independent. They all thought they were a hell of a sight better born than Martha and they wouldn't take any oul guff from her. They all knew her history. Their parents insisted on their knowing before they would work for her. People said if you stretched Martha's maids head to toe, lying on the ground, that you could walk over female flesh from Boola to the sea. People were naturally very sorry that Martha was getting into such a mess. They said they could weep for her they were so sorry for her. If so there were enough tears to start a flood. Something will have to bust, they said, below. The only one in the place now that's holding it together is Sheila. And if she goes God knows what'll happen. They were looking forward to what would happen.

She knew them. She knew what they were saying. She knew what they were thinking. The only sincerity she could feel came from the people that owed her money. She wondered if they would be so sympathetic if they could get their bills paid.

Into the shop on top of all this Saturday frustration came Bidelia.

237

She was wearing her hat with the flowers. This was a hat which she had cherished for many years. She kept it in a cardboard box with tissue paper wrapping it around. Bidelia was generally the spokesman. If a county councillor had to be talked to about a new road or the surfacing of an old road, or the priest had to be talked to about things, Bidelia would talk to them and she always wore the hat with the flowers.

She pushed through the women and she slammed a bit of paper down on the counter.

"Did you send me this, dear?" she asked. She was red in the face.

Martha looked up from her parcelling. She looked at the bill on the counter. It said that Bidelia owed Martha eleven shillings and nine pence for goods received and that prompt payment would oblige.

"Yes," she said. "I sent it to you. It was long enough on the books."

"You're a contumelious bitch, dear," said Bidelia, straightening her hat. "How dare you! All my life, all my parents' life, we have left money in this shop. Winter and summer, all our lives, and it has to come about that a little upstart like you with no name to you should insult me and all belonging to me."

"There's no need," said Martha, "to get excited. A business can't go on if people don't pay. There was too much slackness in the old days, that's all. Things have changed."

"Things have changed indeed, dear," said Bidelia. "But things haven't changed for the better. No, dear. Not for the better. We never thought to see the day arrive that we would be insulted by a thing like you. Here is your eleven and ninepence. Little good it will do you. You will never see me or mine inside your doors again, dear. Ah, the sad day. The sad day for Boola that people die and are represented by girls of your class. What's the country coming to? I don't know. But you won't last long, dear, as the world knows. I'll live to see the last of you in Boola, with ivy hanging over the walls of this place and the roof caved in, and it will be you that did it. In two generations you have destroyed what it took two generations to build. But we'll have an end of you. Never again, dear, never again, if I had to walk twenty miles for a loaf of bread."

Then she went out of the shop.

There was a dead silence in the shop. Sheila's face was flaming. The customers all had their backs turned pretending to be reading old posters and things and the small writing on packages of cornflour. But in the midst of the air of embarrassment there was also an air of glee; from a suppressed nervous titter that was covered with a cough, from the way in which a laugh was hidden by the men in a sudden burst of conversation about a pig fair. It took a lot of courage on Martha's part to continue with what she was doing, but later when the customers had departed she left the shop and she went into the kitchen of the house and she sat at the table and she rubbed her temples with her fists.

It was then that Luke came in to her. He was complaining.

Is there no way at all, Martha," he said, "that we could get a man or something into the store? I don't like it. The ploughing is behind and that stookaun below is destroying the tractor. He's destroying it, I tell you, and up on the bog I haven't even the top of the bog cleared and I should be up there at that or we won't have a sod cut before the sun comes in to dry it. This store is too much for me, Martha. I'd do anything except it."

"For God's sake leave me alone," Martha said.

"What's wrong with you?" he asked. "What's wrong now?"

"Nothing, nothing, nothing," she said.

"But, Martha," he said, "we'll have to get the ploughing done and the bog cleared and it'll never be done if I have to be wasting me time all day around the oul store. I don't like it."

"I don't like what I have to do either," she flared at him. "Why should I like it? I'd prefer to be in here in the kitchen than what I'm doing. But it has to be done. Somebody has to do it. Why don't you make your precious brother go up and clear the bog for you?"

"Is it Joseph?" he asked.

"Yes, Joseph," she said. "Joseph. We all have to work, don't we! I sleep four hours a night out of twenty-four and work the rest trying to build something. What does he do? He just sits and sleeps and walks for himself in the spring sunshine. Why can't he help? Why can't he go up in the bog for you?"

"Now, Martha," he said. "You know he's not strong."

"Not strong!" she said. "Not strong! I'm sick of that talk. Sick of it. I've been hearing it ever since I came into the place. He's as strong as a horse. He's stronger than I am. He's as strong as you are. He's been coddled and fussed over and spoiled all his life, that's what's wrong with him. Well, make a man of him for God's sake before it's too late. Send him up on the bog to sweat with a spade in his hand. Let people get a bit of respect for him, instead of watching him wilting like a flower and the children running after him, jeering at him and calling, Bless me, Father, for I have sinned."

"Martha!" he said.

"Well, it's true, it's true, it's true," she said. "They are jeering at him. He's a joke. He's another burden around our necks. I'm sick of the sight of his cow's eyes. He's eating and sleeping and doing nothing, nothing to help us when we need help so badly. You're as bad as his mother about him. She built up that fairy tale about his delicacy. She reared him like a milksop, to build her own position in the world, so that she could get into the back way to heaven with a priest in the family. You all believed her tales about him. But I didn't! I always saw him for what he was. A parasite. A white slug, that's what he always was, and he disappointed his mother into the grave for all that she did for him. Well, he's not going to do it to us. You'll make him work, Luke. You'll make him help. You'll make a man of him. You'll do something about him or I won't be able to go on. I'm at the end of my tether now. And all you can say is Joseph! Joseph! He's delicate. Delicate! Well, he's not. And unless you make him do something to help us instead of being an uneconomic load on us, I'll do something, I'll make it a choice, Luke, if I have to. I swear to God I will. Between Joseph and me. I'll make you choose."

Her face was inflamed. Her hands were clenched. He was dumbfounded at the depths of her anger. And the door of the room opened and Joseph came out. He had his black suit on. It was getting shiny. Luke had noticed it before and had spoken to her about it. She said they hadn't the money now for a new suit. Later. The tractor and the fittings, she said, had used up a lot of money. He'd have to wait.

"You were calling me, Martha?" he asked in his quiet voice. Luke was relieved. He looked at his eyes but there was no knowledge there that he had heard what she said about him.

"Yes, I called you," she said. "I called you for many things. I said to Luke that things are going bad with us, and we need help and that you are there and you never reach a hand to help us. Never reach a hand to help us."

"I'll do whatever you wish, Martha," he said. "I would help at whatever you wish. But you were displeased with me in the shop and the store. You said I was better out of them."

He wasn't chiding her. He was just saying it.

"It's easy to be bad so that you won't be good," she said. "Easy."

"What is it?" he asked. "How have I vexed you?"

"You haven't vexed me," she shouted. "You haven't vexed me. I'm just saying that if you had any love or obedience for us you would go up and help Luke. You could take a spade and go up and clean the bog. You could do that. And sweat a bit, Joseph, so that you'll know what it is to sweat and raise a blister on your hand so that you will know what it is to have a blister. All that I said. And it's true for me. We can't afford to rear a gentleman like your mother could afford it."

"I'll do whatever you wish, Martha," Joseph said.

"You heard him," she said to Luke. "Go out and get the spade for him."

"But, Martha," Luke said.

"Go on and do what he tells you," she said. "Go out and get the spade for him."

He looked into her red eyes and he went out of the back door slowly.

She looked at Joseph. She wondered again why the sight of his meekness sickened her. His big eyes were on her now. They were big enough to drown in them. His face was pale and the bones very evident. It wasn't her fault if he didn't eat a lot, if there were

241

violet lines under his eyes. He walked a lot at night-time. What brought him out at midnight sometimes, and sometimes at two o'clock in the mornings? Sometimes four. She didn't know. Maybe people were affected by the thin pale saintly look of him, but all it did to her was to make her sick.

"I'm sorry, Martha," he said, "if I have done anything to upset you."

"You don't have to be sorry," she said. "You don't have to be sorry. Something practical is what we want from you, something practical. Like working. Like coming out of your day-dreams and helping us when things are bad. That's all we want from you. Not sorrow."

He remained silent. He was always conscious, when he was aware of his surroundings, of the dislike he engendered in her. He couldn't find a reason for it. It troubled him. He must have some terrible fault, he knew, to make a person dislike him. It couldn't be her fault. There was something about him. Was it his manner, or his behaviour? Could her eyes look deep into him and discover something false in him that he wasn't aware of? Something false? If that were so, then all the rest was false too. All the feelings. All the bad moments of the black despair were true because it meant that the other moments were only imagined.

Luke came back handling the spade as if it was a bomb. He stood there with it. Joseph held out his hand. He was smiling at the hurt bewildered look in Luke's face.

"Thank you, Luke," he said. "Have you the place lined out or what?"

"Yes, yes, Joseph, I did that. It's lined out. But I don't think . . ."

"Thank you, Luke," said Joseph, and he took the spade. It seemed heavy to him. The handle was very thick. His hands hardly went around it. He turned with it and went out of the front door.

"Listen, Joseph," said Luke, starting after him.

"Let him go. Let him go, for God's sake," Martha said.

He stood at the door looking after him. Joseph and a spade didn't seem to go together. He turned into the kitchen.

242

"Martha," he said. "What is happening to you?"

She had her back to him.

"There's nothing happening to me," she said.

"There is," he said. "Listen, Martha, if things are so bad let us sell the shop. Let us get rid of it. Let us just live on what we can make from the land. Will that make you happy?"

"No," she said. "I am going to make a success of the shop. It's only a matter of time until I have mastered it. I'll make a success of it if it kills me, so that I will have the laugh of them. Why should we throw away good money? Answer me that. There's money in a shop. Why should we throw it away?"

"I like the land, Martha," he said. "I'm only happy on the land."

"The land is only for slaves," she said. "Toil and moil, toil and moil."

"Martha," he said, "you shouldn't have done that with Joseph. I tell you he's not strong."

"It will make a man of him, Luke. You mark me. Sweat never hurt anybody. It will take his mind off himself. I have to get back."

She wouldn't listen. She went back to the shop. She felt that she had been humiliated, but it was much lessened now. She could face the lot of them again. She felt fortified.

Luke looked out of the back door and saw the black figure toiling towards the shoulder of Boola. He felt sad. What has happened to us? he wondered. Why has everything gone wrong with us? He wondered if he could chance running after Joseph and taking the spade from him and telling him to go and dream. He looked below at the fields from where the chug of the tractor was coming. He groaned at the little of the earth that was gleaming in the pale sun. It was coming on towards sunset and that was all the bastard had done in that time. Why, even with a single horse I could have done that much in half a day. He wondered would he chance going down there. Then he thought of all that had to be done in the cursed goddam store and he turned out that way. It would never do. Martha would be after him.

I wish nobody had died, he thought. We were all better off then.

Twenty-Six

THERE WAS A sort of road up to the place. It was very rough. It had been formed by throwing down branches of pine trees and putting a layer of scraws over those, then big stones and after that rough gravel. But it served until it petered out near the place where the land started to go over the shoulder of the hill. From there on it was soft ground and rough heather, and the low bushes whose leaves smelled like mint.

From there up you could see the parallel tracks which were made by the rough runners of the sleigh which they used to get the turf down over the very soft ground. The round pools were still there which had been made last season by the frantically digging hooves of the horses.

It was easy enough until he left the road, but as he started to climb – his feet sinking into the soft mud until he felt it penetrating into his feet through the light leather of his shoes – the blood pounded in his ears and his heart started to thump so fast that he had to stop and bend forward and lean on the spade. He could see brightly coloured dots in front of his eyes.

She was perfectly right, he thought, she was perfectly right, I am indeed a miserable and selfish creature. This thought was driving him frantic. What had he done to help them? He was so taken up with his own thoughts, analysing the loss of his father and mother, his own personal loss, as if nobody else in the world was made to feel and suffer except himself, and putting this personal suffering away because it was only part of the burden that was loaded on the shoulders of a seeker of the interior life, the roughly rearing Cross that confronted every soul once it had entered into the valley of resignation.

Oh, he was wrong. He was very wrong. He could see that now. It was an awful imperfection. It was enough to damn him. All his needs had been provided by another person's sweat and toil and worry, so that he could sleep or walk or eat and dream away his life fitting everything into a pattern of perfection, that was like the grey rottenness on a parsnip that you wouldn't notice until it was cooked and the grey bit was brown and you knew then that the vegetable was not perfect and would have to be thrown away and grown anew from a little seed. Oh, so far back, when he had thought he might be going forward. So far back. He could have found his answer in labour and toil, instead of shutting himself away. That was selfishness, wasn't it? He should have come out and worked with sweat and endeavour to help them. Oh, how terrible that he should have been blind right until now, and that it was Martha who opened his eyes to the road he was going. It couldn't have been all wrong. Don't let it be all wrong.

Well, now he would sow the seed.

He started up the hill, his grip firmer on the handle of the spade. He welcomed the dreadful tightness of his chest as his mouth was wide, wide open trying to suck in the air. He tugged at his collar, pulling it away from his swelling neck so that the little white button popped and fled away into the foreign strangeness of the bog. He had to bend forward far to pull his legs from one sticky patch to the next. One of his feet went deep into a green slimy mess that covered a crack. He felt the mud and water up to his knee. It was very cold on his flesh. How wrong it was that he who had been born and bred in the mountains should have such actual physical difficulty in merely climbing the side of one! He forced himself to go on and only rested when the spade slipped and he fell face forward. While he was lying this way he struggled, out of his coat. It seemed to be strangling him. He sat up. He left the coat on one side. He looked briefly below. He seemed to be up near the clouds. The afternoon sun was shining on him, but below he could see that part of its shine was cut off the waters of the lake by the looming peak of Boola ahead.

245

He walked on further. He dragged the heavy spade behind him and pulled himself up with the other hand grasping the tufts of tough sedge. He tried to think of how many times he had seen men walking this hill in heavy hobnailed boots, leaping from tuft to tuft, their bodies inclined, no harsh rasping breaths coming from them. It can't be that hard at all. He covered the last few yards to this particular top of the shoulder on his hands and knees, dragging the spade behind him. It's ridiculous, ridiculous!

From here in, it was flat. The tracks of the sleigh runners ended here. From here the donkeys with the panniers on their backs brought the turf out over the soft plain. That's why they let the hooves of the donkeys grow long and curling. It was against the law, but if you cut their little hooves and shod them they were no use on the soft ground. Each one would sink into it. But when the hooves were allowed to grow and curl like the slipper of a Turk, they didn't sink, they stayed on the top of the softness and could carry their load.

He walked across the plain. He sank at almost every step because there had been a lot of rain. His heart wasn't beating so fast now. He held his free hand tightly across his chest and gripped the place over his heart. It felt as if it would beat its way out of the wall of his chest. He was sweating. A cold sort of sweat that was almost frozen by the wind that blew up here. It was an April wind and it should have been warmer, but the sun was beginning to go behind the peak of the hill and leaving chilling shadows wherever it did not touch.

Then he reached the banks. He knew where Luke's was. He had been up here, once or twice, but coming very slowly on a summer's day. Walking a yard and sitting and walking and sitting and looking down at the place below under the sun, and marvelling at the wonders that God could create, a touch here and a touch there and a bit here and a bit there, and up on a hill looking down, that was the thought you had of God with a brush stroking in the beauty of the world.

The bank had been lined along by a string and then the line dug in with the blade of the spade, so that it was ready. You had to dig deep, about a square foot of the topsoil, tough mossy spring heather mixed with sedge. He dug out a cube. It was too big, he had to halve it. He threw it from him and it fell into the boghole below, splashing into the water. He dug another and another. He had pains under his shoulder. Cold sweat fell from his forehead, from his eyebrows, and blinded his eyes. He rubbed it away. He dug another scraw and threw it away and he staggered and went after it. Into the water below, almost his whole body immersed, but he pulled himself up, scrabbling on the soft bank. The top of him was all right. That was out of the water. He pulled himself out completely. He didn't pause. He collected the spade and he climbed back up on the bank. It's merely an excuse for idleness to say that it can't be done. Because the body is lazy, that's why. Because this is good for the body, this whipping of the old man. That's right. But he was very tired. His foot could hardly rise to dig in the spade. The water seemed to have made it very heavy. His arms were very tired. He found it very difficult to raise them. Then he fell to his knees, his arms holding on to the handle above his head, his face resting, panting against the wet smoggy mass of it below. And he said, Oh, I am trying, I am trying, but I am so tired and I am so lonely. Oh, I am so lonely and I don't know where I am, because everything I have done has been wrong. Has everything I have done been wrong? Have I always given offence because my thoughts are wrong? That all tears must be shed inside, inside, and now they weren't inside but outside, and that's weakness, oh, terrible weakness, but it is because I am tired.

The sun passed down by the peak of the hill and threw himself and his bog into cold shadow.

"Well, that's what I told her, dear," said Bidelia, "and now in a way I'm sorry. I am. I shouldn't maybe have said some of the things, but I am not quick to anger as you know, but I get terrible vexed when my dander is up."

"You shouldn't have done it," Breeda said.

"Well, they flew out of me," Bidelia said apologetically, like a stream coming down the side of the hill. I was livid, dear.

Imagine eleven and ninepence. I never owed anybody anything. You know I never owed anybody anything. I always paid."

"I know that," said Breeda, "but things are not going well for them. She's new. She doesn't know how to handle things. She'll learn. You shouldn't have taken offence."

"I'm always in the wrong," said Bidelia. "Always in the wrong with you, Breeda." She started to sniffle.

"Oh, no, you're not," said Breeda. "Honest. You're very kind and you hardly ever hurt anybody with your tongue and maybe you should go back if you can at all, and say that you're sorry."

"Breeda!" outraged.

"I said if you can at all," Breeda said. "It takes very big people to be generous, and everybody knows that you are very big and very forgiving, and maybe it would soften her up a bit and make things a bit easier for her. That's, of course, if you want to do the big thing."

"H'm!"

"It's only a suggestion, of course. There's too many people too quick to take offence and if she injured you what harm is there in you sort of forgiving her, in a big way?"

"Well, perhaps since you say so, dear, I might do the big thing. Although it takes great courage, Breeda. The looks she gave me, and that eleven and ninepence. Really, dear, it was unbearable."

"I'm very pleased that you can be so magnanimous," said Breeda.

"Well," said Bidelia, "there are some that are and some that aren't. And then when I was coming back who do I see ahead of me coming out of the house but Joseph, and he going up towards Boola bog with a spade."

"What did you say?"

"That's right, dear, Joseph going up to Boola with a spade. Somebody was outside the door heard a great rumpus. She was shouting at him, dear, and at poor dear Luke who wouldn't say boo to a goose. Sort of shouting they tell me and then this little Joseph comes out with a spade and the spade is bigger than himself and off he sets towards the Boola staggering with the weight of it."

"Oh, what stupidity" said Breeda.

"Just what I said, dear, what can you make of it at all? So I thought how sorry I am and that I would go back and tell her that I forgive her and find out what all this is about, I said."

"Do. Go," said Breeda, feeling for a cardigan and pulling it on and making her way to the door.

"Breeda!" she shouted. "Where are you going?"

"Just up a bit of the bog," said Breeda, going out of the gate and turning left towards the mountain.

"But, Breeda!" said Bidelia. But Breeda was gone. So Bidelia looked at herself in the glass and settled the flowered hat on her head. She didn't want to relinquish it yet. She thought, looking at herself: I'm still a presentable person, dear, not many lines on the neck and a clear skin and a good form below, and isn't it a great pity that my poor man died! I am a great loss. She wondered how it would be to have another husband. A nice one. But where would one get a nice one? She sighed and went out of the door and closed it after her.

Carrymore was coming into the village and looking for Bart. He was disappointed that he didn't see him at the first turn of the road. Sometimes he came that far to meet him.

Near the village he ran out on to the road, laughing as if he was going to run under the wheels. Carrymore grinned and pretended a great to-do about pulling brakes and edging sideways and then stopped and opened the far door and little Bart came into the cab with him. He leaned an arm on the wheel and looked at him.

"Well," he asked, "anything new, man?"

"No," said Bart. "Mother said you would come today."

"Did she?" Carrymore asked.

'Yes," said Bart. "She washed her hair last night too. In rain water. She says rain water makes your hair softer and shinier. Is that true?"

"I'll tell you when I see her hair," said Carrymore.

"Oh, there was a big row too. In the shop. I was in behind the place. The lady said things to Martha. Martha bit her lip."

"Oh, ho," said Carrymore. "Who was the lady?"

"The one with the funny hat," said Bart. "Did you bring any of the rock?"

"Guess," Carrymore said, starting up, and moving down the street. The boy started to move things, searching and searching. Carrymore would say, You are getting warm or cold or warmer or you are really getting hot, and they both laughed when he found the stick of rock on a ledge facing him where he should have seen it long ago. He sucked it happily.

Into the shop Carrymore went.

Only Sheila. Her eyes lit up. You'd think, Carrymore thought, that she had a couple of batteries behind them.

"Give's a look," he said to her, turning her around with his hand.

"What's up?" she asked.

"It is all right," he said.

"What is?" she asked.

"Your hair," he said. "The rain water made it shinier."

"I told you," said Bart.

"You shouldn't be saying and telling things," she said.

"Where's everyone?" Carrymore asked,

She frowned.

"Oh, trouble," she said. "Nothing but trouble. Rows. Bidelia read her and then she went away and she read Luke and Luke read Joseph, so they say, and sent him out to top the bog."

Carrymore laughed, hitting the counter with his hand.

"Are you joking me?" he asked her.

"No," she said. "It's all upsetting."

"Well, it's going to be more upsetting," he said. "I've been thinking. I've been thinking a lot. Late thinking is bad for people. You know what?"

"What?" she asked.

"You tell Martha that you'll be leaving here in three weeks. You tell her that."

Her head fell. He couldn't see her face. It worried him. Was he taking too much for granted? Was he going to get another kick in the teeth?

"Doesn't that please you?" he asked her.

She looked up at him.

"Oh, yes," she said. "Oh, yes, that'd please me very much."

"Well, try and be happy about it," he said. "We'll go far away. We'll carry our house on our backs like the snails."

Little Bart called out to them.

"The lady with the funny hat is gone into the house," he said.

"Oh-ho," said Carrymore. "I must go and join in this. I can't miss this. I will be back, Sheila."

And then he was gone.

Twenty-Seven

THE GIRL WAS there in the kitchen. She was coming in with an armful of turf, but Bidelia, having decided to abase herself, paid no attention to her. She was a streel anyhow, dear, as Bidelia said. A big fat girl with a faded flowered dress on her and a canvas apron, no stockings and big boots and a big mouth that seemed to be always open.

"Martha, dear," she said, "I have come back to say that I'm sorry for what I said in the shop. It wasn't decent, dear, but you vexed me so."

Martha looked at her coldly.

"It's a bit late," she said. "You can take a person's character away but it's not as easy to put it back."

Bidelia's lips tightened. Her face flushed. Very hot words rose to her lips, but she quelled them and sat down in the chair near the table.

"All right, dear, perhaps that's so, but at least you can grant me the grace of being sorry about it."

"Yes," said Martha, "you can be sorry about it. But what's going to happen with all the people that heard you? And the talk they can carry and the way they can exaggerate it. What about that?"

"Dear," said Bidelia, "you pay too much attention to what people think. You are too sensitive."

"I have reason to be sensitive," said Martha. "All I ever wanted was not to be noticed. I have never hurt anybody. I have tried to be fair and decent with everybody, and what you did makes it very hard. Very hard."

Bidelia rose to her feet.

"Well, dear," she said, "I tried to do the decent thing, but as far as I can see I would have been better off at home nursing a grievance. Did you have the courage to apologise for the way you hurt my feelings? What about what people will say of me, that I'm a woman who doesn't pay her lawful debts but has to be dunned, dear, like a tinker, for eleven and ninepence?"

"All right," said Martha, "you have apologised. Now you can go."

"A person would want to be a saint, dear," said Bidelia, "to get on with you."

She was about to go when Carrymore came in. He saw the hot angry eyes of Bidelia and the cold tight-lipped face of Martha. He professed to ignore them.

"Ah, you're here, Bidelia," he said. "Man, but that's a hat. It makes you look as young as a virgin. If I hadn't three wives in China I'd marry you myself."

Bidelia was mollified. She put her hand up and settled her hat.

"Oh, you, Carrymore," she said.

"Any chance of a mug of tea, Martha?" he asked then. Sit down, Bidelia. Dammit, you're not running off when I come in, are you?"

"Well . . ." said Bidelia.

"Sit down, sit down, sit down, woman," he said, practically forcing her into the chair. "We are all friends together, aren't we?"

He sat on the other chair. He was enjoying himself.

He met Martha's eyes. She flushed at the look on his face. Sardonic. She hated the sight of him.

"We're very busy," she said. "It's Saturday."

"You're not going to turn me away from the house where I was born," he asked her, "when I ask for a sup of tea?"

"Make the tea, Julia," said Martha.

"Good girl, Julia," said Carrymore. "You should see the way they make tea in some places. A cup of hot water and a grain of tea in a bag. Man, it's like dried horse-droppings. There's no place like your own home where you can come in and sit in the seat where you spent your happy childhood and watch the kettle boiling on the hob. A great thing! That's what you miss most when you are away. The sight of your relations. It's an agony to be separated from them. Don't you feel that way, Martha?

"I don't know," she said. "I have never been away."

"Well, you can take it from me, it's the truth," he said. "I hear that Joseph has taken to the bog. Is that so?"

"He went up to the bog," said Martha.

"That's good for him," said Carrymore. "Bog life is very bracing. It's good for the health and the muscles. Particularly when you are a big strong man like Joseph. I'm sure he'll be able to do a lot up on the bog. He'll be able to do twice the work that Luke would do."

"Luke is busy," she said.

"I'm pleased to hear that," said Carrymore. "That makes me happy. I hope he doesn't overwork himself. But it will be all right now, when you have trained Joseph to do the dirty work."

"Don't talk like that," she said. "I had nothing to do with it. It was of his own free will that he went up to the bog. He wanted to go."

"I can understand that," said Carrymore. "He must have been bursting to get at it."

"You went on too about him," she said. "The delicate business. He's not delicate. You tell a person a thing often enough and they'll come to believe it themselves. That's all."

"You have turned into a colossal bitch, Martha," said Carrymore. "I didn't think you had the makings of one. I can't understand how you became one. One time you wouldn't be like that. Listen, you are safe. Do you hear? You are safe. I don't want anything you have. And Joseph doesn't want anything you have. Nobody wants anything from you. You can rest easy at night. Nobody is going to try and take what you have away from you."

"Only happiness," she said. "Only happiness."

"Happiness is a thing nobody can give you or take away from you," he said. "That's something you make or mar all on your own. Now look, Martha, I'm telling you something. You leave

Joseph alone. I'm telling you now. You leave him alone to go his own road. If you want to kill him off fast put poison in his tea or something, but for God's sake use whatever bit of intelligence you have left and keep him off bogs."

"Now, dear," said Bidelia.

"I don't think I'll wait for the cup of tea after all," he said, rising. "Something tells me that we're not welcome here, Bidelia. What do you think?"

"I think we'd brew better tea at home, dear," she said, rising with satisfaction. After all she had apologised. It wasn't her fault. She had kept her temper. It was Carrymore that had said all the things.

They would have gone, but Joseph came in at the back door. He held on to the lintel. He saw Carrymore facing him.

Bidelia gasped.

He was a sight. His shirt was brown dirt all except the neck of it. His trousers hung around him in wet dirty folds. His hands and arms were black with bog. There were smadders of it across his forehead. His narrow chest was heaving convulsively, and his mouth was open and gaping. But it was his eyes that riveted Bidelia. They were like two glowing lamps opened to their full extent.

The sight of him shocked Carrymore. He hadn't seen him properly since he came home. He made nothing of Joseph. Joseph was all right, like a pup you'd have about the place that you'd be indulgent with. He was amazed at the change in him, at how thin he had become. His dirtied arms were like two sticks, his neck thin and pitiful, it was so white, and the burning eyes that were turned on him made the cheek-bones stand out naked and shining.

None of them spoke.

Then Joseph did.

His words came in breathless croaks. He held on to the lintel. Behind him the sun that was setting in front of the house had coloured the sky and the land almost vulgarly in broad stripes of dark red and purple.

"I saw her," Joseph said. "Like a flower. Like a great shell opening and inside a flower, so beautiful, pink and white. And she spoke to me. I was lonely. What have I done to be worthy of it? I was grovelling in the mud and she raised me. And her smile was like the sun, like the sun and the love, and the love and she will come again, on the May-day at the same time when the sun is gone behind the peak."

Bidelia felt a shiver going up her spine. For a moment the hair on the back of Carrymore's neck rose. He is gone mad, Bidelia thought, the poor boy is gone mad, and it's all her fault.

"What are you saying? What are you saying?" Martha asked, going over to him.

His eyes moved to her. But there was no recognition in them.

"I saw the Mother of God," he said.

Carrymore's hair stopped crawling, and deep down in his stomach a laugh formed. It wasn't a nervous laugh. It was one of rich amusement. He looked again and the figure of Joseph that a moment ago he had been feeling sorry for became a figure of fun, a sort of scarecrow. It was all he could do to stop a shout of laughter bursting out of his mouth.

Then Martha had reached Joseph. She raised her hand and she hit him a blow across the face, and with the other hand she pulled him inside and slammed the door. Joseph fell to the floor. Carrymore would have moved to save him but he was too late. He was trying to stifle his laughter. Even the sound of the blow and the sight of the boy on the floor didn't conquer the laugh that had been born in his stomach.

"You idiot," Martha was shouting down at him. "You idiot. Do you want to destroy us? Do you want to ruin us? Aren't we bad enough? Aren't we bad enough?"

"Oh, you cruel thing," Bidelia said. "Oh, cruel." She ran forward and she got on her knees beside him. "Get up, Joseph, get up," she said. "Pay no attention to her, pay no attention to her."

She helped him to his feet.

Carrymore was watching.

The light had gone out of Joseph's eyes. He looked around him. There was a red weal on the side of his face where she had hit him.

"I'm sorry," he said. "I'm sorry. But it's true. It's true."

Bidelia was supporting him.

"Don't say it," said Martha. "Don't say it again or I won't be responsible. Listen, you, Bart, don't talk about this. Promise you won't talk about this. He's gone mad. We'll have to get the doctor for him. You won't talk, Bart. Promise you won't talk. And you, Bidelia, if you have any feelings for us, don't talk about it."

Why should Martha be the first to see the enormity of it, Carrymore wondered.

"But he did and it's true," said the voice of Breeda then. She had come to the front door. She was panting.

She felt them looking at her. She felt the sort of crawling silence. "I went up after him," she said. "I was up near the bog when something made me fall to my knees. It was very still. There were no birds singing. There was a sort of silence with instruments playing that you couldn't hear. And I saw Joseph kneeling on the bog and he was facing a light. And there was movement in the light, and my eyes pained me and I had to cover my face. And he came away and the silence went and Joseph was gone when the pain went out of my eyes."

Carrymore said: "So you can see! So it is a miracle!"

"No," said Breeda. "I cannot see. Not now. But I saw then."

Carrymore laughed. He laughed out loud. He couldn't help it.

Martha was furious.

She said, "Go home, Bidelia, and take her with you. Take her home to hell out of our sight. What sort of plot have ye concocted? Is this the thing ye dreamed up from yeer books and talks to shame the lot of us?"

Joseph said, "Breeda, you saw!"

Martha turned on him again. Carrymore held her hand and hurt her arm or she would have hit him again.

"Shut up! Shut up! Shut up!" she shouted.

"I saw, Joseph," said Breeda. "Nobody can take it away from you. No matter what they say nobody can take it away from you."

"Take her home from here!" Martha shouted. "Go on and take her home from here."

Joseph spoke then.

"Martha, please," he said in a quiet normal voice. "I shouldn't have come and spoken. It was such joy, that's all. I shouldn't have spoken. I didn't mean to hurt anybody. I didn't mean to hurt anybody."

He moved to the door of his room. Martha shouted after him.

"You won't talk about it any more, you hear. You mustn't talk about it any more or I'll get the priest for you, do you hear, do you hear?"

The door closed behind him.

Martha said, "None of you must speak. Do you hear that? None of you must speak. It won't be too bad if none of you speak."

None of them answered her. It was almost dark in the kitchen. The maid stood like a block of wood in the corner of the fireplace.

"You, Julia," said Martha, "you mustn't say anything about what you heard, you hear that. If you say a word about what you heard . . ."

"Breeda," Bart said, "you know what you are doing?"

"What am I doing?" she asked.

"You'll kill Joseph," he said.

"Not me," she said. "It's people like you will kill him."

"Look, Breeda," he said. "What's come over you? You are not the same girl I knew. What's come over you? Do you really mean this thing?"

"I told the truth," she said.

"I know you feel sorry for him," he said. "You always felt close to him. But this business. There was no need out of loyalty to back him up. People will laugh at you, Breeda, and of all things it would be terrible to have people laughing at you."

"We have drifted very far apart, Bart," said Breeda. "Haven't we drifted terribly far apart?"

Then she turned and left them. Bidelia hurried out after her. Martha shouted, "Bidelia, she mustn't talk. None of you must

258

talk." She followed them to the door and shouted after them into the darkening night. In a sort of shouted whisper. "You mustn't talk. Please remember, you mustn't talk."

Then she turned back to Bart.

He was looking at her. One of his eyebrows was lifted. She could see him grinning.

"Bart," she said. "Bart, if you ever had the slightest regard for John Willie or your mother or your brother, you won't say anything about this anywhere. Anywhere. Please, Bart, for the love of God."

He didn't answer her. He went out. She heard him laughing. Outside she heard him laughing. She went over to the door of Joseph's room. She tried the handle. The door was locked.

"Joseph!" she shouted. "Come out and talk to me. Joseph, I want to talk to you."

But the door remained closed and Joseph was silent.

Twenty-Eight

I T IS VERY easy to drop a rock into a placid pool, and you get
amusement or fantastic dreams out of watching the commotion it sets up.

He felt like a creator. In different places, the approach could
never be the same.

Like down in that pub near the docks, where all the men
gathered who were hard cases, labourers and foremen and sailors
and respectable factors. In the evening, in a haze and fug, tightly
packed bodies, gesticulating hands, emphatic obscenity, all the
men he knew, and the one or two women who drank in a corner
with their coats and hats on, since it wasn't respectable to be
drinking without a hat.

Set it up, and what will you have, and small talk, and then
suddenly you emphasise a thought with a laugh and a bang of
the glass on the counter. A funny thing. The funniest thing you
ever heard. What's this? What's this? You know the place well?
What place is this? Out there beyond out in Boola. Man, the
back of beyond. I know. Snug in the mountains, a bleak place.
Bought some wool back there. A bleak place. What's wrong
about it? You haven't heard? No, man, haven't heard. What's it?
About the young fella out there that saw the Blessed Virgin. No,
man! You're foolin'! On me oath! Saw the Blessed Virgin? You're
foolin'! Back there. On me oath! And what's more she's coming
back again to talk to him next Saturday night at eight o'clock.
That's a fact. That's what he says. Oh, no, hold me up! It's a
joke. The Blessed Virgin! Is he a dim-wit? No, he seems to be

rational. My God, that's a laugh. Did you hear that, Jack, about your man back in, where did you say the place was, Boola, hah? The Boola Boy, Jack, that saw the Blessed Virgin back on the bog. Isn't that a laugh? He must have been drinking some of your man's bad stuff. Laugh at that.

But he watched them out of the corner of his eyes, grinning. They made more jokes about it, but he was questioned, carefully although very casually it seemed. Like whereabouts was this place? How long would it take to reach it? I must tell the wife about that. Man, won't she have a laugh about that! Because he knew that severe drinkers were frightened people. No man drinks just to drink. If that was the case you might as well drink water to satisfy a thirst. Severe drinkers drank because they were burying something deep in the subconscious, and always even with the worst of them there would be a guilt complex. They would almost look over their shoulders with fear even when they were nearly unconscious. They knew that it was wrong. What was wrong maybe they didn't know, or maybe they did. But dimly they knew that excess would always bring a train of pain in the wake of it, so they would grab at straws to bolster up the barricades they built to ward off the consequences of their gluttony. No drunkard going home late and staggering would fail to pause and raise his hat passing by the closed door of a church. If he went at all, once a week to a late Mass on a Sunday, he would be right at the very back, his mind blotting out all the things he was looking at because if he looked at them closely enough all that they meant would clash with the things he was doing. So you joked about going to sleep at Mass, that you couldn't keep your eyes open when your man was giving the sermon about temperance. All that. Even the sacredest part was just where you put your cap under your knee and knelt down while the bell was ringing and you thought how it would be possible to slip into the pub near the church directly after Mass, that your man did a good trade on Sundays after Mass. You daren't let yourself think about the meaning of it all because it was all so contrary to what you were doing. Carrymore understood all this well, because he had been through it himself and he only found freedom when he had discovered that all the church business was a fraud and that every man was a god in himself if he could see it that way.

One of the drinking ladies blessed herself when she heard the tale. She didn't laugh at it although they encouraged her to laugh. Bet that fella never took a drink in his life, that's what's wrong with him. If he took a drink or two like a man he wouldn't be goin' around thinkin' he saw the Blessed Virgin. And where did you say it was again? Oh, up in Boola. And when did you say? Saturday, May-day. Man, he has it all worked out, hasn't he? Right down to the time of eight o'clock. The time that the sun goes behind the tip of the mountain. Man, that's something, isn't it? Man, that's something!

He left the seed to germinate.

You wake up in the morning. Being sort of crawsick in the morning has become a regular part of living, part of the hazards. It's worth it. And maybe your wife has rifled your pockets to get a few quid to keep the house going. She is down below. And you rush because you are going to be late out. And you wallop a cup of tea and you avoid looking at her hard lips and the straight way she holds her back, and you shout at the kids maybe, and she looks at you with loathing. And anger, and fear for the future, and if she says anything about her fear you can say, Ah, for God's sake, I can hear all that in the church. In the church, and you say uneasily, A very funny thing last night. You won't believe it. You have to force out a laugh here about the young fella back beyond that saw the Blessed Virgin out on a bog and she's coming back again, she says, he says.

Isn't that funny! Imagine that! Wouldn't a fella be an eejit to take him at his word! Maybe we'd all yank up there to have a look. Wouldn't it be great gas? Where? she asks, and when, and what are you talking about? It's a fact. I heard it for a fact. I know, I know, but they are also places where you hear many interesting things, meet interesting people, and if I hadn't been there last night I'd never heard about this fella back the way that saw the Blessed Virgin and she's coming back again to him next Saturday. I don't believe it. It's all damn superstition. The

262

police should lock up people like that. But I'm only telling you about it.

Other people heard it outside pubs. There was the good lady who had a shop up the way. Carrymore sold her things like eggs and butter. She had a small shop with a few groceries and sweets and holy pictures and he knew she was one of the types that went to Mass every morning and wouldn't dream of cheating over anything and she belonged to sodalities and she lived as well as she could, and he told her very casually. But the approach was different here. It was a little ironically reverent. She accepted the news with almost complete belief. It was what she had been praying for all her life. The people were so bad it would take a miracle to bring them back to their ancient beliefs and the road to salvation. She was avid for details. She wrote them down in a little book and she closed the shop for two hours and she went and she spread the word here and there.

He dropped his tale casually at many other places. People always want news anyhow. People are always avid for news. Even when there were no newspapers it was proved that a piece of news could travel to over a hundred thousand people in a few days, just by somebody telling somebody else. A murder in a town is a great source of conversation. About who and what and where and why, and shivering How Awfuls, and did he really cut her throat and was the floor all over blood? Yes! My sister said that he this and he that. Or if a person is found flagrantly in sin this word spreads too with great righteousness, so it was really no wonder that all over the town the word spread about the young fella who had seen the Blessed Virgin. If he had just seen, that would be fairly good. You could deride or jeer or pray. But what you had heard about her coming back a second time. Oh, that was lovely! There were some people who didn't hear a thing at all about it until it was over. They could afford to say, Well, it's a good job I didn't hear about it, and even if I did hear about it I wouldn't have paid it the least spark of attention.

But it was a good talking point, and on the second or third day when people started telling Carrymore about it he knew that the word had spread. So what did he do then? He loaded up his van with grosses of rosary beads and mineral drinks and boxes of biscuits and penny buns, the big round biscuit with the currants in it, as dry as a dog biscuit but sort of traditional at race meetings and sports meetings and gatherings. He got great amusement out of it. He laughed many times about it. He puffed out his chest to himself and said, Well, it's all my own work. It never struck him that Joseph was his brother; that Joseph had been born from the same womb as himself, and that Joseph might be injured by what he was doing. It never even entered his mind, because his mind at that time was just filled with amusement.

Somebody was not amused.

That was the Canon. He was lying on his sick bed. He was afflicted with very bad varicose veins and he had got a few of them tied off, and it wasn't until Saturday itself that a servant brought him this story. The servant brought it with a sort of apologetic laugh, and nearly jumped out of her skin when the Canon roared at her. He extracted as much as she knew and sent for his curate, and the curate couldn't be found at the time, and no wonder, because he was terribly overworked. One other curate was away and the Canon was on the broad of his back, so he had a tough time saying three Masses a day and bringing Holy Communion to sick people in scattered parts of the diocese and he didn't get the message that he was sorely needed until late in the day, and then he went over to see the Canon.

The Canon waved his fists at him. Where was he and what was he doing when the Canon was hors *de combat* and was there no soul at all in the world that could be relied upon in a crisis? And what is it? And the Canon told him about it, distastefully. In my parish, he would say! In my parish. I will be the laughing-stock of the whole country. Go on up for the love of God and call him off! Call him off! He can't do that to me.

It took a long time for Larry to come around to the meaning of the Canon's words. Joseph said he had seen the Blessed Virgin. Joseph? Was it Joseph Baun? Yes, yes, the lunatic. The same fellow that had been at the College with him. That's what they got for taking these simpletons into colleges and half-educating them without finding out if they had vocations at all. But it couldn't be Joseph. But it is. It's the same fellow. You know him well. Now, go up and do something about him. Shoot him if you have to, but get him out of the place. Shut his mouth. Tell him to go into an asylum and have his head examined. Do anything, anything at all, but stop him and the disgrace he is bringing on the whole parish.

Larry left. His heart was in his boots. He tried to see Joseph in the role of a phoney visionary, but he couldn't fit him in. What could have happened? What in the name of Almighty God could have happened?

And he headed for Boola and he prayed.

The village of Boola felt like a grub under a stone. Living away contented enough, eating and sleeping and working, and then suddenly a giant hand lifts the stone and exposes the grubs under it. That was the way the people felt about it. None of them believed it. Even if it was true they wouldn't have believed it. They wanted to be left alone. That was all they wanted, to be left alone. They didn't want to be dragged into the daylight. That mad Joseph, they said. We always knew there was something wrong with him. He never behaved like a normal person. And this was what he was brooding on, this was what he was working up to. They prayed that nobody would hear. But tales started to creep into the valley, and in ones and twos and threes during the week, strangers came enquiring. Nobody told them anything. Their investigations were met with tight-lipped and hostile silence. In this all the people were at one almost for the first time. The only mistake they made was that they hoped if they didn't talk about it that the whole thing would be miraculously forgotten. All except Bidelia. Bidelia believed. She had to be shouted at and insulted a few times by other people before she would keep her mouth shut.

Boola became a village of closed doors and darkened windows and a deep desire that Joseph Baun had never been born.

And on midday of the Saturday, Carrymore with a laden van came driving cheerfully and full of anticipation into the village of Boola.

Twenty-Nine

"OH, DEAR, OH, dear," said Bidelia, pulling aside the curtain of the window and looking down below.

"What is it?" Breeda asked.

"You've never seen such a sight, dear," she said, almost whispering. "The whole of the village is packed with vehicles, dusty cars and bicycles and horses and traps and pony carts. Oh, I wish they had stayed at home. Why in the name of God didn't they stay at home?"

"Where is he?" Breeda asked.

"He's still there at the bridge, dear," she said. "Oh, may God forgive him, that's all I can say, because nobody else will find it in their hearts to do so, the things he has done to us."

"He is still selling?" Breeda asked.

"Yes, dear," she said. "He's standing up at the back of the van taking money as quick as he can. It's just like the time we had the sports, dear. Young people around him drinking lemonade out of bottles and sputtering, laughing. And old ladies and he selling them rosary beads. It's terrible. It's like blasphemy. And he is laughing, actually laughing with them. I swear to God, dear, he is like the devil with his yellow face and the turn-up of his eyebrows, and laughing. He has his coat off and his sleeves rolled up, like he was a grocer behind a counter. Oh, he's selling, God forgive him, he's selling away the life of his brother. This will kill his brother, but a lot he cares. I can't understand him. Has the man no liking or love in him for anybody at all?"

"I don't know," said Breeda. "I don't know."

Bidelia came over from the window and sat down.

"It's terrible. What could have happened to us all in such a short time? It's so terrible. Everybody in behind closed doors as if we had something to be ashamed of. We have nothing to be ashamed of, dear, if only all those people hadn't come down on us like locusts. If they had left us in peace, then just a few of us could have struggled up there with him, and even if it was all a dream, nobody would have been any the wiser. But what's going to happen under the thousands of eyes?"

"It wasn't a dream," said Breeda, rising and walking. "You were there. You heard what he said. Do you think it was a dream then?"

"No, dear," said Bidelia. "I thought it was very real. I went all goose-pimples and things started walking over my grave. But if it was private like, dear, if there was only a few of us – but the people will never forgive him for bringing all that down on us. Never forgive him."

"It wasn't his fault," said Breeda. "That was the doing of his brother. It would have been so much better for all of us if that Bart had never been born. I thought when he came back, the things he went through away, I thought he might be changed. But nothing changes him, nothing changes him."

"Dear," said Bidelia tentatively, "are you quite sure that you saw the light? That you weren't dreaming?"

"I don't want to talk about it," said Breeda. "I won't talk about it any more. I'm sorry I followed Joseph. What was beautiful to him was just terror and bewilderment to me. I don't know. Maybe I didn't see anything. But my eyes have been closed for so long, how could I be mistaken when I saw them opening again, even for a second? I saw six stacks of turf on the side of the bank and I saw Joseph kneeling and I saw a seagull hovering. I saw the sky. Unless I am mad."

Bidelia was back at the window.

"It's like a river in flood the way they are coming in. They are black around the shop now, and all up the hill there are some of them streaming away to the bog. Why didn't they stay at home? Why in the name of God didn't they stay at home? Look, Breeda,

267

you know who's coming now? The young curate with the fair hair. There he is. He has to shoulder his way through them. God forgive them. Now there will be trouble. Now there will be trouble indeed. He will never let him go up. God forgive me, but it might be better if he never let him go up at all."

Breeda was at the door, she had it open.

"I'll have to go to him," she said. "Whatever Joseph wants to do is right. If he wants to go I will have to help him.

"Breeda! Breeda!" Bidelia almost cried. "Don't go out into that crowd. Wait, Breeda, until I get my hat and coat and I'll go with you to guide you, Breeda!"

But Breeda was gone, out of the gate and down the hill. She was taking a chance, but she thought she could always ask somebody to guide her. She didn't feel the crowd until she got down to the bottom of the hill near the bridge. She wanted to cross the bridge and get in behind the wall, so that she could get around to the back of Joseph's house. She felt herself caught up in bodies. Sweating bodies. Not much noise. People talking. People laughing. People joking. The smell of women and men in the mass, and the churned dust of the road coming up into her nostrils. She raised her arms above her head to force her way through, saying, "Please let me pass! Please let me pass!" Then she was horrified when she heard them talking to her. "Hey, it's the blind girl! Is she the one? Yes, she's the one. Hey, miss, did you see it too? Tell us, did you see it too? What was it like? Hey, miss. Tell us, miss! Was she dressed in blue or white? What did she say? Hey, miss, what did she sound like? Leave the girl alone. Let her pass. Here, where do you want to go, miss?" She felt hands, sweating and hot and terrible, on her bare arms. She thought she would choke. Her sense of direction was completely lost. Oh, God, she thought, send me someone.

She felt the arm about her shoulders. Strong arm. A man with strong arms and the smell of sweat, and laughter in his voice.

"Here, make a way, make a way," he shouted. "Pull away there! Pull away!"

"Not you," she said. "Not you. Go back to your buckstering, you, and leave us alone. Leave us alone."

"Why, Breeda, have sense," he said. "I'm your benefactor. I'm the benefactor of the lot of you. Listen, girl, by the time I'm finished the village of Boola will be better known than New York." He was laughing.

"I don't want you to touch me," she said. "I want you to take your hands off me. I want you to go away, and make more of your filthy money over the tears of your brother."

"Have sense, Breeda," he said to her. "Have sense." He hauled her alongside of him. She could feel the strength of his whole body as his muscles worked to push his way through the people. She heard voices shouting at him. "Hey, Carrymore! This better be good. This better be no swiz. Hey, Carrymore, where have they him hidden? Hey, Carrymore, the priest has gone in. They won't let us see him. Hey, Carrymore, go in there and tell them they'll have to let him out. Priest or no priest they will have to let him out." There was talk and sweat and dust and suffocation and the sound of bad words as men were stepped on or elbowed in the teeth, and somewhere she heard the sound of old women's voices saying the rosary and this horrified her more than any of the other things.

It was taking them a terrible long time to reach the front door.

All the doors in the village were closed and bolted. It was as well they were because there wasn't room to lift an elbow. With all the vehicles parked anyway and the obstruction they caused, there was so little room to move. There wasn't a cloud in the sky. The sun shone hotly. The dust rose in a cloud from the rub of rubber and the scuffle of leather and the stamping of the iron hooves.

The doctor had a terrible job getting out of his place. The tall man from the back of the mountain whose wife was expecting had called. Just at that hour, God bless him, and his wife was in a bad way. The doctor couldn't believe his eyes or ears when he struggled into the street. Fortunately his car was pointing the right way, but he dented the front and the rear bumpers trying to get out of the street. He honked and honked and people moved an inch or two, all gazing below, looking for something to see, and seeing nothing. "God damn ye to hell!" he roared at them,

269

leaning out of the car. "Get out of the way. I'm a doctor, I have to get to a sick patient." It took him half an hour to clear them and get into the freedom of the road, but all the time as he went out other vehicles were coming in. It was incredible. Incredible. He thought of Joseph. He thought what he'd like to say to him. And that brother of his that was reported to be the cause of it all. A pair of bloody neurotics. He never liked Bart anyhow, never liked him, and the other frail fellow had so little to say that the doctor always thought he was a half-eejit. And now wasn't it proved? He couldn't breathe until he got into the road that went back by the sea and then got on to the other road that went back behind. He looked at the man with him. He was a big awkward fellow with a worried face and huge awkward hands. "Is she bad?" he asked, knowing well that she would be because she always was, and she should never have babies at all, but she would have no matter what you told them. He chuckled and then looked back from his eminence at the village below. Sun glinting off chromium and a veritable cloud of dust, a cloud of dust. Thank God I'm well out of that, he thought. I'm well out of that.

Sheila had to close the shop.

Nobody had expected the crowds. First there were just one or two people who wandered aimlessly and sheepishly about. Nobody to answer questions. Nobody at all. Most of the people shut in, and some of them up on the surrounding hills looking at the scene below them with disgust and cursing Joseph Baun and all belonging to him.

Then the shop was filled with people. Jam-packed with people. Porter and whiskey and it all being avidly gulped by men, and young people drinking minerals. And then Martha was in there, shouting at them, "Get out of here! Get out of here!" And they looking at her foolishly. And one fellow saying, "Here, man, you can't shut a place like that. We'll have the licence taken away from you. You can't do that." They all protested, and they would be there yet if Luke hadn't come into the place and started pushing them out. He was in a frenzy. And he was strong, but they resisted him and he couldn't have done anything but rave at them, his face red and spittle on his lips, but Sheila's brothers

270

Suck and Willie came in and they started pushing at them and they put them outside and they bolted the doors, and Luke got the heavy shutters closed on the windows and barred down, and Sheila handed young Bart over to Suck and he said: "I'll get him out of this. I came down to get him and you out of this." But Sheila said: "No, take him. I'll wait. I might be able to help." So Suck swung the child to his shoulder and carried him out and pushed his way roughly and blindly through the crowds and carried him up the hill to the home of his grandfather.

And Larry had to leave his car away out beyond the road into the village. He would have had a lot of trouble getting through. But the sight of that milling mob and all it entailed made him terribly angry, so that he went pale, and when they saw his face they fell silent and made a way for him. First he had to shoulder his way savagely, but when he had done that a few times they respected him and when he shouted at them, "Let me through! Let me through!" he got their attention, and a path of respect opened for him right to the closed door of the house. He knocked on the door and he turned and looked at all the people. He felt like reviling them. If he had had a whip he would have felt like belabouring them. They were packed in front of the house, their noses up to the glass of the windows. The look of Larry silenced them. The bolt was pulled back and the door opened and he went in and it closed again behind him.

"Thank God you came," Martha said to him.

He threw his hat on the table.

"Where is he?" he asked.

"In his room," she said. "He won't come out for us. He hasn't been out of that room for seven days, except at night when we are sleeping, he creeps out then. I have no voice left for talking to him. It is up to you now, Father. He mustn't go out today or it will be the end of us. You are our hope. If you can't persuade him to stay, I'll block the door with my body. I tell you that."

Luke was standing helplessly and Sheila was there.

Larry went up and knocked at the door.

"Joseph!" he called. "Joseph! This is Larry." He had to call it out loudly. It was only when you were locked up inside four

271

walls that the sound of the crowd outside really was heard. The key turned in the lock and Larry went into the room and closed the door behind him.

Joseph stood facing him.

If Larry had expected to find a cowering figure unshaven and haggard with soiled clothes, he was surprised. Joseph's face was freshly shaved. He wore a spotlessly white shirt and a pair of black trousers held up by black braces. The big eyes that looked into Larry's were calm. The face was white and emaciated-looking. There seemed to be no flesh on his bones. That shocked Larry, and then the sight of the patient eyes seemed to repel him and he turned away and sat on the bed, and tightened his lips and dropped his head for a few seconds. He thought back to the Joseph of the College who had been called names, ironically. He had always defended him and liked him, but now the sight of him seemed to bring a wave of dislike beating into his brain. He tried to prevent it. He said a quick aspiration, and then he raised his head again.

"Joseph," he said. "What have you done?"

"I haven't done anything, Larry," said Joseph. "I told the truth. That was a mistake. I should have kept my vision in my own heart. I shouldn't have said about it. I don't know. Maybe I was meant to say it so that all that could happen" waving his hand at the window. "But I didn't do that, Larry. Please believe me, I didn't do that."

"I know, Joseph," said Larry. "I heard all about that. That was mainly the doing of your brother Bart, but fundamentally you did it, Joseph. You see that. The main fault lies with you."

"Yes," said Joseph, "I am mainly responsible."

"Joseph," said Larry. "Do you really and with your whole heart believe that you saw what you saw?"

"I do," said Joseph. "Oh, I do. She was the radiant rose of our prayers."

"I see," said Larry, and bent his head and ran his two hands through his hair. "Now listen, Joseph. I'll tell you the way we feel. You will listen to me."

"I will, Larry," said Joseph.

272

"All your life," said Larry, picking his words carefully, "you wanted to be a priest. I don't know if your mother influenced you in this but we'll say she didn't. Right. You go to college. You see that your vocation will be fulfilled. Now in a short space of time many things happen. Your father dies tragically. You are told that you must leave the College, that you cannot be a priest, and this news has a severe effect on your mother. She might have suffered anyhow, but in your mind you are certain that the news was such a shock that it hastened her death. You are deprived of your mother who was very attached to you and you to her. You were deprived of your father. And worst of all you were deprived of the priesthood. Now, Joseph, don't you think when all that happened when you were left so alone, feeling dependent on your brother Luke, that the day you went up to the bog what you think you saw was just a wish fulfilment, that it wasn't real? That it had no basis of a true vision. Don't you think, Joseph, that it was all false, based on your terrible losses and your terrible loneliness?"

"No," said Joseph, "it was real."

There was silence between them. Larry had his head down. He was knuckling one palm with a closed fist.

"Have you thought of the consequences?" Larry asked then. "There must be several thousand people out there, Joseph. Most of them are sceptics. They have come along for a thrill, like they would go to see a strange animal at the Zoo. Some of them are genuinely saintly people. Have you thought about this?"

Joseph's face was twisted. Larry, looking at him, thought he was going to cry.

"Yes," said Joseph. "I have thought about it. I didn't want it to happen. I wanted to be alone."

"But you're not," said Larry. "You are not alone. You have virtually told all these people that you are going up a mountain this evening before sunset and that when you go there you will see your vision, and they have come to see you seeing your vision. Have you thought of the effect it will have if there is no vision?"

Joseph seemed to be in agony.

"Yes," he said, almost in a whisper. "I have thought about that."

"The danger to the faith?" Larry insisted. "Even if there is only one soul out there whose faith may be destroyed for ever, Joseph. You know the consequences for the destruction of a single soul?"

"Oh, I do, I do!" said Joseph, his hands up covering his face.

"Then in the name of God," said Larry, "do the right thing. Go out there now like a man, and face the people and tell them to go home, that you have dreamed what you have dreamed and that they must go home, that you will not go up the mountain."

"I cannot do that, Larry," said Joseph gently, "because what I saw was true and I must do what I believe is right. I believe it is right for me to go up the mountain."

"Knowing the consequences?" Larry asked.

"Yes," said Joseph, "knowing the consequences."

The door behind them opened.

Bart stood there. The priest's eyes and his own met.

"You weren't thinking of keeping him under lock and key, were you?" Bart asked.

"What stake have you in this?" Larry asked him.

"Goods," said Bart laughing. "Goods and chattels, and he is my brother and I will see that he gets a fair deal and that if he wants to go up the mountain nobody will stop him."

"You have heard about the money-changers in the temple?" Larry asked him.

"Yes," said Bart, grinning. "I have heard about them, and I have seen them too. There isn't a shrine in Christendom where the money-changers aren't. With beads and sacred objects and food and drink. Have you heard of the merchants of Lourdes or the grocers of Jerusalem?"

"Bart," said Joseph, "please don't say any more. Don't say any more."

Bart looked at him. Something about the bewildered emaciated look of him caught at Bart's heart. If I have a heart, he thought. He thought of this frail little brother going into the rancid breath of the multitude outside and for a moment his heart smote him. Then the sight of the priest's eyes examining him hardened him up.

274

Breeda said, "Joseph, are you there? Are you well?"

She came in from behind Bart.

"Yes, Breeda," he said. "I am well."

He looked at Larry.

"I know you find it impossible to believe me, Larry," he said. "I don't blame you, honestly. But Breeda was there. Breeda saw something too."

"I heard about Breeda too," Larry said. "You are blind and you saw Joseph talking to a moving light."

"Yes, Father," she said. "That's right." But he caught the note of doubt in her voice.

"But you're not quite sure?" he asked.

"Father," she said, "I'm not a very good person. I'm too taken with the pride of life and my own misfortunes. How can I have the faith of Joseph? Joseph is wholly good. I am not as fervent as he. I can be moved and swayed by multitudes and dust and dirt and my own little emotions. I said what I saw. For me it might have been a dream. But if Joseph said he saw, then he saw. I believe in Joseph."

"All right," said Larry. He went into the kitchen. "Open the door," he said to Luke who stood there, "and let Joseph out."

"No, no," said Martha. "You can't do it! You can't let him go! It will ruin us. It will ruin us all for ever. You can't do it! You can't let him go!"

"There's no other way," said Larry. "You know the crowd that's out there. If he is prevented they will get ugly. Nothing will ever be resolved. It must be resolved. This is Joseph's task. He is the only one who can do it. All the consequences lie with himself. And only with himself. Are you ready, Joseph?"

Joseph was coming out of the room, pulling on a coat.

"Yes," he said, "I'm ready."

"Joseph," said Larry, "I'll wait for you until you come back. I'll pray for you."

He still disliked him. He disliked the pale look of him, the way his eyes were widening, the way his mind was already going away from listening to them. He would pass through the crowds and he mightn't even see them. Was it just false, he wondered, or were his eyes really directed on the mountain? He couldn't tell. But he couldn't believe him. God protect us from the phoney visionaries, he thought, and the terrible damage they do, and then wondered at himself to be thinking like that about Joseph, and he watched the door opening and the pressing people falling back and shouting, "He's coming! He's coming! Here he is now! He's coming!" And Joseph went out and they fell away from him and Bart and his big body blocked out the door and Breeda followed behind him and then the door was closed and Martha was saying, "You shouldn't have let him go. You are a priest of the Church and you shouldn't have let him go!" And Larry said, "Excuse me," and he went into Joseph's room and closed the door behind him and looked at the white austerity of the room, and then he took his breviary from his pocket and sought what he wanted and he went on his knees beside the bed and he started to read.

Thirty

ALL THE WAY down, a lane opened up.

The eyes of the curious were upon him. Remarks were made as he went past. He couldn't hear. People in the press behind leaned over other people's shoulders, jumping to catch a glimpse of him. There were people on both sides of the way all over the rough road and right up the shoulder of the hill.

The sun was low in the sky. There was a cold nip in the air.

Bart had his hand on Breeda's arm, guiding her. Several times she shook it off, but when she stumbled his hand grasped her again. She left it there in the end.

Watching the thin boy going up the road, off the road, and up the steep place. All in dead silence. It was terrible. It began to affect even Bart. He felt trapped with the thick lines of people on each side. It could be that you were walking to a scaffold. There was silence as Joseph climbed. There was silence as he stumbled on the soft ground. Silence as he paused and held his arms across his chest to hold in the thumping of his heart. The silence was only broken at times by the groans of a few old people following behind, as the climb got at the back of their legs, or threatened their hearts. Silence except for an odd suppressed curse as a city shoe went into slime and the cold muck met a foot. They waited in silence as he topped the shoulder of the hill, as he lay there for a time almost stretched out, panting, his face held down, his eyes closed.

There was the silence of anticipation as he walked forward again towards the distant turf bank around which thicker crowds were grouped, like, Bart thought, the crowds around a grave at a funeral.

The small black figure walking across the soft ground towards his destiny. What destiny? What was he thinking about? Did he really believe all this? Bart wondered. Had he really fooled himself to the extent that he could believe it?

And then he was there at the spot and he fell on his knees on the wet ground.

There was an awed hush. The sun was shining on the place. A big-looking sun that was about to be smothered by the top of Boola. Many people looked at the sun and they looked at the kneeling boy, and many of them didn't wait for any decision, they just knelt in the wet place. Bart wondered how silence and imagination could clothe this bleak unfriendly place with an aura of something that was brooding; of anticipation; of what? He didn't know. He had seen places before where mystical people were supposed to tread. They would bear the solemn feeling of the groping of men's minds.

Then he thought: What happens if Joseph is not a good actor? What happens if he is disappointed in his dreaming? You can dream well once. But suppose your second dream does not come true?

Everybody watched the sun. And when a third of it, and a half of it, and three-quarters of it had gone behind the hill they took their eyes off it and they riveted them on the place where the boy knelt and as the rest of the sun disappeared they watched the shadow racing across the ground towards him to engulf him.

And they held their breaths.

Now. What would happen? Would they, ordinary people, see any sign? Was it only granted to him to have a sign? If he saw, what would they see? Would they see a twitch in his face or ecstasy or would he be levitated? Would there be a mysterious breeze on the calm air and would they see the movement of heather where the sacred feet would rest?

Nothing at all happened. Nothing at all.

It was at that point that Bart felt as if he was looking into a deep black pool with his face over the water and no reflection of

278

himself coming back to him. Instinct made him move a pace or two towards his brother. Nothing at all happened.

People looked at one another. And they looked at the sky and they looked at the boy, but nobody was willing to break the silence, until one voice did. It was a man's voice as hoarse as the crowing of a crow. "A bloody fraud!" the voice said.

This seemed to be a release to pent-up breath.

Out of the release there grew a laugh, and out of the rueful laugh there grew a murmur, and out of the murmur there grew loud voices laughing, and Bart never knew who threw the first clod.

It's very easy to find clods on bogs. The first wet clod that flew was thrown with an accurate aim. It hit the kneeling Joseph on the back of the head and it threw him forward on his face. Then more clods flew and Bart was in the middle of them, standing over his brother, his fists clenched, shouting at them. But nobody could hear his voice because there were women screaming and men shouting and people had given it up for a bad job and just turned away, down, writing it off to experience. But a lot of men were bending and throwing and cursing and jeering. Bart bent and lifted Joseph. His eyes were closed but there was movement in him. Bart tried to protect himself and Joseph. But the clods flew very thick, so he didn't wait, but gathered him up in his arms and turned towards the way down.

They shouted and he shouted back at them. Nobody opened lanes for them now. There was no respect.

Bart shouted curses aloud at them, but they were drowned in the roaring. He thought of Breeda and turned his head to look for her. She was behind him. She was guided by a very big man, who was Suck, who had his hand around her arm.

There was a clomp, and a clod stuck sickeningly on the side of Joseph's face. Bart freed one hand and tried to scrape the dirt away. He was frantic. Joseph said: "Let me down, Bart. Please let me down," and Bart put him down and Joseph walked ahead stumbling and the clods flew from all directions. It was like a scene out of hell if hell could be like this. There was nothing they could do.

The people all the way seemed to be in a frenzy. The women who were running down the hill were screaming. Some men were running up the hill preventing them from running down, and when they finally reached the bridge the people were packed there, and Bart had to fight a way through with his fists, feeling blows landing on the body of his brother behind him. What have I done? Bart thought, in the middle of the pain. What have I done at all, at all? Suck was behind and Bart saw that they hadn't even spared the girl. From head to feet she was covered in the bog muck, as if she had been rolled in it. Suck was dirtied, but he was shouting, his mouth opening, swinging his great arms, swinging and swinging. Breeda was crying. Her mouth was open and she was crying, but Bart knew that she wasn't crying for herself.

And then, of course, they ran out of clods, so the men bent and dug the stones from the dirt road and Bart got a blow of a stone on the temple, that staggered him and made the blood flow. He tried to protect Joseph with his body. Suck closed up behind him, and Joseph reached his hand for Breeda and put it on her arm and held to her.

Jack, Jim, and Joe, the bastards! Bart thought. They were there near the bridge shouting at him, "Carrymore! Bloody swindle, Carrymore! What did we say? Leading us by the nose, man," and the stones flew and there were screams and shouts. "Let me free. Oh. Let me through." And Bart saw the fellows heaving at the van. He tried to work over to them. He couldn't. He saw the van keeling over from the lift of them and canting towards the river, and he saw the underneath part of it and the swinging wheels and then it was gone, and they were over the bridge and fighting their way to the yard of the house and then to the door, and the door opened and there was the priest confronting them. He had a deep voice and he was roaring, but you could hardly hear a word he was saying. But he stood there and came in front of Bart, and Bart got Joseph behind him and into the kitchen and followed after him, and then Breeda was in there and Suck, and the noises were dwindling away and they heard the voice of the priest.

"Go home, you fools, go home!"

And he came back in after them and he closed the door.

Martha was saying in a sort of moan, "I knew! I knew! I told ye what would happen. I knew what would happen."

And Joseph said, "I'm sorry, oh, I'm sorry," and he went towards his room, staggering. There was blood on his face and dirt. And Breeda was over on a chair hunched up, crying, her hands up to her face, and the priest went into the room after Joseph. Joseph lay down on the bed and the priest bent over him.

"I'm sorry, Larry, I'm sorry," Joseph said.

"Don't mind. Don't mind," said Larry. All his dislike and distaste had gone from him, and he pulled the quilt down from under Joseph and pulled it up over him, wet and muddy and stained as he was. The face was so pale and so pitiful and it was nearly an accident that he put his hand on his forehead and it was as if he had put his palm on the hot lid of a stove.

He covered him up fully and went into the kitchen.

"He's ill," he told them. "He is very ill. Somebody will have to get the doctor." And he looked at them. None of them dare go and get the doctor. He would have to go himself. So he went to the door and opened it. He went into the street.

The place was smothered in dust. The sun was about to sink into the sea. Cars were moving and people cursing and crying. The whole village was a hive of noise.

"I knew it! I knew!" Martha was saying, and only Luke of them all thought of taking a glass of clean spring water and going with it to the room and standing there with it in his hand.

He was about to say to Joseph, "Joseph, have a drink. Come and have a drink." He looked at the face. It was deathly pale. The great eyes were open and unseeing and it seemed to Luke as if they were looking at something that he could not see. And it seemed to Luke as if the room was being brightened. As if somebody was turning on a very powerful lamp in the room. That's what he thought. And suddenly his mouth went very dry and the hair started to rise on the back of his neck and he backed out of the room, and the sight of his tense back coming out of the room gathered the attention of the people in the kitchen so that

281

they stood, and Luke, still staring at the room, said in a terror-stricken voice:

"There is something back in the room with him. I couldn't stay in the room. There is something back in the room with him."

And Martha said, "You're mad, Luke. You're mad." And Bart went to walk towards the room, but as he walked towards it it seemed to him that a bright light was being lit in the room. He didn't know what. He backed away from it.

Martha said, "Can't ye see? It's the sunset on the window-panes. I tell ye it's the sunset on the window-panes!" She was pointing out where the dying sun was going into the sea and casting radiant and red light all around the edges of the world.

But nobody answered her.

Luke took off his cap and he went on his knees.

Martha went over and shook him. She was frantic. "Get up, you fool! Get up!" she said.

"S-sh, Martha!" said Luke, stopping her with his hand. "S-sh!"

"I tell you it's the sunset on the window-panes," she shouted at him.

Big Suck removed his cap and he went on his knees.

Breeda was over at the door. But she didn't go in. She went on her knees. Sheila was in the corner, and she was very frightened and her eyes were terrified, looking at the brightly lighted room. And she went on her knees.

And Bart was there standing looking at the kneeling people around him. I don't know them, he thought. I don't know them at all.

And Martha said again in a sort of subdued sob, "I tell ye it's the sunset on the window-panes."

And the door opened and the priest came in.

He said, "The doctor is gone away. We will have to wait until he comes back."

Then he said a thing that brought their eyes on him.

He said, "It is very dark in here. I can't see a thing." And he went to the mantelpiece and he took from it a candle in a

282

candlestick and struck a match and lit the candle and went towards Joseph's room. And as he went towards the room the light in the room seemed to fade away as if it was giving way to the much more feeble light of the candle, and they kneeled or stood there in terror. They saw him go in and they saw him leave the candle by the bed on the little table and they saw him come out and they heard the bewilderment and sadness in his voice.

"It's too late now, anyhow," he said. "Joseph is dead. I can't believe it, but Joseph is dead."

And Bart backed away from the voice of the priest and he felt for the door and he backed out of it and he ran on to the street and he ran away from the street, up, up, out of the village that was littered and torn and tattered by the passing of the multitude. And at their doors some of the people stood now that it was all over, looking out, and they remembered the sight of Bart with a terrible face on him running away from the house of his brother, a tortured face, people said he had on him, and he was running and running and it seemed to some that he was crying, and when he got farther on, clear of the houses, he heard a young voice behind him calling, "Carrymore! Hey, Carrymore!" but he didn't heed the appeal of the young voice. He just ran and ran, his arm up over his eyes.

OTHER BOOKS
from

Walter Macken

The Grass of the People

This new collection from one of the most popular masters of the Irish short story includes twelve previously unpublished stories. Marked by Macken's own distinctive style, they present a rural world teeming with characters and life.

256 pages; ISBN 0 86322 248 X; Brandon hardback £12.99

City of the Tribes

"A vivid evocation of Galway and 'the plain people' of that city in the forties, full of insight and humour but free of romanticism, as they fight against the sea, poverty and political conservatism." *Irish Post*

256 pages; ISBN 0 86322 228 5; Brandon hardback £12.99

Brown Lord of the Mountain

"Walter Macken's dramatic, almost mystical tale, with full-blown romantic hero, reveals his theatrical background. Macken knows his people and his places and his love of them shines through; this final work is a fitting tribute to them." *Examiner*

284 pages; ISBN 0 86322 201 3; paperback £5.95

God Made Sunday

"The charm of Walter Macken's leisurely, lyrical tales is real but deceptive. . . Macken's scene is a western Eden, moments after the Fall – a setting of ecstatic beauty for a life of tribulation and toil." *The Scotsman*

222 pages; ISBN 0 86322 217 X; paperback £5.95

Green Hills

"More valuable than sociological studies, [these stories] show the skill of the dramatist . . . Brandon's uniform series of reprints is modest but dignified: just right." *Books Ireland*

220 pages; ISBN 0 86322 216 1; paperback £5.95

Quench the Moon

"Where the writer knows and loves his country as Walter Macken does, there is warmth and life." *Times Literary Supplement*

413 pages; ISBN 0 86322 202 1; paperback £5.95

Rain on the Wind

"It is a raw, savage story full of passion and drama set amongst the Galway fishing community . . . It is the story of romantic passion, a constant struggle with the sea, with poverty and with the political conservatism of post-independence Ireland." *Irish Independent*

320 pages; ISBN 0 86322 185 8; paperback £5.95